CALLICOE RNVR

Callicoe RNVR

By

Vincent Formosa

2020

Copyright © 2020 by Vincent Formosa.

1st Edition created 2020.

This is a novel. The characters, situations and military organisations are an invention of the author, except where they can be identified historically. Any other resemblance to actual persons, living or dead is purely coincidental. Likewise, names, dialogue and opinions expressed are products of the author's imagination to fit the story and not to be interpreted as real.

ISBN: 9798672940878

3D meshes of Chance Vought Corsair and Ki84 created by Anders Lejczak. Contact him on his website at www.colacola.se Textures for the Corsair created by Vincent Formosa. Cover layout by Vincent Formosa.

All rights reserved under International and Pan-American Copyright Conventions.

No part of this book may be reproduced in any form or by any electronic or mechanical means; this includes but is not restricted to information storage and retrieval systems, without written permission from the author or publisher, except by a reviewer who may quote passages in a review.

This book would not exist if it were not for the help and hard work of a number of people. Particular thanks go to my diligent beta reader, Barbara Boon, for spending many hours going over my manuscript, making suggestions and discussing their ideas with me for which I am truly grateful.

Other titles by the same author

The Eagles Of Peenemunde
Run The Gauntlet (Book 1 of the Blenheim Series)
Channel Dash (Book 2 of the Blenheim Series)
Maximum Effort
Prototype

Available in both Kindle and paperback formats on Amazon.

Contents

01 – Wish Me Luck	1
02 – Ugly Ducklings	12
03 – Swans	28
04 – Roll Out The Welcome Mat	37
05 – The Danger Of Expectation	48
06 – Get Your Feet Wet	57
07 – Work Up	67
08 – One Last Time	81
09 – Jewel Of The Med	91
10 – Out Of The Frying Pan	105
11 – An Expensive Way To Learn	112
12 – Operation Velvet	123
13 – Sleight Of Hand	132
14 – Fetch And Carry	141
15 – Close Run Thing	151
16 – 不運 Fuun	162
17 – So This Is India	171
18 – I Met A Girl On The Way To The Circus	187
19 – Gather Together	199
20 – Leading With Your Chin	211
21 – All Change, Next Stop Japan	217
22 – Merry Bloody Christmas	225
23 – Black Gold	233
24 – Road To Palembang	247
25 – Graduation	255
26 – Down Under	269
27 – Good Fortune	277
28 – Back And Forth	297
29 – Logistics And Damn Lies	307

30 – Sydney Blues	310
31 – Taffy 57	322
32 – Divine Wind	334
33 – Taketh My Name	344
34 – Hot Work	350
35 – Again, Again, Again	357
36 – Tooth And Nail	370
37 – All Hands On Deck	378
38 – The King Is Dead, All Hail The King	387
39 – Carnival	397
40 – The Next Generation	411
41 – When You Think Of Me	419
42 – Gathering Storm	434
43 – Land Of The Gods	437
44 – Paper Tiger	447
45 – Tilting At Windmills	454
46 – In The Navy He Was	460

1 – Wish Me Luck

The reception room lacked its usual warmth tonight. James Callicoe knew why of course. The underlying current of disappointment had been made very clear to him. They were all there, the whole family with smiles painted on their faces to send him on his way.

His father, Martin Callicoe was sat in his favourite armchair nearest to the window. Close enough that he could catch a breeze from the garden but stay in the shade on the bright summer days. Callicoe's stepmother, Margaret sat opposite him, legs elegantly crossed. She nursed a gin and tonic, the glass balanced on her knees. His older brother, Frank and wife Ariadne stood behind the sofa. They leaned over the back of it while their daughters read their books aloud to the room.

"Ah, the man of the hour," his father said. Every face turned in Callicoe's direction and he straightened his shoulders at their scrutiny. He felt like a sample under a microscope.

The children rushed over to cries of, "Uncle Jim," and grabbed his legs. He took a few steps with them clinging on, before he shooed them back towards their father. They sat down on the settee and turned their attention back to their books.

He walked over to his brother and Ariadne. She leaned towards him and he skimmed her cheek.

"James," she said. Callicoe shook his brother's hand.

"Fashionably late, old man," Frank commented.

"Just double checking a few things," Callicoe replied. "I've got an early start in the morning so I just want to walk out of the door."

Ariadne made a face. Early starts were anathema to her. As far as she was concerned, it was one more strike against the whole enterprise.

"And you're still sure about all this?" Frank asked, trying to keep the disapproval out of his voice.

"It's a bit late now darling," Ariadne chided him. "Our little, Jimmy's off to war. Aren't you dear?" she said.

Callicoe remained mute, not wanting to be drawn into another debate about his decision. There had been plenty of those the last few weeks after he'd dropped the bombshell he'd been accepted for pilot training in the Fleet Air Arm. Their first reaction had been disbelief, then it had turned into a horrified dissection of why he'd done it. The arguments had raged all Christmas and into the New Year.

"Damn fool thing if you ask me," Frank had told him without hesitation. Firmly entrenched behind his Ministry desk, his older brother's world was sharply defined. Everything had its place, a structure. His little brother enlisting to have his head shot off violated his carefully constructed rules.

Callicoe had been surprised by their reaction. He'd made no secret of the fact that he'd wanted to join up for a while. The difficulty had been actually managing it. It wasn't easy getting out of a reserved occupation.

At the start of the war, his father had pulled a few strings to get him a minor job in the Home Office. Frank was already well established at the Ministry, so it was only natural his father would do the same for his other son. It had seemed like a good idea at the time, the war would be over soon enough and then he could go back to his studies.

Once it was clear the war would not be over by Christmas after all, Callicoe changed his mind. With England fighting for her survival, he'd felt like a coward sat on the sidelines while others went off to fight. The only difficulty he'd had was getting his status deferred. He submitted numerous requests and each time he was turned down. In response, he just wrote more of them. In the end, he thought they agreed just to get rid of him.

Ariadne detached herself from her husband and went over to the sideboard on the back wall. She picked up a crystal tumbler and tapped the lip of it with her finger.

"Drink?" she asked Callicoe, already reaching for the decanter on the tray. He gave her a ghost of a nod and she poured a measure of scotch into the tumbler. She added a glimmer of water and brought it over to him.

He took a sip. It was too strong, but then she knew that and he saw the mocking challenge in her eyes as he looked at her over the glass. He went to the sideboard himself to top it up. He used his finger to swirl the brown liquid round to mix it.

His step mother joined him by the sideboard. She was as elegant as ever, her lithe figure draped in pastel shades. She'd pinned her blonde hair up to show her long neck to its best advantage. She was thirtyfive now, trim from tennis and swimming in the pool. She poured herself another gin and tonic and added some ice to it.

Margaret looked at him, remembering the boy he had been when she first met him. James had been a moody fourteen year old mourning for his mother when she had appeared on the scene ten years ago. Young Callicoe had expected his father to tire of her. Despite his teenage provocations, Margaret had stayed the course.

Callicoe considered her a siren who had charmed his father in a moment of weakness. She had done little to change his opinion in the intervening years. There had been no loving care for him and she'd left him to his own devices.

He'd heard the story how they'd met enough times. His father had been at a Ministry function when he saw her charming her way around the room. He'd been a coming man then, being groomed for greater things; perhaps even a Permanent Secretaries post. She'd latched onto him, seeing a bright future in front of her despite the appendages of two children.

The wedding had followed swiftly and Margaret had moved quickly to secure her place. Ever the practical sort, she solved the issue of children quite easily. With not a maternal bone in her body and having no interest in having offspring of her own, Callicoe had been packed off to boarding school. Frank had gone off to Oxford to read English.

Extended time away from home changed Callicoe's view of his family. They became planets in the same orbits but forever apart. Frank had drifted away, the four year age gap between them becoming a distance too far to bridge. With his sons grown up, his father's focus shifted away to his own interests, work, collecting stamps and Margaret.

While he'd been absent at school, Margaret had redecorated the house to suit her own tastes. The last vestiges of Callicoe's mother were wiped away and he'd hated Margaret for that. He'd found a photograph of his mother shoved in a drawer, out of the way, forgotten. He rescued it and put it in his bedroom. The house became somewhere he just happened to live in. Joining up was his way of getting out.

The six week wait before getting his call up papers had been the worst. Callicoe had never been one to count his chickens. People could change their minds. His application could have gotten lost. He'd experienced disappointments like this before and until he had it in his hand in writing, he'd said nothing. He only broke the news to his father when the letter confirming everything arrived.

He'd not been prepared for the reaction. Of all of

them, he thought his father would have understood but he was sadly mistaken.

"You're a damn fool," his father had raged at breakfast. He slapped the newspaper down on the table and Margaret jumped in time with the toast rack. "Do you have any idea what it took to get you your position? You'll tell them you're not going," he demanded. Callicoe shook his head.

"It's my choice father. No one else's. It's done." The elder Callicoe went red in the face at such an open challenge to his paternal authority. For once, Margaret had remained quiet, leaving them to have it out without any comment from her.

"I can't hide in your shadow father. I must make my own way."

"Then get another job. I'll get you moved to another department if you like, I've heard good reports about you, you've earned it. Anything but this."

"Other people have joined up."

"You've not seen the horrors I have." His father's voice had cracked as he'd stared off to one side, his eyes straying to the photograph of himself on the sideboard. His lip curled at the memory of it being taken. His breast had been full of patriotic fervour, all primped up in his uniform, going off to war. The mud of the Somme had cured him of that. "Sheep to slaughter," he muttered to himself, his eyes distant.

Callicoe had tried discussing the matter with him a number of times since, urging him to see his point of view but his father would not be moved.

Callicoe's remaining time at the Ministry went fast while he tidied up his department. Reports were compiled, his successor was briefed; and then there was the round of farewell drinks. Some were mystified at his decision, others wished it was them going in his place.

Then it was Christmas before his deployment. The

holidays were always torture, when the family got together. His departure had given things an extra edge this year.

Callicoe returned with Margaret back to the family tableau in the middle of the room. His father listened intently as the girls finished reading a Beatrix Potter story aloud. He applauded and then Lucy held the book to her father, asking for one more story.

"I'll read you one more," he promised, "in bed."

The girls said goodnight. Frank took them upstairs to the guest bedroom. Callicoe took their place on the settee and Ariadne sat down next to him. Silence descended. Margaret did her best to keep things civil. She'd had enough practice over the years dealing with excruciating Ministry functions that she had a fund of harmless questions ready to fill uncomfortable silences.

"Where do you have to report?" she asked him, "Is that the right word?" Callicoe gave a ghost of a smile.

"I believe so. I've got a travel warrant to go to Gosport. After that; who knows?"

"Well I'm looking forward to seeing you in your uniform," Ariadne commented. He might have been crazy for joining up, but there was something about the officers uniform with its white peaked cap that she found quite thrilling. His father said nothing, remaining stoically quiet.

"I can't say I like the idea of flying myself," Margaret commented. "I've always preferred to keep my feet on the ground."

Callicoe knew that all too well. In all the years he'd known Margaret, whenever they travelled on family holidays, it had always been by a combination of car, train or boat.

That had been his first introduction to sailing. He'd gone out in a ten foot sail boat with Frank when they holidayed on the Isle of Wight. They hadn't gone very far, but it had been fun splashing about. He remembered being sat at the stern, working the rudder while Frank mucked about trying to trim the sail.

Conversation continued but it was stilted, topics kept circling back to his departure. Finally, Ariadne and Margaret discussed some dress they had seen in town so Callicoe was left on his own. His father did not engage in the conversation, remaining a mute lump in the corner. Callicoe fidgeted under his father's scrutiny and he fished his pipe out of his pocket, clamping it between his lips. Frank had once referred to the pipe as Callicoe's comfort blanket and he wasn't far wrong.

When he needed to think, or to pause and reflect, the pipe would come out of his pocket and get stuck in his mouth. Callicoe found it a marvellous way to deflect conversation for a moment while he packed the bowl with tobacco or he lit it. Finally, he could take no more.

"Nothing to say father?" he asked. That stopped Margaret and Ariadne in their tracks.

"What would you like me to say?" was the reply.

"No words of wisdom?"

That produced a reaction, albeit a fractional one. His father grimaced, shifted in his seat and hitched forward, his arms resting on his legs. He barely blinked as he stared at his son, his blue grey eyes iron hard.

"If you think I'm going to applaud a shambles of a war, you're sadly mistaken." He snapped his fingers as he sat back. "France, Poland, Czechoslovakia all sacrificed on the altar of hubris. We should have taken the Nazi buggers on at the time of Munich and what did we get? Bits of white paper waved in the air instead. Then we got Churchill. He's brought us to the brink. We shall fight them on the beaches? Pah. I won't give you my blessing for this adventure."

"I see," Callicoe said quietly.

Frank came back into the room and Callicoe was

grateful for the interruption.

"I had to tell them two stories," he said in mock outrage. He picked up on the tension and quirked an eyebrow at his wife. Ariadne said nothing, she kept her head still but moved her eyes towards Callicoe.

"Who's for cards?" he asked breezily, trying to provide a diversion. Margaret went to get the small folding card table and they arrayed themselves around it to play Bridge. Callicoe hovered at Margarets shoulder. He could play, but not very well and he didn't fancy a scolding for laying a bad card. He made himself useful by keeping score and fetching drinks.

His father's mood improved as they played, loosening up once he had a few whisky and sodas under his belt. He was a competitive player and with Margaret, they were a sharp pair. Conversation turned to life at the Ministry, who was on the way up, who was on the way down. Callicoe zoned out to some extent, that was no longer his world and hearing the same old gossip was stale.

He emptied the ashtray and as he brought it back to the table, he turned it over in his hand, running his finger over the rounded edge of the brass. His father saw him looking at it.

"My one and only souvenir," he said brusquely. "About all a shell is good for." He took it out of Callicoe's hand and put it on the table. It was the bottom of a shell case, cut down to a small circular container.

Callicoe took the packet of tobacco from inside his suit jacket and busied himself packing the bowl of his pipe. He tamped the flakes down with his thumb and then lit it. Clouds of sweet smelling smoke surrounded him as he got it going. He sat down by the fire with a book and flicked through the pages while they continued to play.

Every so often he glanced up to see them frowning over their cards, the ladies in their finery, the men in their suits. His father sat bolt upright, shoulders back. Frank slumped forward, guarding his cards.

Despite the years between the brothers, they were similar in appearance. Both of them short at 5'6", medium build with jet black hair. Both of them had a narrow square jawed face with a long nose, a Roman nose, their mother had called it once. Frank had spent the time to grow a beard which he fastidiously maintained. Callicoe had never bothered, he couldn't stand the itching and scratching you got after a few days.

Frank and Ariadne ran up the white flag after Margaret and his father won their fifth straight rubber. The game broke up and everyone returned to their seats.

Callicoe shifted over to give them room but Ariadne was still squashed between him and her husband. He hitched over again but her thigh was still pressed up against his. He was about to get up but she put a steadying hand on his leg.

"Don't move on my account," she told him.

"Where will they send you do you think?" Frank asked as he lit a cigarette. He closed the lighter with a snap and blew a puff of smoke to the ceiling.

"Not a clue. Where they need me I suppose. Convoys in the Atlantic, convoys to Russia perhaps-"

"Oh no, Jimmy. Don't say Russia. I can't imagine you going to such an awful place. All that cold and ice, positively frightful."

Callicoe contained a smirk. It was typical Ariadne. She had a knack of distilling weighty issues into simple things like cold and ice. If he'd said the Mediterranean, she'd have said it was too hot.

"Maybe they'll make you an instructor," Margaret suggested, trying to think of a lesser evil than flying into battle. Callicoe grimaced because such a thing was a possibility.

"Gosh, yes," said Ariadne, latching onto the idea. "He might not even leave England at all."

Callicoe took this as his cue to leave. Ariadne's narrow horizons and his father's simmering silence was enough to draw things to a close.

"Well I'm for bed," he announced. "Early start on the morrow."

Frank, Margaret and Ariadne stood up. Ariadne gave him the most sincere goodbye, hugging him with genuine warmth.

"Goodnight, Jimmy. You'll send us a letter when you get sorted won't you?"

"Yes, I'll do that, when I've got time. They might keep me quite busy to start with you know," he joked. Ariadne was good enough to laugh. Margaret offered her hand as she always did.

"Goodnight James. Will you be wanting breakfast in the morning?" she asked, her voice cool. "I'll have cook sort something out."

"Good lord no," Callicoe replied. He was getting up at five. He couldn't possibly get the poor woman up just to sort him out. "Just some bread and cheese and I'll make myself a cup of tea and be on my way. Goodnight, Margaret."

"I'll see you up, old man," Frank said, taking him by the arm. They walked up the wide stairs side by side, in step for the last time. As they got to Callicoe's bedroom door, Frank offered his hand. Callicoe shook it.

"Good luck and take care of yourself," Frank said with an edge of finality. Callicoe nodded and went into his room.

He undressed and put his pyjamas on. Before he put the light out, he did a final sweep around his room. He noted where a few things were that he would need in the morning but he thought he'd covered everything. His eyes strayed to the suitcase he'd put at the foot of the bed. Everything he'd need was in there. The instructions had been that he was to pack light. Callicoe knew that once he got there he'd discover he'd forgotten something missing.

The small travel clock buzzed at five to five. Callicoe forced himself to get up. He dressed quickly and gave the room one last look. He was leaving his old life behind.

He wrapped some cheese and bread in greaseproof paper and contented himself with a glass of milk. The kettle made a racket when it whistled and he thought better about waking the whole house up. He didn't want another awkward goodbye.

He was about to open the front door when his father's voice stopped him. Callicoe turned to see him stood at the door to the front reception room.

"You've wanted this for a long time, haven't you?" Callicoe nodded, not quite trusting his voice. "You know, it all seems bloody silly fighting about this now."

"I never wanted to fight at all, father."

2 – Ugly Ducklings

Callicoe took the train to Portsmouth, missed his connection and caught a later one. When he pulled in, he could see the station and the surrounding area was a bit of a mess. Heavy raids earlier in the war had flattened the station down by the docks. A makeshift one had been built to save people the walk from town. He took the ferry to the other side of the harbour and reported to the gate of *HMS Saint Vincent* at Gosport. He was shown to a waiting room where men dressed like him sat with their suitcase, looking a little lost.

Ages varied. There was an old man of twenty seven who, like Callicoe, had fought for months to get out of his reserved occupation. Two baby faced eighteen year olds sat at the end of the bench. One was visibly nervous, the other radiated sublime confidence.

A Chief Petty Officer appeared and barked out names, dividing them up into groups of twenty five. Callicoe was put into class D. A, B, C and D were pilot candidates, classes E and F were prospective observers.

The CPO rounded them up and took them to their new digs, a dingy barracks block out of the last century. It had thick walls and small windows and smelled of damp. There was one toilet for twenty five men and the beds were straw stuffed palliasses. Paraffin lamps gave them light in the evenings. Callicoe thought it was something out of Tom Brown's schooldays.

"Cor, salubrious it ain't," announced a chirpy type from Norfolk. He leaned across the gap between their beds and introduced himself. "I'm Gabriel Veriker, everyone calls me, Gabby."

Callicoe quirked an eyebrow.
"Gabby?"
"Allegedly I talk too much."

After an uncomfortable night's sleep, the second day was devoted to administrative tasks. They lined up in a hut that smelled of mothballs and were issued uniforms and a plethora of other knick knacks. Callicoe thought the bell bottom trousers were ridiculous. The visorless cap wasn't much better. The worst thing they had to wear were the stupid black handkerchiefs as a tribute to Lord Nelson.

Night time reading was a copy of the *Admiralty Manual of Seamanship (Vol. 1)*. Callicoe didn't bother asking if there was a second, the first volume was boring enough. Each class was taken under the wing of a Petty Officer or Chief Petty Officer, they were the backbone of the service with years of experience.

For seven weeks it was early starts, long days and hard work. They did rifle drill, they painted walls, cleaned up the barracks blocks and were taught how to tie knots. For a week it was interesting. By the third week they were bored to tears and climbing the walls. They had joined to fly, not do square bashing and make work.

Slowly; they were moulded to the ways of the Senior Service. Rooms were cabins, toilets were heads, it was all very confusing to a layman. Badges of rank were explained. They suffered innumerable lectures on the ships of the Navy and where they operated all over the world. They also started to learn the unwritten pecking order, the differences between regulars and the reservists, what CPO Atkins called, *the Wavy Navy.*

There were few regulars at *Saint Vincent*, most of them were hostilities only officers. Some were very keen, but *Saint Vincent* seemed to have more than its fair share of officers who were bitter at being left behind from the action. That resentment manifested itself in a harsh regime with little latitude for transgressors. Aircrew candidates had to march from place to place and woe betide the man caught doing otherwise. Those who transgressed the rules walked the grounds, picking up cigarette butts and sweeping the gravel drive by the main gate.

After a month they were allowed out in the evenings. With accumulated pay burning a hole in their pockets, they went to the pubs around the base and made up for lost time. A shilling got you into the cinema or play house.

The following morning, CPO Atkins had them lined up on the drill square. More than one of them swayed back and forth on parade.

"Look at you," Atkins raged, examining them with a beady eye. "Officers? Not yet you ain't. Embarrassing I's call it. There are three types of officers as my old man used to say, gor bless 'im." He held up a finger.

"Regulars is gentlemen trying to be sailors." He held up another finger, "Reservists are sailors trying to be gentlemen." He held up a third finger, "and then there's you lot, Wavy Navy." He gave them a pitying look. "Neither a gentleman or a sailor, trying to be both. Well, we'll sweat that booze out of you so 'elp me."

He braced them to attention and marched them for two hours. Just as they were flagging, he let them have a five minute break and then had them at it again before breaking for PT. They hated PT more than marching. Every day, it was a run, or a game of football, or exercises in all weathers.

Commander Billiers RN gave short shrift to those he caught complaining in his hearing. It was not uncommon for him to hand out extra guard duties for such comments. People learned to keep an eye out for him stalking the base.

They learned to keep their cabins spotlessly clean. Floors were scrubbed, windows were cleaned ready for Atkins daily inspection. Brass was polished to within an inch of its life. Atkins raged over the uniforms. He expected creases, he wanted buttons to shine, he wanted shoes polished so you could see his face in them. Some were very good at it, others weren't.

After the whole block was penalised for deficient uniform, the men pulled together. That was the whole idea. They started helping each other and becoming their own worst critics. Atkins smiled to himself one morning when he heard Callicoe patiently explaining to Gabby how to bull his boots for the umpteenth time.

The final week was exams on most of the things that had been drummed into them. It was hard, but not impossible. If you couldn't get a reasonable mark in a test, there was little hope on your progressing any further. The dullards were culled from the herd at this point and sent for other training.

After seven weeks the change was remarkable. They were leaner, tougher and more organised. They knew who was strong, who was weak and who needed help. It was a start.

At the beginning of the course, they were asked if they would like to start their flying training in the UK, or do the whole course in the USA. Callicoe had picked the USA but never really thought he would get it. He was pleasantly surprised when he and forty others received orders to go to America.

Contrary to their expectations, there was no embarkation leave. A ferry took them to Portsmouth where they transferred to a troopship called the *Strathallen*. The ship weighed anchor at dusk in company with two other transports and a destroyer escort. They slipped into the English Channel, rounded Land's End and went up to Liverpool. Forty RAF types came aboard for flying training as well.

In peace time, *Strathallen* had been a passenger liner coming to the end of her career. After a lifetime plying the Atlantic route, she was about to be scrapped when she was pressed into service. Her worn out cabins were stripped out and every available bit of space was turned over to accommodation.

It was cramped, but there was an air of excitement, it was all a big adventure. Unlike the normal convoys that crawled along at eight or ten knots, this was a fast troop convoy. They went north at fifteen knots and headed for New York.

Callicoe discovered that messing about in a ten foot boat on the Solent was no preparation for winter weather in the North Atlantic. The *Strathallen* was a big ship but she still pitched around in ten and fifteen foot waves. Heavy rain lashed the decks and ice clung to the rails. It took Callicoe a few days to find his sea legs but he wasn't hanging over the rail like some of them did.

The RAF types were the worst hit and Callicoe took some pride that most of the navy men were better at dealing with it. At least he did until the storm front hit. Waves as big as a house tossed the *Strathallen* around like a toy in the bath. The passageways stank from a mix of seawater and vomit as hundreds of men voided their stomachs. Gabby spent hours groaning in his hammock as did Callicoe.

Seven days after they left Liverpool, they crowded the deck to see the Statue of Liberty. They'd seen it in the newsreels but it was something else to actually see it come into view over the horizon. Beyond it, New York was a sprawling metropolis that filled the skyline. To lads from rural towns like Norwich and even industrial towns like Leeds and Birmingham, New York was big.

Everything about America was big. The customs men

that met them at the dock were larger than life, the accommodation building they were housed in was big and everything was new. There were no mouldy century old barracks blocks here. The food was excellent. After suffering years of rationing, getting bacon and eggs for breakfast was a treat. They discovered the joys of pancakes and maple syrup before moving onto ice cream and coca cola.

They went south to warmer climes, leaving the winter cold of New York behind them. They rode the train down to Richmond, through Atlanta, Charlotte and on to Mobile in Florida. From there, transport took them to *Naval Air Station Pensacola* for flight training.

The cradle of US Navy aviation, *Pensacola* was a small city with thousands of personnel. The men were agog to find it had two bowling alleys, a huge sports ground and even a large theatre of its own. The accommodation blocks were long two storey wooden structures. Each dormitory housed up to one hundred men, split eight to a room.

"They don't do things by halves do they?" Gabby commented when they were shown their new digs. Callicoe was housed with Gabby, an RAF man called Barker, two US Marines and four US Navy officer candidates. One of them, Asher, had been a pilot in the mid west as a crop duster.

Contrary to their dreams, they did not step straight into an aircraft. The whole course was shuffled into the theatre and the timetable was outlined. There would be weeks of ground school first, followed by basic flight instruction. The pace of instruction would be intense. They would be expected to show progress in their skills before going solo.

"Be under no illusions gentlemen," the schools CO informed the assembled throng, "dead wood will be culled. We're training you for war, there are no passengers here."

Days were busy. Reveille was at 0530 hours. They rushed from class to class, having their heads filled with the theory of flight, navigation and other esoteric subjects. After dinner, more classes went into the evening.

In between all of that, they had to adjust to the American way of doing things. Most of the instructors were friendly, almost informal, but for other things, the Yanks pernickety beyond belief.

The biggest bit of high comedy was the fuss they made over being Officer of the Day. In the evening, every few hours, two men took over from the ones sat at a desk, one at each end of the dorm. The outgoing OOD would hand over a clipboard and a web belt and an armband designating their status.

The Yanks did it with military precision like it was some kind of public show. The incoming man would crash his heels together on the lino as he came to attention and went through a very formal script to relieve the outgoing man. The sheer over the top pomposity of it made it a rich source of humour.

It became a battle of wills as two distinctly different mindsets clashed over how things should be done. The Brits flung web belts at each other and turned the air blue as they relieved one another. They turned up ten minutes late, half an hour late, stretching the patience of the man at the desk. The Yanks fought back, their way, insisting that the script was adhered to.

Time off was precious. One evening a week and every other Saturday was their own and jealously guarded. If you failed an exam, you had to revise and keep on going until you passed it. If you didn't, you weren't going anywhere.

When they did go out, the locals made them feel welcome. Their accents and uniforms were a curiosity that got them free drinks and interested female company.

The attraction was mutual. Back home, after four years of war, there was little exuberance left in England what with the black out, rationing and war news. Florida was another world. The lights were bright, the food was plentiful and the girls were confident and forward.

Callicoe saw a girl called Charlotte once a week, making up a pair with a Marine Lieutenant called Christopher. Christopher had a car; a red Cadillac and they would pick up their girls and go for food and a movie on their night's offf. Callicoe didn't see much of the movie, he was always otherwise engaged.

The biggest cultural difference was in general demeanour. The American pilot candidates were a serious bunch. He never heard them curse, they rarely drank and if they did it was in moderation. That wasn't to say they didn't enjoy themselves on evenings out, but there was a built in reserve and a dim view taken regarding excess.

Callicoe thought he was fairly civilised. He wasn't a hard drinker but compared to them, he was some sort of heretic. Fish Salmon and Gabby were worse, they were the devil incarnate, hard drinkers who whored as much as they swore. When Callicoe suggested they tone it down a bit, he was hit with a barrage of abuse.

"We're all big boys, Jimmy," Gabby replied. "You've seen the planes we're going to fly. I thought it better to live a bit before we meet our maker."

Callicoe made a face. That was the whole reason they were there, but Gabby was right, they were all adults here. During the weeks of ground instruction, they had seen for themselves how cheap life could be.

Pensacola was a busy airfield with numerous courses at different stages of training. Aircraft buzzed around, going to outlying airfields to practice formation flying, basic navigation, landings and aerobatics. With so many aircraft in the sky at once, rarely a day went by without some sort of incident. Callicoe saw two biplanes collide in the landing pattern. They crashed to the ground like two flies with their wings plucked.

After completing the course of ground instruction to a satisfactory standard they were finally allowed near an aeroplane. They weren't much, just biplanes with a radial engine and a low top speed but they were an aircraft. They were flying at last.

A Reserve Navy Lieutenant called William Luke was Callicoe's instructor. A Georgia native, his accent was so thick, Callicoe had to fill in the blanks like some crossword puzzle to figure out what he was saying until he got used to him. He talked incessantly, chivvying Callicoe to get a feel for the aircraft.

The pressure to show improvement was a constant. After each lesson, he was expected to show that he could apply what he had learned. The boozing and the partying naturally died off. Spending all day concentrating was very tiring. Even Gabby and Fish Salmon curtailed their night time activities as the pressure increased.

Asher, the crop duster soloed first after seven hours. Callicoe managed it later in the week after nine hours of instruction.

"You'll do fine, kid," Luke assured him. "Do you think you can land this kite?" Callicoe nodded. "Then there's nothing more I can teach you at the moment. If you can't get this thing down on the ground then there's no point showing you anything else. Off you go."

Callicoe swallowed hard and got in. The cockpit in front of him was a gaping hole, a reminder that he was on his own. He started the engine, tested the controls and when he was clear, he taxied out. It was an exhilarating feeling, taking off for the first time on his own.

He did a few circuits and then flew to the satellite field at Ellyson. Taking his time, he setup to land. He was too cautious on his first approach and came in too high on the round down. He abandoned the attempt and went round again, burning with embarrassment. The whole field and he couldn't even land on one of the runways.

Setting up for a second time he brought the N3N biplane down neatly. As soon as the wheels kissed the ground, he opened up the throttle to make another circuit. Luke had told him to make five touch and go's before landing. Callicoe did six, doing an extra one to make sure before committing himself to a landing.

His caution was unfounded. He descended smoothly like he was on rails. Just before touchdown he cut the throttle and pulled back on on the stick to make a perfect three point landing. The wheels touched and he kept the stick pulled back to stay on the ground.

He taxied round to get into the wind at the bottom of the runway and took off to return to *Pensacola*. He'd done it once, now he just needed to do it again with his instructor watching. It wasn't perfect, but he got down without bouncing and parked next to the hangar where Luke was waiting for him.

"See," Luke said. "I told you, you could do it." He wagged an admonishing finger. "You should listen to me more; I know what I'm talking about."

One hundred men started the course, eleven failed to solo, one of them from Callicoe's room. Gabby and Salmon soloed after eleven hours of instruction. Everyone else passed except the RAF man Barker, he killed himself, trying too hard to get down. He flared too early, stalled out and buried himself in a coffin of wire and canvas.

Now that part of the course was over, the staff rewarded them with a weekend to relax.

"Enjoy yourselves while you can," Luke told Callicoe. "It's only going to get harder from here on out. If you go anywhere, be back Sunday night, 11pm at the latest."

The six men left in his room went out as a group to

celebrate. They piled into two cars and headed for the main gate. Quite a few men owned vehicle but Callicoe didn't bother himself. They weren't going to be there long enough to make it worth his while. Callicoe sat in the front of Christopher's Cadillac with Gabby in the back. Christopher was driving. A broad shouldered Marine Lieutenant, he was used to the saltier side of life so Gabby's antics didn't shock him so much.

"How wild do you guys want to get tonight?" he asked as they drove through the gate and turned left towards Mobile.

"Booze," said Callicoe.

"Women and booze," Gabby answered.

"In that order?" Christopher queried with a smile?

"Hell, in any order you like," Gabby enthused.

"You randy little polecat," Christopher laughed. He knew just the place. Five miles down the road was a nice little boudoir that served a more exclusive clientele, at least that's what he'd heard. The prices certainly reflected their boast anyway. After that they could go on to Mobile and find somewhere to stay, take in a movie, have a feed. Christopher had an Aunt living in Mobile and he was duty bound to make a call.

Christopher turned off the road to the track leading to Madam Giselle's. In times past it had been a summer home for a banker from New York with southern roots. Now it was a bordello of some repute where the booze wasn't watered down and the women's beauty was commensurate to the price. They parked outside and Christopher led the way.

Inside, the hall was white wood panelled walls, polished floor and expensive rugs. The place was buzzing with the sound of music and spirited conversation. Stairs went up to a broad landing and a few scantily clad lovelies hung over the upper balcony.

"Hallelujiah," Gabby whispered. He was about to set

foot on the stairs when a portly woman of advanced years interposed herself in front of him.

"What'll it be fellers?" She asked smoothly. She looked them up and down in the calculating appraising way all women seemed to have down cold. Christopher screamed money. Although he was only a Junior Grade Lieutenant, his uniform jacket was well tailored, an obvious sign of wealth. She could see the other two weren't officers because of their bell bottom trousers and round hats. Gabby got straight down to the negotiating.

"Now look here, mother, I've been working very hard." He flashed her a glimpse of a money clip and peeled off a few Dollar notes, almost waving them under her nose. Somewhat mollified, Gabby was allowed up the stairs to make his choice. Eyes bulging at the delights on offer, he zeroed in on a brunette with a dancer's figure and stocking clad legs.

No blushing virgin; Callicoe left Gabby to it and followed Christopher into one of the room downstairs. On the drive over, he had warred with his conscience, wondering if he was being disloyal to Charlotte by coming here.

"It's not like you're engaged," Christopher had told him. "A few more months and we'll be gone. We made it pretty clear at the beginning it was going to be nothing more than friends."

Callicoe knew he was right, but it didn't stop his British sense of fair play trying to mess with him.

The room was full of patrons sat in easy chairs. Ladies circulated around. They made sure their drinks were topped up and they didn't lack for company. Christopher relaxed on one half of a couple's chair and it wasn't long before a statuesque blonde in a barely there negligee joined him. Callicoe circulated round before settling himself on an elaborate Queen Anne style settee with spindly legs and velvet cushions. A petite red head brought him a glass filled with whisky and ice.

"You look like a whisky man to me," she told him, her voice a rolling husky drawl. Callicoe took a sip and winced, the only water in there was from the melting ice. She slid next to him with a sibilant hiss of silk and draped an arm over his shoulders. She ran a finger around the black handkerchief at his neck and fixed him with a hooded look, her tongue licking her lips.

He turned his attention to the girl. She was very pretty, with a heart shaped face, her hair cut short, framing her cheekbones. Her hand descended and started rubbing in small circles. Callicoe felt a stirring and he shifted, a little uncomfortable at being in view of other people.

"Don't worry about everyone else, honey," she whispered. Callicoe tried to relax. Sensing his discomfort, she pulled on his hand, getting him to his feet. Callicoe went along without any resistance, across the room, into the hall and up the stairs. His last glimpse of Christopher was the American giving him an encouraging nod while he undid the laces of his girl's negligee.

It didn't take Callicoe's girl long to get down to business. She sat him down on the bed and straddled him, her fingers deftly undoing the handkerchief at his throat. He put his hat on her head and she pushed him back onto the soft mattress. She leaned over him, arms either side of his head. Her ample breasts brushed against his chest.

"Now then, tell, Sarah about home," she said as her head went lower.

Callicoe drank a bottle of beer while he sat on the bonnet of Christopher's red Cadillac, waiting for the others to emerge. His wallet may have been a few dollars light but he was in a very relaxed frame of mind.

Christopher came out five minutes later, his tie awry. He sorted himself out as he walked down the steps of the veranda. Callicoe handed him a beer and a bottle opener.

"Thank you." Christopher sat on the curved bonnet as well, his feet perched on the chrome bumper. "I thought you just wanted some booze?" he asked his friend. Callicoe shifted and cleared his throat.

"Well you know; when in Rome," he said airily.

"We ain't in Rome, Jimmy."

"You got that right," said Gabby as he clattered through the entrance to join them by the car.

"Did you have second helpings or something?" Callicoe asked.

"Please, sir, can I have some more?" Gabby replied, snickering at his little joke.

They piled into the car and headed to Mobile.

"So how was it?" Christopher asked.

"A gentleman never tells," Gabby said, tapping the side of his nose. He was grinning from ear to ear so Christopher assumed he'd had a good time.

They were still extolling the virtues of the place when they got to Mobile. Christopher found some digs at a motel and then they went off in search of food. They came across a late night diner and feasted on steak and ice cream close to midnight. Christopher watched in horrified fascination as Gabby polished off two bowls of ice cream and a huge glass of ice cold Coke.

"I don't know how you do it."

Gabby wiped his mouth on his sleeve and burped.

"We don't have this at home. I'm not missing the opportunity while I'm here."

They slept late. After a hearty breakfast, Christopher went to see his Aunt. He dropped Callicoe and Gabby in the centre of town and told him he'd meet them outside a cinema. He wrote the address down on a piece of paper and gave it to Callicoe. They found the town of Mobile was a hive of activity awash with uniforms. They saw the shipyards going full tilt churning out liberty ships for the

Atlantic.

Worn out from all the walking, they caught a bus back to town. The bus was quite full but they went to the empty back seats to claim them before anyone else did. It took a minute for them to realise they hadn't moved. When they looked around, they saw everyone glaring at them, black and white people alike. Callicoe saw a yellow line painted on the floor of the bus in front of the last three rows of seats. The bus didn't move an inch until they got off the seats and stood in the aisle.

They talked about it in hushed whispers over ice cream in a diner. It was their first direct experience with segregation in the American south. Callicoe had seen signs in some shops, saying things like *'No Coloured'*, but it had never really sunk in before now that there was such a blatant division.

Their mood perked up when they met Christopher. He took them to a dance at a music hall. Gabby consoled himself with a raven haired goddess. Callicoe felt a little uncomfortable when he noticed everyone dancing were white, the band playing were all black.

They drove back to the station in good time and got to the main gate close to 10pm. The barrier was down and Christopher impatiently tapped his fingers off the steering wheel while they waited for a guard to appear.

After a few minutes, no one showed up and Gabby lost patience. He got out of the car and flounced over to the wooden pole barring their way. He laid one finger on it when he was tackled from behind and clattered to the ground.

He rolled over to find a rifle muzzle poking him in the nose. At the other end was an MP Corporal, his face a mask of stern authority.

"State your business," he ordered. Gabby was about to move but the muzzle pressed into his cheek. "I said state your business, boy."

"I'd like to get onto the base please," Gabby said, his voice a squeaky parody of its normal confident self.

"You don't just let yourself in here, pal."

"I wouldn't have to if you'd been here," Gabby argued back. "Aren't you supposed to be on guard?"

The MP was about to yank him to his feet when Christopher's steady voice cut across the argument.

"Corporal, if I might have a word?"

3 - Swans

Within a week of going solo, the course had its next casualty. A candidate's engine cut on take off and he stupidly tried to get back to the field to land. Another one died the same way the day after. Luke had told Callicoe time and again that when your engine cut, you got down any way you could, but you landed straight ahead. With limited airspeed, you had to trade height to stop yourself from stalling. There was no reserve to try and turn and make it back to the field.

That opened the floodgates and there was a rash of accidents in the next few days. Two aircraft crashed at the remote fields. One did a low pass and clipped a hangar. The other thumped down too hard and folded the undercarriage, slithering to a stop on his belly.

Two other aircraft were written off during formation flying. The trailing aircraft got too close to the one in front and their propeller chewed through the tail. The leading aircraft went straight in. The other pilot managed to bail out but banged his head on the tail plane when he went over the side. He managed to pull his ripcord before he passed out. He was found unconscious in a field with two broken legs and a fractured skull. He lingered in the hospital for two weeks before he died.

That brought home to them all the dangers of flying. Up until the time they went solo, their instructor's warnings had rung in their ears, but it was all so abstract. The crashes made it very real.

Once technical failure was removed from the equation, most accidents were down to inexperience and youthful exuberance. Luke knew why of course. Flying was a thrill. If you let young men loose with a powerful aircraft, then they were tempted to push things to see what they could do. They would dare themselves to make a turn that little bit tighter, pull a loop a little lower than the instructors let you. Sometimes they went too far and paid the price.

Callicoe went to more funerals in a month than he had in a lifetime. For Luke, it was par for the course and he faced this struggle every time a new intake came through *Pensacola*. When you flew with someone and saw them at the bar in off duty hours, you got to know them and sometimes even like them. It was hard to put them in the ground. He' d lost count of how many students he'd lost in the last year.

Flying could be cruel. The principles of flight were quite simple, but not everyone had the knack or the touch to fly. Fish Salmon demonstrated his lack of spatial awareness with heavy landings that brought him to the attention of the course commanders. In the air, he was a capable pilot, but he just couldn't judge his height when he got close to the ground. Despite his protestations that he would get better, his flying career was over.

A Navy Lieutenant from Callicoe's room threw up every time his instructor demonstrated a loop or a roll. He was grounded too. The prevailing view being that a man who couldn't keep his lunch down on a simple training flight would not improve with time.

Luke worked his students hard in the months to come. Every day he gave them instruction in the morning and time to practise in the afternoon. Luke wanted to see progress and he gave Callicoe and his other pupils as much room as he could.

"All I want is to see improvement," Luke told them. "You aren't all going to be General Doolittle. Natural pilots are rare. Similarly, you aren't complete idiots, but you can't make too many mistakes. You can't force an aircraft to do things, you have to finesse it."

He demonstrated the point simply enough. He got up to altitude and threw the aircraft around beyond its limits. The airframe would vibrate, one wing would drop and they would go into a spin. Luke cut the throttle, centred the stick, put on opposite rudder and then forward elevator. The engine picked up, they stopped spinning and Luke pulled out of the dive.

"Do that too low and you'll make a neat little hole in the ground. I'd just rather you do it without me around."

Luke demonstrated basic aerobatics, loops and rolls. Once he was happy they could manage those he started to throw in some more complex manoeuvres. That was when Callicoe came alive. Flying straight and level from A to B was not the same as chucking a kite around the sky.

During their lessons, Luke always tried to impart little grains of knowledge. Invariably they were stories about mistakes he'd made in his own flying career. It put a human face on things rather than a bland admonition in a training manual. He talked about the Japanese fighters and how nimble they were. He'd seen them firsthand for himself at Midway eighteen months before. They'd danced rings around him when he'd tried to turn with them in his tubby Grumman Wildcat. He'd been lucky enough to bail out and spent four hours bobbing in the middle of the Pacific before a PT Boat picked him up.

Towards the end of the primary course, they progressed onto blind flying training. Callicoe spent hours in a Link Trainer sat in a wooden box, which mimicked an aircraft's cockpit. He had a set of flight controls and instruments. He had to keep an eye on his dials, using the climb and descent indicator, the turn and slip indicator, artificial horizon and airspeed indicator. If his speed increased, he must be diving, if it dropped, he was climbing.

It was all very simple in theory but it took a lot of concentration to get it right. He had to focus on the instruments while navigating using a map and a stopwatch. Outside of the box, Luke had a set of duplicate instruments to see what he was doing. Callicoe's position was marked on a huge map board.

To begin with, it was a challenge just to stop himself from crashing into the hypothetical ground. After a few goes, he started to get the hang of it. Once Luke was happy he could manage he introduced the next level of complexity, blind landing. Callicoe thought he was crazy when he first told him but again, it was straightforward.

When you approached a runway with a beam landing system, you heard a noise in your headphones. Different noises told you if you were on track, too far left or right or high or low or even on the right speed.

After hours sweating in the Link Trainer, they went out to do it for real in an airplane. A hood was fitted over the rear cockpit and Luke took Callicoe out for some real life blind flying. It was very strange, being sat in the cockpit in the dark. More than once he told Luke they had arrived at their destination to find they were over the water. Things like that dented your confidence.

Luke kept him at it. He felt this was something the students needed to be good at. They had to have belief in their own abilities and had to learn to trust what the instruments were telling them.

The course averaged at least one accident a week, particularly after they started formation flying. Once more the instructors took them back to basics, building up the student's confidence until they felt comfortable flying alongside another aircraft.

Final check rides rounded out their time at *Pensacola*. They progressed to *NAS Opa Locka*, south of Miami.

"Coo that's a mouthful," Gabby commented as they were packing their things in the billet. "I wonder what the women are like?"

Callicoe rolled his eyes. Ever since Christopher had taken them to the brothel down the road, Gabby had been a regular patron. He was bereft at the thought of leaving his favourites behind.

"I'm sure they've got two legs and two arms just like everywhere else," he reassured Gabby.

Luke was all smiles when he saw Callicoe off.

"Don't do anything I wouldn't," he told his younger charge.

"I'll try not to," Callicoe replied, touched by his concern. Luke leaned in close as he shook his hand.

"Watch out for the instructors there, they're a ruthless lot." Callicoe didn't know if he was kidding or not.

Opa Locka was another big well appointed station. The Americans certainly didn't do anything by halves. It had eight runways, numerous hangars, workshops and hundreds of aircraft. The place was a constant hive of activity. Twelve Thousand pilot candidates had gone through the place in a year. Despite the quantity, the staff prided themselves on turning out a high quality of airman.

The accommodations were to the usual high standard they had come to expect. When he thought about the state of conditions at *Saint Vincent*, Callicoe was appalled at how much privation they had put up with in those Victorian barrack blocks.

Going from *Pensacola* to *NAS Opa Lacka* was like being promoted in the football league. They traded in their old biplanes and obsolete trainers like the N3N and the OS2U Kingfisher for the more powerful AT6 Texan. A modern, monoplane trainer, it could do up to 200mph in a dive, had a fully enclosed cockpit, flaps and retractable undercarriage.

Opa Locka was ideal for more advanced flying. The airfield was surrounded by the Everglades, miles and miles of mangrove swamps, low lying marshland and forest. With no locals to upset they spent hours roaring over the soggy terrain practising their formation flying.

Luke's warning to Callicoe about the instructors proved to be more prophetic than he thought. Callicoe was assigned a Lieutenant called Curlew who was a stickler for discipline. Where Luke had kept up a constant flow of good natured banter while he instructed, Curlew was as silent as the grave, only speaking to criticise. He was sparing with his praise and seemed to harbour a particular dislike of Englishmen.

He was quick to show his power, in the air and on the ground, expecting to be shown deference to his every utterance. Callicoe was sure he deliberately washed out one RAF candidate just to show that he could do it. How Gabby survived was anyone's guess. His flippant character put him firmly in Curlew's firing line, but in the air, he was exemplary, doing exactly what he was told and flying by the book.

Their training progressed to aerial gunnery and they sat through hours of lectures, learning the complexities of deflection shooting. Films and lectures laid out the principles of how to get into a firing position and how to bounce a target from out of the sun. They listened with rapt attention to a guest speaker who told them about fighting the Japanese at Coral Sea.

The next plane they were checked out on was the Brewster Buffalo, a tubby short winged fighter that was obsolete before the war had even begun. Armed with two machine guns in the wings they went out in groups and tore up the everglades. Flying at two and three thousand feet, they would shove the nose down, line up on paper targets and blast them to bits.

Christopher led a group of four Buffaloes including Gabby east over the Everglades. They flew in a loose pair's formation at five thousand feet. When they'd gone far enough, Christopher took them lower. There were so few people living in the Everglades it wasn't like flying at *Pensacola* where you would get spotted. They shifted into line astern and tore across the tops of the mangrove trees.

They flashed over a clearing with a pond of brackish water in the middle. That would do perfectly for some strafing. Christopher zoomed up to two thousand feet and levelled off. He waited until everyone was in position and then checked that they were clear. There wasn't another aircraft in the sky.

"Okay boys. Follow me in. Just remember to leave yourselves plenty of room." He stood his Buffalo on its port wing and went screaming into the attack. A heavy fighter, the Buffalo was good in a dive and rock steady as a gun platform which made it perfect for training. Gabby watched Christopher continue to go down, expecting to see the familiar puffs of smoke as he opened fire with his wing mounted guns.

The Buffalo never pulled out of its dive. It went straight in at over three hundred miles per hour. There was a huge splash as it ploughed into the pond and buried itself in the mud. When the spray died down, the stubby tail stuck up out of the water. Gabby called it in immediately. They circled the crash site until a swamp boat came out from the station to investigate. Christopher's body was dug out of the wreckage and the funeral was held the following Sunday.

The last few weeks at Opa Locka were bleak for Callicoe. He'd come to accept accidents during training, but Christopher's death shocked him deeply. Inspection of the wreckage failed to provide an obvious reason for the crash, which left a bad taste in everyone's mouth. They needed to trust their aircraft and suddenly there was a question mark that couldn't be wiped away.

Callicoe wrote Ariadne a long letter, his first for many months trying to put into words how he felt. When he was finished, he binned it, it wasn't what he wanted to say at all.

The Chief Flying Instructor had Callicoe on the mat the following day after a landing accident. Still distracted by Christopher's death, he'd hit the brakes a little too smartly while taxying and stood his Buffalo on her nose. There was a loud tearing sound as the propeller was turned into scrap. He ended up hanging in his straps, staring at the runway.

The CFI threw the book at him, marked him down and told him if he did it again, he'd be going home. So close to the finish line, Callicoe swallowed hard at that. It took the intervention of the Royal Navy Liaison officer, Commander Willows to pour some oil on the troubled waters.

"It's a lapse, I grant you, but considering his record I think we can afford to be a little more forgiving," he said smoothly, his voice a nasal drawl. "You've got how many hours now, Callicoe?"

"Over two hundred, sir."

"Two hundred and twenty to be precise," Willows informed him, glancing at his record. "I also note a letter from your primary flying instructor, Lieutenant Luke USNR. He spoke quite highly of you." Callicoe perked up a bit at that. "Just don't do it again will you?"

His path crossed with the CFI again two weeks later but this time he wasn't in trouble. After passing the final exams, he had one last assessed solo ride to graduate from the flying program. Callicoe performed the required manoeuvres, did a touch and go, landed, took off again and then brought the Buffalo in. The CFI kept a poker face as he wrote up his notes.

A list was posted the following morning saying who had graduated, Callicoe's name was on it. The course paraded at the theatre to be awarded their diplomas and Navy wings by the Station Commander. He went down the line, spending a few minutes with each man and shaking their hand as he pinned wings on their chest.

After the parade, they made a beeline for Commander Willows office. He was waiting for them, taking the lid off a tin box which contained gold thread Fleet Air Arm wings.

They were awarded their commissions as Sub Lieutenants a few days later. The local tailors did a roaring trade in outfitting these new officers with the dark jackets and white topped peaked caps to complete their wardrobe. Callicoe couldn't help himself from preening as he admired the single gold stripe and the wings on his arm. The surviving RAF and Fleet Air Arm candidates had a course photograph outside the control tower to record the event.

4 – Roll Out The Welcome Mat

Eleven months after he'd said goodbye to his family, Callicoe returned. He walked up the drive just as the light was starting to go. With a kit bag under one arm and suitcase in the other he couldn't be bothered to fish for his key so he pushed the door bell.

There was a moment's pause and then he heard Margaret's light tread on the wooden floor inside. There was a rattle as she took off the chain and then a click as she opened the big front door. For a moment, all she saw was a dark shape in a thick coat with gold braid at the sleeves. She gave a sharp intake of breath as it registered in her head who it was.

"Why, James. Come in," she told him, her voice a little unsteady. She stepped back and he walked into the house. Once she locked the door, she put the hall light back on.

"Who is it?" Ariadne's voice called from the rear parlour.

"You'll never guess," Margaret replied.

Callicoe took a few moments to get used to the heat of the house. His cheeks tingled from the cold outside. He unbuttoned his greatcoat and took off his peaked cap, hanging them both on the hooks by the door. He noticed Margaret didn't give him a hand with that, nor did she go anywhere near his kit bag or suitcase either. Some things never changed.

"You should have let us know you were coming," she admonished him. "Your rooms not been turned over or anything."

Callicoe wasn't bothered. After the barrack blocks at

Saint Vincent, a room was a room. He was just surprised she hadn't rented it out, but then father probably hadn't allowed her. He assured her it was no problem.

"I've been travelling since early this morning. I didn't think you'd have appreciated a call at 5am when I left Liverpool."

Her lips pulled tight in annoyance at his arriving unannounced. She didn't like surprises. She offered her cheek and Callicoe leaned in and kissed her in the European way as she preferred.

He took his bags up to his room. The air was musty and there was a strong smell of mothballs. He could tell the place hadn't been touched since he'd left it at the beginning of the year. The only evidence of interference was his mother's picture was missing from his bedside. He opened the top drawer. The picture frame lay on a bed of rolled socks. He took it out of its hiding place and put it back by his bed where it belonged.

He went downstairs to the parlour. This was Margaret's favourite room in the house. As his father had his office, Margaret had the parlour as her personal space. If you needed to find her, that's where you would expect her to be.

Ten feet square, the walls were painted a lemon yellow. The south facing windows went from the floor to the ceiling, just like the reception room. There was a delicate fireplace with two armchairs and a chaise longue arrayed around it. The only other thing in the room was a small walnut bookcase on the back wall. It contained heavy tomes such as Shakespeare and a variety of trashy romance novels. Margaret kept them strictly in alphabetical order according to genre. Young Callicoe had taken great delight in creeping into the room when she was otherwise engaged and moving them around.

He found Margaret and Ariadne at their repose in the armchairs, legs crossed at the ankle. They were nibbling on fresh baked biscuits and drinking tea from fine bone china. The room was stifling, a good blaze going in the fire. Ariadne stood up, brushed down her skirt and hugged him warmly.

"Welcome back," she said.

Margaret didn't offer him the chaise longue. Callicoe sat down anyway. Margaret pointed at the pilot's wings on his left sleeve.

"So, you made it then?"

"I did," he said with some pride. "Lots didn't." Ariadne arched an eyebrow in enquiry but Callicoe didn't elaborate further. Of the starting group at *Saint Vincent*, fifteen had fallen by the wayside. Six had died in accidents, nine had washed out and been sent back home.

"How long have you got?" Ariadne asked.

"Two weeks," Callicoe replied. "I'm to report to *RNAS Saint Merryn* in the New Year."

"Where's that?"

"Cornwall. I had to look it up."

Margaret excused herself to let cook know there would be another one for dinner.

Throughout their journey back to England they had debated what was going to happen to them. They could end up flying Swordfish or Fulmars or something more modern. Gabby was certain Curlew had marked his card and thought he was going to end up flying a Walrus seaplane.

He was delighted to find out he was going to *Saint Merryn* too along with some of the others from the course. At Liverpool they were issued rail warrants, passes for a fortnight's leave and orders to report on a certain date. Callicoe would have asked Gabby to stay with him, but he knew what Margaret would be like, he'd never hear the end of it.

"You're not normally here at this time," Callicoe commented.

"Bridge night," Ariadne told him. "We started having them about six months ago. Once a week like clockwork," she said with little enthusiasm. "Frank's suddenly become very interested in the game. I suppose he thinks it'll get him noticed for a promotion."

Callicoe nodded his understanding. He was intimately familiar with the politicking that went on at the Ministries. His father had played the game for a long time; hitching his cart to projects to get noticed and get his name mentioned in the right ears. There were regular soirees where civil servants gathered to exchange ideas and show off their wives. There was a subtle order of rank at those sorts of dos.

Callicoe had never had the patience for all of that nonsense. Besides, he wasn't married and you could only really get ahead if you had a wife. They didn't hand out senior positions to lone wolves. In Ariadne, Frank had the perfect foil to his talents. She was smart, with a sharp line in humour when she could be bothered and she did a good turn as dutiful hostess when required.

Even with two daughters, she looked after herself and there was rarely a hair out of place in her attire. "The kids keep me fit," she had told him once. "You try chasing after two girls all day and see what it does for you."

They looked up when there was a noise in the hall and the men came home. Frank appeared at the door to the parlour.

"It was deathly quiet so we-Jim!" he exclaimed. "My word, it's good to see you."

He shook his brother's hand warmly. He grazed Ariadne's cheek with a kiss and said hello to Margaret.

"Have you been here long?"

"An hour or so."

"Well," Frank was at a loss for a moment as his mind whirled with questions. "Fathers in his office," he said in the end. Callicoe nodded and left them in the parlour. He went back into the hall. The light was on in his father's office, the light spilling through the doorway at the foot of the stairs. Callicoe knocked on the frame.

"Father?"

Callicoe senior had his back to the door, pulling folders out of his battered leather briefcase. Callicoe saw his father's shoulders stiffen before he recovered himself. He put the briefcase down on the top of the desk and slowly turned round.

He looked at his son, seeing the uniform, the braid at his sleeve. He straightened, shoulders back, almost like he was on the parade square.

"James," he said, his voice formal. Callicoe took two steps into the office. The room hadn't changed. It was the same disorganised mess it had always been. Piles of papers occupied the windowsills. Pink folders with red ribbons were shoved in between volumes of the Encyclopedia Britannica.

Callicoe had always been a little mystified by this aspect of his father's character. At work, everything was in its place; he ran a tight ship and expected exactitude from his staff. At home, he worked in a looser manner. The secret was, it might look a mess, but he knew what was where. Margaret was forbidden from tidying up in that room. It was his one small act of rebellion in a home life otherwise kept in order by his wife.

"So you didn't kill yourself," he stated to his son.

"No father."

Callicoe took two more steps into the room until three feet separated him from his father. It might as well have been the Grand Canyon.

"Well, I'll see you at dinner," he gestured to the folders. "I have some work to do."

Callicoe sighed and left the room. As he heard his son going up the stairs, Martin made to call him back and then stopped himself. He stood listening to the clock for a few minutes before sitting down behind his desk. He took his pince nez out of their case and settled them on his nose.

Dinner was a strained affair. Cook had done her best, but at short notice she'd had to think on her feet to provide enough dinner for everyone. She resorted to boiling some carrots and extra potatoes to extend the rabbit stew she had produced. Callicoe found he did most of the talking, telling them about his time in America.

Ariadne helped keep the conversation going, getting him to expand on things he had written about in his letters. She was enthralled at his descriptions of life at *Pensacola*. No one quite believed him when he talked about the food. After years of rationing, the thought of limitless amounts of steak and ice cream seemed like a fairytale.

"I know two people who'd like to go there," Ariadne said with a smile, thinking about Lucy and Emma at home with her parents. She smiled brightly for a moment before her thoughts turned darkly to other things. She shot a glance at Frank on the other side of the table, watching him as he sucked on his spoon.

Callicoe saw her demeanour change and followed her look to his brother. Frank used a napkin to wipe some sauce off his chin.

"You know, we should get the recipe for this," he told his wife. "Lovely sauce."

"I'll let cook know," Margaret said.

Ariadne made a mental note to make sure she had the recipe before they went home. Frank would expect to see it on his own dinner table in the near future. That was his way, what he wanted, he got.

They retired to the living room for after dinner drinks before playing Bridge. Callicoe watched for a little while before pleading fatigue. He left them to it and went upstairs to his room. He took some time hanging his uniform up. He brushed down the jacket and then fussed when he put it on its hangar, straightening the shoulders. The gold braid glinted in the glare of the sidelight. He stroked the wings for a moment before putting it in the wardrobe.

He was asleep before his head hit the pillow.

Callicoe woke late. After the stress of nearly a year of non stop study to get his wings and commission, it had finally caught up with him. He spent most of the morning in bed in that fuzzy place where you're not quite awake and not quite asleep. There was no reveille, no need to get outside in the cold to do PT and no instructors hounding you to get to class or do a perfect flat turn.

He dragged himself downstairs at eleven, yawned and trailed into the kitchen. Cook rapped his knuckles with a wooden spoon when she caught him in the pantry cutting a corner off a block of cheese.

"If you want something, ask," she told him sternly. Fifteen years she'd worked for this family and he had never changed. As a boy it had been biscuits, when he got older, he had progressed to snaffling cheese.

"Sandwich," he pleaded. She pointed to the door.

"I'll bring it out to you."

Callicoe did as he was bid. He went back into the hall, located the days paper and sat down at the dining table. The Russians were pushing back against the Germans and there was a feature about the meeting of the Big Three, Roosevelt, Stalin and Churchill. There was a big photograph of them sat together on the front page. There was an article about the campaign to retake the Gilbert islands. It had started in November and the Americans were going island to island in tough fighting. Callicoe assumed events had moved on since then.

Cook came in with a sandwich and a cup of tea. She

departed silently while Callicoe pondered what to do with himself. If Margaret stuck to her usual routine, she would be at some society meeting and wouldn't be back until mid afternoon.

He went back upstairs, had a shave and then changed into one of his suits. He looked at himself in the mirror with some concern. The trousers were loose and the jacket hung on his frame a little large. He went into town, catching a bus into Kingston.

He pottered around the streets and bought a few things for Christmas. He came back in the afternoon with a number of items and a roll of brown paper. He was wrapping them in his room when Margaret returned.

"Good afternoon," he said from the top of the stairs. Margaret jumped slightly, not expecting him to be in.

"Oh, it's you," she said in ill humour.

Callicoe sighed. So, it was going to be one of *those* days. He left Margaret to whatever it was she did and returned to his room, descending when the dinner bell rang.

During dinner, his father talked at length about a proposed change to rationing which had been the doing the rounds at the Ministry. Soundings were being taken about how the new proposals might be received. Callicoe didn't bother commenting, certain whatever he said wouldn't be right.

That was the pattern for the next few days. He rose late, went out for a few hours, endured dinner and drinks with his father and Margaret and then either listened to the radio or read a book. When he'd been in America, he'd been looking forward to some leave. Now he was on leave, he couldn't wait to go back to strap himself into a Seafire or a Hurricane.

On Christmas Eve, Frank and Ariadne arrived with the children to stay for a few days. That had become the family tradition the last few years. One year, Frank and his family would come here, the next year they would go to Ariadne's parents. For a few days the house was alive to the sounds of delighted children enjoying themselves.

Callicoe managed to make it a little more special with his presents which he'd purchased in the USA. Ariadne and Margaret received a silk dressing gown each. Frank and his father got Cartridge pens he'd bought in New York. The girls went mad for the toys he'd bought from Bentalls.

"You spoil them," Ariadne told him later, "but thank you."

Callicoe shrugged.

"Christmas comes but once a year."

She kissed him on the cheek, her hand lingering on his arm.

"You're too sweet."

Callicoe played with the girls. He helped them set up the board game and did his best to lose as often as possible. Ariadne kept him supplied with drinks but he had to ask her more than once to add more water. She had quite a few drinks herself as did Frank.

After the girls had gone to bed, Callicoe put on the radio while the others set up the card table and sat down to play bridge.

Ariadne tried to interest him but Callicoe declined. He puffed away quite happily while he started a new book he'd bought in town.

Callicoe listened with half an ear as they played. The game was bad natured from the start with Frank admonishing Ariadne for some bad bidding for tricks during one rubber.

"You must try harder, Ari. Really." Frank said as he began shuffling the pack for another hand. He spilled the cards and cursed as he scrabbled around on the floor to pick them up. His mood only improved when he won a game.

45

Callicoe noted his brother was the worse for wear and he thought back to how many drinks he'd had. Frank had started early in the morning and continued steadily since then. Ariadne wasn't far behind him either. He knew there was no point mentioning it. It would only cause embarrassment all round and he didn't want to spoil the day.

On Boxing Day, they went to the morning service and Callicoe made his peace with god. He reckoned he'd used up a few of his lives already and he decided a little bit of spiritual top cover wouldn't go amiss.

Ariadne had her hands full keeping the two girls in line. They fidgeted throughout the service and when they got outside, both of them earned a smacked bottom from Frank for not doing as they were told. There were tears and Callicoe didn't know where to look as the congregation filed past. Before they left, the Priest came over to see him.

"Merry Christmas to you, James."

"Thank you, Father."

"You've been away a long time."

"I might be away longer still after New Year."

The Priest nodded in understanding.

"You know where I am if you wish to see me. I hope you enjoy your leave."

The atmosphere in the house was tense when they got back. His father didn't like public displays of emotion and he remonstrated with Frank over his lack of restraint in his office. Callicoe heard the raised voices through the door and he did his best to distract the girls by putting the radio on and telling them a story.

"It won't do, Frank. You know how people gossip." Frank was abashed.

"Father-"

"Do not interrupt!" Martin gripped the arms of his

chair, his knuckles white. "I've told you time and again about public displays. Things like that get noticed."

"Yes Father."

"What's bothering you my boy? Everything in your Department's okay isn't it."

Franks jaw tensed, the muscles in his neck standing out.

"It's not that."

"Well whatever it is, sort yourself out."

Frank emerged from the office, slamming the door behind him. He stalked into the reception room and made a beeline for the drinks cabinet. He sloshed scotch into a tumbler and drank it quickly. It had been a few years since he'd been lashed like that. He swallowed his pride and painted a smile on his face. He clapped his hands and went over to the girls.

"Now then," he said, "who wants to play a game?"

Cook had Boxing Day off but she had prepared food for supper, there was a selection of cold meat, cheeses, bread and some Mackerel. Callicoe made up a plate and topped the cheese with some pickled onions. Ariadne came into the kitchen while he was at the table.

"Top shelf," he said as she started hunting on the shelves.

"Is it that obvious?" she asked, her voice echoing. She found the tin she was looking for and came into the kitchen. She spooned out some Alka-Seltzer into a cup and filled it with water.

"That for you or for Frank?" he asked.

"Both," she replied tightly. For a moment, her shoulders sagged and her head dropped before she recovered herself. She smiled brightly, eyes sparkling slightly. She wiped a hand across her face and left the kitchen.

5 – The Danger Of Expectation

The next day, the weather was cold but clear and they went for a walk in Richmond Park. Frank and his father stalked ahead, setting a brisk pace. Margaret did her best to keep pace with them while Callicoe took his time, walking with Ariadne and the girls. They were keen to see deer but there weren't any in view.

"We'll see them next time," Ariadne assured them. The girls nodded, half listening as they skipped along. She took Callicoe's arm as they walked.

"Tell me more about the American girls," she urged him and Callicoe laughed.

"What would you like to know?" he asked her.

"Are they like they are in the films?"

Callicoe had to think about that.

"I think yes," he said after some consideration. "The ones I met were confident, dressed well, stylish. I suppose that's more to do with the place. No blackout, no rationing on clothes."

Ariadne playfully slapped his arm.

"Brute. Gosh, I'd love to go there and see what you've seen."

"When it's all over you will," he assured her. "But perhaps you don't have to wait so long," he said, his tone teasing.

"And what's that supposed to mean?"

"Ah, that would be telling."

She was good enough to laugh.

When they got back to the house, she bid the girls up to their room and asked them to get changed for dinner.

While they were getting out of their clothes, she went into Callicoe's room.

"So, what have you brought me?" she asked him. She opened the wardrobe door rummaged around inside. She saw his uniform hanging there and ran a hand down the sleeve, her fingers lingering on the gold braid at the cuff. She picked up the white peaked cap and perched it on her head. She turned and gave him a little twirl.

Callicoe rose from his bed and took it back. He returned it to its shelf in the wardrobe and closed the door. He stretched to reach to the top of the wardrobe and pulled down a parcel and handed it to Ariadne. She clapped her hands in delight.

"I knew it."

She opened the parcel and pulled out four pairs of silk stockings. There was a ruby red silk scarf in there as well.

"Oh, James, thank you."

"I had bought them for you and Margaret. I know things like that are in short supply but I, er, well, after thinking about it I didn't think it was the most appropriate thing to give your stepmother after all."

"Her loss, is my gain," Ariadne said as she opened one of the packets of stockings and ran her fingers over the material. She fixed Callicoe with a smile and kissed his cheek.

He taught the girls how to play Hearts in the afternoon and Ariadne made up the four. Frank retired to his father's office and the pair of them spent a few hours drafting a response to a Ministry proposal. Margaret went to her parlour and caught up on some of the correspondence from her committee work.

Callicoe stopped after two whisky's but Ariadne continued drinking. After three whiskies of her own she moved onto a bottle of blueberry wine. Callicoe put a hand over the glass at one point and eyed her with some concern.

"Ariadne," he cautioned.

"I know what I'm doing," she said. She moved his hand off the glass but drank no more. She kept her focus on the children, encouraging them to play a certain card.

"Your leave finishes soon."

"Yes."

"What happens after Cornwall?"

"I don't know. I don't even know how long I'll be there. The Navy runs to its own schedule."

Ariadne snorted.

"Like the Ministry then," she said. Callicoe looked at her quizzically as he caught a slight catch to her voice. She shot him a look, daring him to say something, her eyes flaring in challenge like they had last Christmas.

It was late when Callicoe awoke. He lay there for a while, but his stomach was grumbling so he crept downstairs and went prowling in the pantry. He was making up a plate of some crackers, an apple and some cheese when he felt a hand on his shoulder.

He jumped in shock and luckily caught the plate before it hit the floor and smashed into a thousand pieces. Margaret would have gone beserk if he'd broken a plate.

"Jesus, Ariadne, you scared the daylights out of me."

"I'm sorry," she whispered. She bent down and picked up the apple. Callicoe put the plate on the shelf while he steadied his nerves.

They stood close together in the pantry, her breath warm on his chest. He saw she was wearing the silk dressing gown he had brought her for Christmas. She looked up at him and suddenly she lunged forward and kissed him on the lips. Callicoe backed up until he was pressed against the wall. His eyes had gone wide in shock.

"Ari-"

"James. I-" She was about to flee when he stopped her.

"No. Not like this." Her eyes darted around the kitchen, looking for somewhere to run. "Ariadne." Her head snapped back to look at him and she stopped pulling against his arm.

"I'm sorry; I-This is wrong."

She burst into tears and sagged onto the chair by the table. Callicoe pulled the kitchen door to. He stood listening for a few minutes, straining to hear if anyone was moving around upstairs. When he was satisfied they would be undisturbed he sat across from her.

He sat watching her, his mind racing at this turn of events. He thought things through, everything he had said and done for the last few days, wondering if he had made an improper comment. He came up blank.

Struggling for something to fill the void he lit the gas and put the kettle on. He studiously avoided looking at her while she sorted herself out. He got two cups, found the loose leaf tea and put two spoons of it in the teapot. Sniffing, Ariadne got the milk while he poured.

"Are you going to tell me about it," he said quietly, his voice barely above a whisper.

"It's; complicated," she said with a lopsided smile, her left cheek dimpling.

"It usually is," he gave her an encouraging smile. She reached a hand out to touch him but she paused in mid air and then withdrew it, wrapping her arms around herself. "Everythings not all right between you and, Frank, is it?" he ventured.

His question dropped into a pit of silence. He waited, not saying anything further. It was up to her to respond and say something next.

"No, it's not," she said, her face etched in despair. "That's one thing you learn being married to a civil servant. Appearance is everything. How did you know?"

"The little things. I don't think I've ever seen either of you drink so much before, certainly not in the day time.

His shortness with you when you were playing Bridge the other day. That's not a good sign. "

"He's become obsessed about forging a legacy," she told him. Callicoe cocked his head at that revelation. "The thought of promotion is everything."

"That doesn't sound like him."

"No, it doesn't. I suppose I'm to blame really."

"You?" His eyebrows shot up in surprise. "What did you do?"

His mind started whirring at the possibilities. The only answer he could come up with was that Frank had caught her in some indiscretion. Considering she'd kissed him; it wasn't impossible to conceive of the possibility. Her response surprised him.

"It's more what I didn't do."

She hesitated and looked at him, wondering if she should say any more. He saw her shrink into herself again, her courage deserting her. He gave her hand a reassuring squeeze. She drew some strength from that and carried on.

"I didn't give him a son," she said her voice bleak.

"But that's not your fault," Callicoe protested.

"Isn't it? Not long after you left, he told me he wanted to have another child; and I said no."

She thought back to that moment. It was not something she was likely to forget as long as she lived. She had been sat at her dressing table, brushing her hair as she did every night before going to bed. Frank had been working downstairs for hours. He came up to their room and told her he had made a decision and made his demand of her. Her whole world had collapsed in around itself as Frank upended everything.

"I mean, I can." She gestured towards herself with her hand. "There's no medical reason why I couldn't; but.." Her voice trailed off.

"You're worried," Callicoe finished for her.

"What if we had another girl? What would he do then? Demand a fourth, or a fifth? How many would it take?" She got up suddenly and paced around the table, the dressing gown wrapped tightly around her. Callicoe let her speak as the rest came rushing out. "So I said no. I didn't see what else I could do. It's tearing him up inside you know. This thought of not having a son. He's focused so much on work he barely speaks to me."

She sat down and started crying again, great shuddering silent sobs that shook her whole body.

"Does, Margaret know?" he asked, Ariadne recovered herself and shook her head.

"No. You know what her views on children are like."

Callicoe nodded slowly. Yes, he knew about that well enough. Ariadne laughed, her voice just that side of sane as she thought about Margaret, the porcelain goddess, never to be marred by the travails of childbirth.

"I'm not sure I know how to advise you, Ariadne. We've known each other a long time. I hate to see you so unhappy but I'm not sure what I can do."

She nodded in understanding. It had felt good just to get it out at last. Bottling it up all these months had put her under a great deal of strain.

"You won't talk to Frank, will you?" she asked, suddenly fearful.

"No. No, I won't do that," he reassured her. "I'm not sure I know how to even broach a subject like this. Obsession is a strange thing. It can't be reasoned with. I should know," he said with a laugh.

They sat in silence for a few minutes, each lost in their own thoughts. Callicoe moved his chair sideways so she was next to him. She leaned against him, resting her head on his shoulder.

"Do you hate me?" she asked.

"No. I don't blame you either. Maybe those stockings weren't such a good idea after all," he said ruefully. She laughed then and it was good to hear some life come back into her voice.

"Familiarity breeds contempt," she said, it had a tone of finality to it that Callicoe didn't like. "Maybe people aren't supposed to stay married for the rest of their lives?"

"People do change," he agreed. "But give him time. Frank's a bit slow sometimes. He doesn't have a lot of imagination. He'll get there, it'll just take him a bit longer."

She nodded, not entirely convinced but willing to give it a chance.

At breakfast you would never have known anything had happened. There was no puffed face or red eyes to betray her tears of the night before. She paid particular attention to Frank and made sure his breakfast was how he liked it. Margaret looked at her with some scrutiny but made no comment.

"You'll have dinner at our place before you go back?" Frank asked his brother as they said goodbye.

"Of course," Callicoe assured him.

The remaining few days of his leave went fast. He spent a pleasant few hours at Frank's house. Ariadne made the rabbit casserole they'd had a few days before and it was the perfect domestic scene. Afterwards, Callicoe played his brother at chess. Frank's plodding defence wore down Callicoe's aggressive play and eventually he conceded.

"Just write a bit more often, old man," Frank had asked him as he left. "Ariadne enjoyed your letters and the girls liked the stamps. They've decided they should collect some more."

"I will," Callicoe assured him.

He was just about to leave on the last day when

Margaret asked him to see his father in his office. Sighing heavily, Callicoe went downstairs in his uniform. He put his suitcase and kit bag by the door.

"You wanted to see me father?"

Callicoe senior looked up from his work. He half stood and gestured to the spare chair in front of his desk.

"Yes, my boy. Have a seat."

Surprised at his apparent warmth, Callicoe ventured into the room. He sat down, trying to calm his nerves.

"Just putting the finishing touches to a report. You know, it could have used your input. Your replacement isn't as good as you were."

Callicoe was warmed by the compliment but he was on edge. It was unlike his father to be so forward with his praise.

"This is difficult for me, you know." He cleared his throat and clasped his hands on his desk in front of him. Callicoe felt inside his pocket for his pipe. His hand closed around the bowl but he didn't pull it out just yet. "I never wanted you to join up, never; never."

He sighed and turned tired eyes on his son. It was like looking in a mirror, how he had been when he joined up himself to serve King and country.

The old hurts bubbled to the surface as he thought about the Yeomanry, his Battalion. He didn't need to see his leg to picture the scars, the torn flesh and what the pain had felt like. The thing he remembered most of all was the smell, the smell of death. When you went up the line, it clung to your clothes, it filled your nostrils, it permeated everything like a miasma of poison gas. It had taken him a long time to leave the demons behind.

He was scared now. Scared he'd lose his son and there was nothing he could do to stop it. He'd tried to protect Callicoe as best he could when the war started. He'd bent a lot of rules to get him into the Ministry and he'd been hurt when his son had defied him to join up.

"You said to me before that everyone needs to make their own way. You were right. It just took an old man a long time to see it."

"Is that an apology?" Callicoe asked slowly, doing his best to make it sound like a query and not a smug observation.

His father cleared his throat. His brow pinched as he looked at his son. That had been an uncharacteristic question. He searched Callicoe's face, seeing a difference there. He was harder somehow. He hadn't seen something like it since the war, when the threat of death had made men of boys.

"I suppose, in my way it is. I can't say I approve of your choice. I hate the idea of you going off to fight; but..I'm proud of you, my boy."

He came round the table to embrace his son. Taken off guard, Callicoe could only stand and put his arms around his father for the hug he had been waiting many years for.

6 – Get Your Feet Wet

It took him a moment to realise they were saluting him when he arrived at *Saint Merryn*. He flicked off a casual salute in return. The guards shared a look. Another fresh one. They bid him wait and gave him a cup of tea until some transport came.

A few minutes later, a Lieutenant turned up in a Tilly, a small utility vehicle with a two seat cab and a canvas covered flat bed on the back. The Lieutenant waved away Callicoe's salute and grabbed his kit bag, chucking it into the back of the car.

"Don't worry about that around me," he said cheerfully, "I don't go in for that sort of nonsense with brother officers. I'm Harry Barret."

"Jim Callicoe."

"Super. Well get in. I'll drive you to your digs."

Barrett put the Tilly in gear and sped off. He ignored the speed limit and went round the perimeter track. He pointed out particular buildings as they went. He talked non stop and Callicoe was reminded of his instructor, Luke back at *Pensacola*.

Barrett was a lean beanpole, all teeth and elbows with a shock of blonde hair on his head. Callicoe noticed the two wavy rings and pilot wings on his sleeve.

"Where did you train?" he asked.

"Here, then Canada. Yourself?"

Callicoe hung on as Barrett swung out from behind a truck and stamped on the gas.

"America."

"You lucky blighter."

"I only got back before Christmas."

Barrett nodded with a smile.

"So, you're fresh off the boat?"

"Literally."

They pulled up next to some Nissen huts and got out. Barrett pointed to a line of duckboards.

"Here we are. The Wardroom is a bit of hike I'm afraid."

"After *Saint Vincent*, this is a step up."

Barrett laughed. He carried Callicoe's kit bag and led the way to the second hut.

"A few others have turned up already." He opened the door and went inside. "Stand by your beds," he announced. The hut had rows of beds down each side, eight in all. Four were occupied. Barrett dumped the kit bag on the nearest bed.

"Jimmy!" Gabby exclaimed, getting up from his bed. "Happy New Year!"

"Good, you know each other," said Barrett. "That makes it a bit easier. I'll leave you to it then. See you later."

Gabby picked up Callicoe's kit bag and put it on the bed next to his.

"Be just like old times," Gabby told him, already chattering away, talking about his leave.

The CO had them in his office later in the day. There were five of them in all, Gabby, Callicoe, a short New Zealander called Aubrey Cook, a handsome blonde called Lee Becker and a beefy northern character called Frank Gardner.

"I don't know how long you'll be here but use your time to good effect. We'll get you checked out on the types and then off you go. For now, we need to get you up to speed, polish off those rough edges so to speak," he said with a smile.

For the next few days, they familiarised themselves with the Fairey Fulmar, a two seat Fleet reconnaissance fighter. It looked a little bit like a Fairey Battle with a wide wing, slender fuselage and a long glass canopy. An Observer would fly in the back seat to navigate and report fall of shot for ships. It was quite well armed with eight machine guns but as a fighter it was outclassed by land based opponents.

Once the CO was happy they could fly without killing themselves, he put them to work practising deck landings. Lines had been painted on the runway marking out the length of the deck on an aircraft carrier. At each end six lines were painted roughly where the arrestor cables would be. Stood off to the left was a batsman.

A qualified pilot, he would stand holding what was basically a table tennis bat in each hand. He would gyrate around as you approached the deck, giving directions so you could correct your course for landing. What you wanted to see was a bat held out level on each side. That meant you were on the glide path at the right height and speed. Both bats up in a V you were too low. Down in a V, too high. If they started rotating you were too slow.

Callicoe began to appreciate why Luke had always banged on about crisp landings.

The largest fleet carriers had a flight deck over seven hundred feet long. Escort carriers were much smaller than that. He had to get used to hitting a very small part of the deck to be able to catch one of the cables in the hook under the aircraft. If you missed, you would go into the crash barrier and write off a perfectly serviceable kite.

It was tiring, going round and round and getting lined up. To start with they came in from way back but were encouraged to make tighter and tighter circuits. It was quite tricky keeping one eye on the batsman while sneaking a glance at the instruments.

When they weren't flying, life at *Saint Merryn* was dull.

Callicoe had no doubt that the northern shores of Cornwall were quite pretty in the summer, but in the depths of winter it was bleak and uninviting. In all the time he was there he only ventured out once for a walk along the cliffs near Haryln Bay. He didn't bother to repeat the experience.

On occasion, Gabby winkled him out of the Wardroom for an excursion to Padstow a few miles away. There was a nice pub down by the waterfront and they often saw the fishing boats going out to ply their trade. The rest of the time he either stayed in his hut or in the Wardroom acquiring a taste for pink gin.

Despite his promise, he didn't write to his brother for a few weeks. He kept it simple, wishing the family were all okay and imparting a little bit of news. He explained about learning to do a deck landing, playing on the more humorous aspects of watching someone wave their arms around. He made no mention of the three crashes and one death they'd had.

Callicoe had a front row seat for the fatality. He was the next one in line to land when he saw a Fulmar pile in from fifty feet. A gust caught them on their final approach, the port wing dropped and it was all over. The batsman barely managed to jump clear of the wreckage. Fire engines went screeching round the peri track but all they could do was put out the flames.

It was another month before Callicoe replied to a letter from Ariadne. She made no mention of the episode in the kitchen. It was just a chatty letter with news about his nieces, their school play and life in Surrey.

They spent two months at *HMS Vulture* before being sent up to Liverpool in their Fulmars. It was a less than perfect day when they flew over the Irish Sea to rendezvous with *HMS Argus* for their first deck landing practise.

Argus was one of the first Royal Navy carriers.

Completed too late to participate in the Great War she was obsolete now, but she'd still seen action on the Malta convoy runs. Callicoe was pleased when he saw there was no island structure on the starboard side giving him a completely clear deck.

After a few dummy runs to get a feel for it, Callicoe's first landing was hair raising. Flying over the water he became very conscious that he was aiming for a very small target indeed. At *Saint Merryn*, if he made a muck of it, it didn't really matter. If he missed here, he was going for a swim and it was a very choppy day. Coming in to land, everything seemed to happen very fast. No sooner had he lined himself up and started making his approach then he was over the stern. He didn't even remember seeing the directions from the batsman.

He thumped down, close to the number one cable which meant he was within a hair of being too low. If the stern had been on its way up, he could have hit the round down at the edge of the deck and lost his hook or hit the tail.

His second landing was better. He got into more of a rhythm, looking at the instruments, the batsman and then checking his horizon in that order. On the third one he was battling gusting wind conditions and was too high. The batsman gave him the wave off and he went round again, nailing it on the second approach. His wheels touched the deck before he opened up the throttle to go round one last time for his final attempt. For this one he would go all the way, land on the deck and then take off again.

While he was circling round to get into position, Gabby came in for his fifth approach and his third landing. He flew smoothly, going down the glide path like he was on rails. The batsman offered few corrections; he was on speed and in line.

In the last few hundred feet it all went wrong. The

engine note of Gabby's Fulmar changed. His airspeed dropped and he gasped in horror as he shoved the throttle through the gate. The Merlin XXX engine should have picked up but it didn't. Gabby tried to stretch his descent but he knew he wasn't going to make it.

The batsman started waving the bats in a frantic circle and then held them up in a V. Gabby cursed, he didn't need the batsman to tell him he was too low or too slow. The stern of *Argus* was looming in front of him and he had the choice of a hard or a soft landing. He plumped for soft and just had time to sideslip to the left before the Fulmar plunged into the freezing waters of the Irish Sea.

He was flung forwards as the Fulmar came to an abrupt halt. Water cascaded over the canopy and the fighter started to settle. Gabby wasted no time, released his harness and hauled the canopy back. He was over the side like a greased pig. The temperature of the water took his breath away, it was freezing. He inflated his Mae West and started doggy paddling to get away from the sinking aircraft. He rolled onto his back and watched as it went down, bubbles and a slick of oil surrounding the tail.

He went numb very fast. His arms went dead and his feet felt like blocks of ice. The only thing keeping his head above water was his lifejacket. He kept spluttering as waves broke over him. The motorboat got to him just in time.

When it came up alongside, the rating in the bow had to fish him out by snagging his lifejacket with the hook on a wooden boat pole. He was dragged on board and taken to a nearby Destroyer. They gave him a hot water bottle, wrapped him in blankets and filled him up with rum.

Callicoe saw the tail of the Fulmar going down for the last time as he made his final approach. He remembered to drop his hook and then it was check wheels, checks flaps and make sure his harness was tight. He eased the throttle closed as the stern drew nearer. He made final corrections to straighten up and flew the Fulmar onto the deck, flaring to keep the nose up. The hook snagged a wire and the Fulmar was dragged to an abrupt halt.

He chopped the throttle and the Fulmar rolled backwards a few feet. He dabbed the brakes and raised the hook as the deck crew waved him forwards.

He hauled the stick back in his stomach, put the throttle to the stops and kept the brakes on, feeling the power build up. The Flight Deck Officer gave it two more seconds and then waved a green flag. Callicoe let off the brakes and the Fulmar started rolling. The speed increased, air got under the wings and the tail lifted. Callicoe used the rudder to keep the nose pointed straight and then he was up.

He raised the undercarriage and the flaps and trimmed for level flight. Rain started to lash the canopy and he was relieved he'd done his four landings before it started. He orbited east of the carrier while the other two Fulmars completed their landings. When they were finished, they formed up and went back to Liverpool.

Gabby returned two days later after he'd thawed out. After being picked up, the weather had deteriorated rapidly. He'd spent the night on the Destroyer, spewing his guts up while the little ship was tossed around on the sea. They stuck him in the hospital in Liverpool overnight to monitor his condition. Gabby was so listless he hadn't even made a pass at a nurse.

The weather cleared and they went back up for some more landing practice on *Argus*. Gabby got back on the horse again to show he could do it. They had two more days of practice before going back to *Saint Merryn*.

They did more ADDL's virtually every day and when they weren't practising landings, they were honing their gunnery skills. Barrett schooled them in tighter formation flying, trying to impart his hard won experience from his convoy runs to Russia. Every opportunity he got; he would bounce you when you least expected it. He was like some stalking horse and would go up in a Seafire, trying to catch you out.

Gabby was subdued for a few days after his dip, it was a reminder that you could be here today and gone tomorrow. He woke up one night, dreaming he was trapped in his cockpit as the Fulmar sank under the dark waters. He perked up once he got more landings under his belt and confidence was restored.

The weather clamped down with heavy rain and then thick fog. Nothing moved for over a week until Barrett persuaded the CO to let him take a flight up. He'd flown in worse weather than this and he thought it was a good opportunity for some more practice.

He took them up and deliberately went hunting for clumps of cloud. The winds were gusting and the Fulmars bounced around as they ploughed through the driving rain. Callicoe had difficulty staying on his wing and Barrett nagged them constantly. He shouted at Gabby to get closer.

"I don't want to run into you," Gabby explained.

"I understand," said Barrett, "but if you get too far back, you'll lose me in all this muck. Believe me it's safer if you're closer."

Not at all convinced, Gabby edged back in until Barrett was satisfied.

"That's more like it."

Gabby found himself leaning away, expecting to blend wingtips at any moment.

Barrett undid some of the work that had been drilled into them at *Opa Lacka* and *Pensacola*.

"The US Navy have their way of doing things," he told them, "we have ours."

Two months at *RNAS Saint Merryn* went by in a flash. Barrett, Gabby, Gardner, Callicoe and another Sub

Lieutenant, Fortescue received orders to report to Liverpool. Two new fighter squadrons were forming up to ship overseas. The excitement was palpable as they packed their gear and headed to the train station.

Barrett was relaxed on the journey; he'd done all this before. For the others it was the final step to becoming operational. Immediately, they started to speculate what they'd be flying and what ship they'd be assigned to.

Barrett wasn't bothered about what they flew. He'd tried just about everything in the Fleet Air Arm arsenal the last two years. His only concern was the ship. A ships company was its soul. That soul was shaped by the officers but more importantly by the Captain. A bad Captain could break a man's spirit.

He also wanted the carrier to be something big. After convoy runs in *Fencer* up near the Arctic Circle; he wanted to fly from something that was a little bit bigger.

At Liverpool, they joined a bunch of other pilots waiting to board a liner bound for the States. They stood around in little clumps, doing the rounds as they saw familiar faces from their service life. There were people Callicoe recognised from *Pensacola* and a few more from the early days in *Saint Vincent*. They sat around yarning, exchanging news about other people on their courses and where they might be. A bigger clump of bodies stood looking very confused. Fresh from Gosport, they were destined for primary flight training in America.

"Christ, did we look like that?" Callicoe asked.

"I hope not" Gabby replied with genuine concern. Some of them looked like they were barely out of shorts and blazers.

They went across the Atlantic in a ship just as worn out as the *Strathallen*. They were jammed in like sardines as every inch of cabin space was put to good use. Every day, the Captain had them on deck for lifeboat drill. It was a bind being stood on deck fiddling around with lifebelts until they were counted.

The weather was kinder this time and they docked at Newport News in the lovely state of Virginia. The weather in spring was gorgeous with lots of green, rolling hills. It could have been England. They boarded a train to take them to *NAS Quonset Point* near Rhode Island.

Like most things it made little sense. When they'd come over the first time they'd docked in New York and then travelled south for days to get to Florida. This time they docked in the south and spent days on the train going north to *Quonset Point*, right past New York along the way. The CO got on the train when they transferred at Grand Central Station.

Commander Vivian Williams DSC, RN was a short, dark haired martinet who bristled with energy. A veteran of the early days, he'd flown Sea Gladiators off *Furious* in the Norwegian campaign and Fulmars in the Med. For eighteen months he'd been in the centre of the action until they pinned a medal on his chest and sent him for a rest. A rare survivor, he was sent to the Fighter Training School at Yeovilton to advise on tactics.

On the way to *Quonset Point*, he pinned their ears back, preaching his mantra of position, height, speed and manoeuvre. They arrived at dusk where the rest of the squadron were waiting for them. Twelve pilots had come direct from deck landing training on the *USS Charger* in the Chesapeake.

7 – Work Up

1771 Squadron officially came into being on the 1st March 1944. A Corsair was parked on the apron and the men paraded in front of it. Williams had a squadron photograph taken to mark the moment.

1782 Squadron was the other Corsair unit working up with them. The Fleet Air Arm had been forming squadrons at *Quonset Point* for over a year and the station personnel had the process down to a fine art. The aircraft were ready and serviced; huts had been set aside for classes and ground training. Groundcrew were on hand to demonstrate and instructors were ready to talk them through the cockpit.

Over the coming weeks they got to grips with the aircraft they came to call the 'bent wing bastard', the Chance Vought Corsair. In all respects, it was a monster. Designed from the ground up for speed, Vought engineers had somehow managed to shoehorn the huge Wright Cyclone eighteen cylinder Double Wasp engine into it. It mounted a propeller so big, they had to cant the wings down four feet, almost like a Stuka. It could go 400mph straight up in level flight, but it also had a stalling speed low enough that it could operate from an aircraft carrier.

That performance came at a cost; the Corsair had a number of vices that could catch out the unwary. As you flared to land it had a tendency to float the last few feet before touching down. If you opened the throttle up on a landing approach, the torque of the massive engine could almost twist the Corsair around its own prop, flicking the left wing down. If you slammed it down too hard, the undercarriage had a wicked bounce. More than one Corsair had missed the wires altogether and gone straight into the crash barriers.

These issues were enough to see the US Navy turn to the Grumman Hellcat as its main carrier fighter. The Fleet Air Arm on the other hand could not afford to be so choosy.

English aircraft designers had neglected the field of naval aviation for years. All of the homegrown naval fighters were adapted designs, no better than having a hook added and other modifications. Sea Hurricanes were robust but obsolete. Seafires were too delicate. Their narrow undercarts were no match for the rigours of carrier operations. The Royal Navy took the Corsairs and was grateful to have them.

Working with the engineers, the myriad of sins were cured one by one. A small metal strip was put on the leading edge of the starboard wing so both wings would stall together. Cowl flaps on the top of the nose were fixed shut to stop oil leaking over the windscreen. A bleed valve was added to the undercarriage oleos to stop the bounce. Gradually, the beast was brought under control but it was still a handful for a novice pilot.

A final modification to make it possible to operate the Corsair from British carriers had an unintended advantage. The hangars were 16ft high. For the Corsairs to fit inside with their wings folded, they had to lop 8" off each wingtip. Clipping the wings increased the sink rate on landing and stopped it floating along.

The men went back to school. After a few days in the classroom, they spent hours sat in the cockpit, their noses buried in the pilots notes while they figured out what was where.

Williams pushed them hard. Every daylight hour was spent learning about the aircraft. He had them in the hangars working alongside the groundcrew so they knew what made it tick. He didn't want chauffeurs, he wanted men who could understand their machine and get the most out of it.

Gradually, they got to know one another too. Most of them were just over twenty. It made Callicoe feel ancient and next to Williams he was the oldest man on the squadron. Two men, Curly Richardson and Dicky Farthingdale were Royal Marines which made them a pretty rare animal. At *Saint Vincent*, CPO Atkins had encouraged them to think of Marines as knuckle dragger bootneck boys, which clearly wasn't the case here.

Some evenings Williams let them off the base to play. A particular haunt just off the base that became popular was a bar called *The Flat Hatter*. The owner, Billy Coker was ex US Navy and the name was an in joke.

At *Pensacola* and *Opa locka*, it had been drummed into them by their instructors that stunting around at low level was dangerous. The US Navy called it *'Flat Hatting'*. If you were caught doing it, you'd have to come up with a staggeringly good excuse not to get grounded. The interior of the bar reflected the owner, the walls adorned with mementoes of Navy life and souvenirs of men that had passed through. Pictures of squadrons hung in frames behind the bar. Once the Royal Navy started forming squadrons there, space was found on the walls for the Senior Service to add to Coker's growing collection.

The place was warm and welcoming and they were soon on first name terms with the staff. Callicoe just had to motion to the bar as he came in and they started setting up the drinks. On this evening, Callicoe handed over a dollar note and told the barman to keep the drinks coming. Gabby dropped onto the stool next to him. He pointed at Callicoe's beer.

"Same."

The bar was heaving tonight, full to bursting with

khaki Navy uniforms and a smattering of locals. Richardson and Farthingdale stood off to one side. A vision in red polka dots floated over to Farthingdale but he brushed her off. Happily married, he fingered his wedding ring and kept himself occupied with his drink. She turned her attention to Richardson, draping an arm over his shoulder. The tall Marine basked in the glow of her attention while she played with his lapels. A few minutes later Williams and Barrett turned up, deep in conversation. Callicoe walked across and handed each of them a pint.

"To get you started, sir," Callicoe explained. He wasn't sure what to make of the CO yet.

Since joining them on the train, he'd been all business. His blue eyes rarely smiled and his voice was a rasping flail when you got things wrong. He had this incredible knack of being able to fix you with a gaze that could reduce even the most confident individual into a stammering simpleton. Williams didn't shoot a line in the Wardroom; he didn't have to. He just went out and showed everyone what he could do. He was the first to take a Corsair up and he'd brought the big fighter in as light as a feather. His level of skill was even more evident when the next three to go up bounced their landings.

Habergast was the first one to bend a Corsair. He blotted his copybook by being a bit too keen on his brakes. He stood his Corsair on its nose, wrecking the prop and tearing a deep gouge in the concrete of the taxiway. Callicoe was content just to get up and down again without breaking it.

By and large, the first flew flights had gone well. No one had been killed anyway which was a start. Williams was pleased he'd not had to write any letters yet. When he'd first looked over the personnel files of his men, he'd been dismayed at the lack of combat experience. Apart from himself and Barrett, only two others had done some convoy runs on Martlets and that was it. Almost by default he'd had to make Barrett senior pilot because of his time on *HMS Fencer*.

So far, he liked what he'd seen. The men had a lot of rough edges, but the standard of training in America certainly seemed to be up to snuff. The other benefit was that they were all used to American instruments and cockpit design. Coming from Fulmars and Gladiators, Williams found he was the one having to play catchup.

He parked himself at the corner of the bar, content to watch what was going on. Ever since he'd been clattered round the back of the head in a bar fight in Valletta he tended to stick to walls.

Wicklow, the youngest lad in the squadron was stood over by the jukebox. Aubrey Cook was next to him, arguing over his selection. Wicklow shoved in some coins and pushed buttons. Callicoe was drinking at the bar with the irrepressible Gabby, Frost and Gardner.

Williams wasn't so sure about Gabby. His reports from flying school had made interesting reading. He'd shown a cool touch in the air and was a nightmare on the ground. Of all his officers, Gabby was the one who had to make the final witty remark in a lecture. He could have had Gabby on the mat, but Williams had met his sort before. You could light a bomb under them and it would be like water off a ducks back. Gabby was one of those types who ambled along at their own pace, expecting everyone else to bend around them.

"More," Callicoe ordered, drinking the shot of whisky as soon as it was put on the bar. Gabby wasn't far behind him. Gardner wasn't faring so well; he felt a bit light in the head.

"Come on my son, don't stop now."

Gabby pressed another drink into his hand and encouraged him to drink up. Gardner turned a bleary eye on him. His gaze wandered while he tried to decide which of the three versions of Gabby were speaking to him.

"Ish all very well, old man," he slurred, "but you shtarted before me."

"That's why you've got to catch up," Gabby assured him. He handed another shot of whisky over.

Talk turned to flying. Using a matchbox, Callicoe was discussing the finer points of the curved approach. Gabby had made the mistake of admitting being nervous about trying it at sea. Frost had asked if he was windy and Callicoe had to step in as peacemaker. He pulled the matchbox out of his pocket to demonstrate.

At *NAS Pensacola*, they had been taught to come straight in on their landing approach. It was what they had spent hours practising at *Saint Merryn* and on their deck training on *Argus* and the *Charger*. The thing was, this wasn't such a good idea in a Corsair. The Corsair had a long nose because of the engine. Even with the pilot's seat cranked up to the maximum, you couldn't see much directly in front of you.

Landing on a runway like that was hard work. Landing on a carrier deck would have been impossible, so a curved approach had been adopted. Originally devised for landing the Seafire, it was perfect for the Corsair.

The mechanics of it were simple enough. You flew downwind with the carrier on your port side. You then reversed your course, going 180 degrees to the left in a descending turn, to keep the batsman in view. At the last moment, you straightened up as you crossed the stern to snag a wire.

They started practising that and it had taken quite a few of them out of their comfort zone. It needed fine judgement and you had to put a lot of faith in the batsman to know if you were in the groove.

Gabby snatched the matchbox out of Callicoe's hand and mimicked an aircraft pranging with the appropriate sound effects.

"I'd have preferred a right hand turning approach," he moaned. "We're already low and slow as we come in and you know there's a tendency for the wing to drop first."

Callicoe didn't have an obvious answer to that. The only real remedy would be to come in a little bit faster and give yourself a cushion of airspeed.

"I do' fel s'good," Gardner mumbled. He sagged at the knees and Gabby grabbed him to stop him slumping to the floor.

"Come on you dozy bugger," he said, "lets walk you around a bit."

Callicoe took hold of Gardner's other arm and they marched him out the side door. As soon as the fresh air hit him, Gardner was a goner. He lurched to his right and as Gabby hauled him back up, Gardner threw up all over him.

"Thas better," Gardner mumbled.

Callicoe had to laugh. Gabby was stood there, with Gardner held up at arm's length while sick tumbled down the front of him.

"Terrific."

Gabby looked at his uniform. Callicoe offered him a hanky but Gabby shook his head. That would just mash it all in. He needed to rinse the jacket. He thrust Gardner into Callicoe's arms and went back into the bar. There was a roar of surprise when they saw him covered in vomit.

"It's not me," he protested. He went through to the head and took his jacket off. He ran it under the tap but he knew it was going to need a dry clean when they got back to the base. Water splashed and he huffed and puffed as he got the front of his shirt wet. Dripping, he went back outside.

"Come on, let's get him into bed," he told Callicoe. They walked to the corner of the street and parked Gardner against a lamp post. Gabby flagged down a taxi.

"Where to boys?" the driver asked.

"Main gate," said Gabby. Callicoe steered Gardner onto the back seat.

"If he's sick, you're paying for it," the driver warned them. Gabby shoved ten dollars under his nose to show they were good for it. That settled the argument and the driver drove at breakneck speed to get them out of his cab as soon as possible.

He dropped them off and Gabby paid him while Callicoe frog marched Gardner towards the main gate. His skin had a waxy sheen to it and he was distinctly green around the gills.

"Christ how much has he drunk?" Callicoe asked.

"Less than us," Gabby shot back. As they got to the gate, one of the white helmeted MP's came out of the guard hut and asked to see their ID.

Gardner was still feeling the effects the following morning. His throat felt like sandpaper and he was ravenous when he woke up. He attacked his breakfast like a starving man. He washed everything down with cup after cup of coffee.

"What happened last night?" he asked Callicoe, who was sat across from him.

Callicoe gave him a baleful look. He wasn't in the best of moods. If there was one thing he couldn't abide it was someone who couldn't hold their drink. Gardner had thrown up on the MP at the front gate. It had taken twenty minutes of fast talking to stop the MP writing them up on some sort of charge.

"Don't you remember?" he asked shortly.

"Not a clue. I know we were in *The Flat Hatter* but that's it."

Callicoe pointed a fork to the right.

"Ask him," he said as Gabby came in.

They went up three and four times a day, singly then in pairs and then in flights of four. All the time, Williams was piling on the pressure for them to get used to flying as a unit. He knew they got along well on the ground, but it was no easy thing putting your life in another chaps' hands. They had to trust each other and the only way that was going to happen was through lots of practise.

"He's like an old woman," Gabby moaned as they walked back to their billet. He rolled his neck and windmilled his arms. His shoulders hurt from the straps of his parachute pack. It felt like he'd been wearing it all day.

"Stop moaning," Callicoe told him. "He's only looking after you."

"He reminds me of me mum."

"What? Manly with dark hair and a deep voice?" Callicoe asked in good humour. Gabby blew a raspberry.

"That's not what I mean and you know it. It's all the nagging. Close up, do this, do that." Gabby shuddered.

That was how the CO earned his nickname 'Lady' Williams. Considering his first name was Vivian, it wasn't a stretch but no one dared say it to his face.

He put them on formation flying. He sent them on long navigation exercises. They fired thousands of rounds at target drogues. They chased each other in mock dogfights. He handed round a booklet that outlined current Fleet Air Arm attack techniques.

"I've bored all of you enough the last few weeks with the sound of my voice," he told them. "Everything you need is there. Read it and then we can put it into practise."

Gradually, it was all coming together, but Williams kept them at it. He knew their departure date was looming.

Beck was the squadron's first casualty. One of the less confident pilots on the squadron, his landings left something to be desired. Coming in low and slow on a landing approach, he did everything wrong. After his fourth wave off, he slammed the throttle forward in impatience and that was it. His Corsair flicked onto its back and he went in.

Wicklow nearly followed him a few days later. He came in on a lovely approach, the only problem was he forgot about his undercarriage. His Corsair sagged to the ground and careened along the runway in a shower of sparks. Wicklow hung on for grim death as it slithered along on its belly.

Once it stopped moving, he undid his straps and shot out of the cockpit in double quick time. In his haste, he missed his footing and fell the six or so feet to the ground on his face and knocked himself out. The crash crew found him sprawled out in a puddle of leaking petrol. He spent a few days in hospital with concussion. Williams would have flayed him alive for wrecking a perfectly good aircraft, but a chap tended not to forget mistakes like that.

They wrote off two more Corsairs before they left *Quonset Point*. Gabby came in too fast and folded his undercart in a heavy landing. Barrett rounded out the field by thumping his Corsair down and bursting a tyre. His Wingtip dug in and the fighter ground looped. The big prop hit the ground and the engine tore out of its mount. Fuel went everywhere and Barrett recorded the fastest sprint Callicoe had ever seen as the Corsair burst into flames behind him.

1782 suffered lost two pilots in an unfortunate accident when they collided in mid air. Neither managed to bail out in time and they joined Beck in the cemetery.

Eventually, their time ran out. Although they had crammed a lot of work into a short time, Williams one regret was that they'd not been able to practise deck landings on a carrier. They had done over one hundred ADDL's each by the end of the work up, but there was no substitute for the real thing. They weren't even going to land on a carrier for the transit back across the Atlantic. They would fly to New York and their Corsairs would be loaded onto an escort carrier for transport to England.

Before they left, they had one last blow out at *The Flat Hatter*. Coker was presented with a framed copy of the squadron photograph to go on his wall.

Richardson had a few drinks for appearances sake and then slid unnoticed out of the side door. He walked a few streets to a tenement block and went inside, going up to an apartment on the third floor. He knocked on the door and only had to wait a moment before he was invited in.

Back at *The Flat Hatter* the songs had started. They kicked off with the Eton boating song which the Americans boggled at and then segwayed into Hearts of Oak. Gabby led a stirring rendition of the A25 song, a glowing tribute to that horrible little form you had to fill out whenever you crashed an aircraft.

> *They say in the air force a landings okay,*
> *If the pilot gets out and can still walk away,*
> *But in the Fleet Air Arm the prospect is grim,*
> *If the landings piss poor and the pilot can't swim,*
>
> *Cracking show I'm alive,*
> *But I still have to render my A25*
>
> *I fly for a living and not just for fun,*
> *I'm not very anxious to hack down a Hun,*
> *And as for deck landings at night in the dark,*
> *As I told Wings this morning, 'Blow that for a lark'*
>
> *Cracking show I'm alive,*

But I still have to render my A25

When the batsman gives lower, I always go higher,
I drift o'er to starboard and prang my Seafire,
The boys in the Goofer's all think that I'm green,
But I get a commission from Supermarine,

Cracking show I'm alive,
But I still have to render my A25

Everyone joined in the for the next verse, their voices building to a crescendo.

They gave me a Barra to beat up the Fleet.
I shot up the Rodney and Nelson a treat,
I forgot the high mast that sticks out from Formid,
And a seat in the Goofer's was worth fifty quid.

They finished off with Rule Britannia and nearly brought the house down. Every time they got to the chorus, they all banged their beer glasses on any level surface and made a racket.

When the clock rolled round to midnight, Williams and 1782's CO rounded up their men. Even Gardner was vertical, which was no mean feat in itself. In the intervening weeks, he'd become more used to alcohol but he was still a cheap night out. When they did the head count, Williams came up one short, Richardson was missing.

"I know where he is," muttered Farthingdale. "I'll be fifteen minutes." He set off at a jog.

"Ten!" Williams shouted after him. "Be back here in ten minutes!"

Farthingdale knew exactly where he was. He pelted up the stairs, taking them two and three at a time. He was puffing by the time he got to the third floor. He ran down the corridor and hammered on the door. He kept on going until he heard someone approaching from inside the apartment. He heard the lock turn and the door opened an inch, a chain stopping it from going any wider.

"Oh, it's you," a plain blonde said. The door closed for a moment and the chain rattled as it was taken off. "You'd better come in," she muttered, gathering her night dress around herself, arms crossed. "You've made enough noise to wake the dead. I bet you the Super will want to talk to me in the morning," she pouted. "Wait here."

Farthingdale waited in the corridor, impatiently tapping his foot while she went to one of the bedrooms. The apartment was five rooms, a long corridor with two rooms either side and a kitchen dining room at the end. The blonde poked her head around the bedroom door and hooked a thumb at the front door.

"You're pals here," she said coldly. Richardson was sat on the bed, already pulling his trousers on. The girl was sat on the bed, the covers pulled up around her chin.

"Sorry, I thought we'd have more time," he muttered. He leaned across the bed and kissed her. It had been a crazy few weeks for Richardson, a heady mix of flying in the day and passion in the evening. Mary was the girl for him

A short brunette with a heart shaped face, she had cute dimples when she smiled. Her father was a Major in the Marines, getting shot at somewhere in the Pacific. She was a secretary at the Navy yard and shared the apartment with two friends. Richardson had seen her when flying allowed and it had been a whirlwind romance, a few hours snatched here and there. He shrugged on his shirt and she smoothed down the lapels, her fingers lingering over the buttons.

"Do you think your father will say yes?" he asked her.

"I think so. Daddies a practical man, he knows when

his girls made up her mind," she replied, her eyes twinkling in good humour. Richardson had proposed, but he was a little old fashioned, he wanted her father's approval. With him on active service it might take a while to get organised. "You've got the address?" she asked, knowing he did. Richardson patted his trouser pocket.

"All sorted."

She stood on tiptoe and kissed him. There was a pounding on the door.

"Come on, Curly," Farthingdale bellowed in the corridor.

"Go," she said, her eyes getting damp. "I'll still be here waiting for you."

Walking fast down the street, Richardson kicked a pebble along.

"Well? Did she?" Farthingdale asked.

"Yup. Yes, yes, three times yes."

"Congratulations."

Richardson didn't look very happy. Farthingdale reflected that he'd probably look the same if he was dragged away from his wife. "Come on, chaps," Barrett shouted from the corner of the street by *The Flat Hatter*. Everyone was crowded outside on the pavement, cramming into some taxis to go back to the base.

8 – One Last Time

1771 and 1782 left *Quonset Point* with a bit of a show. After they took off, they formed up in sections and did two low passes of the field before heading west. They landed at the Navy field in New York and spent two days and nights painting the town red.

Callicoe, Gabby and the rest did a tour of the bars and eateries. They went up the Empire State Building. Barrett didn't have half the fun he thought he'd have. As Senior Pilot, Williams expected him to know roughly where they all were. The only way he could manage that was to go out with them. He spent two days fussing around like some sort of sheepdog.

Richardson managed to get Mary to come down by train and they had two final days together before he went off to war. He took her to Tiffany's with lofty ideas of getting a ring. The prices took his breath away. Mary took mercy on him and dragged him out to a more modest Jewish jewellers in the lower east side. She didn't care what he spent; she had her ring.

Their Corsairs were towed through the streets to the docks and lifted onto *HMS Lynx*, a small escort carrier. American built, she and her sisters had been provided to the Royal Navy under the terms of lend lease. The fighters were packed in the hangar and lashed to the flight deck.

Part of a fast convoy, it was a five day run to England. The weather was good which made it easier. Callicoe didn't relish having to go through another storm in the middle of the Atlantic. The final bit of the voyage was fog bound as they rounded Ireland and crept into the busy Irish Sea. Docking in Liverpool took hours as the tugs fussed around the carrier to bring her alongside the quay. Cranes began offloading the Corsairs as soon as the lines were made fast.

The men got two weeks leave as soon as they stepped ashore. Gabby, Callicoe, Frost and Cook decided it was time to broaden Wicklows horizons and they took the youngster to London. They checked into a hotel and hit the town.

Having experienced the bright lights of America, London was a bit of a let down. After five years of war, the battered capital was drab and colourless. There was no ice cream, no Coke, prices were steep and portions were small. There were few cars on the road, the buses were crammed and, in the evenings, the blackout made the city a dark forbidding place.

They made the best of it. Callicoe knew a few places that were worth a visit so they started there. A suitable female was located to complete Wicklows education. Money exchanged hands and she approached the lad in a bar, paying him lots of attention before they retired to the hotel and did the deed.

After a few days, they split off around the country to see friends and family. Callicoe had an open invite from Gabby to go to Norfolk with him but he felt he needed to go home. He bid farewell to his friend at Liverpool Street Station.

"If you change your mind," Gabby said, shoving a piece of paper in his hand. Callicoe looked at the address scrawled on it.

He got a taxi into central London and went to the Ministry. It felt odd going back. It had been eighteen months since he'd last set foot through those doors. The man at reception hadn't forgotten him though.

"My word, Mister Callicoe. A pleasure to see you, sir."

He warmly shook Callicoe's hand, gave him a visitor pass and took his bag. "It'll be here when you come back, sir."

Callicoe took the stairs to the fourth floor. The Ministry never really slept in the day time. Each floor was humming with the sounds of typewriters tapping away and telephones ringing. Callicoe went to his father's office. There was an outer room where his secretary and five assistants worked and a door that led through to his own office where he ruled his department.

Arriving in the middle of the afternoon, he walked in to be met by a frosty glare. Military men were rarely seen in the building.

"Can I help you?" asked a mean looking mousy brunette with dark rimmed glasses and a blue cardigan. None of his father's usual staff were visible so Callicoe decided to play with this shrew.

"I wondered if the Under Secretary was available?" he asked, hands grasping his peaked cap in front of him.

The assistant gave him her best stare, looking down her nose at him and adding a short sniff of disapproval for good measure.

"Did you have an appointment?" she asked, already knowing the answer.

"Gosh, I was rather hoping he could squeeze me in."

She clicked her tongue and made a show of flicking through the appointment book.

"I'm afraid the Under Secretary's very busy at the moment. What was it regarding?"

Callicoe walked over to her desk and craned his neck to take a look at the diary. She closed the book to stop him looking at it.

"Would it help that I was his son?" he said simply.

The change was immediate. A look of anger, then horror washed over her face and she shot to her feet, her mouth flapping. Her hands fluttered in agitated fashion.

"Oh, I'm dreadfully sorry-"

Callicoe ignored her and made for the door to his father's office. She scampered to get in front of him, opening the door just as he got there. There was no time to announce him as Callicoe strode into his father's inner sanctum.

It was a richly decorated room as befitted a man of his station. A book case filled with red leather bound volumes filled one wall. A thick Wilton carpet was underfoot, a swirling pattern of gold and red. Tall windows covered in blast tape let in lots of light from the end of the room, affording a fine view of Whitehall outside. Souvenirs of empire hung from the walls, including a Zulu shield, Assegai and Knobkierrie. Two green leather Chesterfield settees faced each other where the grandees could sit and plot over whisky and cigars. His father sat behind his desk, a heavy Italian art deco piece of oak and walnut veneer inserts. He liked sitting behind a big desk, using it as a metaphorical wall he could hide behind like a shield.

He looked up from a report he had been making notes on. It didn't register at first who it was. All he saw was a uniform striding unannounced into his office. He was just about to protest at the interruption when he recognised his son.

"James!" he exclaimed. "My word, what a surprise." It was the most emotional thing Callicoe had ever heard his father say. He noticed his assistant at the door and scowled, embarrassed at such an outburst in front of his staff. "Thank you, Miss Lloyd, that will be all."

She retreated from the field, closing the door behind her.

He came from behind his desk and shook his sons' hand, pumping it warmly. He kept a grip of his hand, directing him towards the Chesterfields.

"Drink?" he asked. Callicoe demurred, his father made himself one and sat down. "I assume you're on leave?"

Callicoe nodded and brought his father up to date

with his news. His father in turn said what he could about his work.

"Of course, it might all be over soon," he told his son. "All we hear about at the moment is the second front and when it might happen. Hitler and his maniacs won't last long once we get back into Europe." He gestured to some newspapers neatly folded and piled on a side table. "You'll have joined up for nothing."

Callicoe bristled a little at the casual remark. He'd been following the news himself. The second front had been the hottest topic going. Speculation on the squadron was rife they were going to miss the big show.

His father checked his watch. It was passing 2pm. It wasn't every day his son came home on leave; his department could do without him for a few hours he decided. He went back to his desk and called Frank.

"Frank, you'll never guess who's here with me. It's James. He's got some leave for a few days. I thought dinner tomorrow if you could manage it?" He nodded as he listened to the response. "Excellent, we'll see you tomorrow then."

He gathered his coat, umbrella, bowler hat and briefcase and told his son to follow him. He walked into the outer office just as his other staff returned from a meeting.

"I'm going home, Mister Smith," he informed his secretary, his voice brisk and peremptory. Callicoe saw the staff accept this without comment. They walked out the building, his father maintaining a brisk pace. Callicoe had retrieved his kit bag and hung the strap off his shoulder.

"Margaret will be pleased to see you," his father said. Callicoe doubted that but didn't comment.

Margaret didn't betray a glimmer when she saw him at the door. She was sufficiently surprised seeing her husband home in the afternoon on a Wednesday. Callicoe went up to his room and dumped his stuff and got changed. It felt odd being out of uniform, he'd worn nothing else for ages.

Margaret stayed in her parlour, probably fuming at the disruption to the order of her day, Callicoe thought. He picked out a book and relaxed in the reception room with the radio on. Cook brought him a cup of tea and some buttered muffins and left him in peace.

Dinner was relaxed. Margaret had a civil defence meeting to go to and for the first time in ages, Callicoe had an evening alone with his father.

Martin did his best to bridge the gap between them. He'd never been one to express his feelings. His reserve at work extended to his home life, a reflection of his own Victorian upbringing. A father was the head of the house; children were a mother's domain.

They played chess. In his youth, he'd been a student of the game and it was one of the few things he'd done with his sons when they were growing up. For once, he was talkative while he played. He asked Callicoe about his friends on the squadron and about Williams.

"He sounds a hard man," he commented.

"I think he just wants us to concentrate," Callicoe replied. "He's seen it for real, it would be stupid to ignore what he's telling us. He's a fine man."

That seemed to mollify his father somewhat. Callicoe showed him a photograph of the Corsair and tried to describe what it was like to fly one.

"So, what makes a good pilot?"

Callicoe had to think about that one. He remembered something Luke had told him when he first started flying at *Pensacola*.

"Mindset is everything kid. You have to live and breathe flying. I don't mean becoming some sort of whizz, I mean touch. You handle the stick like it's an egg. You have to be delicate."

After a few games they settled themselves on the settee. His father was generous with the whisky and added ice and water the way Callicoe liked it. For the first time, Callicoe felt his father saw him as a man, not as a child.

Margaret came in late, looked in the reception room and went back to her parlour. After his father dozed off, Callicoe thought he should make an effort so he went to see Margaret. He poked his head around the door to see her sat by the radio listening to the final programs of the night. She nursed a cointreau in a small stemmed glass while she pressed the palm of her other hand to her forehead.

"Not a good moment?" Callicoe asked.

"No, not at all," she said, but her heart wasn't in it.

"Not a good meeting?" he commented.

"The usual farce. Squabbles over fines, the blackout restrictions. I don't know why I bother sometimes."

"So quit," he told her bluntly.

Margaret shot him a look, wondering if he was playing with her. She'd had to endure his teasing for years and she had no patience to be mocked by him. Picking up on her mood, he said it again.

"I mean it, Margaret. Quit. One thing I've learned in the last year is life's too short. If you're not enjoying it, it's not worth it."

She arched an eyebrow.

"I'll consider it."

Seeing that he'd used up his reserve of goodwill for the evening, he said goodnight and left her to it. Callicoe turned in, glad to be back in his own room.

He went to the park in the morning and just walked wherever his feet took him. After the intensity of the last few months, it felt good to be in wide open spaces but even here, the war wasn't far away. He saw some barrage balloons in the distance.

He had a pint in a pub and then browsed the shelves in a book shop. A small volume on air fighting in the RNAS in the Great War caught his eye. It was two shillings. Happy with his purchase he went home and let himself in and got straight down to reading.

He went up to get changed for dinner and came down just before Frank and Ariadne turned up. Frank was his usual self; Ariadne seemed a little subdued. His father was quite animated during dinner. Callicoe wondered if his father had imbibed a long liquid lunch in the afternoon although none of the usual signs were there.

Callicoe answered question after question from his brother and Ariadne. He ended up using the cruet to explain deck landings. He saved demonstrating what a batsman did until after dinner, pantomiming the arm movements in the reception room to great amusement.

The evening wore on and Callicoe went into the kitchen to make some tea. Cook had gone hours ago and the washing was piled up in the sink. He put water in the kettle and then whistled to himself while he waited for it to boil.

"Need a hand?" Ariadne asked from the door. Callicoe started at the sound of her voice. She walked in, hands behind her back, chewing on her lower lip.

"How have you been?" he asked her.

She sat on the big Victorian kitchen table, her legs swinging back and forth.

"Oh, you know, getting by."

The kettle began to whistle and Callicoe took it off the gas, putting it on the stand by the side of the oven. Ariadne lined the cups up on a tray while Callicoe added six scoops of loose leaf tea to the pot, one per person and one for the pot. He gave it a stir and then closed the lid, letting it stew for a minute or two.

He was very conscious that Ariadne was stood right next to him. He'd been in this position before. He coughed and took a step back to give himself some space.

"Milk," he said, going over to the fridge.

"Thank you for your letters, I know you've been busy. The girls liked the stamps."

He was about to pour milk into the cups and then stopped himself. Margaret would go mad if he brought in cups with milk in. He sighed, another sign of change. In the Wardroom, if you were 'mashing' as Gardner called it, it was milk, strong tea, serve. He poured milk into the porcelain jug and put the bottle back into the fridge.

"Jim," Ariadne said quietly. Callicoe froze as he closed the fridge door, his back to her. He didn't turn around. "About before..." The silence dragged across his nerves as he wondered what she was going to say. "Thank you for not saying anything; to, Frank."

"Why would I have said anything?" He turned around finally. Her eyes were as big as saucers, she was so pale she seemed ill. "Nothing happened, nothing more to be said."

He gave her arm a reassuring squeeze before picking up the tray and going through to the reception room.

He stayed a few more days but he found the house too confining. All the years he had been here, he had merely existed. He realised he'd grown beyond this old world and was no longer constrained by the ghosts of the past.

He packed his things and said goodbye to his father and the rest of them. He dug out Gabby's address from his tunic pocket and caught the next train to Norfolk.

Gabby's family lived in a small village just outside of Aylsham, north of Norwich. Callicoe spent the last few days of his leave walking in the Norfolk countryside. Gabby took him fishing. For most of his life Callicoe had lived and worked in London, it was relaxing being surrounded by nature for a change. Soon enough there would be nothing but water for as far as the eye could see.

9 – Jewel Of The Med

The squadron reported to Liverpool bright eyed and bushy tailed. At least, most of them did. A few of them had spread their wings to the big city and indulged themselves.

Their ship was waiting for them in the harbour. Barrett had gotten his wish; they were going to war in a Fleet carrier. Their Corsairs had been loaded aboard *HMS Lancer* the last of the Illustrious class carriers constructed.

The biggest carrier Callicoe had been on was *HMS Lynx* which wasn't the same thing at all. The Escort carriers were based on freighter hulls with a hangar and a flight deck slapped on top. They were basic, with a small bridge structure on the starboard side. *HMS Lancer* was a top of the line armoured Fleet carrier.

She had been ordered when the clouds of war were starting to gather. Even though the threat of Munich had come and gone, the Lords of the Admiralty had recognised the need for more aircraft carriers. Four of the Illustrious class had already been laid down in 1937 but even before they were completed, they started tinkering with the design. There was a growing realisation that they would need to carry more aircraft. They also wanted to make the design faster but they would have to find some way to squeeze in more boilers and an extra shaft.

Not willing to wait until the redesign was ready, *Lancer* was ordered on the same pattern as *Illustrious* and laid down in early 1938. For all the sense of urgency when she was ordered, she wasn't completed until 1941. When the battle of the Atlantic went against them, her construction was delayed so more escorts could be built instead.

The flight deck was 745ft long and 95ft wide. It had been shorter than that originally, but the round downs at the bow and stern had been removed on her last big refit, giving her 65ft more of usable deck space. Callicoe liked the sound of that. There were nine arrester cables at the stern. Twenty feet between each wire gave Callicoe a 180ft long target to hit if he was going to safely land on board. Ahead of the wires were two safety barriers. Consisting of steel hawsers linked together, they were metal nets to catch an aircraft if it missed the wires to stop it ploughing into aircraft parked forward on the bow.

Amidships on the starboard side of the deck was the island. It was here the ship was fought and from where flight operations were controlled. The flag officer cabins were located near the top. Below that was the Bridge, Flight Direction Office, Navigators chartroom and the Air Operations Room which served as the pilot's ready room. At the back of the island was a balcony where people could watch aircraft landing which was known as the Goofer's gallery.

The main hangar ran the length of the ship below the armoured flight deck. There were two lifts, one aft and one forward along the centreline.

Seventeen hundred men were crammed on board to run the ship, man the defences, service the aircraft and run air operations. Below deck most of the space was devoted to the hangar and the storage of spares, munitions and aviation fuel. Everything else was squashed in around them. Living conditions were snug.

Any hopes Callicoe had of getting a porthole for some fresh air were dashed when he was shown his berth with Gabby, a tiny cabin off one of the inner passageways. They had a bunk each, a tiny desk and a wardrobe. There had been the usual argument about who had what bunk. Gabby caught the gleam in his friend's eyes so he tossed his kit bag up top first and claimed the high ground.

Callicoe found getting used to the food the hardest thing. After being spoiled in America, he thought it was basic but boring. It filled him up but he found himself craving steak and ice cream, lots of ice cream.

Once he stowed his gear, Callicoe found his way to the Wardroom and found the place awash with gossip about the invasion in Normandy. Gabby had a drink waiting for him.

Like the rest of the ship, the Wardroom was just grey painted metal walls but efforts had been made to make it more homely. There was linoleum on the deck, a few easy chairs were at one end of the room and a piano had been manhandled on board. It was lashed to the bulkhead to stop it from going anywhere. There was a gramophone, a selection of records and a pile of books and magazines.

The other good thing was that the Wardroom bar was well stocked and the booze was provided at duty free prices. Gin was 2d per tot, whisky and brandy were only 3d. Ratings from the lower deck served as stewards.

Despite being in the Navy for over a year, this was his first ship and it was an eye opener. He'd been so focused on learning to fly and getting operational he hadn't thought about what shipboard life would be like. He discovered ships were living, breathing things, shaped by the men who served in them, a floating community. If you needed a hair cut or some tailoring done you were sorted. Some men formed themselves into little syndicates to do laundry, ironing or other little jobs for a small consideration. Mini industries could also provide art and pieces of furniture. There wasn't much they couldn't turn their hand to.

The Corsairs got a thorough check. They hadn't flown since being lifted aboard *HMS Lynx* in New York and they'd spent five days getting sprayed by Atlantic salt water on the flight deck. While the mechanics were doing that, Callicoe took the opportunity to look over the other aircraft on board.

There was another Corsair squadron, 1783 and the offensive side of things was covered by a squadron of Fairey Barracudas.

Ungainly underpowered things, they were the ugliest aircraft Callicoe had ever seen. They had a shoulder mounted slab of wing with large trailing edge flaps to enable a diving attack. They had a chin radiator for the Merlin engine, a high tail and a Fairey favourite, a long glazed canopy that ran the length of the crew compartment. For all of that, their pilots said they were a doddle to land, with good visibility from the cockpit. Callicoe wasn't sure it was a fair trade. He was perfectly happy with his Corsair and he wouldn't swap her for anything.

HMS Lancer put to sea on a foggy morning. The city was wrapped in a thick white wall and tugs helped nudge her into the main channel. It was a brief work up; she was needed in action.

For ten days, they circled the Isle of Man while the Air Group practised launches and deck landings.

The Corsairs and Barracudas were brought up on deck. Callicoe took his time getting ready. It was his first time flying off a Fleet Carrier, he didn't want to make a hash of it. He was starting to sweat in his flying suit and he went out onto the flight deck.

Up near the bow, a deck hand held his arms high and motioned a Corsair to come forward. The big wings folded down into place. There were final checks and then it was off, thundering down the deck. As it went off the edge, it climbed away. The next Corsair ready followed it, then a Barracuda went up.

The key to carrier operations was speed. Tactical doctrine at the beginning of the war was for small strikes of a few aircraft sent in waves. In the Pacific it was the exact opposite. The Japanese and the Americans made massed attacks and it wasn't just one carrier either, they hunted in packs of two or more carriers. The Japanese had attacked Pearl Harbour with six carriers. At the battle of Midway they had four.

It may have seemed chaotic to Callicoe but there was method in the madness. The aircraft needed to be spotted on the deck, tightly packed together to make maximum use of the limited space available. Then they needed to get into the air as quickly as possible, form up and go so that they weren't wasting fuel.

Callicoe went over to his Corsair and did a walk around. He checked the undercarriage and made sure the locks had been removed from the control surfaces. He got into the cockpit to start up.

He set the propeller to fine pitch, mixture to rich and put the elevator trim to neutral. At full power, the engines enormous torque would want to drag him left as he started rolling forward so he fed in eight degrees of right rudder trim to counteract it.

A fitter looked up at him. Callicoe turned on the master electrical switch and pumped the primer. The fitter gave him a thumbs up that he was clear and Callicoe switched the magnetos on and pressed the starter. Up front, a Koffman starter cartridge fired. The prop jerked into life, kicking, stuttering and then blurred into a disc with a roar. Callicoe's Corsair added to the cacophony of noise on the deck. He let the engine settle down and did his tour of the instruments.

He checked his radio and cringed as a burst of static almost took his head off. He brought the revs up to 1,000 and tested for mag drop, getting sixty from the left and twenty from the right. He was ready. He crossed his arms in front of his face and the fitter ducked out of sight, reappearing with the chock ropes in his hand.

He kept the brakes on, waiting to be called forward. The Barracuda in front of him was off next and Callicoe's nerves started to jangle. The Corsair to his right had Barrett in it and would go after them. Butterflies fluttered in his stomach and he flexed his fingers to stop his hands from shaking.

The Flight Deck Director stood off to the left in his yellow bib and cap. He waved a green flag and with a cloud of exhaust smoke, the Barracuda accelerated down the deck. As it got to the end, it dipped out of view and then climbed away, retracting its undercarriage.

Barrett was next. He ran up his engine one last time, the green flag waved and he was rolling. Even before he was off, Callicoe was waved forward. He double checked he'd locked his wings after he unfolded them. He'd heard the story of someone who'd taken off without locking them. When he raised the undercarriage, the wings had folded and the Corsair had dived into the sea like a lawn dart.

Callicoe kept his brakes on and waited. Not a lot of deck was ahead of him and the horizon went up and down as the ship ploughed through the waves. He swallowed hard. This was it. All those months of training had come to this. He knew he could fly, but none of that mattered if he couldn't get off the deck.

The green flag waved. The engine gave a roar and the fighter surged forwards. The end of the deck came up awfully fast. The tail lifted and then he was airborne. After months of training, muscle memory kicked in. Wheels up and reduce the revs to climbing power.

Now he was safely airborne he closed the hood and that helped dull some of the noise that was battering his ears. He lost himself in the moment as he revelled in the thrill of flying again. The engine was purring like a kitten as he cruised along and he made a few gentle turns, looking around him. Below him, *Lancer* looked like a model in a bathtub.

He shook himself back to reality and found Barrett. He formed up on his left side, tucking in behind and below. Gabby tucked in close to Callicoe in similar fashion. Wicklow formated on Barrett's starboard side.

"Very pretty chaps. Now follow me, we'll wait for a few more to get up, then we've got to make four landings to qualify."

"Do we get a teddy bear?" asked Gabby. Barrett laughed. Williams cut in.

"I know what I'll do to you if you don't make four landings," he said. That shut Gabby up.

They all got up okay, the fun came when they came back down. Williams got his four in smoothly. He came down, cleared the wires and then took off again. After his Corsair was struck down in the lift he went to the back of the flight deck and stood with the batsman to watch his men come in.

Lancer's senior batsman was Lieutenant Commander Gilliard. He had trained with Williams when they first learned to fly but their careers had diverged a lot since those early days. A qualified pilot, he happened to be in the wrong place at the wrong time when his CO had been casting round to nominate someone for a Batsman training course.

Barrett caught the three wire on his final go, a textbook landing. Wicklow had a tendency to keep landing long, just managing to catch the last wire. For obvious reasons it was called the Jesus Wire. Miss that you ended up in the barrier. Gabby consistently came in low, grappling with the Corsairs sink rate. Twice he caught the number one wire. Gilliard shook his head in disapproval.

"Low all the way, I give that stooge three or four goes and then…"

"They'll get it," Williams shouted in his ear.

"They better." Gilliard turned back to his job. The breeze ruffled his trousers and he had to brace his legs to keep steady. He held his arms out as the next Corsair came in.

Callicoe came in for his last landing. He flew the upwind leg with *Lancer* on his port side and dropped the undercarriage and his hook. He flew a mile beyond the carrier and then broke to port, flying the downwind leg on the carrier's port side. He locked his harness, opened his hood, reduced speed and lowered the flaps to 10 degrees. He dropped them to twenty as he drew level with the stern. Then it was a descending turn to port, full flaps and et voila, you'd landed. If only it was all so easy. Landing on a moving carrier deck was nothing like the ADDL's at *Saint Merryn*. Landing on *Lancer* wasn't even anything like his practice on *HMS Argus*.

She may have been bigger, but up in the air, her flight deck still seemed to be the size of a postage stamp with nine tiny bits of string across the back to aim for. He concentrated on flying a smooth approach, keeping Gilliard in view in the crook of the wing.

Callicoe was finding it difficult to get comfortable. He was fine until the final bit when everything seemed to move very fast. On his last three approaches, he'd been overly cautious and as he straightened up to land on he committed two cardinal sins, he was high and he was fast. This time he stamped on his doubts and tried not to second guess Gilliard as the Batsman gave him direction.

Callicoe made an adjustment and straightened up as he crossed the stern. Gilliard gave him the cut signal and this time Callicoe nailed it bang on. The Corsair dropped neatly, the hook caught and the wire went taut, dragging the fighter to a dead stop. He cut the throttle and let the fighter roll back a few feet to release the arrestor wire from the hook. Then it was flaps up and once the deck crew lowered the crash barrier, he taxied forward to clear the deck for the next man to land on.

Gardner was the first casualty. The deck dipped away from him as Gilliard gave the cut signal and Gardner's Corsair sailed over all of the wires. He went straight into the crash barriers and there was an almighty bang as he ploughed through the first one and was stopped by the second. Wires wrapped around the wings to bring it to an abrupt stop.

Deck handlers rushed out of pits in the walkways at the edge of the deck. One climbed up onto the wing and helped a shocked Gardner out of the cockpit. The rest of them circled while the deck was made ready again. The barrier was lowered and the Corsair was dragged out of the way.

Cook and Frost landed, then Wicklow came in. His approach was good, but as he flew down the chute, his Corsair bobbled in the air turbulence from the island and he got off line. Gilliard was frantically giving him the wave off as Williams grabbed the back of his vest and dragged him down to the deck. Wicklows Corsair roared over their heads as he veered to the left.

Williams looked over his shoulder to see Wicklows Corsair sinking towards the surface of the sea, hovering on the edge of a stall. The boy's mouth was dry as he opened up the throttle to go around again, keeping a firm grip of the stick to catch the wing if it tried to drop on him.

His nerves were still raw on his second go and Gilliard waved him off early. Confidence crumbling, he finally got down on his third try but it was clumsy. He thumped down hard and the port wheel burst, stranding the Corsair.

It was only when the rest made it down without incident that Williams relaxed. He went down to the hangar to have a look at Gardner's Corsair. The fitters had taken the cowlings off and were in the process of looking at the engine.

"It looks worse than it is," said the fitter. This was why they had some spares. Above him were engines, props, drop tanks and spares in overhead storage.

They changed the wheel on Wicklows Corsair, then they jacked it up to test the undercarriage.

For ten days, they circled the Isle of Man to conduct air operations, practising launches and recoveries. Fresh from a refit, half of *Lancer's* crew were new recruits. The old sweats had their work cut out moulding them into an effective machine. They did fire drills; they did lifeboat drills. Captain Austin had them running full tilt to action stations. He timed them and had them do it again until he was happy. Swordfish dragged drogues behind them so the gun crews could get some practise shooting at something that moved. Gradually, they were coming together as a crew.

At the end of the workup, *Lancer* put back into Liverpool to take on supplies. Crates of fresh produce were brought on board. She topped up her aviation gas tanks and took on fresh provisions. In the Wardroom, speculation was rife about where they were going. The newspapers were full of the landings in France and they wondered if they would be kept at home to support the invasion.

At high tide, *HMS Lancer* went out into the Atlantic with four Destroyers and two 8" Cruisers for company. She moved fast. It only took them a few days to make Gibraltar but there was no flying. Captain Austin had orders to make best speed to Malta which didn't allow any time for further deck landing practice.

Williams kept his pilots busy, getting them to lend a hand in the hangar. Unlike the American carriers which had open hangars to allow air flow, British hangars were an armoured box. That was fine in the freezing weather of the North Sea and the Atlantic. Under a beating sun, the ship gradually started to cook. The hangars began to stink of sweat, oil, fuel and cordite so they lowered the lifts to try and let some fresh air in.

The aircraft were brought up on deck and run up. Callicoe sat in his Corsair, went through the checks and started the engine. The big three bladed prop started turning, kicked and then blurred with a roar. He watched the oil temperature climb. Once the engine was warmed up, he looked out of the cockpit and motioned to the mechanics. They gave him a thumbs up that he was clear. He unfolded the wings and worked the controls. He lowered and raised the flaps and checked the rudder and elevator in his rear view mirror. Satisfied that everything was working, he cut the switches and the propeller windmilled to a stop.

The Corsairs were struck down to the hangars and the Barracudas were brought up on deck to take their turn. The work occupied most of the day and when he wasn't helping move aircraft around, Callicoe was content to lounge around on the edge of the flight deck and enjoy the scenery. It was hot below decks and he made the most of the fresh air.

A tanker came alongside to refuel them when they arrived at Gibraltar. The rock loomed large in the background, an impressive vista, a sign of strength. There was no chance to go ashore. At nightfall, *Lancer* put to sea with her escorts, slipping into the Mediterranean with the Battleship *HMS Jellicoe* and the Battlecruiser, *HMS Hawke* in company.

Two years ago, the Mediterranean was a dangerous

place to be for an allied ship. *Ark Royal* had been sunk on the way back to Gibraltar. *Illustrious* had nearly been blown out of the water in 1941, suffering heavy damage that kept her out of the action for almost a year. *Lancer* herself had been bombed while providing cover for Operation Husky, the invasion of Sicily. Now, it was almost a summer cruise, sailing through waters that had previously proven lethal for so many ships.

Once they got clear of Gibraltar, they went east, rounded the island of Pantelleria and headed south east for Malta. Here, *Lancer* would form part of the forces being gathered to liberate Greece. Even before they arrived, the operation was postponed. The allied effort was focused on Europe and *Lancer's* orders were changed.

They sailed into Grand Harbour to much fanfare. Thousands of people came to see them in and the ships company lined the deck. Callicoe was impressed by his first view of Malta. Grand Harbour was massive.

To the north, it was overlooked by the city of Valletta. Aside from the main anchorage, to the south were four creeks lined with docks and wharves. All of it was surrounded by the three cities of Cospicua, Vittoriosa and Senglea. The other side of Valletta was another large bay where the Navy had its submarine base, *HMS Talbot* at Fort Manoel, an eighteenth century stone fortress. Passing the breakwater at Ricasoli Point, the torpedo boom was moved out of the way and they were warped to their berth.

The place was crowded. Three other carriers were already there, their ride across the Atlantic, *HMS Lynx* and two of *Lancer's* sisters, *HMS Victorious* and *Indomitable*. A number of destroyers were berthed at Kalkarra Creek.

As soon as the anchor dropped, small boats came alongside. Command staff went ashore in the Captains gig. Fresh supplies came on board. The port side watch got shore leave.

Callicoe was glad to stretch his legs and go for a walk. Dressed in summer whites, shorts, knee length socks and white short sleeve shirt, they walked around Valletta. He found the place a mix of beauty and despair. Callicoe was reminded strongly of London as he walked past burnt out houses and piles of rubble.

Between 1940 and 1942, Malta was the most bombed place on earth as the Luftwaffe and the Regia Aeronautica tried to pummel the islanders into submission. Malta had been a giant stone aircraft carrier, a thorn in Hitlers side. Every day, a meagre number of Spitfires and Hurricanes had gone up to try and disrupt the raids. The city was quiet now. The air raid sirens hadn't gone off for months and it had a peaceful air.

Buildings were constructed from local stone, a yellow sandstone that almost glowed in the dusk sunlight. Gabby wasn't interested in any of that, there was only one place he wanted to go and that was The Gut. Famous throughout the Navy, The Gut, or Strada Stretta, Straight Street to give it its proper name was where off duty sailors went for beer and women. To the devout Catholic population, Straight Street was a blot on the landscape. The bottom end of the street towards the citadel at Saint Elmo was a writhing den of iniquity with pubs and bars piled one on top of another.

"After a week at sea with you lot, I need some female company," Gabby complained. The rest followed in his wake, content to wander. The street was crawling with randy matelots going from bar to bar seeking skirt and booze. Ratings tipped them lopsided salutes as they rushed past.

They passed a few places that were strictly bottom drawer and then Gabby spotted something a little more upmarket. The paint on the doors wasn't peeling, the floor was polished and the man on the door was turning away the undesirables. He sat perched on a little stool in tan pants and a crisp white shirt. He only marred the look by having a cigarette hang from his lips and holding a blackjack in his left hand.

They put on their best boy faces and presented themselves. The man looked them up and down, saw the gold braid on their epaulettes and let them in. A fan was spinning in the ceiling providing some measure of cooling and after a week of sweating in the hangar, Callicoe thought it was wonderful.

They sat at the bar and ordered beers. When the drinks were set in front of them, they sat looking at the tall glasses coated in condensation. Callicoe ran a finger up the side of his glass.

"Bloody marvellous."

They attacked, finishing them off and ordering more.

"Keep em coming," Gabby told the girl behind the bar. The evening got a bit hazy after that.

It was late by the time they got back down to the jetty. They almost fell into the liberty boat and were taken back to *Lancer*. Callicoe sat in the stern looking at the big carrier as it loomed over them.

10 – Out Of The Frying Pan

They were on their way at the break of day. The Destroyers went first, sniffing for trouble, then the big ships followed them out. Tugs helped *Lancer* turn around and the horizon was a vibrant orange as they got underway. Once Malta was behind them, they formed up in two divisions, *Victorious* leading *Indomitable*, *Lancer* leading *Lynx*. The Destroyers cranked on eighteen knots and they were off.

Flying training continued. More take offs, more landings. Commander Oates, Commander (Flying) raised the difficulty level by pushing them to take off and land at shorter intervals. To start with, it was taking over forty seconds between each launch and nearly a minute for landings. They had to do better than that.

One Barracuda was lost over the side, another was wrecked on landing. 1783 lost a Corsair of their own. Coming in low, the pilot was lucky enough to just clear the stern, rip off his undercarriage and slither into the crash barrier.

It was over eight hundred nautical miles to Alexandria. The Task Force covered the distance in just over forty hours and arrived at the Egyptian coast close to midnight. They anchored off shore, waiting for the dawns early light to show them the way in.

Callicoe rose early to watch the sun come up. Day came quickly in the desert. There wasn't a cloud in the sky as the sun crept over the horizon, a glowing ball that bathed the land in an orange glow. The city was silhouetted against the light. The sea glittered as the ships rode a light swell at their anchors.

The coast was very low lying around the city, miles of sand as far as the eye could see. A lot of ships had come to grief here over the centuries, not realising how close to shore they were. It was one of the reasons why the Egyptians had built the Pharos in ancient times.

The ships entered the harbour. The starboard watch got an evening ashore this time and Callicoe spent a relaxing evening in the Wardroom. The portholes were opened and a nice breeze was coming in from the shore. He thumbed through an old newspaper, sipping on a beer.

Gabby came into the Wardroom and sat next to him. He held up two chess pieces. Callicoe looked at him over the top of his paper. He paused for effect and then folded it, dumping it on a chair.

"All right. Loser buys."
"You're on."

After taking on more fuel and fresh food, the fleet set sail from Alexandria and headed east to transit through the Suez Canal. The canal was cleared of northbound traffic and the ships came through one after the other. It took four days for all of them to get through. There were moments that Callicoe thought they were going to collide with the great sloping stone sides as they crept along at a few knots. They stopped again at Port Trewfik and then struck south down the Gulf of Suez, into the Red Sea.

Now they were on their way, Oates gathered all three squadrons together in the Wardroom. The Air Staff stood at one end of the room to let them know what was going on.

"You'd have to be blind to notice that we're heading south and we're not on our own." There were good natured grins and they nudged each other. "All these months you've been working hard to get ready. You've been begging for action and I think we're going to get it." There was a rustle of interest. "We'll make a short stop at Aden for fuel and victuals-" the rumble went up a few more notches, "before we join the Eastern Fleet against the Japs."

Oates voice was drowned out at the end as they cheered.

Callicoe wandered around the ship and snapped a few photos as he went along. He'd picked up a camera and rolls of film when he was in America. It wasn't much, just a simple Kodak but he thought he'd try his hand at recording some history. He took a few shots from the Goofer's gallery as some Barracuda's landed on. No one crashed so he went below. He took a snap on the Mess deck and then wandered along to the hangar.

As they'd journeyed south, the temperatures had gone up. The mercury in the hangar started nudging over 100 Farenheit and higher. The heat hit Callicoe like a brick wall when he went through the hatch. His skin prickled with sweat and pools of damp gathered under his arms immediately. There was a slight breeze as the forward lift went up and down, bringing aircraft from the flight deck. The mechanics were stripped down to their shorts, the sweat glistening on their bodies as they worked.

Callicoe moved around, looking for something interesting to photograph. A Corsair had its cowlings off and some trays were underneath so they could drain the oil out of the engine. Callicoe fiddled with the camera, trying to do a long exposure. He braced off the tail of another aircraft to try and keep steady after he pressed the shutter.

Amidships, two ratings were refuelling a Corsair. One had passed the hose up; the other was stood holding the nozzle to fill the 350 litre tank behind the engine. They had just started fuelling when CPO Nelson barked at them.

"Get a move on," he shouted. "You'd move fast enough if this was real."

The two fitters shared a look. Nelson never let up. It always had to be right now. As soon as the fighters were brought down, he would be on your back to get them ready to go again. He was all business, hard as nails and a right bastard when it came to discipline.

Even with the forward lift down, it was absolutely roasting in the hangar and the fitter on the wing straightened up to wipe the sweat off his brow. He looked up at the ceiling. In between the storage racks, vents, and metal firescreen curtains were hundreds of sprinkler heads. They were part of the fire suppression system. He'd have given anything to turn them on and dampen everything down.

At that moment, the deck lurched as the ship dipped into a trough and he lost his footing. He flailed to grab something but just pulled on the hose. He crashed to the deck below and screamed as he felt his arm break under him. The hose fell out of his hand and the nozzle sprayed aviation fuel across the hangar.

Directly across from the Corsair was a Barracuda with electrical problems. A trolley accumulator had been plugged in to provide additional power. They were stood around debating whether the battery was duff or there was some other problem when they were sprayed with liquid. The trolley acc sparked as it objected to being drenched in liquid. In the next instant, the men were screaming and rolling around, wreathed in fire.

The Barracuda went up in flames. Burning fuel turned the deck into a sea of fire. Alarm bells rang. Thick choking smoke started to fill the hangar as the fire spread. A Corsair exploded, then the ammunition in the wings cooked off and bullets started flying through the air. A box of Very cartridges added to the conflagration and the choking smoke was turned lurid colours as the flares went off.

Callicoe's first reaction was to flinch and hit the deck. On instinct, he put the camera to his eye and took a photograph. He berated himself for being an idiot and ran to the back of the hangar. Two ratings were running forwards with a hose and he joined on the end. The hose stiffened as water rushed through it and they started working the spray back and forth to contain the spread of the fire.

Damage control parties shut down the aviation gas pumps and activated the sprinkler system. Salt water covered everything in the forward section of the hangar. The deck got slippery from patches of oil and hydraulic fluid when it got wet. Callicoe clung on to the hose to keep his footing. The fire curtains were released and they dropped to the deck to contain the conflagration. Men in asbestos suits went behind the curtains and advanced with hoses.

Other ships could only watch as *Lancer* hove to, her alarms wailing plaintively across the water. Smoke billowed out of her forward lift. The air rushing in fed the flames like a fan and efforts were made to raise it. Once the lift was up, the hangar would be almost air tight but it wouldn't move. The sprinklers and fire curtains did their job and after twenty minutes, the fire was under control, but the damage had been done.

Five men had been killed, eighteen more were badly burned. The casualties were transferred to a Destroyer and sped off ahead of the fleet to get to the hospital at Aden. Eleven of them didn't live long enough to get there.

Once the fire was out, the stern lift was lowered to help vent the smoke. Attempts were made to raise the forward lift but it was jammed in the down position. It took six hours before it could be persuaded to move again but it was painfully slow. The walls of the hangar were soot blackened raw steel. The grey paint had been scorched off with the heat of the fire.

When the smoke had cleared, four Barracudas and five Corsairs had either been burnt to a crisp or drenched in so much salt water they were unserviceable. Spares stored in the roof spaces were destroyed and tools and other equipment had been damaged or lost. The av-gas system was also damaged and until it was repaired there was no way to refuel the aircraft in the forward part of the hangar. The wreckage was pitched over the side and the aircraft that had been drenched were brought on deck to be checked in the fresh air. They could fly but needed to be overhauled before they'd be considered operational again.

Callicoe came up on deck and sat with his back to the island. His uniform was blackened with soot, his eyes were raw and he kept sneezing, trying to clear his clogged nostrils. His throat felt like sandpaper. One of the deck hands brought over a bucket of water and Callicoe washed his face. He used a rag to wipe his arms. His skin was an angry red and the hair on his arms had been singed off.

It felt good to be up on deck in the fresh air after the hell in the hangar. He'd been scared stiff, seeing the wall of flame coming towards him, but the ratings hadn't run, so he could hardly do so himself.

When they put in at Aden, engineers came aboard to inspect the damage. Aircraft and tools could be replaced, there were stocks of those at Ceylon, but until the equipment in the hangar could be repaired *Lancer* was no longer operational. Alexandria wasn't equipped to do the work, nor were the port facilities at Trincomalee. Signals went back and forth to the Admiralty and Eastern Fleet command while they debated whether to send her back to

Malta or on to Bombay.

The other ships loaded up with munitions and fuel oil to top off their tanks. Three days after arriving, they set off for Trincomalee in eastern Ceylon. *Lancer* wasn't there to see it; on the second day, she put to sea with two Destroyers in escort for Bombay.

11 – An Expensive Way To Learn

It took four days to get to Bombay and another week to put the damage to rights. The dockyard staff worked non stop, fitting new equipment and slapping paint over blackened steel. For seven days, the Air Group kicked its heels. Within sight of Bombay they had flown off *Lancer* and landed at the RAF station just outside the city. Replacement Barracuda's were made available from stocks. They would have to wait until they got to Ceylon to replenish their lost Corsairs.

Williams put the time to good use. They might not be able to conduct any more deck training, but he had the squadron up practising as much as possible. They strafed a sunken wreck off the coast and dropped bombs on it. He had them practice section attacks, one half of the squadron going down while the other half flew top cover. He talked the RAF into some dogfight practise. The Corsairs could run rings around the Hurricanes and the few Mk V Spits based there, but that wasn't the point of the exercise.

Williams put his men at a disadvantage. They got bounced out of the sun, they would be low on fuel, they had to protect the Barracudas. Any tactical situation he could dream up, he flung at them. Time and again he preached watching their fuel state.

"It's a big ocean," he told them. "A carriers a small thing to find when you're low on fuel."

Once the yard had put *Lancer* back together, she put to sea and headed south. The aircraft followed her, landing on without incident. It was a three day run to

Trincomalle but they did it in six. Captain Austin wanted to get his ship into action as soon as possible, but there was no point arriving at Ceylon with an Air Group that wasn't up to snuff.

For three days they flew off and recovered four strike packages. The got the launch times down to twenty seconds and a recovery time of thirty. Not the best, but a lot better than they had been. Williams went up with the CO of the other Corsair squadron, a Canadian reservist called Matthews to test the CAP of four Corsairs. They flew thirty miles west and then came in low.

Lancer had received new radar in her last refit. Five different sets helped control air operations and direct the anti aircraft defence. Williams knew the type 281 air search radar on the mast was very good, but its detection range was reduced the closer you got to the surface of the water. Targets could get lost amongst the ground clutter. Williams and Matthews skimmed along at fifty feet at full throttle. Down low, it was exhilarating, the blue sky above, the blue water below. Sunlight caught the tops of the waves making the sea glitter.

They saw the smoke from *Lancer's* funnel long before they saw her.

"They'll get us any time now," Matthews said.

"We'll see how sharp they are. Let's see if we can't fox them."

"Any time you're ready, Viv."

Williams pulled up sharply and Matthews watched the Corsair curl away, admiring the sleek lines, the bent wing and the long snout. Williams levelled off at 3,000ft and made a target of himself.

As he got closer, he saw the carrier dead ahead. She was turning to port and he could see the cream of her wake trailing behind her. The Destroyers were in outer picket position and would be tracking him with their guns. If this was for real, the AA fire would have started by now. The sky would be filled by dark blots and shrapnel as *Lancer's* 4.5" guns opened fire. As he got closer, the 40mm pom-poms and 20mm Oerlikon cannon would have joined in.

He shoved the nose down, keeping the carrier squarely in his gunsight. He caught a glint of sunlight off perspex and looked up. Two Corsairs were coming down on him, going like the clappers. He broke off his attack run and reefed hard over to the right, standing the Corsair on her wingtip.

The two CAP fighters followed him, chasing him away from the carrier. He dived down away, letting the speed build up, keeping a close eye on the fighters in his rear view mirror. After chasing him for a few miles they broke off to return to guarding *Lancer*.

"Not bad, not bad," Williams said on the squadron frequency. "But er, what about the other one?"

Gardner froze when he heard Williams warning tone. He craned his neck, looking ahead to see what was in the air. He breathed out a sigh of relief as he saw the other CAP pair chasing Matthews Corsair.

"All right, knock it off ladies," Williams told them. "We'll bring it in and talk about it in the Wardroom."

Williams kept the post mortem light. He focused on the good. The radar had picked Matthews up late. The Fighter Controller had provided the CAP with an intercepting course, but it wasn't soon enough to stop him from making a strafing run. There were arguments afterwards about whether the AA gunners would have got him but it was still a poor show.

Captain Austin wasn't impressed either. *Lancer* could have been seriously damaged if that had been for real. He was quite sure the Japanese would happily trade a few aircraft for a Fleet carrier. To be fair, the late intercept wasn't the CAP's fault. They could only go where the controllers sent them.

It was the turn of the Barracuda's next. They practised torpedo attacks. Some of the Corsairs flew cover, some of them flew CAP. After the previous hiccup, the Air Operations centre was more on the ball. Then again, picking up a mass of twenty aircraft was not the same as a lone speck on a radar screen.

The only thing to mar the occasion were the accidents on landing. One Barracuda went into the barrier and one Corsair ditched after the engine conked out. The pilot was picked was up by one of the Destroyers. Considering all of the incidents they'd had on the trip out, it seemed minor.

After the Japanese had captured Singapore and Hong Kong in 1942, Trincomalee had become the home port for the Eastern Fleet. At the southern tip of India, it was on the north eastern side of the island of Ceylon.

Everyone had been through Ceylon over the centuries. The Dutch East India company had been there since 1640 and the Portuguese before that. Authority had been transferred to Britain during the Napoleonic Wars in 1796. One of the few sources of cinnamon in the world, the British East India Company had jealously guarded this valuable possession.

Horatio Nelson had once described Trincomalee's harbour as one of the finest in the world. Over the years, the Royal Navy had developed the port facilities and built fuel oil storage tanks to support operations. The Fleet Air Arm had a station there called *HMS Highflyer*.

As they rounded Elephant Island, the great harbour spread out before them. Wide and deep, it was perfect for capital ships. Slender inlets ran into the central bay. All of it was surrounded by dense jungle.

West of the main harbour was an RAF airfield called *China Bay* and north of that, Cod Bay, where the MTB's and ML's berthed. RAF Catalina's were moored in Malay

Cove. The big ships were in a line in the main harbour, the escorts anchored around them. Two submarine depot ships were next to a floating dock and hospital ships. Fleet oilers were moored near the storage tanks in Malay Cove.

The list of the ships in port was like a who's who. The Battleships *Queen Elizabeth*, *Valiant* and *Renown* were there along with the newly arrived *Jellicoe* and the Battlecruiser *Hawke*. Williams had never seen so many aircraft carriers in one place.

HMS Victorious and *Indomitable* had made good time after leaving Aden. They'd arrived at Ceylon the same time *Lancer* had dropped anchor for repairs in Bombay. Their sister ship, the famous *HMS Illustrious* had been out here for months. Another new arrival was the fleet carrier, *HMS Reliant*. *Ark Royal's* sister, she had sailed from Durban after repairs to a damaged turbine.

Lancer's command staff went over in the Captain's gig to *Indomitable* to see Rear Admiral Moody and Somerville. The air staff went over in a second boat. Somerville was an imposing figure and almost a legend in the carrier community. He'd commanded the famous Force H during the hunt for the *Bismarck* and fought hard in the Mediterranean in 1941 to reinforce Malta.

With the arrival of *Lancer* and *Reliant*, he finally had the force he had been promised for nearly a year. All through 1942 and 1943, he had been on the defensive; operating with slow battleships, few escorts and slender carrier resources. Now he could go on the attack.

"I'm not one for making long speeches, gentlemen," Sommerville began. "I hope you're ready for some action, because you're going to get it." He was talking their kind of language.

"An operation has already been planned in fact. *Victorious* and *Illustrious* will sortie the day after tomorrow to attack facilities at Sabang." He saw their disappointment and smiled with a gleam in his eye. "Don't look so despondent. I'm not having ships lie idle when there's work to be done. What shape are you in?"

Captain Austin spoke for *Lancer*.

"We're ready, sir. We've worked the Air Group all the way here. I'm confident we can conduct operations. We just need to load some Corsairs to replace our losses in the Red Sea."

Somerville's staff officer made a note on a clipboard. Austin had already signalled his requirements when they arrived at Bombay. The aircraft were waiting for them, they just needed to be loaded.

"We can manage that, sir. The replacements are on *Minerva*, they can be transferred over tomorrow."

Somerville nodded approval.

"Captain Manson?" he asked *Reliant's* commander.

"I'd say so, sir. It was a long run from Durban, we can do it. The deck crews are experienced and we've calibrated our radar on the way."

"Good. With that I mind, I'll want you to make a spoiling attack on the Andaman Islands and draw attention away from the strike on Sumatra." He motioned them to come forward and look at the map spread out on the table in front of him. "This is what I propose."

There was no rest for *Lancer* at Trincomalee. She was refuelled, her aviation fuel was topped up and replacement aircraft were loaded aboard. The duds were put ashore. The hangar crews worked nonstop to check over the new aircraft and make them ready.

HMS Lancer raised anchor at 0450 on the 22nd July and headed east. In company with her was HMS *Reliant* and a light escort comprising only cruisers and destroyers. They moved fast. Somerville wanted them to be in position a clear twelve hours before the main strike force. It would be their job to make a demonstration and pull the Japanese north, away from the real target.

It was a muggy, sticky day and Callicoe hung off the stern by the port side 4.5" gun turrets. He turned his face into the fresh breeze that swirled around the guns and ruffled his shirt. He was slated to fly in a few hours. Everyone was taking a turn at flying CAP over the Task Force. Four were up now and four were ranged on deck. *Reliant* had put up a similar number of Seafires.

Callicoe took his camera out of its pouch and steadied himself against the rail, focusing on the aircraft carrier a mile away. She was older than *Lancer*, a copy of the famous *Ark Royal*, Somerville's flagship earlier in the war. Although she was virtually the same length as *Lancer*, *Reliant* appeared stubbier in appearance because of her higher silhouette. She had two full height hangars and could carry far more aircraft than *Lancer* had any hope of accommodating.

"Should we shoot you as a spy perhaps?" said a voice behind him. Callicoe stiffened and whipped round to see Williams with an amused look on his face.

"Sir, I-was just-"

"Relax, Callicoe."

Williams joined him at the rail, sweat glistened on his forehead and there were damp patches on his shirt. Callicoe put his camera away and extracted his pipe from his pocket. He kept his hands busy, shoving some tobacco into the bowl and tamping it down.

"I came up for some air, it's too hot below."

"Some cooler weather would be nice," Callicoe agreed. Williams smiled, showing a row of even teeth, marred by a chipped front tooth.

"Careful what you wish for," he said, his voice taking on a faraway tone as he thought back. "I've been in weather you can only imagine." He gestured along the flight deck. "We were tossed around like a rag doll. Waves as high as the bow, water inches deep in the hangar, howling gales." He pulled his shirt off his chest. "No, I'll take mill pond seas and hot sun any time."

Callicoe just nodded and lit his pipe, cupping his hands around the bowl. Wind whipped away the cloud of sweet smelling smoke. He'd been compelled to ration himself lately. He was running low on his favourite tobacco which he'd bought in England before shipping out.

Williams lit a cigarette of his own and they stood like that for a few minutes, enjoying the relative calm. Callicoe asked about the coming operation.

"How many will we put up?"

"Oh, the lot," Williams said. "A few on CAP, the rest escorting I should think. It depends on the old man I suppose."

They both looked over to the other carrier. Commodore Moore had raised his flag on *Reliant*, taking command of what Somerville had designated Task Force 71.

In the island of *HMS Reliant*, Commodore Moore was in the Navigators office. Hunched over a chart he measured off the distance with some calipers. One more day and they would be in position, ninety miles southwest of the Andaman Islands. Moore pursed his lips and pondered times and distances. He wanted to raise holy hell on Port Blair. He would have preferred to launch from further away, but the range of the Seafire's and the Barracudas was limited. He needed to factor in enough of a reserve for them to loiter before landing back on.

"Whens sunrise?" he asked again.

"0450 hours, sir," the navigator said. Moore leaned on the chart, blocking out the day in his head. *Reliant* had eighty aircraft ready to go, Thirty two Seafires, thirty six Barracudas and twelve Fulmars. Some would be the protective CAP, the rest would be the main strikeforce. The Fulmars would be kept for scouting duties, his eyes and ears while the attack was going in. Allowing time to take off, assemble, strike, return and land, it should be possible to get off a second raid.

A short dark haired man, Moore was an intense individual. He was a firebrand who had chafed at the staid requirements of the service throughout his career. At Jutland he had been a junior Lieutenant on HMS *Invincible*. Stationed in the fire control top in the tripod mast, he'd had a grandstand view of the two greatest fleets in the world blazing away at each other. It was the only thing that had saved his life. When *Invincible* had blown up, he'd been cast into the water. Choking and spluttering he'd been dragged, half drowned from the North Sea by a Destroyer.

After a period of convalescence, he'd seen the aircraft carrier *Furious* at dock in Portsmouth and fallen in love with the romance of naval aviation. When the RNAS had been merged into the RAF in 1918, he'd spent years between the wars agitating for the Royal Navy to have its own air arm again.

Even when the Navy had built new carriers, Moore was kept on the sidelines. He learned to fly and wrote papers on the study of carrier warfare. To keep him out of the way, he'd been sent to America to see how they did it. He came back, more vociferous than ever for bigger carriers.

That had made him few friends in the upper echelons and he'd spent the later years of the 1930's on the China station. Moore knew it for what it was, exile. Promotion had been slow and he'd been resigned to a career that would fizzle out with a whimper.

On the cusp of retiring from the service, he was in England on a long leave when war was declared. Suddenly, firebrand officers were the flavour of the month and he'd been flung into action. He'd commanded a Destroyer in the Norwegian campaign and run the gauntlet of fire on the Malta convoy runs.

He went on to command three different escort carriers in the Atlantic. Covering convoys with his aircraft, he'd operated in some of the worst weather he'd ever seen. Promoted to Commodore, he had been transferred to the Far East to study the Royal Navy's return to the Pacific.

It was Moore who had pushed for Somerville to request another auxiliary carrier to be sent to the Far East. From his time on the China station, Moore knew what it was like to operate in the Far East. The distances in the Indian Ocean were small compared to the Pacific.

Moore knew it was going to take a large amount of support ships to keep the carriers supplied with fuel, aircraft and munitions. Submarines had tenders, so did Destroyers. *HMS Unicorn* and *Minerva* were going to be a vital link in the supply chain.

Moore had also requested more escort carriers to support operations. A number of them were expected in the coming months and Somerville was relying on Moore's experience to make the best use of them.

When *Reliant* and *Lancer* were delayed, Somerville had tried an experiment earlier in the month, pairing *Illustrious* with an escort carrier to attack Port Blair. Somerville liked the idea of having a spare deck in case *Illustrious* had been damaged but it was a mismatch. The escort carrier couldn't keep pace with the bigger ship and it was an experiment not to be repeated. Since then, he'd had them patrolling the supply lanes, hunting for submarines and commerce raiders.

It was Moore who had urged Somerville to send *Reliant* and *Lancer* out in support of his operation against Sabang. *Indomitable* and *Victorious* had spent weeks working ship since they arrived. Moore had advocated action. All the practice in the world was no substitute for operational experience. A strike on Port Blair would be a good introduction for everyone.

12 – Operation Velvet

Callicoe stayed tight on William's wing. At seven thousand feet, he was surrounded by aircraft and he felt hemmed in. Two thousand feet below were the Barracudas from *Lancer*. Ahead, *Reliant's* aircraft were leading the second strike of the day. The Seafires were above and behind, covering everyone.

Callicoe yawned and worked his jaw, trying to make his ears go pop. He was tired and feeling it. He'd been up since two in the morning and running on adrenalin ever since. As planned, the carriers had approached within one hundred miles of Port Blair and launched everything they had. The first aircraft had been launched at 0530 as the first rays of dawn were lightening the sky.

Callicoe had never taken off so early. Everything had an eerie dreamlike quality in the half light of dawn. Deck crew scurried around in the gloom like rats. There was no green flag to signal take off, Callicoe couldn't see it. The Deck Officer used a hooded torch instead, a dim red light that flashed twice when it was time to go.

Moore had to keep his patience as both carriers were slower at launching their aircraft than he would have liked. The strike force shook itself out into good order and set course for the Andaman Islands. Port Blair was on the southern tip and they had flown a dog leg, coming in from the south so they could attack from the sea.

The cloud base had been low, the warm humid weather of the last few days continuing. The strike force had been compelled to descend so they could see the target and get into position.

The Barracudas flew into stiff AA fire. Port Blair had been attacked a number of times the last few months and the defences were well schooled. They had a good fire plan and they threw everything they had at their attackers.

The Barracudas dove into the middle of that to lay their eggs. Explosions had blossomed in the dockyard and amongst the ships moored alongside. A freighter in the middle of unloading caught the worst of it. A 500lb bomb went straight into her main hold and detonated amongst bundles of kapok. Within minutes, she was a blazing inferno.

The Corsairs went for the airfield but the AA guns were waiting for them. The airfield was a narrow strip of land surrounded by jungle. Dispersal bays for aircraft had been hacked out of the treeline. AA guns were at both ends of the runway because there was only one way an aircraft could attack, straight down it.

Williams led them in, peeling off at two thousand feet and going down almost vertically. Flattening out, the CO skimmed over the tops of the trees with the engine going full belt. Nudging 450mph, the Corsair screamed into the attack. Six lines of tracer from the wings scythed the ground. A bowser blew up and took a two engined bomber with it. Men ran around on the ground like ants.

The second section sprayed the AA gunners to keep their heads down for the third section following close on their heels. Two fighters taxied out and tried to take off. Wicklow skewered the first one. The second actually managed to get its wheels off the ground before it was stitched nose to tail and went cartwheeling across the runway. They made one run each and went back over Port Blair on the way home.

Smoke billowed into the sky from burning warehouses and ships. A Frigate was sunk in the southern channel. It had tried to get underway during the attack and been hit by two bombs. The first had hit the bridge. The second went in amidships and penetrated two decks before exploding. The shockwave broke her back and she sank within minutes, her stern and her bow poking above the waves.

Casualties had been light; one Barracuda had been shot down over the harbour. Another ditched on the way back. The rest made the carriers without incident and landed on. Reserve aircraft took off to strengthen the CAP during this vulnerable period. Moore put up two more Fulmars to provide extra eyes.

Two Seafires missed the wires and crashed into the barriers. Two Corsairs did the same on *Lancer* which caused some delays while they were pulled clear. It took over an hour to recover all of the aircraft back aboard.

As soon as the last of them were down, Moore went north at full speed to put some distance between themselves and their launch point. Next, he sent a destroyer south east and had them transmit signals like a carrier taking on more aircraft.

While the ships steamed north, the deck hands got to work refuelling and rearming the aircraft. Conscious of the recent accident, *Lancer* was a little slow, taking nearly as long as *Reliant* did to refuel all her aircraft.

Two hours at flank speed had them seventy miles away from their previous position. When the aircraft were ready, they turned north west into the wind to launch their second strike. To the north and east, a bank of iron grey clouds was threatening but moving towards the island fast, pushed along by the wind. The aircraft got off faster the second time.

Callicoe was on Williams wing again. The weather had changed in the intervening period. The clouds on the horizon thickened over the island, bringing light rain and gusting winds. The strike group descended and everything got very dark. Rain lashed the canopy and the formation spread out slightly, everyone giving themselves room to move.

Callicoe's Corsair bucked up and down through the turbulence as he fought to stay on Williams wing. Port Blair hove into view. Some of the fires had been brought under control but the freighter at the docks was still ablaze.

The AA started up again. This time, the Corsairs were going in first to clear the way for the Barracuda's. The squadron split up into Sections and spread out as they went down for the final approach. Callicoe made sure his safety was off and turned on his gunsight. He tightened his straps and hunkered down in the cockpit.

The Corsairs pulled ahead of the Barracudas and went in. Williams spotted some guns on the bluff overlooking the harbour. He pointed his nose at them and bore straight in. He walked his guns through the battery, dropping men like rag dolls. Callicoe added to the carnage, picking out a pair of guns surrounded by sandbags.

He flinched as a line of holes appeared in his left wing. He banked left and then kicked the rudder to drag his nose back round. He followed Williams, flattening out over the water. Callicoe looked back over his shoulder to see the Barracudas starting their runs.

They dived from four thousand feet. Their big flaps gave them all the time in the world to line up, settle down and release their bombs. Four Barracuda's had hang ups and had to clear the area, still weighed down by their bombs.

Williams led his section on, heading for the seaplane base. The slipways were ahead of them, large concrete ramps where flying boats were winched on trolleys onto dry land. Workshops and a hangar were behind that. Williams took the hangars, pouring his fire into the building. Something exploded inside, blowing the wall out on one side.

Callicoe lined up on an Emily flying boat, half in, half out of the water. The men on the winch ran for their lives and left the aircraft to its fate. It was a big, four engined high winged flying boat, with outrigger floats on the wings. The upper turret turned its gun towards him so Callicoe opened fire. His first burst fell short, the bullets churning up the water into a fine froth. He pulled the stick back ever so slightly to adjust and his next burst hit home. The wing tanks exploded and the Emily tore apart, bits flying into the air.

The second section of Corsairs worked over the warehouse district, shooting up the guns on the roof. It was carnage on the ground. Men hugged the earth, crawling to trenches and shelters as the bombs and bullets rained down among them. A Corsair was hit pulling off the target. It went straight in at high speed, scything through a line of trucks like a battering ram.

The Barracuda's escaped at low level racing for the rise of land to the west. Once they were over that, they were beyond the reach of the guns. The Corsairs covered them out, shooting up anything that dared to poke its head above the parapet. A Barracuda trailing behind the rest was singled out for special treatment. A burst of flak caught it in the tail and it wobbled to stay in the air.

Williams dived on the gun position, Callicoe following close behind. They were in a bad position; it was a steep dive leaving them only a moment for a snap shot before they had to pull up. Williams missed, but it got their attention. They fired on him as he passed overhead and Williams felt the jolt as he pulled up. Callicoe destroyed the gun, but the damage had been done.

Williams was struggling to stay in the air. The controls had gone slack and he checked his instruments. The Hydraulic pressure was close to zero but there were other things wrong as well. He must have been hit in the engine because he could feel it surging.

With no hydraulic pressure, he knew the hook would drop automatically but he'd have to use the emergency bottle to blow down the undercarriage when it was time to land, provided he made it that far.

Once they were clear, he got a little height and had Callicoe look him over. Callicoe slid below for a look. The underside of Williams Corsair was peppered by holes. Oil streaked back from the cowling and there was a whacking great hole in the starboard wing inboard of the undercarriage. Halfway back to the carrier, the damaged fighter started to labour. The oil temperature shot up and he started to lag behind. He sent the rest on ahead but Callicoe stayed with him, glued to his wing.

Contrary to his expectations, Williams made it back to the task force, but he knew there was no way he was going to risk a landing. Even with the throttle to the stops, he could barely stay above stalling speed and the engine was dying all the time. If he tried to land, he had no reserve of power to go around again. He made contact with the carrier and then peeled off to ditch next to one of the Destroyers.

Callicoe was his shadow, watching the CO as he brought the Corsair in light as a feather. Callicoe was reminded of the time he saw Williams go up in the Corsair for the first time back at *Quonset Point*.

He approached the destroyer down the port side. He had his hood back and he was lovely and level as he brought it in. The hook left a trail in the water as it touched the sea first. The underside of the wings kissed the surface of the waves and the Corsair slid to a halt, like a toboggan in the snow. Callicoe circled as he saw Williams step out of the cockpit. He inflated his Mae West and jumped into the water, swimming to get clear of the sinking fighter. He was barely in the water five minutes before a boat from the guard destroyer picked him up.

Callicoe was one of the last to land on board. The forward end of the flight deck was covered with aircraft. The forward lift was moving up and down to transfer them down to the hangar. On the downwind leg, he saw the crowd of spectators on the platform at the back of the island. Callicoe grimaced. On the ride back, he'd started to wonder if he'd been hit himself. There was a vibration in the controls he didn't much like.

He pulled back the canopy and double checked that his straps were tight before making the final turn in. Gilliard held his bats low and Callicoe finessed the stick, trying to lose some height. He didn't want to do it by throttling back in case he had to go round again. The wind had picked up since they took off a few hours ago and he was having to work to stay on track. The bow was going up and down as the carrier flew into the wind.

Gilliard's bats stayed low and the deck was looming large in front of him. Callicoe had a matter of seconds to adjust. He gritted his teeth as he aimed for the deck and straightened up. Gilliard gave him the cut but Callicoe thought he was a little high. He floated down the deck. Just as he thought he was going into the barrier; he caught the last wire and was jerked to a stop. The Corsair touched down with a thump, engine straining to go forward.

It took a few seconds to register in his head that he was down. One of the deck crew stood ahead of him off to his right, waving his arms for Callicoe to cut the throttle. He did so and the Corsair rolled back, allowing the deck hands to work the wire free. The crash barrier was lowered and Callicoe was waved forward as he folded the wings.

There was a knock on his cabin door and Moore looked up from the chart.

"Come," he said curtly. His Flag Officer came in with a

piece of paper.

"Aircraft availability figures, sir."

Moore took the paper and put it on the table.

"Assume I can't read," he said. His staff officer was new, he wasn't used to Moore's little ways yet. There was a pregnant pause while the man dredged up the details.

"Three lost from *Reliant*, two from *Lancer*, one of which ditched. Five others damaged from landing accidents, four on the first strike, one on the second."

"That's what, ten percent?"

"About eight, sir."

Moore nodded sagely.

He flirted with the idea of a third strike. It was still early afternoon, there was time to do it, but the flight crews had been up for twelve hours already, the maintenance crews longer. Tired men made mistakes. The weather was another consideration. The wind had stiffened and the sea had been whipped up. He could launch and then find the aircraft might not be able to get back aboard. He needed to preserve his aircraft for the next phase of operations tomorrow.

"Get me the launch and recovery times for both decks. We'll see if they can do any better tomorrow, what?"

The task force reversed course and went south. In the gathering dark they skirted round the Andaman Islands. In the morning, Moore wanted to be south of Port Blair and heading for Sumatra.

On board *HMS Lancer* the squadron was jubilant at the days success. They'd been blooded at last, although the elation was tempered by losses. The Corsair that had gone in on the second strike was from 1783 and the drinking and singing was as much of a wake as it was a celebration.

Williams was brought back aboard at dusk. He'd dried out by then and he was welcomed aboard like the prodigal son returned. He had a quick drink in the

Wardroom and then gathered with the carrier's senior staff, Captain Austin, Commander Oates, Gilliard and the other squadron CO's and senior pilots. Now that they'd seen action, they had something to dissect, looking for improvements.

13 – Sleight Of Hand

After yesterday's dunking, Williams had gone up at first light to get a good landing in and settle his nerves. He chewed over the results of the previous evenings post mortem while he flew around the Task Force.

It had been agreed that the squadrons had formed up in good time after take off and the formation had been good. The Barracudas were more than happy at how well they'd been covered going in which was something.

Flying into the teeth of the flak had put some pilots off but he was pleased with the strafing runs overall. No matter how much practice they'd had, there was no substitute for the real thing. They'd get used to it.

The main sticking point had been the handling of the aircraft on the deck. Launches, particularly on the first strike had taken too long. There was general agreement that the poor light hadn't helped. The squadrons had never practised launches that early in the morning and it was something they were going to have to work on.

Gilliard had been critical of some of the landings and singled out a few men that needed to improve, Callicoe among them. He had come within a hair of missing the wires altogether.

"Some of them are correcting far too late," Gilliard had said. "At the last moment, they're either shoving their noses down and diving for the deck or coming in too fast."

"Nothing that practise won't solve," Oates had said. He knew Gilliard had high standards but it was a young group of pilots with little experience amongst them.

The good news was that they had less barrier engagements than *Reliant*. Williams didn't think that was anything to shout about. Seafires were notoriously delicate.

Still, considering it was first time out, he couldn't grumble too much. No doubt Commodore Moore would have plenty to say when they got back to Trincomalee.

While Williams contemplated the previous day's events, Task Force 71 passed the small flat island of Car Nicobar. It was the northernmost spit of land in a chain of islands and atolls that stretched three hundred miles to Sabang and mainland Sumatra. Four Seafires shot up a rough strip on the east of the island to get their attention before returning to the carrier.

The Task Force carried on east into the Andaman Sea. Callicoe was up in the CAP with Gabby on his wing. They were flying five miles ahead at fifteen thousand feet. Another section was out to starboard. Aircraft from *Reliant* were out behind and to port. The radar teams on both carriers passed information back and forth, keeping a close eye on their displays.

Callicoe landed on two hours later and Barrett took up a section to do a stint. Food was a hurried sandwich, bully beef and onions. The Fulmars from *Reliant* were ranging far and wide, radar was taking care of everything else close in. Both carriers had eight fighters spotted on deck, ready to respond to anything that showed up.

Tension rose slowly, the further east they went. Seaplanes operated from Malaya and no doubt Port Blair would have been screaming their head off after yesterday's mayhem. Intel had no information of what Japanese units were at sea so a submarine or a Destroyer could appear at any time.

In the middle of the afternoon, the radar plotters got excited when they picked up aircraft to the south. Extra

CAP aircraft were put up but no attack materialised.

An hour later there was another contact to the south but nothing that came close to the carriers. They could have been long range patrol aircraft from Sabang or from the Malayan mainland. They could also have been a scout plane from a ship, there was very little to say one way or another. After a while, the contact faded away, never coming close enough to cause any concerns.

They reversed course at dusk and headed back, accelerating to twenty five knots to get them clear of the Andaman Islands by first light of the 26th. They arrived back at Trincomalee on the 29th. Until they dropped anchor, they'd had no idea how Moody had fared at Sabang.

Somerville had a conference of Captains and key staff the following day. Williams thought it theatrical but there was the touch of the Nelsonian about it; we happy few.

Somerville gave a general overview of the operations. The Battleships and the Cruisers had stood at range and bombarded the port. The Destroyers had gone in at close range and added to the mayhem, launching torpedoes at targets of opportunity. The ships were fired on by shore batteries and all of them had suffered damage to some degree which would take some time to repair.

It was hard to say if Moore's raid on Port Blair had provided much of a diversion but it had provided the new carriers an opportunity to show what they could do. Considering they had never operated together before; it was a positive start.

There was some debate as to future dispositions. With five fleet carriers, it was the most powerful force the Royal Navy had put into action. Fleet doctrine didn't really cover this eventuality. Carrier operations had always been about short sorties for specific missions.

Mooore thought they should work towards operating

as a single task force as the Americans did. With the new reinforcements, Somerville was at last able to do something that had been pressing for some time, he released *Illustrious* for refit to Durban. She had been in action almost continuously for the last year and it was long overdue.

For now, the remaining ships would continue to operate as they were, making spoiling attacks to marshal their strength and gain experience. *Indomitable* and *Victorious* would continue to operate together, *Reliant* and *Lancer* would go out with one addition, *Minerva* would go out with them.

It would give them a spare deck in case of problems and a stock of aircraft for replenishment. Besides, *Minerva* looked exactly like a small Fleet carrier. Perhaps there was some advantage to letting the war correspondents say she was. The Japanese were bound to hear about it. It would force them to react if they thought there was a sixth Fleet carrier in the area.

Callicoe took in the lines of *HMS Minvera* as he rode the boat across the bay. He'd had to visit the gunnery officer and look her up in the data books. Maintenance carriers hadn't been mentioned during his Navy education at *Saint Vincent*. No other navy had one that he knew of.

They were welcomed aboard and Callicoe and Williams were given the tour. A mobile repair shop, *Minerva* was equipped with repair workshops to service aircraft at sea. She was fully stocked with spares, tools, engines, airframes and some complete aircraft as ready replacements when required. She had a 600ft long flight deck and was fitted with arrestor cables at the stern.

Her official designation before the war had been a masterstroke of semantics. Officially, the design was designated as an auxiliary tender. At the time, the Royal

Navy was still constrained by the tonnage requirements of the Washington Naval Treaty. If either *HMS Unicorn* or *Minerva* had been classed as carriers, that would have been a portion of the allotted tonnage allowed. They were classed as depot ships instead. Destroyer tenders looked like destroyers, the fact that *Unicorn* and *Minerva* happened to look like aircraft carriers was just a consequence of what they were supposed to do.

The only difference between them was that *Minerva* was faster. During construction, a third shaft had been fitted so she could maintain 30 knots and keep up with the ships she was supposed to be supporting.

Williams walked to the side of the flight deck. Callicoe peered over the edge, looking down at the water over sixty feet below. A work party was fiddling with the accelerator on the bow. Callicoe brought out his pipe and looked at the harbour of Trincomalee spread out around him. It was another humid day and he was grateful to be in the middle of the bay where the breeze off the sea did good work.

"What do you think?" Williams asked him.

"She's a tidy ship. I'm just not sure why you brought me along."

Williams grinned.

"I like my officers to see things first hand. It makes their job easier."

Callicoe's antennae twitched. Williams was pulling another one of his strokes. Callicoe had noticed this over the months. Williams rarely approached something directly. He liked to show his hand in a more circumspect way. He was a show, rather than tell man.

"I've decided to make you Squadron Maintenance Officer."

Williams looked at Callicoe, trying to gauge his reaction. Callicoe didn't flinch if that was what he'd been expecting. He was just bowled over by the vote of confidence in a mere Sub Lieutenant.

It wasn't a mystery. Williams knew about Callicoe's civil service background from reading his personnel folder. He was methodical and had an eye for detail, exactly what the job required.

"Come on, lets meet your opposite number," Williams said over his shoulder as he walked back towards the island.

The following day *Illustrious* departed for her refit and Moore took his Task Force to sea for practice. He had the ships work at station keeping, turning into the wind for launches. He was a stickler for good ship handling and a flurry of signals flashed out from signal lamps in an almost continuous stream.

He had the Corsairs and Barracudas make mock attacks to challenge the ships radar teams. One of the keys to the integrated air defence measures was the radar operators passing information to the other ships. The numbers of aircraft increased, working up to full launches and recoveries. Moore had them on a stopwatch and he expected to see improvement.

Like any carrier operation, there were incidents. A Fulmar on patrol ditched. By the time a destroyer got to their position they found a dinghy and no crew. *Lancer* lost a Barracuda in mysterious circumstances. It had been flying in the outside position in a section of four. When the leader looked again in his mirror, they weren't there. One of the escorting Corsairs saw it go into a nose dive and that was it. It never pulled out and went into the sea vertically, shedding its wings and tail on the way down.

On the way into port, the Air Group flew off the carriers and landed at the RNAS station. It was a relief to be ashore. Life on board had its moments, they had films, music evenings and parties in the Wardroom but the ship was a closed environment. On a shore posting, you could go to town to see a film, or a girl, perhaps even a few civvies you were friends with. On board ship there was none of that, it was an all male preserve. Since leaving Portsmouth, it had been non stop pressure, Trincomalee was their first chance to relax in months.

Deciding where to sleep came down to a simple choice, primitive but cool ashore, or facilities and a constant roasting heat. Even with the hatches open, the ship was a simmering hot box and it became a contest to find somewhere you could catch a breeze. Men would have slept on the flight deck but Captain Austin drew the line at that. They had to keep some standards.

Living conditions ashore were interesting. They lived in huts at the edge of the jungle, single story wooden frame huts where snakes abounded. Rarely was there a morning when Callicoe didn't hear a high pitched squeal as someone woke up under their mosquito net and saw something slithering across the floor.

Mosquitoes were the biggest irritation. They swarmed at night to feast on human flesh and cases of illness started to rise. Callicoe was bitten to pieces one night when he didn't set his net properly. He spent days scratching and it was very uncomfortable when sweat trickled over irritated skin.

Callicoe woke early. It was a natural thing. The harbour came alive at first light. Destroyers would pap their sirens as they went to sea. Aircraft came and went, the air split by the roar of their engines. He shifted around on the narrow bed, obsessively making sure the mosquito net was tucked in. He did his best not to scratch but he couldn't help it. The MO had given him some cream to put on the bites but it didn't last very long.

He got up, made sure nothing had crawled into his shoes and put them on. He stretched, yawned and chucked a spare pair of socks at Gabby's bed. They bounced off the mosquito net and hit the floor. He picked up the wash bowl and walked out of the hut, covering the thirty yards to the river bank.

He had a good look around before going down to the edge of the water. The place was swarming with crocodiles and they were often seen basking on the opposite bank around midday. He edged down to the water and dipped the bowl to fill it before scampering back to the hut.

He sat on the sand in front of the hut and put the bowl between his legs. He rubbed some shaving soap on his face and wielded his razor. He rinsed it in the bowl and started on the right side, pulling on his sideburns to make the skin taut. Gabby appeared behind him.

"Good morning," he said.

"I'm nearly done," Callicoe told him.

"I might go for a swim," Gabby said, pondering the delights of immersing himself in cool water. Callicoe made a face.

"Your funeral," he said. He moved round to his chin, using small strokes with the razor.

As soon as Callicoe found out the place was infested with crocodiles, you couldn't have paid him to go for a dip. It didn't stop some of the others though. Halfway along the creek was a high pile of rocks. A chap could stand there to watch with a rifle, ready to take a pot shot at anything that got too close before an arm or a leg got nibbled.

Breakfast was basic. With so many ships in harbour, food ashore was no different to food on board. Entertainment ashore was negligible. There was no transport to go into the town, the bar at the station was primitive and the films were ancient. It didn't matter anyway, the racket from the nocturnal insects and animals in the jungle drowned out the speakers. The only thing they watched were newsreels that came periodically from new arrivals.

They watched reel after reel about the Normandy invasion, seeing the allied armies shoving the Germans back. They saw the first mention of things called Doodlebugs, unmanned flying bombs that crashed when their fuel run out. With a large warhead they were wreaking havoc in the south and around London.

Callicoe wondered if the family were okay and it reminded him to write a letter to Ariadne.

14 – Fetch And Carry

While they continued to practice there was a flurry of activity at the RAF base. Heavy machinery was moved in and the runway was lengthened. Men filled thousands of sandbags and started building huge bays to hold aircraft. Metal mats were laid to construct taxiways. Callicoe flew over every day and saw the work progress.

"What do you think they're doing all the building for?" he asked. They were all sat on the sand by the huts.

"I heard it's a secret plot to kidnap the Emperor," Gabby replied in good cheer. That remark was met with the seriousness it deserved.

"Whatever it is, it's big," said Callicoe. "Have you seen the size of the bays? They're not putting fighters in there."

"None of our concern anyway," Barrett said as he took a swig from a bottle of beer. "From what I'm hearing we're back to sea tomorrow."

That stopped everyone dead.

"How the hell do you know that?" asked Callicoe.

"Because when I was on board earlier, I heard them discussing the tides. Now why would they do that, I wonder?" He took another swig from his beer and smiled innocently.

They went down the rabbit hole, speculating wildly about what was going on. It could just as easily be another one of the Commodores practice runs or an operation.

The Task Force put to sea before first light. They went out through the boom one by one and then formed up, heading east. They flew off from *Highflyer* and landed on two hours later. At sea, Captain Austin broke the news.

"Training has been cancelled. There are reports of some Japanese Cruisers causing some havoc on the shipping lanes. We've got orders to go out after them. I'm sure the next few days will be quite busy but an excellent chance to show what we can do. So good luck to us all, and good hunting!"

Off they went, chasing the proverbial needle in a haystack. They had two radio reports made eight hours apart to go on. Two Japanese warships, type undetermined heading in unknown direction. All the Navigator could do was stick a pin in the last reported position and draw a circle, assuming best speed. After that it was a guessing game, that's what Admirals and Captains and Commodores were paid to do.

Moore considered the two signals they'd received. The first had been from a tanker, the *Sophie*. It was only a partial message, giving their position and course, a sighting of a Japanese warship closing from the north. That was it. There had been no transmission from the *Sophie* since.

The other signal was little better. Twelve hours later, another ship had given a sighting of a Japanese warship. They were under fire and gave their position before this abruptly ended. Without the second signal, Moore doubted that they'd even have been dispatched to go hunting.

Moore tried putting himself in the Japanese Captains shoes. They would have to move fast. They couldn't afford to hang around too long in one place, particularly when a transmission had been sent. It was transports they were after and Moore had the benefit of knowing where the convoys were. They wouldn't go east towards Australia. There would be too much of a chance of running into long range patrol aircraft. He stabbed a finger at the chart.

"Here, west of the Cocos Island group. That's where I'd be, heading west to sniff out some more victims." He tapped his teeth with the end of a pencil. "Assuming he maintains a constant speed, that's a two day run?" Moore looked at the Navigator to confirm it but he knew he was right. "Plot me an intercept to get us in range to fly off a strike mid afternoon."

The Navigator did some sums on a scratch pad.

"At twenty knots, we should be in position, 1400 hours, day after tomorrow."

"Very well, make it so. Commander Keller, devise a search plan for your Fulmars, I want them up as soon as possible."

"Yessir."

They came into the wind and launched a CAP, then the Fulmars went up to scout ahead. The Task Force kept up a steady pace all day and into the night. The Fulmars went up again as soon as the sun was peaking over the horizon. Commodore Moore sat on the bridge for hours, staring at the horizon, trying to will the Japanese ships into existence. He knew the odds of finding them were small, but it didn't stop a man who had known many disappointments clinging to hope.

He retired to his cabin to dine, kippers and bread with some pickles from a jar. When he was finished, he hovered over the Navigators shoulder as he plotted their progress on the chart.

On *HMS Lancer*, Captain Austin felt a treat was in order. Two days without any landing accidents was something to be cheerful about. In the evening, he had the ships entertainment officer break out some films they'd been holding for a special occasion.

Films were screened in the after lift well. The biggest vertical space on the ship, a white screen was suspended on the back wall of the well to turn it into a cinema. With the lifts in the down position fore and aft, there was a nice draught to make the conditions bearable.

They had a double feature, a comedy and then a David Niven film. The comedy was dreadful but David Niven was excellent, oozing charm in typical British fashion as he led his men to victory.

Callicoe went to the Wardroom after the film for a snifter. Some of them were talking or playing cards but Callicoe didn't feel up to it tonight.

He retired to his cabin. He sat in shorts, feeling sticky in the hot air. He tried reading but found it hard to concentrate in the heat.

Gabby clattered through the door a while later, three sheets to the wind.

"Cut, cut, cut!" he called and then clambered onto his bunk, giggling to himself.

"Had a good time, did we?" Callicoe observed. Gabby stared down at him

"A very good time," Gabby hiccuped.

"Well don't throw up-"

"Yes, I know mother," Gabby interrupted. "If I'm not well I'm to take myself elsewhere."

"See that you do," Callicoe said sternly. The thought of Gabby being sick in such a small cabin turned his stomach, the smell in this heat would be horrific. He lay back down again and rubbed his temples; his head was pounding.

Sleep eluded him. He knew they'd be flying again in the morning and being up on CAP was mind numbingly boring. The latest rumour was they were chasing ghosts. Callicoe wasn't particularly bothered, he was just glad they hadn't strayed far from the carrier. They were hundreds of miles south of Ceylon, in the middle of nowhere.

He went for a wander up to the flight deck. It was a

different place at night with no aircraft flying. Five Corsairs were lashed to the deck in front of the island, their wings folded.

The wind across the deck was refreshing and helped clear his head. He stood there for a while, watching the bow go up and down as they sailed along. It was almost a full moon and the ships looked almost ghostly, their grey hulls shining under the moon light. The ships were running dark, not a light shining from any porthole. The sea was a dark cloak, the bow waves carving a path through it.

He clamped his pipe between his lips and sucked on the stem, tasting the residue of tobacco, the sweet cherry flavour he was so fond of. He sighed. He'd nearly run out of it and he'd have to start smoking the tobacco they were issued with. He'd hoped he could find something at Trincomalee but he'd had no luck.

"Trouble sleeping?" Williams asked, appearing out of the dark by the crane. Callicoe stiffened. Williams seemed to have this uncanny knack of catching him out.

"A little sir. The damn heat."

Williams chuckled in the dark.

"It's no better in my cabin," said Williams.

There were flashes of light on the horizon away to port.

"Electrical storm?" Williams suggested.

"Or gunfire," Callicoe countered. "The Japanese ships?" he pondered.

"Do not be anxious about tomorrow, for tomorrow will be anxious for itself. Sufficient for the day is its own trouble," Williams murmured, his tone almost reverential. Callicoe cocked his head. He'd never taken the CO to be a religious man.

"Proverbs?" Callicoe queried.

"Yes," Williams confirmed. He felt foolish for quoting the bible to a subordinate but it seemed an appropriate moment. The deck was quiet, like a church and he'd put his faith in god for a long time now. Flying off carriers was dangerous and luck would only get you so far.

"You ever fly at night?" Callicoe asked him.

"No. I missed Taranto. I can't say I'd be thrilled at the prospect, it's hard enough landing these things in daylight." Callicoe grunted agreement on that point. "Are we on top line?" Williams asked, becoming all official again, the mask back in place.

"Yes sir. And *Minerva* has spares, just in case."

"Goodnight, Sub."

"Goodnight, sir."

Callicoe woke up with a sneezing fit. He dragged himself to breakfast and went up on CAP. He felt groggy as he went through his startup routine but a whiff of oxygen sorted him out once he was in the air. He felt tired throughout the time he was in the air but put it down to lack of sleep. He'd tossed and turned all night in the heat, thinking about what Williams had said.

From the beginning, Williams had always been so serious, Callicoe had found his quoting the bible a strange revelation. He'd lain awake for a while in his bunk, sucking on his pipe contemplating what he believed in. He'd never really pondered this question before but then, he'd never been as close to death before.

The Task Force continued steaming south. The tension on *Reliant's* bridge ratcheted up as they got close to the area Commodore Moore identified as the target zone. The remaining Fulmars went up to scout ahead. The air groups were armed and brought on deck. *Reliant's* Barracudas had torpedoes, *Lancer's* AP bombs. They were ready, all they needed was a sighting and they would be off.

The hours ticked by as the Task Force reached

Moores point on the map. He left the bridge and retired to his cabin and stared at the chart.

"They've got to be there," he muttered to himself. He rolled the options through in his head and kept coming up with the same answer. If they weren't here, then the only other possibility could be was that they'd turned around and headed back to Singapore.

There was no sighting that day, nor the following morning either, the trail had gone cold. Two days head start was a difficult obstacle to overcome. The Task Force kept at it another day, running a line towards Perth. Moore knew he didn't have to worry about the west, a hunting group of Destroyers was covering that area.

The whole thing was an anticlimax. The pilots commiserated in the wardroom. They had been promised action and had nothing of the kind.

"It's a gyp," Gabby complained. "Old fashioned bait and switch. They tell us it'll be bombs and bullets for breakfast and all we do is run a CAP and dash around like headless idiots."

That tickled them. Wicklow tinkled a few notes on the piano. Gabby leaned against the side of it, humming along.

"Be fair," said Gardner. "They can't just magic up ships for your convenience."

"Hogwash," Gabby shot back. "This was no better than playing with toy boats in a bath, it's just a bigger bath."

The room cracked up. They were in a rebellious mood after being worked up into a lather. There was a big difference between going out to do some training and steeling yourself for going into action. It had all been a bit of a letdown. Barrett clapped Gabby on the shoulder.

"Careful tiger. You'll get your chance."

Gabby's eyes went wide, his eyebrows high.

"Gosh, will I? Please, sir, can I lead the next one?"

"I don't see why not," Barrett replied, his face

deadpan. "We're always looking for leaders."

With no enemy contact, Somerville recalled the Task Force. Halfway back to Trincomalee, they were met by three oilers and the pilots saw their first at sea replenishment. In principle, it was very simple. Two ships would sail in a straight line one in front of the other. The ship in front would put a hose over the side that the trailing ship would bring aboard to pump fuel. Keeping the same speed was difficult. Hoses often broke and it took hours to transfer fuel.

To transfer supplies, lines were passed and boxes and crates pulled over. It called for some fine station keeping. The supply ship held a straight course while the aircraft carrier came up alongside. It would edge in until there was no more than fifty yards or so between them. The sea was churned up, becoming roiling crests of white as the water funnelled down the gap. The helmsman had to work hard to keep the gap consistent and not put any strain on the lines.

The Task Force returned to Trincomalee, a week after putting out. When he flew over *China Bay*, Callicoe saw what all the building work had been for. The sandbag bays had been filled by big, shiny, B29 Superfortress bombers, lots of them. The Americans were in town.

It was the hot topic of conversation that evening while they sat drinking beer outside their huts. The size of the B29's took their breath away, they had seen them flying in the afternoon, air testing. They were massive in every dimension, with big long wings, huge rudder and a blunt glazed nose up front. The bomb bays were massive.

China Bay almost become an American airbase. The few RAF aircraft were moved to *HMS Highflyer*. Their pilots joined the squadron down by the river. They were horrified by the state of the accommodations.

"Gad, our spares tents are better than this," a Pilot

Officer commented.

"You're quite welcome to put one of those up if you prefer chum," Gabby said acidly. He knew that the RAF bods had proper accommodations with ceiling fans at *China Bay*. It was a bone of contention that the RAF lived in apparent comfort while the Fleet Air Arm did not. Gabby pointed over towards the river. "You can set up over there if you want."

The Pilot Officer went over for a look, seriously contemplating it. He went beyond the circles of light provided by the hurricane lamps placed around them and disappeared into the gloom.

Gabby counted down to himself from ten to zero. He got to two before there was a yelp and the Pilot Officer ran back into the group.

"There are bloody crocodiles out there," he said, pointing towards the river. The squadron cracked up.

"What's the matter?" Gabby asked between gasps, tears running down his face, "is it a bit bumpy?"

They descended into more giggles, clutching their sides. Callicoe handed the Pilot Officer a bottle of beer and motioned for him to sit. The man sat down in a huff. A Flight Lieutenant plonked a crate of bottles down in the sand.

"It would be churlish to turn up without bringing a gift," he said. He chucked a bottle to Gabby. "The huts will be just fine. I don't think the Yanks are staying for very long."

"You know what? I always liked the RAF," said Gabby as he popped the top off the beer bottle. It was warm but he didn't care, beer was beer. He heard a noise behind them, a sibilant hiss and the rasping of sand. He picked up a stone from a small pile he had by his side and pitched it into the dark. There was a low growl and then the rasping sound and then a splash.

"Croc," Callicoe said. It had been creeping towards

them. He hefted another stone into the dark and they heard some more thrashing.

"Bloody crocs," said an Australian Flying Officer called Mobson. "We've got enough problems with the bloody things back home." He pulled a Webley revolver out of a holster on his hip. "Want me to sort them out for you?" he asked with a gleam in his eye. Callicoe put a steadying hand across the cylinder of the gun and pushed down so the barrel was pointing at the sand.

"I don't think we need to go that far," he said slowly. He had visions of half the squadron getting plugged in some mad crocodile killing frenzy.

All of the RAF men were browned off. Some of them had been at Trincomalee for months, flying endless patrols over the ocean. They hadn't had a sniff of action and were quite jealous when Gabby and some of the others started describing their attack on Port Blair.

Soon enough, the conversation turned to the relative merits of their aircraft. Everyone knew theirs was the best and it ended at a good natured impasse. The biggest laugh was when Mobson boasted he'd have no problem landing on a carrier. There were hoots of derision at that. Of course, there was no way they were ever going to be able to prove it.

"I could too," Mobson insisted hotly. He sat down in a huff and before anyone could stop him, tugged out his pistol and started firing towards the river. "Bloody crocs!" he shouted. He kept on pulling the trigger even after the firing pin clicked on spent cartridges. There was a struggle for the gun. Callicoe and the Flight Lieutenant rolled around with Mobson trying to get it off him. Callicoe sat on the Australian until he calmed down.

They were rudely awakened by the sound of hundreds of engines being run up. Gabby sat up as the constant thrum and vibrations drilled into his skull. Callicoe got out of bed and stumbled out of the hut, bleary eyed. His head was throbbing and his tongue felt like a piece of carpet. He kicked a bottle out of the way as he walked away from the huts to get a clear view of the airfield.

Mechanics rushed around seeing to lots of last minute things. Bombs were wheeled out on long trolleys and loaded on board the big bombers. Their bare polished metal gleamed under the harsh sunlight.

There was only local flying that day. The powers that be decided they wanted to keep the air clear for the Americans. In the middle of the afternoon, the air shook as the bombers started up again. Fifty six B29's edged out of their bays and took off into the afternoon sun. One after another they roared overhead and circled round to take up a course towards the oil fields at Palembang. It was a marathon mission, a three thousand six hundred mile round trip.

Fifty six B29's went out, fifty five came back. When the smoke had cleared, intelligence said major damage had been caused to the refineries. The Americans left the following day in a roar of noise and power.

Commodore Moody watched them depart, jealous of the power at their disposal.

With the departure of the Americans, life got back to normal. The Air Groups continued to practise. The RAF made mock attacks on the ships at sea, their big Beaufighters coming in at low level. The Corsairs returned the favour. They beat up *China Bay* and the docks to give the AA gunners something to aim at.

By the middle of August, Admiral Somerville was gone, shuffled off to head the naval delegation at Washington DC. Officially, it was at the request of Admiral Cunningham, but there were all sorts of gossip. One that got some traction was that it was because of Mountbatten. The head of South East Asia Command had clashed with Somerville a number of times and the relationship was never harmonious. Many felt sorry for Somerville. He'd been criticised after the Japanese attack on Ceylon in 1942 and had been fighting on the defensive ever since with a motley collection of ships. Now the Royal Navy was going on the offensive and he wouldn't be here to see it.

Two new faces appeared in the form of Admiral Fraser and Admiral Powers. They ensconced themselves at headquarters and had conferences with Moody and Moore about what they were taking on.

Fraser's arrival was particularly welcome. He had a reputation as a fighting Admiral who took the fight to the enemy. He had commanded the old carrier Glorious before the war so it was comforting to know they were getting someone who knew about carrier tactics and operations.

Fraser soon showed them that he intended to go forth into battle. The carriers had been here since July, consuming valuable supplies while they worked up their Air Groups. It was time for them to start earning their keep.

"I want results," he told Moody and Moore. "Results to show that we can do it, that we can operate at sea and replenish and keep on operating." He gestured to the map on the table, his hand encompassing the water between Ceylon and Sumatra. "This is *our* backyard. This isn't two years ago. The boots on the other foot now. Show me what you can do."

Fraser told the intelligence types to prepare a list of top targets in theatre and start planning to make it happen.

15 – Close Run Thing

A flurry of orders went out from Fraser's headquarters. Moody would be in overall command with Moore's broad pennant remaining on *HMS Reliant*. Fraser had picked the target but he left the overall planning to Moody and Moore.

This one was going to be a fast dash. A sharp thrust into the Japanese belly and then back again before they could do anything about it. If they were going to go on extended deployments like Fraser wanted, then they were going to need more accurate fuel consumption figures. In addition, there was a question mark over how much aviation fuel they'd use in multiple strikes.

It was an awesome sight as the entire Eastern Fleet put to sea. The battleships led the way, the newly arrived *HMS Howe*, followed by *HMS Jellicoe*. Then the carriers slipped their moorings and passed by the boom. All four carriers put to sea with *Unicorn* and *Minerva* providing spare flight decks and material support.

The Task Force sailed in two divisions, with a battleship each at their head. The cruisers and destroyers surrounded them in a screen.

It was a three day run to get in position and they didn't see a soul and that made Moore nervous. There hadn't been sight or sound of a Japanese ship since the beginning of the month. Moore didn't like that. A heavy cruiser or two appearing at the wrong moment could wreak havoc. If the carriers were in the middle of recovering aircraft it could be a disaster.

Even with the benefit of radar, it was still possible to

spring a surprise or two. He wasn't impressed when one of the officers on Fraser's staff espoused the belief that the Japanese were done. Wounded yes, but they still had plenty of life left in them.

On the second day out, they maintained a larger CAP. The carriers turned into the wind briefly to launch the fighters before resuming their base course. Williams was happier once the aircraft were up, he didn't like the air of confidence that seemed to be pervading everything.

The mood in the Wardroom was buoyant. They gathered round the piano and sang the old favourites. The noise was terrific. Even Williams mood lifted. He hadn't seen wardrooms like this since the beginning of the war, the bravado, the confidence. Gabby turned to Williams and waved him over to the crowd at the piano.

"Come on boss, your turn."

Williams tried to squirm out of it but the crowd started baying for him. Even Matthews joined in, egging everyone on. Williams shoulders sagged; he wasn't getting out of this one.

"What'll it be, skipper?" asked Wicklow. He'd turned on his stool and looked over his shoulder. Williams took up position at the corner of the piano.

"How about A25?" he suggested with a grin. The room erupted. He'd barely managed two lines before everyone else joined in, singing at the top of their voices.

They finished their drinks and cheered, chanting 'skipper, skipper, skipper'. Williams left them to it with a smile on his face. Some things never changed. Form A25 wasn't bothered if you were a regular or Wavy Navy. Everyone had filled one out.

They were called to briefing early. Oates Matthews, Williams and the Barracuda CO, Commander Birkenfield stood at the front by a blackboard covered in white chalk with a map and times on it.

"I'm sure you've heard the rumours," said Oates. "We're going to knock on Johnny Japs door." He motioned for quiet. "If I may?" he fixed them with a look and they settled down. "The Americans are making a landing in the north of Dutch New Guinea. We are going to make a demonstration in the south west of Sumatra to provide a distraction. We will sneak in from the west."

"When we get in range, we're going to fly off a strike against the harbour at Emmahaven," he pointed to the chalk map and circled one bit of it, "also the airfields around Padang, the cement works at Indaroeng and the repair yard at Kajuara."

"I know that doesn't sound very exciting, but the cement works at Indaroeng is the only facility of its kind in south east Asia. If we destroy or damage it, we interfere with every aspect of their defence. They can't make cement for bunkers, or blockhouses; they can't make runways or repair buildings."

"Questions so far?" There were none.

He started going through the details. *Victorious* and *Indomitable* would go for the cement works.

"We will start to take off from 0600 hours. *Reliant's* Barras will go for the airfield south of Padang, we've got the repair yard at Kajuara. 1771 will cover the strike to the yard, 1783 will cover the airfield."

Oates left for them to brief individually. Williams did his down in the hangar. He leaned the blackboard against the side of his Corsair and gathered his men round.

"Eight of us go first, ten go second; who wants what?"

"As long as I'm not on CAP again," Gabby said.

"Don't worry, Veriker, everyone goes on this one. You have my word. *Reliant's* Seafires will cover the Task Force, they'll also cover both strikes on the way back in case the Japs want to play. Happy now?"

"Yessir, very happy, sir, thank you, sir."

Even Williams had to laugh. Gabby had that ability to lift the mood.

At one hundred thirty miles from the coast of Sumatra, the Task Force turned into the wind. Moody had to compromise when he picked the launch point for the strike. On paper, the Barracudas had a range of over 600 miles, but that wasn't what they could do in the Far East. Already underpowered with the Merlin engine, the hot air reduced their performance even more. Loaded down with bombs, the Barracuda's could barely make one hundred eighty miles each way. If they lingered over a target, there would be little margin to spare to get back to the carrier.

Moody would have gone closer, but one hundred miles or so offshore was a chain of islands. He wouldn't risk the carriers going beyond them. It was bad enough that they were sailing so close to them as it was. There was a very good chance the Japanese had watchers on these islands, maybe even AA guns. There would be little chance of a surprise attack here, but there was no other way to do it.

The first strike had none of the problems in the early morning light like they'd experienced before. They averaged a launch every eighteen seconds, not bad in the half light of dawn. The difficulty was the state of the sea.

Williams had grimaced when he saw the conditions. The ocean was almost glass smooth and there wasn't a breath of wind. Days like this made for difficult launch conditions. Just like taking off into the wind from a runway, the more wind over the bow, the easier the take off. The carriers would have to go flat out to stop anyone going into the drink today. The carriers accelerated to flank speed. To Moody's alarm, the battleships started to lag behind.

With their powerful engines, the Corsairs got up easily, but the Barracudas struggled. Each one went over the bow and there was a heart stopping moment where they dropped from sight before climbing away.

The aircraft formed up and headed east. As Moore had feared, the Japanese were ready and waiting for them. They threw up a wall of flak as the strike went in.

The Barracuda's held tight together and dived into the middle of it. They throttled back, lowered their dive brakes and went straight down. At fifteen hundred feet they released their bombs and pulled out. The 250lb bombs pummelled the repair yard, blasting buildings and slipways to bits. A freighter took two bombs through its deck and settled at the stern, grounding itself on the bottom of the harbour. Spilled fuel oil ignited and the water of the bay turned into a sea of flame.

Not hanging around, they turned back for the carriers. The Seafires from the *Reliant* met them fifty miles out and guided them in, covering them on both sides. The Barracudas landed first without incident and were struck down to the hangars. The fun began when the Corsairs came in.

One after another they thumped down on deck. Frost made a good start, then Wicklow blotted his copybook, bobbling on a pocket of turbulence. The left wing dipped before he could catch it, his undercarriage leg clipped the deck and his Corsair plunged over the side. The fighter sank fast and he was lucky to get out before it took him with it.

Farthingdale was next and bounced. He missed the arrestor wires entirely and went into the crash barriers. One wire cut across the canopy frame and nearly took his head off. He was pulled out of the cockpit and the fighter was dragged clear.

Moore simmered in frustration. Every minute spent clearing wreckage was more distance between them and Padang, stretching the range of the Barracudas to breaking point.

The second strike got off ten minutes late and out of position. There was no racing into the attack this time. The Barracudas reduced their speed to conserve fuel and gained as much as height as the overburdened engines could manage.

Callicoe cruised above them in his Corsair. Gabby was on his right, Gardner and the CO to his left. They knew where to go long before they got there. Smoke rose from Padang and the repair yard. Further inland there were flames rising from the cement works.

"Boxer Leader to all Boxers," Williams called over the R/T, "keep your eyes open. The Japs have had enough time to get organised."

He peeled off to clear the Barracudas and circled to the south of the bay. The Barracudas went down into the teeth of the flak, drawing all the fire. One of them was hit during that mad dive. It turned into a streak of flame and plunged like an arrow into the middle of a large warehouse. Its roof went up as the bombs went off. A second Barracuda was blotted from the sky as they sped off at low level. What was left of it fell into the harbour in a hiss of spray.

Up above, the Corsairs had their hands full. Japanese fighters had fallen on them out of the sky above. Williams had caught the glint of sunlight on perspex as they came down.

"Break, break! All Boxers break!"

His section scattered like a covey of partridge. Williams went left with Gardner, Callicoe went right with Gabby stuck to his tail like glue. The Japanese fighters flashed between them like avenging angels. It was every man for himself as another group of Zeros closed in from the north and went for the other section.

Callicoe pulled the stick into his stomach and grunted as the G forces built up. He sagged in his seat and struggled to keep his head up, straining to see where the

Japs had gone. He caught a glimpse of a green tail through the top of his canopy and maintained his turn. He got behind it and closed in for the kill, but before he could fire, he saw a black nosed fighter in his rear view mirror. In the same instant, Gabby shouted a warning in his ear. Callicoe rolled left, kicking on the rudder bar to drop the nose.

Tracer flashed past his canopy. Callicoe pulled back on the stick for all it was worth, tightening the turn. The Zero tried to stay with him and couldn't, the high speed of his diving attack stiffening the controls. As he slid wide, Gabby got onto his tail and stayed there. The Zero reversed its turn, rolling to the right. Gabby led the target and opened fire, giving the Zero a long burst. The nimble Japanese fighter went right through it and fell apart. It shed a wing and burst into flames.

"You're clear, Boxer three," Gabby called.

"Roger, forming up on you," Callicoe replied.

Gardner had his work cut out. A Zero latched onto him and followed him through a series of gyrations. This one was good, trying short bursts every time he got the Corsair in his sights. Each time, Gardner was able to twist out of the way at the last moment. Williams couldn't come to the rescue, he had two after him and the other Corsairs were occupied as well.

It was a vicious dogfight, a whirling mess of fighters that twisted and turned, jockeying for position. Another zero fell, then a Corsair. Finally, the Corsairs broke for home.

The Barracudas were long gone, there was no reason to stay. They dove for the deck and opened the throttles, leaving the Zeros behind. Coming out of the target area low, their engines screamed at full power, eating up the miles. They left Padang behind, shrouded in smoke and flame.

Callicoe landed, then Gabby. Frost, Barrett and Farthingdale made it down after that. Gardner came in delicately, his tail a mess, a hole in his rudder and elevators.

Callicoe watched from the island as Williams was the last to come in. Gilliard crouched, leaning into the thirty knot wind on his back. He kept his arms straight as Williams flew to perfection. The ship was barely moving up and down, the sea perfectly flat.

Williams straightened up and Gilliard gave him the cut signal. The Corsairs engine note dipped as Williams chopped the throttle and floated the last few feet to the deck. Callicoe had just turned away when there was a screeching twang and the arrester cable snapped.

The thick cable whipped across the deck like a flail. The deck crew who had raced forward to secure Williams Corsair were in its way. They were bowled over like skittles. One man had his left leg taken off below the knee. Another rating saw it coming and managed to jump over it like a child does with a skipping rope. He landed in a heap on the deck, his heart pounding at his good luck. He crawled over to his mate who was screaming like a stuck pig, hands clutched the stump of his leg as blood squirted between his fingers.

Williams felt the cable go, but before he could do anything about it, his Corsair veered to the right. His starboard wing caught the island and ripped off. The undercarriage leg collapsed and the fighter span round, nose down, tail high in the air. Fuel started spilling across the deck. Williams pulled on his straps, trying to release the harness but the catch was stuck. Two deck crew ran over to help him but couldn't figure out how to get up there. Someone shouted for a step ladder.

Callicoe was running to lend a hand when leaking fuel spilled over the hot engine. Flame licked out from the cowling and began to consume the fighter. Williams was surrounded by a sea of flame. It rushed up the underside of the fighter, orange tongues of fire that hungrily consumed the metal. As the flames got higher, Callicoe could see Williams frantically clawing at his harness, twisting to get out.

Hoses appeared and started spraying water on the nose. Before they could get water on the fire, the heat of the flames got to the wings and the six machine guns started firing. Bullets ricocheted off the island and went in all direction. Men dropped the hoses and ran as tracer exploded at their feet.

Callicoe ran for a hose and landed on it, fighting to get control of the writhing wet canvas sausage. Pinning it to the deck with his body weight he worked his way along, trying to grab the nozzle. Gabby rushed over to help and the two of them got it under control. Rolling to his knees, he trained the hose on the Corsair but it was too late. The heat of the fire was terrific, the intensity of the flame added to by the magnesium alloy in the engine. Williams sagged in his seat and was then mercifully hidden from sight by thick plumes of smoke as the flames consumed the fighter.

Two ratings rushed in to try and save him but the fuel tank exploded. The blast showered them head to toe in burning petrol. One collapsed screaming, the other was blown off the deck into the sea.

Asbestos clad fire crews sprayed foam onto the fighter and got the flames under control. The fire was choked to death, leaving a blackened bit of twisted wreckage. It was all over in a matter of minutes and just like that, Williams was dead.

16 - 不運 Fuun

The deck crews extricated Williams charred remains from the cockpit of his corsair. There was nothing recognisable, just a shrivelled figure with tatters of clothing attached. Callicoe stood rooted to the spot, numb at the suddenness of it all.

A chain was put around the fuselage and the deck crane lifted it clear, pivoting on its mount to dump it over the side. It made a splash and then slid into the depths. Callicoe was dragged out of his funk by the screeching of the klaxon. The tannoy called the crews to battle stations and ordered them to close up. Below decks, hatches were dogged shut, sealing men into their compartments.

Callicoe went into the island and collided with Barrett coming the other way. They landed in a heap in the passageway, a tangle of arms and legs.

"Aircraft approaching!" Barrett shouted. "We've got to get into the air."

He ran out to the flight deck. Chaos reigned. Not everything that had landed had been struck down to the hangar yet. The forward deck was covered with aircraft and there was no room to launch. Barrett pointed forward.

"Get that catapult clear and get me two Corsairs ready to go," he ordered. The deck crew looked at him, blinking at this Lieutenant who was issuing orders. They sprang into action. The forward lift went up and down, cycling every forty seconds as they cleared aircraft out of the way.

The carriers increased speed, surging forward as they

went to maximum revs. The battleships began to lag behind but Moore didn't care, the only ships that mattered right now were the carriers. Radar had detected a double threat, surface ships approaching from the north and aircraft from the east. The aircraft would get here first and he was faced with a stark choice. If he wanted to launch fighters to head off the enemy strike, he would have to head into the wind. That meant going north, bringing them closer to whatever these ships were.

He knew they weren't friendly, everything they had in these waters was with the Task Force, they had to be Japanese, but what? They couldn't be battleships, but destroyers or cruisers could make life interesting. Moore took the lesser of two evils, he carried on heading south west, trusting to the AA defences.

Barrett went up to the bridge, looking for Oates. He found him in conference with Commander Matthews. The Canadian towered over the diminutive Oates, his face mottled red.

"But that's madness!" he exclaimed. Oates didn't look very happy either.

"I'm sorry, but there it is. Orders from the flagship are to maintain course. Excuse me," he said. The deck phone buzzed and he put the handset to his ear, listening intently. "Get the aircraft below as quick as you can."

"What's going on," Barrett asked.

"The Commodore won't turn into the wind. So we'll have to rely on whatever is already up."

Barrett blanched. He peered down at the flight deck. Aircraft were disappearing below rapidly.

"But that's-" words failed him.

"I know."

They looked at each other, aghast at the choice being made. Barrett turned to Oates to appeal but the Commander Flying cut him off.

"I know what you're going to say. Commander Matthews has already said everything you're going to."

"What about the catapult?" Barrett blurted. That stopped Oates. "That'll accelerate us to sixty knots. We've got thirty knots over the deck."

"It's never been done," Oates said, horrified at the prospect. All he could picture was a Corsair being launched over the bow and plunging straight into the water.

"It's worth trying," Barrett persisted. "I'm willing to risk it."

The silence was deafening. Barrett could see Oates considering it, dissecting the pros and cons.

"I'm sorry," said Oates, "but I can't let you try it. We've lost Williams, I'm not going to sacrifice you too."

Oates absented himself from the bridge before anything else could be said. He went down to the Air Operations Centre to look at the radar screens and stare at the blobs that were rapidly approaching form the east.

Barrett went down to the hangar with a snarl on his lips, frustrated at the decisions being made. They were an aircraft carrier and they weren't going to use their aircraft to defend themselves. He found Callicoe deep in conversation with CPO Nelson and Lieutenant Willis, one of the engineering officers.

"How long till you can get some ready to go?" Callicoe asked.

"I've got three now," Willis said, pointing forward to the lift. "The rest are being rearmed, but we can't refuel while this is going on."

Callicoe turned to Barrett as he noticed him approaching.

"We've got three," he reported.

"Forget it," Barrett snapped. "The prevailing wisdom is we'll tough it out."

Callicoe and Willis just looked at him, disbelieving

looks painted on their faces.

The approaching aircraft ate up the distance. The CAP of Seafires were sent into the attack. They intercepted them thirty miles short of the Task Force. It was a mixed bag of Japanese aircraft; all they'd managed to scrape up from the aftermath of the airfield attacks. It wasn't much, six Betty bombers escorted by some Ki43 Oscars and Zeroes.

The Seafires buzzed around them, claiming one Betty but losing two of their own. They chased them all the way, sniping at their heels. Another Betty was hit in an engine and dumped its bombs to stay in the air, turning back for Sumatra. The Seafires let it go, focusing on the bombers that were still going.

The big guns opened up first as they came into range low on the horizon. Every ship in the task force covered the sky in puffs of dark smoke.

HMS Lancer shook as her own deck guns contributed to the weight of fire. Callicoe went up to the Goofer's gallery at the back of the island so he could see what was going on. As he wasn't flying, he didn't have a post as such. It was a matter of grin and bear it.

Barrett pointed as he spotted the incoming aircraft coming in from astern. The Seafires were still going, nipping at their heels but there was only so much they could do. They were mobbed by the Japanese fighters. One Seafire dived for the sea, a dead hand at the controls. His wingman avenged him, sawing the wing of an Oscar clean off with a concentrated two second burst.

The Betty's pressed on. A Seafire burst through the protective ring of fighters and chased after them. Just as he was about to fire, the Betty's opened up with the 20mm cannon in their tails. The first burst smashed the engine, the second exploded the fuel tank and the Seafire flew apart like a firecracker. The remaining Seafires sheared off, giving the AA guns a clear field.

Coming in at three thousand feet, the Betty's selected their target and dived for the water for their run. The flak increased, converging on them. A shell exploded directly in front of one bomber. The airframe came apart. The fuel tanks split and the fragments tumbled into the water.

The remaining bombers pressed on. Callicoe could only watch, helpless as they headed straight for *HMS Lancer*.

"Here it comes," he said through gritted teeth.

Coming in from the port side, they aimed ahead of the big carrier, allowing time for the torpedoes to run. An AA cruiser was right across their line of approach. Her 4" guns laid down a fearsome barrage, her quick firing pom poms lacing the air with tracer.

Lancer's own 4.5" guns and the Oerlikon mounts along the port side blazed away. The water around the Betty's was churned into froth as they came on. Callicoe had to admire the courage of the Japanese pilots. Flying into the teeth of a vicious barrage they pressed home their attack. Closing to within four thousand yards, the three surviving bombers released their torpedoes and turned hard to starboard to get away.

The five metre long torpedoes slid into the water and accelerated to over forty knots. The first missed in front, the second hit the cruiser amidships. She was in the wrong place at the wrong time. She shook and heeled over, a massive plume of water shooting into the sky. The third carried on, oblivious to the carnage around it.

Captain Austin ordered the helm hard over and rang down for the port engine to be put into reverse. Moments after the ship began to turn, *Lancer* shuddered as splinters ripped through her hull. The windows on the bridge were blown out. The dustbin above the bridge that housed the Type 72 radio direction beacon was swept away. The radar on the mast that directed the AA guns was shredded. Screams came from inside the island.

Callicoe and Barrett ran inside to find carnage painted on the walls of the Air Operations Centre. Oates lay across the plotting table, a gash across his temple. There were holes in the steel plate. Callicoe could see daylight outside. The body of a rating was slumped over the radar display. Callicoe had no idea who it was, he was missing his head. Blood covered the floor. The compartment stank of burnt wiring and singed flesh.

Wounded, *Lancer* heeled through the turn, the great deck tilting over as she manoeuvred. They got away with it by the skin of their teeth, the torpedo missed the bow by a matter of yards. The helm order had saved them but the radical turn had put them in the line of fire of another AA cruiser.

Concentrating on the retreating bombers, it took a second for the cruiser to check her fire, but one second was all it took. Two 4" shells had hit the island superstructure. Another hit near the stern, going straight through the armoured hangar and out the other side. The aft lift well was showered in shrapnel. *Lancer's* starboard side was lashed by 20mm shells. Most pinged off the armour, but a few hit home. An unfortunate gunner at a starboard Oerlikon mount was killed and another wounded.

On the bridge there was confusion as Austin got his ship back under control. His eye stung as blood dripped into it. He held a hand to his head as he looked around him. Men were down, some dead, some wounded. A CPO took over the helm and Austin shouted down to damage control for a report.

The great aircraft carrier turned back to starboard and resumed her course west. The rest of the Task Force closed around her while smoke drifted out of the holes in her side.

The cruiser struck by the torpedo was listing badly to

port but got underway again. Working up to fifteen knots, the crew slaved to shore up leaky bulkheads. Moore detached a destroyer to stay with her.

HMS Jellicoe and *Hawke* took up position to form a barrier between the carriers and the ships approaching from the north. Radar tracked them to within twenty miles and then they turned away. *Jellicoe* put up her Walrus seaplane to see what they were. They spotted a heavy cruiser and two destroyers heading east for Padang. Moore left them alone. There could be more ships out there and he wasn't about to be led by the nose into a trap. The mission had been the strike on Padang, he'd accomplished that.

Barrett found Callicoe stood on deck, watching as two ratings slapped paint on the blackened steel of the deck where Williams Corsair had been. His hands and forearms where covered in dried blood and his uniform was torn and stained. His eyes were fixed on the deck.

"I thought I might find you here," Barrett said softly. Callicoe nodded without moving. Barrett shot him a look, noticing that he was barely blinking. His whole body was wired tight.

He rummaged in a pocket and fished out a crushed pack of cigarettes. He extracted one that had clearly seen better days and fiddled about trying to straighten it. He cupped his hands and lit it. He drew the smoke deep into his lungs and closed his eyes, rocking with the movement of the ship.

"It, er was Hanley that bought it in the mixer with the Zeroes."

"I heard," Callicoe replied. He screwed his face up as he recalled a mental picture of Hanley. A cheery soul with a toothy smile and a thick Welsh accent. He had a good singing voice. Then he remembered Williams singing around the piano only last night.

"Well, er Oates had made me acting squadron commander." Barrett laughed, a faltering snicker of disbelief that it would be him, but he was Senior Pilot, the logical choice.

"Congratulations," Callicoe said.

"So I'm bumping you up to Senior Pilot," Barrett continued. "I realise you're only a Sub, but it's not about rank with me. I want a good pilot."

"Then have Gabby," Callicoe said. Barrett snorted.

"No thanks. No, the boss made you Maintenance Officer for a reason and I'm not going to question his judgement."

Callicoe's right cheek was twitching, his mouth moving like someone was pulling on a thread. His eyes were red rimmed and glittering damp. Uncomfortable at the display of emotion, Barrett patted him on the shoulder and left him to it.

Damage control parties put the ship to rights on the way back to Ceylon. The holes in the island were patched over. Blood was mopped up, glass cleared away and scarred steel was painted over.

By the time they back to Trincomalee you would never have known she had been damaged. Her speed was unaffected, but the hurts were deep inside. One of the shells that had hit the island had caused the most havoc, carrying away most of the radar fit, severing cables and trashing the Air Operations Centre. Their ability to fight the ship and direct air operations was severely impaired. The hit in the hangar had jammed the stern lift. It wouldn't move an inch. Shrapnel had torn through the wiring looms and bent two of the rails on which the lift went up and down.

The lift was a relatively easy fix, a few days in the yard would sort that out, but Trincomalee did not have the radar on hand to fit. An urgent request was made to

Bombay who confirmed they had the necessary equipment. *Lancer* didn't even put into port. With two destroyers as escort she went past Ceylon and up the western coast of India for Bombay.

17 – So This Is India

There was a gloomy air over the ship as Lancer *slunk* into Bombay. Less than three months since they were last here, they were back and this time, from an accident not of their making. The assurances of Captain Austin that it wouldn't be for long fell on deaf ears. The ship had put up a black and no amount of chivvying along could make much difference this time. The carrier was warped into dock and within an hour, work crews came aboard to look at what needed to be done.

The crew were given shore leave. Two watches would be ashore at any one time and they would swap over every two days. The Air Group flew to *RAF Santacruz* and parked up to lick their wounds. All the squadrons had suffered casualties in the strikes on Padang and their tails were down. Bombay was if anything, hotter than it had been the last time, but it wasn't the heat, it was the humidity.

Inland at *Santacruz*, it was horrendous. There wasn't a breath of wind like there was in the bay at Trincomalee. A man could rub himself down with a flannel and by the time he was finished, he'd be streaming with sweat again. Even in tropical kit, uniforms clung to you and it was misery. The only thing that made it bearable was the monsoon rains. When they hit, it damped everything down.

The last time they were here, Williams had kept them too busy to do much off the station. This time Barrett let them off the leash. It wasn't because he was laid back, but when the rain came down, the flying stopped.

Compared to Malta and Portsmouth, Bombay was the epitome of the exotic east. CPO Atkins had told them tales of Bombay when they were at *Saint Vincent*. He'd mystified them with images of streets full of beautiful women, men in turbans and coolies carrying you around in rickshaws.

Callicoe found the area around the docks dirty and squalid. The place was still feeling the effects an explosion in the harbour earlier in the year. The *SS Fort Stikine* had caught fire with a cargo of cotton, gold, explosives and ammunition on board.

When the ship exploded, houses were flattened, hundreds had been killed and many ships in the docks had been damaged or sunk. Thousands were made homeless and it had taken three days to get the fire under control. Hungry for work, the dockworkers had no choice but to return and live in the slums around the warehouses. The shops and the commercial district were smart. The thoroughfares were awash with people going about their business. Policemen stood on street corners with their long Lathi sticks watching everyone going by. It was exotic, but it wasn't quite the dream that CPO Atkins had portrayed.

In the evening most of the squadron bellied up at the polo club a few miles from the airfield. They lounged around, waited on hand and foot while the rain come down. Civil servants and their wives treated them well, doing what they could for the war effort by supporting the troops that came through. The wives did rather more than the husbands did in that regard. More than one illicit liaison was formed while they waited for the carrier to be put back together.

Replacement men came from a pool who had been about to embark for Ceylon. Barrett had Callicoe go and pick them up in a jeep. Gabby went along to keep him company. They drove over to the transit blocks at the other end of the field before the rain started. As they drove along Callicoe talked about something that had been bothering him.

"Have you ever wondered about what makes a ship lucky?" he asked Gabby. Gabby shot him a *'are you kidding me'* look.

"No. No, I haven't," he said emphatically. "I presume this is because of what happened?"

"Sort of? But other things as well."

"What other things?"

Callicoe pulled out from behind a truck and floored it. The engine of the jeep roared and surged forward. Gabby clung on to the side of the jeep.

"Well, I was talking to one of the Bosuns-" Gabby groaned.

"Oh god, not war stories."

"Will you give a man a chance?" Callicoe glared at him and Gabby had to pantomine that he keep his eyes on the road in front of them.

"Sorry. Do continue."

"He's been on *Lancer* since she commissioned and he said it's just been one thing after another. She got hit by two bombs during the Sicily landings. That put her out of commission for a few months. She's had problems with her central shaft producing vibrations at high speed. Now this."

"So what?" Gabby replied in irritation. He pulled on the front of his shirt. "We're in a war, we are supposed to get shot at you know. Transfer to *Reliant* if you're that bothered."

"God no, she's just as bad," Callicoe replied quickly. "I'd rather have been on *Ark Royal*."

"*Ark Royal* was sunk!" Gabby protested.

"Look, I don't go in for all that superstitious mumbo jumbo. We make our own luck. Simple." He leaned forward and stared at Callicoe, forcing him to glance at him. "Now tell me honestly, what would you do without me?" Callicoe laughed. "Are you coming to the club tonight?" Callicoe hummed and hawed. "Oh, come on, a few drinks, some female company."

"Maybe."

Gabby let it go. He had the rest of the day to work on him and get him out of his funk. The Jeep turned off the road and pulled up outside the barracks block.

"Game face mate, we're picking up the sprogs."

They got three men, three wet behind the ears rookies straight from the US of A and landing practice on *USS Charger*. Gabby immediately got to work asking them where they were from, who had a pretty sister he could write to; the important things. They got a mixed bunch. The first was a Sub Lieutenant Beahan who had one of those nasal accents that only came from the very best English education money could provide. The second was a dark haired Liverpudlian called Thomas and the third, an Australian called Stan White.

They helped them shove their stuff in the jeep and drove them back to their new billet. They got in just as the heavens opened and water spilled off the metal roof like a waterfall.

Callicoe stood under the terrace watching the puddles blend into a small lake. He was grateful for the cool air that wafted across the airfield as the rain came down in sheets.

He glanced at the letter in his hand and pondered what to do about it. It was from Ariadne and was dated four weeks before. It had started normally enough like any letter does, how are you? what have you been up to? but then it veered off in an unexpected direction. It was like being back in the kitchen at Christmas. She had poured her heart out, a tale of woe about Frank and her predicament. There was an edge of desperation in her writing as she asked for his advice, almost pleading for him to help her.

Callicoe thought he'd left all that behind. He thought about the first lesson he'd learned in the Civil Service. You never put ideas on paper to be used against you later as Exhibit A. He knew what Ariadne wanted. She wanted to be told what to do to make whatever happened next all right. He could never do that to Frank. Relations may have been strained over the years, but Frank was his brother. Even if he thought Ariadne was put upon, he would never say it. This was a fight he wanted no part of.

He let the paper fall from his hand. The letter fluttered to the ground. Under the pounding of the monsoon, the ink washed away.

He allowed Gabby to persuade him to come out. It had been one of those days. He needed the distraction. They went over to the polo club in their tropical dress uniforms. They handed over their caps as they were ushered inside.

"You know, I've always hated the whites," said Callicoe. "They're a bugger to keep clean."

"I don't keep mine on long enough," Gabby replied with some relish.

They walked into the main room which was buzzing with the hum of conversation. The ceilings were high, the doors were wide and fans turned slowly to move the hot air around. Ladies stood in diaphanous dresses. Men in smart blazers and linen trousers talked in hushed whispers over drinks. Their cheeks were red from the heat and too much alcohol.

The most exciting things in their life were the coming cricket season, the war news from Europe and the national British past time; the weather. Wives and girlfriends were rated as one might evaluate horse breeding stocks.

"Land of opportunity," Gabby said, surveying the talent on offer.

Callicoe made a face. This was no different from the social circle he had grown up in. Dinner parties at home were like this, full of Civil Service types with their narrow little worlds. The women were extensions of that, something he wanted to escape.

They nodded hello to other men from the squadron as they circled the room. Callicoe snagged two drinks off a waiter's tray as he walked past.

"You can get more," he said as the waiter asked for them back. "Put it on Sub Lieutenant Hanley's tab," he told him. The waiter huffed off to get some more drinks.

"Sneaky," said Gabby.

"Practical," Callicoe countered, he knew what the prices were like. He ran a finger around his collar, feeling the damp there. Since the afternoon's contribution to cooling things down, the temperature was climbing again. They went onto the veranda where it was a little cooler.

A lithe brunette came over to them. She wore a silk something in green that was low cut to display her decolletage to its advantage. Gabby openly leered at her as she circled her finger around the top of her cocktail glass. She met his gaze, her eyebrow arched, her tongue wetting her lips.

"You looked lonely, standing here," she said in a smooth contralto. Gabby wasn't one to refuse such an open invitation. He put his arm up to lean against the wall and she slotted right in, looking up at him.

"Now then, what kind of a day have you had?" he asked her.

Callicoe left them to it. He got in the Jeep and drove off. He had intended going back to the billets but he found himself driving down to the docks. He got past the sentries and drove to where *Lancer* had been berthed. The dock workers had finished hours ago and the only men aboard the carrier were the duty watch. A Marine sentry came to attention. There was the slap of hand on sling as he brought the Lee Enfield rifle to the salute. Callicoe returned it and handed over his ID. The Marine scrutinised it then let him on board.

The boilers had been shut down and power was being provided from generators ashore. He went up to the Bridge first and made himself known to the Officer of the Watch.

It was like new. There was fresh paint everywhere, the brass work was shining and the windows had been replaced. It had been the first area of the ship to be put to rights when the workmen came on board.

Callicoe went below deck to his cabin. He dug out a book he'd been looking for and then went to the hangar deck. The ship was as quiet as a tomb, a very hot tomb.

"Hello?" he shouted, listening to the echo. "Hello!"

A face appeared half way down the hangar.

"Hullo?" They walked towards him. "Oh, it's you, sir," said CPO Nelson as he wiped his hands on a rag. "What are you doing here, sir?"

"I was in the area, Chief."

Nelson nodded.

"I've never seen it empty like this," Callicoe said.

"Yes, sir."

Nelson waited for Callicoe to say something else. He was old fashioned. Officers spoke, ratings responded when invited to do so.

Callicoe looked at the repairs to the aft lift. The dock crews knew what they were doing after fixing *Lancer's* forward lift a few months before. The bent runs had been replaced but new wiring looms had not been hooked up yet.

"A few more days then?" Callicoe asked aloud, his

voice booming in the empty hangar.

"Maybe a week, sir." Callicoe arched an eyebrow at him. "Five then."

"Poor ship," Callicoe whispered, "we've not looked after you very well, have we?"

He left then; his mood melancholic. Nelson must have thought he was mad, talking like that. It was a good job there had been no one else around.

Callicoe was surprised to find Gabby in bed when he got back to the billet. He woke up as Callicoe sat on the end of his bed taking off his socks. Gabby sat up and rubbed his face.

"You're back. I wondered where you'd got to."

"I went for a drive," Callicoe explained.

There was a flare of light as Gabby struck a match and had a cigarette.

"You're early," Callicoe commented. "I thought you'd be trailing your tired behind in the early hours. Did she throw you over?"

"God no. She wore me out." He lay back on the bed, cigarette stuck between his lips. He blew a cloud of smoke up at the ceiling. "She was like some rabbit." He smiled at the memory of her all over him. Her perfume, the feel of her silky soft skin.

"Twice," he said, holding up two fingers. "Then she chucked me out before her husband got back. I feel used."

"Poor you," Callicoe said, grinning. He hefted the book he'd brought back from *Lancer* in his hand. He saw the gold lettering on the spine glinting in the dark, Dickens, *A tale of two cities*. It had been a gift from his mother. He'd been angry with himself for leaving it on the ship for someone to swipe.

"What about you?" Gabby said. "She mentioned you, you know," Callicoe turned round at that.

"Did she now?"

"She said a friend of hers had seen you at the club and

wanted to meet you."

Callicoe snorted as he considered it for a half second. "Pass."

Gabby sat up and tapped ash off the end of his cigarette.

"Oh, come on," he complained. "One night wouldn't make a difference."

Gabby nagged him about it all morning the next day until Callicoe gave in.

"All right, all right, enough. Tonight. Now will you give it a rest? I've got work to do."

He went to see Barrett in the office he'd been allocated. A paper dart flew past his nose as he came in.

"Was that aimed at me?"

"No. I was going for the bin."

Callicoe looked, there were three others in there already.

"Two sections are up for a short flight before the rain starts again," he reported. He sat down across from Barrett and fished one of the darts out of the bin. "They've been sat in the wet long enough."

"Agreed." Barrett looked out of the window at the gathering clouds on the horizon. Regular as clockwork it would be chucking down again by 2pm. Barrett sighed, at least at sea there was less of that to worry about.

There was another knock at the door and Commander Oates came in. Both Callicoe and Barrett stiffened to attention but Oates waved them off. A regular officer, he wasn't stuffy like some RN types Barrett had come across.

"Nothing to worry about. I'm doing the rounds, seeing how you chaps are doing. I'm sorry I couldn't do much about the weather," he said with a grin.

Every day he called the ship to find out the current progress on the repairs. He wanted to be back at sea, an aircraft carrier was no use in dock.

"I don't want you getting soft. I want the men trained to a fine pitch before we get back to Trincomalee. All this time off dulls reactions and you know what Commodore Moore is like, he'll be wanting to throw us straight back into the action." He pulled a piece of paper out of his pocket and looked at it. "Anyway, you'll be busy for the next few days." He handed it over to Barrett. Barrett's eyebrows shot up.

"This should interest you," he said, handing it over to Callicoe.

"New kites?"

"In a day or two," said Oates. "They're getting unloaded now down at the docks. Go and take a look would you? You know what dockworkers are like. Stuff gets clattered around."

Callicoe drove down to the docks. It was more crowded than it had been last night. When he got close to the dock entrance he had to slow down to a crawl from the press of people on the road. He leaned on the horn as boys crowded round. Some were trying to sell him something, others had their hands out begging for money.

"Out of the way," he shouted, waving his arm at them. "Out of the way."

A policeman appeared and started wielding his long stick. The crowd scattered and Callicoe accelerated before anything else happened. He signed in at the gate and got directions to the admin building.

Callicoe went up the stairs, found the movements office, and knocked on the door before going in. He went into a large room filled with desks, filing cabinets and telephones that seemed to be ringing off the hook. A row of offices were at the end. A row of windows to the left overlooked the docks. When the *Fort Stikine* had exploded, all the windows had been blown out by the shockwave, showering everyone in glass.

They had a view filled with cranes and the roofs of

warehouses. The superstructures of a few ships were visible in the distance. The windows were wide open to try and catch any stray breeze. Ceiling mounted fans were going full belt to provide some draft on this still day.

Callicoe walked down the middle of the office, looking at desks to see if any of them had a title on telling him what they did. WRENS were buzzing around. Quite a few of them were Indians he noticed which caught him by surprise. He didn't realise Indian women were allowed in the service. He did his best not to be rude and stare.

At the far end of the office, Second Officer Jane Fisher saw him walking slowly towards her. She smiled to herself, her left cheek dimpling. He looked like a little lost puppy, his neck craning to look at each desk as he went along. She noticed his uniform next. There was no visible crease on the shorts and there was a smudge of something on the left sleeve. Commander Forbes would have him for breakfast if he spotted him looking like that.

"Can I help you?" she asked brightly.

Callicoe turned towards her, seeing her for the first time. She wore round tortoiseshell glasses for reading. She took them off as she stood up and smoothed down her skirt.

"Yes, actually. I was wanting to find out about some aircraft we've got coming in."

She noticed the wings on his chest, then the wavy gold stripe of a Sub Lieutenant. That explained his interest in aeroplanes. He handed over the signal Barrett had given him. She sat down and spread out the folded piece of paper, her glasses perched on the end of her nose.

"*SS Eidermorn*," she murmured. She looked up with a faraway look and tapped a pencil off her chin. She bid him wait and walked over to a cabinet. Callicoe followed her with his eyes, noting the figure inside the uniform. She was like a dancer, trim and lean with broad shoulders. He stared at her legs while she pulled out the top drawer of the cabinet and went through the index cards. She walked back towards him holding a card up with a smile.

"Success. Docked yesterday." Callicoe smiled as he heard her Australian accent for the first time.

"I know."

"Unloading now," she read from the card.

"I know."

"Of course," she said, her cheeks colouring. Callicoe perched on the corner of her desk and tried to read the card upside down. "Dock six," she told him.

"Thank you, Second Officer?"

"Fisher," she told him. He stood up and clicked his heels together, putting two fingers to his temple in a mock salute.

"Jim Callicoe," he said. He got as far as the door before he came back to her. "Where do I find dock six?"

She laughed, a light lilt as she rose from her desk and walked him over to the window, guiding him by the elbow. She pointed across the rows of warehouses to the right. He could see cranes and funnels in the distance. Far off to the left was *HMS Lancer*, her island towering over the buildings.

"Over there."

The rain started as soon as he went down the stairs to the Jeep. He splashed the last few yards and got under cover.

Callicoe drove down to the *Eidermorn*. She was a tidy ship. Some freighters had been used hard and it showed, with rust and poor paintwork. The *Eidermorn* was spick and span even if she had run across the Atlantic numerous times in all weathers.

A crane was lifting long wooden shipping crates from the deck and the forward hold. Four crates were on the dock already. Men were shouting to watch it as the crane lowered the next crate down, it was swinging in the breeze.

He stopped next to the crates and peered at them. *Property of the Royal Navy* had been sprayed on the side.

A Bosun shouted at him to get away from there. The man stiffened when he saw Callicoe and fired off a salute.

"I'm sorry, sir. I didn't see who you was."

"That's all right. I do believe these are meant for us."

"I don't know about that, sir. All I know is they've gots to go up to *Santacruz*."

"How long do you think to get them all up there?"

"Tomorrow, sir. The transporter trucks is all arranged."

Callicoe saluted and drove off. He had no idea what Barrett had expected him to see. He wasn't going to get them to open a crate in this weather. He could see what shape they were in once they were uncrated in the hangar back at *Santacruz*. Barrett hadn't specified a time he had to be back by so Callicoe drove over to the carrier and see what they'd done today.

He was let on board and he went up to the Wardroom. There were a few officers there and they exchanged pleasantries. Callicoe asked about the work and had his ear bent about all the radar equipment being fitted. Most of it went in one ear and out the other but it sounded like they were winning.

He stayed for a sandwich and cup of tea and waited until the rain stopped. It felt strange being on *Lancer* with so few crew being on board. There was no thrum of the engines, no hum of activity as eighteen hundred men went about their daily tasks.

The rain stopped at four thirty. Driving back through the docks, Callicoe was leery about going back to *Santacruz*. Gabby would be waiting for him and he baulked at the prospect of the club and some moneyed woman wanting to use him as a catspaw.

An impulse took him and he drove back to the admin

building. It was close to five o'clock as he parked where he could see the entrance. He didn't have long to wait, WRENs started coming outside in ones and twos. Some of them carried umbrellas with them as they picked their way round the puddles. The Indian WRENS wore white saris with their uniform jackets. Second Officer Fisher was one of the last to come out. He started the engine and creeped the Jeep forward as she walked away from the building.

"Going my way?" he asked her.

She jumped in shock.

"Hello, you surprised me. Did you find your little ship?"

"I did. Do you have far to go? The skies not looking very good."

That was a bit of a stretch but he went with it. The sky to the north was darkening and the breeze was picking up again. She looked at him. It was a walk to her billet. Why shouldn't she ride? She walked around to the right side of the jeep and got in, keeping one hand on her skirt to keep it in place.

"I'll tell you when to turn."

Grinning, Callicoe put it in gear and pulled away. The coming rain had thinned the crowds and he had an easier time of things driving back through the city.

"So, you're from the carrier?" she asked him.

"Guilty as charged," Callicoe replied as he concentrated on driving. "Have you been here long?" he asked.

"Long enough to hate the summers and love the spring and autumn." The air was muggy and she could feel a line of damp building up on her back. "It's not much different to home really."

"And where is that? If that's not too forward?"

Jane smiled at his British manner. Typical Pommie, not wanting to cause offence.

"A dusty little town called Kalgoorlie in Western Australia. It's as hot as this place, but not as wet. What about you?"

"Me? London. Jolly old England. As British as roast beef and Yorkshire pud."

"Take a left up here," she told him.

He did as instructed and drove down a wide thoroughfare with a central divide. The buildings were more modern here and maintained by the British administration. There was a mixture of architecture styles, even some Gothic Revival and Art Deco. Callicoe looked everywhere with interest. All he'd seen of Bombay the last time was the airfield and the docks and this time he'd gone to the polo club.

"I can give you a guided tour if you'd like," Jane commented in good humour. "And on your left, a house."

He was good enough to laugh. He pulled up outside a large boarding house with a smart frontage. All the WREN officers were accommodated there.

"So," she said, drumming her fingers on her knee.

"So."

She held out her right hand and he took it.

"Thank you for the lift, Lieutenant Callicoe."

"A pleasure, Miss Fisher."

They looked at each other, neither one saying anything.

"Can I have my hand back?" she asked him.

"Oh, I'm dreadfully sorry." He blushed like a schoolboy and Jane laughed. She alighted from the Jeep and went round the back of it to the pavement. "See you around."

She paused a moment but he didn't say anything else so she made to go in. Callicoe screwed up his nerve and called after her.

"I say, could I interest you in a drink or something? You know town better than me. Do you want to continue

the tour?"
 She took mercy on him.
 "I'm game. Here; at eight."

18 – I Met A Girl On The Way To The Circus

Callicoe was back at the boarding house at eight on the dot. He'd reported to Barrett when he returned to Santacruz and put in hand preparations for the new aircraft. They'd be busy the next few days once they arrived. The fitters would have to assemble them and then they'd need air testing. Gabby pounced on him as soon as he got to their room in the billet.

"You're gonna have fun tonight."

"You're right, I am. Rain check," he said with enthusiasm.

"Wha-"

"I got myself sorted out. Sorry tiger, you're going to have to fly solo tonight."

He changed into a fresh uniform.

"You can't do this to me," Gabby moaned. "I had it all figured out. I was going to do all sorts to that girl. Spill," he asked, wanting details.

"You've been nagging me to get out and meet someone. So, I did." Callicoe studiously ignored him while he sorted his tie out. "Look, I'll tell you all about it later," he said as he went out the door.

He took a breath and went up to the front of the boarding house but didn't even get to knock. The door opened and Jane came out all bright and breezy. Another woman came out behind her.

"*Leftenant*," she said, emphasising the correct pronunciation with her Australian twang.

"Good evening, Miss Fisher."

"May I present, Kaylani Prasad."

She was a striking, tall Indian woman, her black hair styled in waved rolls. She had a red Bindi dot on her forehead between her eyebrows. She put her hands together in front of her and gave him a slight bow of her head.

"Namaste."

"Er, hello, Miss Prasad."

"Shall we?" said Jane. Without waiting for an answer, she swept past him and got into the back of the Jeep. Flummoxed by her taking the lead, Callicoe was caught off guard. The Indian woman copied Jane and got into the front passenger seat of the Jeep.

"Well, do you want to go on this tour or what?" Jane asked him.

He grinned and got in.

"Where to?" he asked.

Jane took him through Bombay, towards the cities administrative centre. Callicoe saw raw expressions of Colonial power, great government buildings even grander than those found in London. The grandest of the lot was the Victoria Terminus, the headquarters of the Central Railway, a huge edifice in the Italian Gothic style. They talked as they rode along, Jane pointing out places of interest. Kaylani corrected her on a few things.

"What do you think of our city, Mister Callicoe?"

"Very pretty, Miss Prasad."

"I hope you don't mind, Kay coming along?" Jane said. "The Senior WREN gets a bit twitchy about her girls going out with men they've only just been introduced to?"

"I thought it would be something like that," Callicoe said. Jane suggested they go to the Esplanade.

"It's by the government buildings. We can go for a walk there after some drinks."

Callicoe went where he was directed and they pulled

up at the Eros Cinema. They sat on the veranda out front of the Art Deco building. They had Masala chai served with condensed milk and sugar cane jaggery. Callicoe sipped the scalding hot concoction. He stirred in some more sugar while he waited for it to cool down.

"I'm afraid I must apologise," he said, addressing himself to Kaylani. "I'm embarrassed to say I had no idea there were any Indian women in the service. My experience is rather limited."

"It's all right Lieutenant. I'm quite used to it. They do not sing of our accomplishments. Many feel it is not right for an Indian woman to don a uniform."

"But you did."

"I had the benefit of an education and an open minded family," she said with an earthy chuckle. Her father was one of the most senior KC's at Bombay's High Court. With four daughters and no sons, he'd encouraged them to be outgoing and carve out a niche for themselves, something quite radical for Bombay society.

She regarded Callicoe critically, intrigued by what kind of man could get her friend talking non stop about him for over an hour. He seemed charming enough. He was well polished with no rough edges and he'd clearly had a good education.

When they finished their drinks, they went for a walk. Kaylani directed them towards the Esplanade, a large recreational ground in the middle of the city. There was lots of green surrounded by trees. It was a balmy night; the earlier heat had died down and a slight breeze ruffled the trees. Jane walked next to Callicoe while Kaylani walked ahead of them.

"You're not annoyed I brought Kay along?" Jane asked him.

"Goodness no. Well, maybe a little bit. She seems nice."

"Oh, she is. All the girls are really great. They work

hard, harder than a lot of others I could name. They've got something to prove, I think. That's one thing I won't miss about India," she said, changing track of conversation. "I've seen some shocking prejudice."

"I can't comment really," said Callicoe. "I don't see much up at the airfield."

"Yeah well, homes not much better," she muttered. "Kalgoorlies a bit rough around the edges."

"You made it sound like a frontier town earlier."

"The Wild West," she said, laughing. "No, it's not as bad as that," she admitted. "There's been gold mining there for years, big claims, small mines, you name it. The towns pretty big, it's got some fancy buildings but its got the feel of a frontier place."

After another turn around, they sat for a while, enjoying the cool of the ground, the feel of the grass.

"Are you in Bombay for very long?" Kaylani asked him. Callicoe shrugged.

"How long's a piece of string?" he said. "Till they put the old lady back together." He picked at the grass, pulling up clumps of it in his hand. "Do I have to get you ladies home by a certain time or do you get turned into a pumpkin?" he asked.

"Maybe we should head back, Jane," Kaylani said. "You have got the early shift."

Jane heard the hint loud and clear and stood up, brushing grass off her skirt.

"Come on, home James and don't spare the horses," she said, giving him a nudge with her foot.

He drove them back to the boarding house and extracted a promise from Jane to see him tomorrow evening.

"You get points for cheek," she said. "All right. Any time after six thirty."

"I'll be there."

Eight crates turned up on transporters mid morning. As soon as they were unloaded, the fitters started unboxing them. The fuselages were jacked up and put on their own undercarriage and the outer wings were uncased. It was like a giant erector set. Callicoe hadn't fiddled around with those things since he was a kid. As Maintenance Officer he had his hands full. Taking an aircraft on charge wasn't difficult, but if he was signing for something, he wanted to make sure they were working.

There was no flying the first day, but three of the Corsairs were nearly ready by the time the fitters knocked off. Barrett was tempted to push them into an evening shift but they'd only be tired in the morning. He wanted it done quickly, but he also wanted it done right. As they broke off for the day, Callicoe swung by Barrett's office.

"We'll get quite a few tested tomorrow," he reported. Barrett looked up from sharpening some pencils.

"Good. The chaps worked hard today."

"They did." Callicoe agreed. He scratched his cheek. "Can I ask something?"

Barrett stopped in mid sharpen, catching the change in tone of Callicoe's voice.

"That depends." Callicoe hesitated and thought twice about asking but he'd done it now. "Spit it out, Jimmy."

"I was wondering if I could get some leave?"

Barrett almost choked and put the pencil down.

"Good lord, you could just as easily ask for the moon."

"Twenty four hours?" Callicoe bartered.

"I'll think about it. I want the new kites checked out before I could even contemplate anything like that."

Callicoe got to the boarding house dead on eight. He was genuinely nervous. He hadn't felt like this since his first solo back at *Pensacola*.

"I'm sorry. It's been one of those days," he said, throwing himself on her mercy.

"It's all right. You can tell me all about it later," she told him sailing out of the door. Callicoe had to skip to catch up.

"Flying solo tonight, are we?" he asked archly, looking for anyone else coming with them.

"Just the one check ride for you. You've got Kay's seal of approval so you must have done something right."

Callicoe laughed as he pulled away from the boarding house.

"You look lovely," he said, a little tongue tied. Jane had made an effort tonight. She'd dusted off her best dress, a red flower print wrap with a sweetheart neckline and cap sleeves. She'd paired it with a red wedge heel and pillbox hat. She'd curled her chestnut brown hair into waves.

"You wielded an iron," she said, mock impressed. He glanced at his right sleeve.

"This? Nothing," he said offhand. He'd spent an hour on his uniform tonight, putting creases in the trousers and shirt and tidying himself up. "Are we driving around? I am at your service."

"Your choice," she said. "I feel like a drink and some music tonight."

"I know somewhere that fits the bill," he said reluctantly.

"Good, I want to feel like a woman."

"Aren't you?" Jane gave a barking laugh.

"Not to Commander Forbes. I think he just wants machines that could work twenty four hours a day. You should see his face when we break for lunch."

Callicoe drove to the polo club. Jane clapped her hands in excitement when she saw where they were going.

"I've always wanted to come here."

Callicoe parked and they went in. Quite a few of the

squadron were here tonight and Callicoe steeled himself for attention. He could feel the eyes on him as they got a table and ordered drinks. As the waiter turned away, the first of the squadron sauntered over.

"Oh, hello, Jim," Gardner said casually. Callicoe made the introductions and Gardner sat down. Wicklow appeared out of nowhere, then Aubrey Cook sat down with a blonde in a revealing electric blue dress. A second table appeared and before you knew it they were having a party. Callicoe's heart sank. He knew this would happen if they came here.

They had a nice time but he didn't feel like sharing tonight. There was spirited conversation, but Callicoe was jealous for every moment that someone else was talking to Jane.

He asked her to dance and got her to himself for a bit. She moved smoothly around the floor and stayed close to him.

"They're a good bunch," she said in his ear.

"They're all right," he admitted, "just not right now."

She giggled.

"Poor, Jimmy," she said, planting a kiss on his cheek. She rubbed the red lipstick off with the heel of her hand.

"At your six o'clock," Gabby whispered from behind them. Callicoe pivoted on his heel, sweeping Jane round, her dress flaring around her legs.

Gabby was dancing with his brunette from the other evening. The pair of them were glued to each other, moulded from top to bottom, his hand brazenly on her behind. They shimmied round in small circles, the woman had a contented look on her face, the cat that got the cream.

"They look like a nice couple," Jane commented.

"I'm sure her husband would agree," said Callicoe tartly, trying to keep his tone light and not sound like his father. Jane's eyes went wide. "It's true. Gabby is not her first conquest. I'm sure there'll be someone else when we're gone."

"Gabby, what's that short for?"

"His mouth," Callicoe informed her. "Gabriel Veriker. He never shuts up on the ground but he's a good pilot so he gets away with it."

"Any other time I'm sure it would be a scandal," said Jane, looking at Gabby and the brunette. "Life's too short."

"That's very generous of you."

"No, just practical," she said simply. "The wars turned everything on its head, when a days a week and a weeks a year."

She looked at him intently, her brown eyes wide and open. He fell right in.

"I tried to get some leave," he told her. She smiled at that, a cute wide smile under her button nose and fluted cheeks. "The pejorative being, I tried. No dice."

"I doubt, Forbes would have given me leave either," she sighed. "It's a shame, there's a nice bay I know with a beach. We had a girl's day out there a few weeks ago to get away from it all. Or we could have gone to the Elephanta caves."

"Oh well," said Callicoe, trying his best not to sound disappointed but she caught the dip in his voice.

The band took a break and they returned to the tables. The party had grown. There were three tables now and most of the squadron with female company. Chagrined at the crowd, Callicoe sat down with Jane next to him. She surreptitiously reached over and took hold of his hand and gave it a squeeze. That calmed Callicoe down.

They stayed till eleven when Jane announced she was tired. She took her leave of the pilots and Callicoe escorted her from the club back to the Jeep.

"Too much for me," she said as she sat down in the passenger seat. "Are they always like that?" she asked him.

"Boys far from home. We've been operating for a few

months. It's been our first real chance to let our hair down."

"I'm not ready to say goodnight yet," Jane said as they drove back towards the city. Callicoe brightened at that.

"Where shall we go?" he asked.

"Not the boarding house," Jane said shortly. "No men allowed, official."

"Hmm, same at our billet. Never the twain shall meet," an idea took him as he pondered where they could go for some privacy. "Have you ever flown before?"

"Gosh no. I've always wanted to give it a go though," she said. "The only plane I saw before I left Kalgoorlie was the Doc. He had this ancient biplane to fly to the stations and check out the workers, oh, and the mines of course."

"Stations?" Callicoe queried.

"You know, sheep and cattle."

"Oh, you mean ranches."

"I mean stations," she insisted, "it's not America."

"I stand corrected," he replied in good humour.

It was a short drive to *Santacruz*. Jane had brought her military ID with her otherwise the sentry wouldn't have let her on the airfield. The fact she was in civilian dress was in itself cause for comment. Callicoe knew Barrett would have something to say about it in the morning.

He drove to the hangars where they had been slaving away all day. He took her in via the side door and fumbled around until he found a light switch. They blinked at the sudden change.

The three new Corsairs that were ready to go were at the front of the hangars. The others were in a state of assembly, some with the cowling and panels off. They walked over to the nearest complete one. Jane held his hand, listening while he listed the specification of the Corsair, rattling off the numbers by heart.

"Do you want to get in?" he asked her.

"Of course, I do, I didn't come all this way just to stare

at it."

He gave her a hand up and then got up himself.

"Now put a hand there," he pointed to the cockpit frame, "you'll have to-oh." She hitched her dress up. Callicoe blushed as he caught an eyeful of shapely thigh when she stepped into the cockpit. She sat down in the bucket seat with a yelp as she sank lower than she expected. He laughed. "I'm sorry, I forgot, you should be sat on a parachute."

She worked the stick back and forth, peering over the lip of the cockpit to see the ailerons moving.

"There's a lot of dials, however do you deal with it all?"

"You don't have to look at everything at once." He pointed out the main instruments, telling her what they did. She saw a different side of him as he talked. He was less diffident in his manner and there was a strength there as he seemed to grow in confidence, talking about the familiar.

When she'd seen enough, she stood up and he held her hand as she stepped out of the cockpit. He dropped down to the floor of the hangar and held up his hands for her. She dropped into his arms and he twirled her round.

"You're a wicked man, if I didn't know better, I'd have said you planned that."

"Maybe I did," he grinned. He lowered her to the ground and she put her arms around his shoulders and kissed him.

"Maybe I did too," she admitted. She leaned into him as he put his hands on her waist and held her close. She broke off and looked at him.

"I've just realised something. I outrank you."

"Yes ma'am, you do."

He was humming away quite happily to himself when Gabby came into their room, half cut and floating on gin and whisky.

"What happened to you and your girl?" he asked. "Pretty little thing she was."

"If you mean, Second Officer Fisher, I took her home."

"Second off-? You mean she's a WREN?" he said in shock. "Why you sneaky-"

"You're only jealous because you didn't think of it yourself," Callicoe told him.

They never did get their leave. *Lancer's* repairs were nearly completed and the pressure was on to get the eight new Corsairs ready to fly off back to the carrier. The squadron air tested each one either in the morning or in the late afternoon after the rain had been and gone. Callicoe and Jane spent the evenings together, making the most of their time together.

On the final night, they went to a point overlooking the harbour. Jane sat on a low wall and swung her legs back and forth as she looked at the ships in the harbour below. The aircraft carrier had been warped into the middle of the bay waiting for first light. The two escorting destroyers lay alongside.

The moment she'd put off had finally come. She'd watched the aircraft flying over the city the last few days with fresh eyes. They were no longer annoying bees buzzing overhead, they were people with names and faces now, Gabby, Wicklow, Gardner and all the others.

Jane hadn't been particularly interested in men for the last few years. She'd found if she threw herself into her work, that was enough. Moving around helped, new places meant new people, new situations to get used to. Her world had shifted with Callicoe and now he was going. She'd tried to blot out the inevitability of this moment.

"I feel cheated somehow," she said glumly.

"Who was it who said a day was a week, a week, a year?" he gently chided her. He sat on the wall next to her and she hooked her arm around his, leaning her chin on his shoulder.

"So, where to next?" she asked him.

"Wherever they send us I suppose. Singapore, Hong Kong maybe? Kick the Jap's all the way back to Tokyo if they let us."

She smiled at his bravado, a wan smile when she thought about the risks that would entail. He'd told her about the attack on Padang one evening. He'd stuck to the sight of the aircraft in the air. She'd seen German bombers going overhead in England in 1940, her imagination could fill in the blanks.

He steeled himself for the final goodbye. She clung to him as he parked round the corner from the boarding house.

"I don't want you to go."

"It's a bit late saying that now," he said. She laughed at that, her control brittle. He wiped a tear away from her cheek.

"I'll write when I can," he told her, trying to buoy her up. She sniffed and gave his hand a squeeze.

"I'll write too, but I don't know when you'll get them."

She went then, before her composure went entirely. She ran inside the boarding house and didn't look back; she couldn't bear it.

19 - Gather Together

HMS Lancer put to sea at first light, nine days after she had docked. The Air Group flew off at ten when the carrier was eighty miles out. Oates gathered his squadron commanders in his cabin. It was cramped but they weren't in there for long. He outlined the flying program for the next few days. Replacements needed time to get deck qualified and to practice operations. Captain Austin was particularly keen to improve their launch time intervals. The new radar needed calibrating. Sections of Barracudas would go up to give the operators something to detect. They would run set patterns so they could accurately plot and adjust for range and height.

Once the CAP launched and four more Barracudas went sniffing for submarines, Oates cleared the deck for the new boys to qualify. He had them go up to do four touch and goes and then another four landings and take offs before he was happy.

White was good. He made four confident landings one after another. Thomas wasn't far behind with three good ones and one wave off. The runt of the litter was Beahan.

His first landing was good, but then Gilliard waved him off late for his second. That seemed to affect his confidence because each pass got progressively worse. One of them was so bad Gilliard waved him off early. He got his four eventually, but Oates was far from impressed. In calm weather, this shouldn't have been that hard.

Barrett wasn't happy either. Beahan's performance reflected on the squadron. Knowing how stringent the training program in America was, he couldn't believe he'd passed. He pulled Beahan's personnel jacket in his cabin.

"Canada," he muttered while Callicoe looked over his shoulder. He snapped the file shut and dumped it on the small square that qualified as his desk. "Well, there's nothing else for it, he's going up again; and again; and again, until he gets better."

"Either that or it kills him," Callicoe observed.

"If that's what it has to be," said Barrett with clipped finality. He wrinkled his forehead as he thought about how one man could screw up a whole strike. Coming back to a carrier, low on fuel with some aircraft damaged, the last thing they wanted to worry about was a pilot who had trouble landing on. They had to have confidence in each other to do the job.

The Fleet was in when they got back to Trincomalee. The only one absent was *Victorious*. She'd had more rudder problems, interfering with her ability to hold station and launch aircraft. A carrier that couldn't hold course was no use to anyone so she'd gone to Bombay for repair. Callicoe was annoyed when he heard about it later. Another twenty four hours and he could have got someone to deliver a letter to Jane for him.

They landed at *China Bay* instead of *HMS Highflyer* as they normally would. Ground crew directed them to the large sandbag bays the big shiny bombers had occupied to park their aircraft.

Transport picked them up and took them to much better huts than they were used to. It felt like being in first class after slumming it.

"The Yanks aren't coming back for a while," a Corporal told them, "so they may as well be used by somebody." There were no complaints. They were far enough away from the edge of the jungle that there was less chance of a stray snake or something else getting into bed with them.

Callicoe wasn't happy to find Gabby had snagged the bed nearest the window in their hut. He was unpacking his kit bag when Callicoe came through the door.

"I might have known," he said.

"First come, first served," Gabby told him casually.

"That's only because I had to sort the kites out. I should pull rank," Callicoe warned him with a smile. "Give me the bed," he commanded.

"Huh, you'll have to fight me for it," Gabby replied, unimpressed. He playfully put up his fists and adopted a boxers pose for a few seconds before laughing.

He spent a few minutes fiddling about with this mosquito net. The last thing he wanted was to muck about with it in the dark after he'd been to the bar. He shoved some rolled up socks into his flying boots. Callicoe did the same, they'd been here enough to know you took precautions.

Once Gabby and Callicoe discovered where the Mess was, they found most of the squadron were already there. It was a brick building with white stuccoed walls. It was lovely and cool inside with big windows and ceiling fans. Gabby thought it reminded him of the polo club back in Bombay.

"How the other half live," said Gabby. "No wonder those RAF types were so annoyed when they bunked down at our huts for a few days."

Barrett and Callicoe were mystified when Oates asked to see them. They went over to an office he had been assigned. There was a tall Commander stood at his shoulder.

"Take a seat gentlemen, I'm afraid I have some news."

Callicoe caught his tone, a little perturbed at his use of words. Oates did not look best pleased so it can't have been anything good. He swallowed hard, thinking the worst. All he could think was that it was a transfer to another ship or a posting to some kind of instructing position. He cursed the day that Barrett had complimented him on his work as Maintenance Officer. He must have put a report or a recommendation in without telling him about it.

Oates ran a hand through his thick brown hair and grimaced. There was no easy way of saying it so he decided to just come straight out with it.

"Lieutenant Barrett, Sub Lieutenant Callicoe, may I introduce Commander Goodfellow; your new Squadron Commander."

It was like dropping a pebble down a well. Oates thought Barrett hid his disappointment quite well.

Goodfellow looked like a prop forward. He had big hands, and his nose took an abrupt left turn like a Corsair did on take off. He cleared his throat.

"Commander Oates has been telling me you've done a good job with the squadron since, Commander Williams was killed." His voice was gentle which was a bit of a surprise. "I'm very sorry, he was a good man. No one wants to take over a squadron in these circumstances but I'm sure with your performance you'll get your own squadron soon enough. In the meantime, I want you to remain as Senior Pilot."

"Whatever you need, sir," Barrett replied with good grace. Goodfellow brightened with a broad beaming grin.

"Good. I'll talk to you later over a drink in the Wardroom. Mister Callicoe, you're my Maintenance Officer I understand?" Callicoe nodded. "I'll talk to you too." He turned to Oates. "If you'll excuse me, sir."

Oates waved him away and Goodfellow left the office. He went to take a look at one his squadrons Corsairs.

"Call it a reward for all your hard work," said Oates. "You've both been bumped up. Barrett, you're a Lieutenant Commander now, Callicoe, you're a

202

Lieutenant, get those stripes up, you're both out of uniform."

They both floated out of Oates office and stood in the stifling heat of the passageway below deck.

"That took the sting off," Barrett muttered. He shook Callicoe's hand. "Lieutenant Callicoe."

"Lieutenant Commander Barrett."

"Come on," said Barrett. "We need to go to stores and get some braid. Are you any good with a thread?"

Gabby was enjoying a beer when Callicoe breezed into the Wardroom.

"Bit early isn't it?" he asked.

"First come, first served," Gabby told him.

"I should pull rank," Callicoe warned him with a smile. Gabby blew a raspberry.

"Belt, you're just a gash subby like me."

"Not anymore," Callicoe said, leaning one shoulder forward, there was an extra gold stripe on his shoulder epaulette. Gabby's eyes went wide.

"Where the hell did you get that from?" he asked. "It's not Christmas yet so it didn't come from a cracker."

Callicoe blew a raspberry of his own in return.

"First come, first served," he said with relish.

"Ah Callicoe," Barrett exclaimed. He got himself bottle of beer. He thrust another one at Callicoe. "Celebration."

In the evening, Goodfellow introduced himself to the troops and stood his pilots a drink. There was no big announcement; he just made his way around the room, shaking hands, spotting one or two faces he knew. Birkenfield roared and gave him a bear hug. They hadn't seen each other since 1942 on *Victorious* in the Mediterranean.

"You duffer," he told him. "I thought you'd have been killed by now."

"I thought *you'd* be dead by now," Goodfellow replied.

He slotted into the mood of the Air Group easily, his old school manner greasing the wheels amongst the men. In the coming days he started putting faces to names. Tonight, he was just one of the boys, a fellow flier sharing a drink and some stories. The time to crack the whip would come later.

Callicoe stayed up late. Like most nights in Trincomalee it was sticky but the breeze from the shore made it bearable. There wasn't a cloud in the sky, the monsoon season wasn't so bad here. It had only rained for an hour in the afternoon. It was barely enough to dampen anything down before the puddles evaporated or soaked into the ground. The moon was a half crescent, a slither of bright light. Enough to write by at any rate.

Gabby had come back from the Mess three sheets to the wind. His friend was too drunk to know what bed he slept in, so Callicoe and Richardson helped him into the bed in the corner.

Callicoe sat up in Gabby's bed under the mosquito net, enjoying the breeze from the window. An insect buzzed against the netting. Callicoe angled himself to catch the light from the window and wrote a letter to Jane, the first real opportunity he'd had to relax since he'd left Bombay.

He crammed as much as he could on the sheets of paper, putting his thoughts down as best as he could. He told her about his promotion and then moved onto telling her about Curly Richardson. Normally, he was cheery and upbeat, but he'd been morbid tonight, surly and taciturn. Callicoe had dragged the story out of him while they'd shepherded Gabby into bed.

"I'm done," he said with some finality.

"What on earth, are you talking about?" Callicoe had asked while he was picking Gabby up off the ground. It didn't escape Callicoe's notice that he was doing most of the lifting.

"Take my advice," said Richardson. "Don't get engaged or married. Bitches only screw you over."

Callicoe gave him a knowing nod, letting him get it off his chest. The Marine came back to himself and grabbed Gabby's other arm, sharing the load. The pair of them half dragged, half walked him back to their hut. Richardson shared the other room in the hut with his fellow Marine Farthingdale.

"Maybe it's not as bad as you think?" Callicoe suggested gently. He'd connected the dots during the walk and figured out what this was about. "The mails slow, anything could have happened."

Richardson gave him a pained look. He tugged a sheet of paper out of his pocket.

"Oh, it's not that," he said, his voice cracking. "Bitch had the decency to send a letter. Threw me over. Met herself, a nice American chap," he quoted from the letter, putting on a dreadful American accent. "Some Lieutenant Commander it says here." He squinted at the piece of paper in the moonlight. "We come from different worlds, she said. Find yourself a nice English girl," he said with a snarl. He stuffed the paper back into his pocket.

"Probably for the best," Callicoe said, saddened by the brutality of it. "It'll look better in the morning?"

"Will it?" Richardson asked sharply. He stopped walking and hauled Gabby up by the shoulder. Callicoe jerked back at the sudden stop. "Why should it?"

Callicoe had no answer for that. He knew the power of letters. He thought about what Ariadne had written in her letter and scowled at the reminder.

They'd put Gabby to bed and Richardson had gone to his own room next door. Callicoe wrote a little about the last few days. He'd taken some more photographs with his camera the last few days. He thought he was getting quite good at it and he remembered the photo's he'd taken of

Jane while he was in Bombay. He'd have to pull some strings to get the film developed, he could send her a print of the photo in his next letter.

> *"I often think of you. The days we had in Bombay feel like a dream. I have to pinch myself to remind me that it wasn't. I miss you very much.*
>
> *Regards,*
>
> *James."*

He hesitated from writing, love, he wasn't ready to say that just yet. He put the letter in an envelope and put it on the shelf by the bed and turned in.

There was the usual change in tempo once they got back to Trincomalee. The ships took on fuel and stores. The skies over *China Bay* were crowded with four Air Groups taking up temporary lodging.

There were accidents. Two Corsair pilots were killed on the runway. One was coming in to land as one was taking off. Both of them thought the green light was for them. It got even more confusing when the tower fired off a succession of red flares. The Corsair on its take off run had just lifted off as the other Corsair went straight through it. The big prop carved through the cockpit. Then it ruptured the fuel tank in front and there was a fireball on the runway. There wasn't enough left of either of them to fill a sandbag.

Two Barracudas failed to return from a navigation exercise. It was a complete mystery as the weather had been perfect and there was no distress call put out to indicate a problem. Another one disappeared the same way a few days later in an electrical storm.

Goodfellow started to put his own stamp on the

squadron. For a few days he was content to watch and see what they could do. He went up on formation and gunnery exercises, watching from above. On the fourth day he gathered them together and told them what his standards were.

"You're too casual on your strafing runs," he said in that quiet voice of his. "The intervals between each plane are too big, you're giving the flak too much time to concentrate on an individual aircraft. You should almost be on each other's tails. I want to see a concentrated punch. You have to press the attack."

With Goodfellow's admonition ringing in his ear, Habergast had the bit between his teeth. He put his Corsair into a steep dive and fixed the target in his sights. His aim was bang on. Oil drums jumped as six streams of 0.50 cal ammunition churned up the ground.

He pulled up a fraction too late. He was still pulling back on the stick as his Corsair mushed lower at the bottom of the dive. The belly of the fighter clipped the ground and the Corsair crumpled like a beer can. The Wright Cyclone engine buried itself in Habergast's chest and killed him outright.

On the 1st October they had a funeral for the casualties. They paraded in their Divisions and the Padre did a good service, keeping it mercifully short in the heat. He didn't really fit the pilot's image of a Priest. Fresh faced, with fine blonde hair, he had piercing blue eyes. Callicoe had heard someone describe him as angelic. Attuned to his audience, he had a number of quotes and verses more suited to aviators.

"I am the resurrection and the life, saith the Lord; he that believeth in me, though he were dead, yet shall he live; and whosoever liveth and believeth in me shall never die," he said in a clear voice, overcoming the drone of aircraft and the noises from the harbour.

"Leonardo Da Vinci wrote, 'once you have tasted

flight, you will forever walk the earth with your eyes turned skyward, for there you have been, and there you will always long to return."

The pilots liked that. The Priest looked amongst the men and saw the usual mix of faces. Some were bored, some serious, others morbidly curious.

"We brought nothing into this world, and it is certain we can carry nothing out. The Lord gave and the Lord taketh away; blessed be the name of the Lord." He finished with a verse from Romans 8, paraphrasing it a little to suit. "Neither death, nor life, nor angels, nor height, shall be able to separate us from the love of god, which is in Jesus Christ our Lord."

He said the Lord's prayer, taking spiritual nourishment from it as he always did.

The coffins draped in the White Ensign were lowered into the ground. The side party pointed their rifles into the sky and fired five rounds. Birds scattered into the air with the crack of the first shot.

There was a rash of mistakes after that. Wicklow damaged a wing tip on a bowser. Callicoe landed heavily and burst a tyre, ground looping his Corsair. Practising a massed take off to bring down the launch times, Goodfellow had the squadron on the runway, tightly packed together. Anticipating the Corsair in front of him moving, Jack Frost let his brakes off too early and chewed up Gardner's rudder.

Goodfellow read them the riot act. There would always be mistakes, but wrecking two aircraft by not concentrating crossed a line as far as he was concerned. The aircraft could be repaired but it wasn't the point. Once they were at sea it wouldn't be so easy to make up their losses.

There was some resentment on *Reliant* and *Lancer*

when the other carriers swapped their Barracuda for Avengers. Acting as fast transports, four escort carriers had pulled into Trincomalee, packed to the rafters with rows of Grumman Avengers with their wings folded.

The Avenger was swarmed by the Barracuda crews at dispersal. A large, tubby aircraft, it had a powered rear turret and an internal bomb bay. The most important thing was it had range, double that of the Barracuda and power to spare. They would be able to launch strikes from further away, reducing the risk to the carrier. The rumour was more Avengers would be arriving soon to replace the aircraft on *Reliant* and *Lancer*. For now, they had to suffer the Barracudas a little longer.

The men did their best to relax. A few boats appeared and some of them went sailing in the harbour. Lots went swimming at the mouth of the river while a few men kept an eye out for crocodiles. Goodfellow had his mob running round the perimeter track and doing PT.

"You get soft on board ship," he said. "I want men who are sharp. Come on donkeys!" he shouted, flicking a towel at Gabby's backside.

He harried them all the way round and sweat was streaming off them by the end. They stood, gasping in the hot air as stitches stabbed them in the side. He had them at it again the following day and threw in some star jumps and push ups for good measure.

A small football league developed, with each squadron fielding a team. It was just a friendly knock around, but it was exercise so it received Goodfellow's seal of approval.

As the days turned into more than a week, behaviour in the Mess got more raucous. At Duty Free prices, the booze flowed freely and with little other distraction, drinking games became a favourite past time. Goodfellow became a nag as the Mess bills increased. He didn't consider it seemly for an officer and a gentleman to live on credit too much. He went round the billets getting them to fork over money to settle up.

Betting on cribbage and Uckers got to some ridiculous sums and paper IOU's fluttered around like confetti. It was all a bit of a jape. Uckers was an adapted form of Ludo popular in the fleet.

There was nearly a fight one night when one of the Barracuda pilots accused Richardson of cheating while they were playing WAFU rules, a variation of the game played in the Fleet Air Arm. Richardson took particular exception to that and made a remark about the Barracuda which raised hackles amongst the spectators.

A hand was placed on his shoulder and Richardson shot to his feet; his face mottled in pent up frustration. He got in the face of the Barra Observer ready for a punch to be thrown. Richardson was wound as tight as a spring and Barrett and Callicoe had to walk him round to calm him down.

"Come on old chap, a breath of fresh air I think," said Barrett as he grabbed an arm.

They both knew what it was. Richardson was still stewing over the letter from his girl. He'd been a pressure cooker for the last week. Callicoe had seen the resentment and anger and frustration building up in him with each passing day. He needed an operation to let off steam soon or he'd snap.

They got word that *Victorious* was on her way back from Bombay and they started having bets on what time she would drop anchor in the bay. Most of them had a go and someone even managed to talk the Padre into a flutter. *Victorious* arrived on the 6th October and dropped anchor at 10.15am. The Padre scooped the pool.

20 – Leadering With Your Chin

As October wore on, the men started getting restless. They craved action and it wasn't long in coming. The Americans made a request for a diversion in the Indian Ocean while they were gearing up to invade Leyte. South East Asia Command selected the Nicobar island group. How Eastern Fleet would do it was up to them, as long as it had the desired effect.

With five fleet carriers, Fraser had options to be more creative. He could fly strikes and cover his ships with little risk.

Eastern Fleet put to sea on the 15th October and headed for their assigned stations. The Fleet would operate as four distinct groups converging closer to the target. This time there would be no quick thrust and away. They would maintain station and attack over a number of days. It would force the Japanese to respond or suffer defeat in detail.

Down in the Wardroom, Oates had a knack of making it all seem so easy. He explained the broad strokes of what their task was and the pilots listened attentively. Sat at the back, Gabby surreptitiously leaned over and whispered in Callicoe's ear.

"Of course, this is all assuming the Japanese do exactly what they're supposed to."

On the 17th, the big ships went in to bombard shore targets. Callicoe flew one of the Corsairs to spot and pass fall of shot. He was glad to be out of the way as the cruisers threw threw their shells at shore installations. It went on for hours, the great ships going up and down the coast in a line, firing non stop.

The cruisers withdrew to let the aircraft have a go. Barracudas and Avengers plastered the airfield and the docks. The Corsairs went in and strafed anything that moved.

A few hours later the cruisers came back in under the cover of darkness to pound the shoreline. If the pyrotechnic show had impressed Callicoe in the daytime, it was even better at night. Even miles away on *Lancer's* flight deck, the cruisers were backlit by the great tongues of flame that sprang from their barrels as they fired.

Overnight, they moved south and on the morning of the 18th, Nancowry took a battering. *Renown*, *Hawke*, *Suffolk* of *Bismarck* fame and other ships got in close. They plastered an army camp, warehouses, another airfield and shore defences. The pounding went on all day. Everyone took a turn at it, pulling away periodically to let the barrels cool before going back into the line.

On the 19th, the carriers got their turn, flying a rolling wave of strikes. Callicoe went on the second strike of the day, escorting the ungainly Barracuda's on their bombing runs. They dived from five thousand feet and got good hits on the harbour. A small destroyer took three bombs close aboard and had her bottom blown out. She ended up on her side.

Once the Barracuda's were done, the Corsairs went down to add to the mayhem. After the first strafing run, Callicoe spotted an area of the harbour covered by large camouflage nets. He told his section to circle overhead while he went down to take a look. He knew he was breaking a cardinal rule but the flak was practically non existent. He got down low and skimmed across the surface of the harbour at fifty feet.

He spotted two patrol boats and a lighter of some kind sheltering under the nets. He gave them a squirt with his guns and pulled up. He called the rest of the section in and they made pass after pass until the netting caught alight. One of the patrol boats managed to get underway. The Corsairs rolled into the attack and lashed it with machine gun fire until it was a drifting wreck.

Well satisfied with their work they flew back to *Lancer* and waited for their turn to land on. The Barracudas went first, then the Corsairs. Goodfellow got down smartly. Gilliard waved off Wicklow and Beahan. Barrett got down, just catching the last wire. It was a procession after that. Each Corsair snagged a wire and taxied forward of the crash barrier. Wicklow landed heavily but managed to get down, which left Beahan.

Gilliard waved him off again and it was getting a bit embarrassing. The Goofer's gallery at the back of the island was full. Barrett and Callicoe watched from the portside AA gallery.

Beahan's third approach was good. He was in the groove and looking bang on until it all went wrong. Anticipating Gilliard's signal, he cut his throttle too early and pulled the nose up to flare into landing. The Corsair sank too soon and bounced up from the back of the deck. The port wing stalled and as Beahan opened the throttle, the fighter shot across the deck at an angle. The starboard wing smashed into the left upright of the crash barrier and tore off at the fold. The Corsair went over the side and landed upside down in the water. Before he could get clear, the Corsair went down for the final time and took Beahan with it.

Callicoe remembered what he'd said about Beahan getting down, *either that or it kills him*. He wished he hadn't said it now.

There was little time to mourn his passing. Carrier ops were like that. The crews started rearming the aircraft, rushing around in the hangar and on deck. The barrels of the machine guns were pulled through, oiled and cleaned and the trays reloaded. Callicoe did the tour, seeing what was damaged and how many they could put on the line. The aircraft on deck were spotted ready to go, not a moment too soon.

Three days of non stop attack had finally stung the Japanese into a response. Radar picked up enemy aircraft approaching from the west. The carriers swung into the wind. Callicoe was one of the first up and he was charging hard to get some height. The controllers passed a bearing to the incoming raid. They were coming in two waves at seven thousand feet. They'd almost got their timing right.

Having just landed strikes on board, there weren't many fighters immediately available to respond. The CAP was the first line of defence, everything else would have to pick up the leakers that got through.

Richardson called out the numbers as soon as he sighted them. It was a mixed force of Betty twin engined bombers and single engined Kate torpedo planes. Fighters flew ahead of them to clear the way.

Seafires and Corsairs dived into the attack. Richardson took care of a Zero and wheeled to get behind the torpedo bombers. He ignored the Betty's. Bombs dropped from altitude could be evaded relatively easily, the real threat were the Kate's. Almost as if they were reading his thoughts, the Kate's went down to start their torpedo attacks. Four went for *Hawke*, the rest went for the carriers.

The ships started to put up their AA barrage. Everything from 20mm upwards was flung into the sky. Richardson ignored it and stayed on target. Diving into the maelstrom he got behind a group of three Kate's heading for *Reliant*. The side of the carrier was sparkling as Oerlikon cannons, pom poms and the 4.5" deck guns trained on them.

One Kate fell to the barrage. It reared up sharply and

rolled onto its back, disappearing in a spray of water. The other two aircraft pressed on; Richardson hot on their heels.

He flinched as a flak burst exploded in front of him. He shoved the throttle through the gate and was pushed back in his seat as the engine screamed. The Corsair closed on the trailing Kate. It made no attempt to jink and Richardson stitched it from nose to tail. Hits sparkled off the fuselage. The Kate caught fire and nosed straight in leaving hardly a ripple.

The lone survivor pressed home its attack. Closing to within one thousand yards, the pilot lined up on the bow. His hand reached for the torpedo release when a chain of 20mm rounds smashed into the cockpit. The left wing dipped and the Kate cartwheeled across the waves as it disintegrated.

Richardson broke off. His eyes were wild as he wiped his hand across his face. He clawed for height and took stock of the damage to his fighter.

Up above, the Betty's were hacked from the sky. The Seafires tore into them. Their cannons and machine guns made short work of them. The Betty's lacked self sealing tanks and armour and caught fire at the slightest hit. One by one, they trailed great banners of flame and fell out of the sky.

The other Kate's fared little better. Two of them managed to drop torpedoes but *Hawke* dodged them, combing the tracks. Callicoe claimed one Zero, Richardson a Kate. Eight Kate's were shot down, the rest got away at low level. The Bettys were shared between the CAP of Seafires and the AA gunners.

Admiral Moody took the raid as his cue to leave. He recovered his aircraft and turned for home. He had *Reliant* and *Lancer* bring up the rear, with a screen of aircraft spread out to make sure they were clear.

21 – All Change, Next Stop Japan

Commodore Moore looked at the ships with a critical eye as he passed each one in the harbour. Some were scruffy and he saw the work parties over the side wielding paint brushes. He never liked seeing ships at rest in harbour. The helmsman showed no reaction having the Commodore on his shoulder, he just focused on his job, delivering him to the dock.

He judged the distance and cut the throttle, putting the wheel over. The gig turned, mushing through the turn. Ratings stood at the bow and stern, ready to put the fenders over the side. The gig nudged along the dock and a line was thrown over, making her fast.

When Moore had been transferred to the Eastern Fleet earlier in the year; it was to consider how Royal Navy doctrine would translate to operations in the Pacific. British carriers usually operated on their own or in hunting groups on short deployments. Rarely had two or more operated together until they had arrived in the Indian Ocean.

Similarly, the scale of Fleet Air Arm strikes had always been small, sometimes twenty or thirty aircraft at a time, split between two waves. That's what the last few months had been all about. Forays to give them a chance to work together and give the Air Groups experience at flying bigger and bigger strikes.

Moore had looked at it almost as a theoretical problem. There had been no time limit specified, and no indication if these plans would be put into effect at all. He'd been required to make regular reports to Admiralty via Fleet Headquarters at Trincomalee, sharing his thoughts with Admiral Somerville and later Admiral Fraser on performance and tactics.

Running Task Force 71 for the last few months had brought into sharp relief a number of issues. Individually they weren't insurmountable. Collectively, they were a line of dominoes that would have to be knocked over if this was going to work.

When he first arrived, he'd already identified the need to use escort carriers to ferry spare aircraft around. *Minerva* and *Unicorn* also had their place as mobile workshops to support the carriers. What had been highlighted most of all was the need for on the move fleet replenishment. Even the two day runs to Sumatra and the Andaman Islands had shown that British warships, particularly the big ships, lacked the range for extended operations.

Moore staff had spent days going over the fuel consumption figures for every operation from the last five months. On one incursion, one of the cruisers had used fifty five percent of their fuel just steaming at nineteen knots. That hadn't even taken into account fuel expenditure running at battle speeds to keep pace with the carriers.

American carriers could range for fifteen thousand miles. The British carriers could only manage half that at best. By Moore's reckoning, a Task Force might have sufficient fuel to operate for two days before they would have to withdraw to refuel.

To operate successfully in the Pacific, they would need tankers, auxiliaries and supply ships, an infrastructure, a supply chain and dockyards and a forward base to operate form. Trincomalee was no good, it was too far away, the same went for Bombay. Moore thought they might retake Singapore and base operations from there.

It had soon become clear that while the army was gaining an advantage in Burma, it would be late 1945 before they liberated Thailand and advanced on Singapore. The only other place they could base from would be Australia but Moore didn't know what facilities were there to make it possible.

Moore wasn't stupid, he knew something was brewing. The very fact that so many British fleet carriers were at Trincomalee obviously meant something was going on. The fact Admiral Fraser had called this conference was the other.

Moore strode ashore, breezing past the Lieutenant waiting for him and headed towards the staff car. A driver held the door open and he got in. His Staff Officer sat next to him, a battered briefcase across his lap. The heat in the car was stifling and Moore demanded some speed while he wound the window down.

He was ushered straight in when he got to the headquarters building. Admiral Fraser's own Staff Officer was waiting for them in the lobby. The conference had enough gold braid to sink a battleship. Fraser, Moody and Power were there of course in their respective roles of Commander in chief Eastern Fleet, Second in Command and Rear Admiral of Carriers respectively. Flag Officer Ceylon, Rear Admiral Nicholson was also there. As a mere Commodore, Moore very much felt like the low man on the totem pole.

Fraser started on a high note, well pleased with the recent performance off Nancowry and the Nicobar Islands. His Staff Officer slid copies of reconnaissance photos across the table. Some had been taken by recce Hellcats during the raid, others by Catalina flying boats a few days later.

He laid out in broad strokes the program for the next few months. He knew the moves being made in Washington and back home to get them into the Pacific.

As early as 1943, the British Government had seen the political need for it. While the policy of the Allied nations was Europe first, Britain needed their contribution to the Far East theatre to be more than just defeating the Japanese on land in Burma. There was a matter of saving face to be taken care of, liberating Singapore and Hong Kong and taking the fight to the Japanese at sea. If the Americans went all the way across the Pacific on their own, Britain would have no place at the peace table and little influence on what happened next.

The difficulty was making that possible. The British Fleet had been stretched to the limit ever since the beginning of the war. The Navy had held its own, but there just wasn't the resources to gather enough ships to venture into the Pacific.

Then the tide had begun to turn. The Germans and Italians had been forced out of the Mediterranean. Sicily had been invaded as had Italy and the South of France. The U-Boat war was being won in the Atlantic and the invasion of Europe had not needed the British carriers to be involved. By combining resources with the free Dutch, French and Australian Navy in the Far East, they were now in the position to do it.

Churchill had made a statement to the House of Commons that it was a priority for the Royal Navy to have a presence in the Pacific. They had a responsibility to share the burden and show they deserved a place in the final victory. At the Quebec Conference he offered Roosevelt the Royal Navy's services.

Roosevelt had gladly accepted the gesture. He knew there would be a great deal of resentment amongst the American public if the British were not seen to take a hand in liberating territory taken from them earlier in the war. The President's decision produced considerable ripples in Washington circles. The Chief of Naval Operations, Admiral King resented what he saw as British interference. Reputed to be an Anglophobe, he considered the Pacific, 'their war'. Allowing the Brits into the theatre was a headache he could do without.

Getting their foot in the door had been the easy bit. Admiral Nimitz had made it clear that there was no spare capacity in the American supply chain. They would have to prove that they could not only provide a fleet that was big enough to be useful but that they were capable of operating independently and supporting themselves.

"Commodore Moore highlighted the issues we face regarding operational range. He was not alone in this. Admiral Daniels has been in Australia for most of the year laying the groundwork for us. However, it will take some time yet for us to gather sufficient numbers of auxiliary ships to support fleet operations."

"Tactically, we are making progress. We've got the next few months to continue training and refining our techniques. More carriers are coming. In time we'll probably have enough to operate in two Divisions to retain tactical flexibility."

Moore was staggered by the news. It would be the greatest mobile striking force in Royal Naval history. Even an advocate of air power like himself had never envisaged operations on such a grand scale.

"*Indefatigable* will be leaving the UK soon," said Fraser. "I'm assured *Implacable* will join us once she's released from Home Fleet but we might not see her until the New Year. *Illustrious* is en-route from Durban as I speak. She should dock in the next few days. That means we can release *Victorious* for repairs. Her steerings still not right and I don't want to give the Americans any reason to find fault once we're operational."

He went through the list of other ships that were being pulled from all over the world to make up the fleet. *Howe*, *Jellicoe* and *Hawke* were already here. The battleship *King George V*, or *KGV* as she was known was on her way as well. Big ships needed escorts. A number of destroyers and cruisers were being modified at Malta, Durban, Sydney and Simonstown to work alongside the Americans.

"I'm keen that we have every resource available to us, sir," said Admiral Power. "Once we move to Australia, Durban and Bombay are going to be too far away."

"What do you propose?"

"Might I suggest that we send *Minerva* and *Unicorn* to do the rounds of the depots? They could load as many aircraft, spares, engines and equipment as possible for transfer to Australia? We're going to need every one we can lay hands on."

"Sort of a Cook's Tour you mean?" Fraser asked in good humour. "Very well, I agree."

Three went out, one came in. *Minerva* and *Unicorn* set with orders to clean out the depots. They would also pick up pilots bound for the carriers and bring them back. *Victorious* headed back to Bombay to get her troublesome steering fixed.

Illustrious' Air Group beat up *China Bay* before coming in smartly to land. They brought with them newspapers, records and sports equipment.

"All the comforts of home," Gabby said, making a few experimental strokes with a cricket bat. Callicoe tossed a cricket ball between his hands.

"Have a knock around?" he asked.

"Yeah, all right."

The knock around turned into a sprawling game. Aircrew dipped in and out, taking a turn at bat or fielding. The years fell off them as they played, going back to their school days.

Sweating, Callicoe braved the crocodiles for once and went for a quick dip to cool off. With a fresh uniform on, he went to the Mess. It was one of the few buildings where the ceiling fans worked and he sat in the shade while he greedily read three letters postmarked India.

Two of them had been written within days of his leaving and the third was from the middle of October. Jane said she missed him and harked back to their time together. Callicoe was amazed she found so much to talk about. She asked after some of the squadron and how they were.

The third letter was more recent and was a detailed description of the leave she'd had with Kaylani Prasad. The Indian WREN had invited her to stay at her parents' home with her in Bombay. Jane had spent three leisurely days being waited on hand and foot by liveried servants with best china and slept on silk sheets.

He read them again, fixing little things in his head and then started writing a reply.

On the 22nd November, the British Pacific Fleet formally came into being. Admiral Fraser hoisted his broad pennant in the battleship *HMS Howe*. Admiral Moody would take command of carrier operations.

Admiral Power took command of what was now designated the East Indies Fleet. He couldn't help feeling he'd been left with the runts of the litter. He got the older battleships and the smaller escort carriers and destroyers to support operations in the Indian Ocean.

It was actually simpler than that. Operations over the last few months had shown that speed was king. If you couldn't keep up with the carrier, you were no use to Fraser. Even *Howe* and *Jellicoe* were a stretch, having struggled to keep pace during Fraser's first operation back in August.

As discussed at the conference, Fraser formed the carriers into 1st Aircraft Carrier Squadron, with sub divisions to provide deployment flexibility. *Indefatigable* and *Implacable* would join them once they arrived.

He started to workup the new formations. While they had operated before, he needed them to get used to the new Divisions. Above all, they needed more practise at mobile replenishment.

22 – Merry Bloody Christmas

Even those not in the know could feel the sense of anticipation. New ships, new men, new equipment. Things were building up.

Goodfellow worked his squadron just as hard as the other CO's. They flew every chance they got. It was a chance to break the monotony of life at Trincomalee. Besides, being at sea was a welcome chance to cool off.

They practised massed launches, forming up over the carrier and tossing 11½lb practise bombs into the jungle on the south side of Ceylon. It took some getting used to and Callicoe wasn't sure he liked it. He'd seen the flak the Barracuda's had flown through, now he was going to have to do the same.

To start with, the bombing results were awful. After the first day they'd barely landed any bombs on the target, a clearing in the middle of the jungle.

"We've got to do better gentlemen," Goodfellow told them in the Wardroom. "The safest place to be was in that clearing today."

They improved but it wasn't as easy as they expected it to be. A steep dive got them more accuracy, but gave them very little time to line up. Shallow dives were far less dangerous but coming in shallow they had to allow for simple things; like gravity. It took some skill to throw the bombs onto the target. They had to hunker down with the Barracuda pilots for tips. The Barra pilots loved it, seeing the cocky Corsair boys meekly coming cap in hand for advice.

Moody had them fly mock raids against Trincomalee

and in all weathers. Flying a strike on a clear day was easy. He wanted to see what they could do in less favourable conditions. Cloud cover was the worst enemy. It played havoc with their formations and the first mock strike wasn't pretty. It got added to the list of things to work on.

Lancer and *Reliant* went south for manoeuvres. Four days out from Ceylon in the middle of nowhere the barometer began to drop as the weather changed. The sea churned up and the wind whipped across the deck. They couldn't go for Ceylon; it would have meant running with the waves and wind on their stern quarter. They changed course towards Addu Atoll, six hundred miles south west of Trincomalee. They never made it. The clouds gathered and the sky went dark.

The Task Force barely made steerage way as it sailed into the teeth of the gale. 100 knot winds rocketed across the flight deck. Below deck, it was hard tack and bully beef. The galleys were shut down and everyone hung on for grim death. Even the hardened sailors were sick as a dog and decks were awash with vomit. Men went out on safety lines to make sure the aircraft on deck stayed lashed down. Five broke free and went over the side, taking two men with them.

Callicoe had never seen anything like it. Bad weather in the Atlantic was nothing on this. The seas were monstrous, fifty, sixty foot waves that crashed over the bow. For three days and nights, they marked time, praying to the gods to get them out of this.

There was chaos on *Reliant* when a Seafire broke free in the hangar and started careening around. It bumped into another aircraft and tore it from its restraining straps, then there were two of them rolling around. With every gyration of the ship, they bumped back and forth across the hangar like wrecking balls, knocking more aircraft free. One man was killed trying to stop them, another had his ribs stoved in when he was trapped between two out of control fighters. It was carnage.

One destroyer nearly went under when a massive wave crashed over her bow. Her forward gun mount, radar and mast were swept away. A freak wave crashed into *Lancer's* port side and carried away one of the Oerlikon galleries on the side of the flight deck. The battering went on and on.

On the evening of the third day, the skies began to clear. The storm veered off to the south and light returned. The seas calmed and the Task Force hove to.

All of the ships had suffered some form of damage. They had to write off fifteen aircraft in *Reliant's* upper hangar. It looked like a scrapyard, a tangle of wings and spare parts.

They limped into Addu Atoll to refuel and lick their wounds. *Lancer* spent two days putting the damage of the storm to rights. They opened every port hole and hatch they could find to air the ship. Captain Austin had the whole crew cleaning up all the way back to Ceylon. Callicoe wasn't happy until they got back to Trincomalee and his feet were back on solid ground again.

A few days later, *HMS Indefatigable* arrived. In most respects there was little to distinguish her from *HMS Indomitable*. She was slightly longer, but the main difference was internal. She had two full hangar bays against *Indomitable's* one and a half. What garnered more interest was her Air Group, a mix of Hellcats, Seafires and a squadron of the new Fairey Firefly.

The Firefly looked like a cross between a Spitfire and a Fulmar. The wing had an elegant Sptifre like curve at the trailing edge and mounted four 20mm cannon, a significant upgrade to the eight .303 machine guns on the Fulmar. The fuselage still had two cockpits, one for the observer and one for the pilot. It wouldn't be able to tangle with top drawer fighters, but it was a significant improvement over the Fulmar which was starting to show its age. It could also carry rockets for ground attacks missions.

Indefatigable brought one other change. Admiral Vian replaced Admiral Moody as commander of carrier operations. He transferred his flag from the new arrival to *Indomitable*. This wasn't the first time this had happened to Moody, Vian had relieved him at Salerno too. Vian was a well known leading personality in the Navy but as a dashing commander of destroyers. Inexperienced where carrier operations were concerned, he had a lot of catching up to do.

He didn't waste any time; he sent the carriers to sea. He had the intelligence officers review previous operations with him to get up to speed. A practical nuts and bolts sort, Vian visited each ship to get a feel for what they were like. Callicoe's eyes were on stalks when he saw the great man come striding down the hangar. He looked at the aircraft and asked questions of Commander Oates as he went along.

Callicoe tried to shuffle himself amongst the crowd of deck crew when Oates singled him out for attention.

"This is Lieutenant Callicoe, sir. He's Maintenance Officer for one of our Corsair squadrons."

Callicoe wished he could disappear. He shook the Admirals hand without thinking and then held out a rag for him to wipe the oil off. Vian was amused.

"You like to get your hands dirty, Mister Callicoe?"

"Something I learned at *Pensacola*, sir. The Americans liked us to tinker and learn our aircraft."

Vian nodded soberly. He liked an officer who could muck in. He walked forward and put a hand on the Corsairs propeller, giving it an affectionate pat.

"And are you happy with the tools of your trade,

Lieutenant?"

"Yessir," Callicoe replied quickly. "She's a handful at times, but I wouldn't change her for anything."

"I look forward to the show."

Callicoe found out what he meant later in the day when Oates had the pilots in the wardroom. Vian wanted to see some mock attacks. There was nothing unusual about that, they'd done them before. Oates saved the surprise for last.

"And you'll be using live ammunition," he told them.

There was a stunned silence.

"Orders from the top," Oates told them. "You come in low and you fire over everybody's heads. Needless to say, watch where you're pointing and be aware of what ships are beyond the one you're flying at."

It was on shaky legs that Callicoe got into his Corsair. Oates had gone through one set of nails and was onto his second before they even took off. With Vian stood next to him, he could only watch as the Barracudas came in at wave top height to make their runs. Next were the Corsairs. They dived from two thousand feet and came in three abreast. There was a shrill whistle as they roared over the deck, their guns chattering as they sprayed tracer over everyone's head.

"Very good, Commander," said Vian, beaming with pleasure. "Good attack."

They went for a late lunch.

The year ended with a whimper, rather than a bang. Never one to rest, ten days after he arrived, Vian seized on a suggestion of the Americans to attack the oil refineries in Sumatra. On the 17th December, British Pacific Fleet made its first official sortie. *Illustrious* and *Indomitable* put to sea.

The raid was a debacle. Bad weather combined with

poor radio discipline and confusion reigned. The strike ended up milling around, dodging in and out of thick clouds, groping their way to the coast. They never did find the target and hit the secondary instead. They flayed the port at Belawan Deli and caused havoc strafing airfields but it wasn't what they had been sent to do.

On the way back to the carrier, Corsairs and Hellcats had clung to Avengers praying their Observers were holding their maps the right way up. Aircraft from different squadrons got mixed up as they struggled to find the carriers. It was a poor reflection of two ships that Vian had been assured were very experienced. As a sop to pride, their fighters had shot up the airfields around Sabang on the way home.

Back in port, escort carriers arrived to deliver *Lancer* and *Reliant's* Christmas presents. Their decks were packed with new aircraft. Avengers were hoisted off the ships and transferred to *China Bay*. The Air Groups finally traded in their Barracudas and Birkenfield had his boys up morning, noon and night to get proficient with them. Callicoe wasn't sorry to see the Barracudas go. They had always been difficult to escort due to their slow speed. For all their faults however, at least they could carry a torpedo. Although the Avenger was rated to carry one, British torpedoes didn't fit in the bomb bay. It also couldn't dive like the Barracuda. The crews plastered the clearings around Koggala, getting used to new shallow bombing techniques.

Callicoe had his second Christmas in the Royal Navy. This time last year he had been home on leave after his flight training. A lot had happened in a year. They had a concert party in the after lift well and various members of the crew did a turn. Gabby showed a previously unknown flair for the dramatic and banged out a passable Saint

Crispins Day speech from Henry V. Three comely greasers from the engine room did what they called the Trincomalee hula. It didn't matter that they had the wrong dance by a few thousand miles, they wiggled their hips and made the grass skirts fly while they shoved their coconut chests forward.

Birkenfield's mob put on a comedy sketch titled, *How many Admirals does it take?* Callicoe had seen them rehearsing it and it brought the house down. They played thinly veiled caricatures of the Fleet commanders stood at a table arguing over how to win the war. Admirals Francesca, Vivian and Margery had tennis balls down the front of their tunics and yellow braid from cuff to shoulder. White table cloths were turned into skirts. Numerous references were made to firing one's catapult too soon and they pillaged the catch phrases of Tommy Handley and Arthur Askey with gay abandon. They brought the house down when Admiral Vivian pulled a little blue book from inside her tunic and asked everyone what joke they'd like to hear.

On Christmas Day, the Padre held a service for morning Divisions on the flight deck. It was a bit strange being stood in shorts and short sleeve shirt in sticky sixty degree heat on December 25th to listen to a sermon.

In accordance with the best traditions of the service, the youngest pilot in the Air Group, in this particular case, 1771's very own Wicklow was made Chief for the day. He pantomimed round the Wardroom and upbraided Gabby as a slovenly sailor. Gabby made the mistake of blowing a raspberry in return. Wicklow's eyes had a wicked gleam as he said, "Make him walk the plank."

Before Gabby could move, they lobbed on him and grabbed a limb each. He was carted from the Wardroom in double quick time and taken to the cable deck. Then it was, one, two, three and he was thrown over the side. A vengeful Gabby had to swim round to the side ladder and haul himself back aboard. He came in, spluttering and dripping everywhere. A pint was pressed into his hand to calm him down.

One of the more portly ratings was roped in to don a red jacket and make the rounds of the mess decks. The men entered into the spirit of things and sat on his lap while he asked them what they wanted for Christmas. Jenkins, an instrument fitter hammed it up, sucking his thumb while he asked for Hitler to fall down a well. Callicoe got a good photograph of that one.

The crew made an effort to spruce the ship up. The mess decks were freshly painted and paper chains were strung up. Someone had put a potted palm in the corner, masquerading as a Christmas tree. The officers served dinner to the ratings and Callicoe went up and down with trays of roast potatoes which were much in demand.

The Officers had their Christmas dinner later in the day. Turkey, roast potatoes, Yorkshire pud. Callicoe leaned back in his chair while he enjoyed a cigar. He was stuffed.

23 – Black Gold

Admiral Fraser was less than impressed with their performance before Christmas. There was no point getting the carriers to the launching point if the Air Group messed everything up. They couldn't even use the excuse of getting used to their new equipment. They'd flown the Avengers long enough to be familiar with them, it was poor performance, plain and simple.

Fraser wanted to prove to Nimitz that they could operate in the Pacific and deliver a knockout blow. Destroying the refineries and oil fields in Sumatra would be a good step towards that. With *Victorious* back from Bombay, they had five fleet carriers to do it. He planned everything with Vian down to the last detail. There would be no repeat of the disaster before Christmas.

The last time equipment limitations had forced their hand. In the northern part of Sumatra, there was a ridge of mountains over ten thousand feet high running east to west down the spine of Sumatra. The underpowered Barracudas would have struggled to get over them so they'd had to come in from the north. The Fleet had gone round the northern tip of Sumatra and ventured into the Malacca Strait before launching. With the Avengers there would be no such impediment. They could go over the mountains easily and launch from further away.

Fraser favoured a single mass strike for maximum punch to overload the target and cause confusion. Vian disagreed. He had built his reputation on dash and daring in destroyers. To his mind, carriers were just big destroyers with a big reach.

Staggering the launches and particularly the direction of attack would confuse the Japanese. It would require careful timing but it would allow them to fly off two strikes in quick succession and minimise the risk.

He proposed a two prong strike. The main force comprising three carriers would do the usual route, across the water to the southern side of Sumatra and launch near Sinabang. The second force would repeat the route into the Malacca Strait and launch from there. The southern force would go in first, cross the mountains and raise hell. Then, while the Japs were looking one way, the northern force would come in to mop up.

Moore threw his weight behind Vian, advocating aggressive deployment of the carriers. Admiral Halsey was bold with his deployments; Moore thought they should try to emulate that. Reluctantly, Fraser was persuaded.

With further to go, the northern force went first. *Reliant* and *Lancer's* crews didn't even get to enjoy New Year. They went through the harbour boom at 2200 hours on New Year's Eve with a darkened ship.

"We can celebrate when we get back," Captain Oates told them over the tannoy.

Avengers went up to sniff for submarines ahead of the carriers when they got close to the Andaman Islands. After giving the place a pasting in October, there had been reports of submarines in the area and Moore wasn't about to take any chances. They timed their approach to pass the Nicobar and Andaman Islands in the dark. They bent on twenty five knots and were clear by daylight before turning to head south east into the Malacca Strait.

They were in position on the morning of the 4th January. They transmitted no messages. The arrangements were that Vian would only transmit in the clear if the southern strike was delayed.

This was the worst bit, the waiting. Callicoe had been awake well before dawn. He rolled out of his bunk, got dressed and went up to the hangar. It was the usual stifling hot box with its unique stink of oil, petrol and sweat. It was strangely quiet so early in the morning. Callicoe wandered up and down the hangar, checked the lashings on the aircraft and then had a nose at his own aircraft. He went up top and hung off the rail on the Goofer's gallery, enjoying the breeze as the air flowed around the island.

The carrier came alive not long after that. The tannoy called them to brief at 0500 hours and they were given their assignments. The southern force was set to go at 0610 hours. They would launch at 0800 hours. By the time they reached the refineries, the Japanese should be chasing the earlier strike over the mountains.

"No screw ups, chaps," Goodfellow told them. "I want good, crisp calls of enemy sightings. If you haven't got anything to say, stay off the air. Anyone who leaves their channel open, don't worry about a chit, I'll have your goolies off."

That raised a laugh. They had all been issued with one of these when they first got to Trincomalee. It was a scarf printed in five or six different languages which promised that whoever delivered the member of aircrew safely into allied hands would be given a reward. Callicoe had sewn his on the inside of the shirt he wore when he flew.

The Corsairs would have their work cut out for them this time. They were going into a target area where the defences would be wide awake. There would be no strafing as they'd have to cover the Avengers. They were covering theirs, 1783 would cover *Reliant's*. If the Japs chased them back to the carriers, the Seafires would be waiting for them.

At 0700, the aircraft were spotted on the flight deck. It was a tight fit. Even with their wings folded, the Avengers took up more room than the Barracudas had done. The engines were warmed up and there was a flap when Goodfellow's Corsair failed to start. The mechanics worked like trojans to get it going. The fact it hadn't turned over was a major embarrassment.

Since taking over, Goodfellow had changed the flight assignments round. Barrett would lead the second section; Callicoe would lead the third as top cover for the entire wave. He'd practised, but this would be his first time leading on a strike.

At 0750, the carriers turned into the wind. Goodfellow started up, unfolded his wings and moved forward. There was a good ten knot breeze to add to the speed of the ship. He was airborne before he even crossed the bow. Wicklow was fast behind him.

Everyone was on the ball. They got the aircraft off every fifteen seconds, a new record for *Lancer*. Callicoe circled the carrier as the rest of the Air Group got up. They went off three short. One Avenger aborted shortly after take off with a faulty engine and returned to *Lancer*. One didn't get off at all and a Corsair went over the bow and straight in the water.

The weather looked bad on the way out. The last strike had been confounded by rain squalls and layers of dense clouds. It was no better this time. The coast was obscured by dark clouds and they flew into a stiff breeze.

If they'd still had the Barracudas with them, Callicoe would have been worried. The headwind would have cut seriously into their range and it would have been touch and go for them to get back.

They ate up the miles, the aircraft undulating up and down on the air currents. Callicoe had the god spot up at Twelve thousand. Barrett was three thousand feet below, hovering over the Avengers. Goodfellow was at the same height a few miles ahead.

They flew into a hornet's nest. The defences around

the refineries were wide awake. The first strike had only finished half an hour before and the AA gunners were still spraying shells into the sky with gay abandon. The first strike had gone in all guns blazing. Corsairs and Hellcats had shot up the surrounding airfields. Fireflies had followed them in, lofting 60lb HE rockets and 20mm cannon shells from eight hundred yards to cause further mayhem. The Avengers dropped 500lb bombs amongst storage tanks, pumps and pipelines. Oil tanks brewed up, spewing gobs of burning oil all over the place. Once they were done, they beat it south as fast as possible.

"Bandits! Twelve o'clock, Joker Leader," Callicoe called. Dots on the horizon were barrelling full tilt towards them. They rolled into the attack, diving for the Avengers, hell bent on getting to the bombers.

Goodfellow lifted his nose and shoved the throttle through the gate, climbing to meet them. It was a mixer. The Japanese fighters were very aggressive, wanting to make up for the damage caused in the first attack.

Going head to head with them, Goodfellow opened fire early, spraying the air with bullets. His target pulled off. Others didn't. Curly Richardson's Corsair folded around an Oscar, neither of them willing to be the first to flinch. He died screaming his defiance as cannon shells thudded into his cockpit. Another Oscar span out of control, its tail a mess.

The Japanese fighters flashed past Goodfellow and his section. Barrett's section was the next barrier and they angled to head the Japanese off. Barrett latched onto the tail of one Oscar and tore it apart. It was an easy kill. They'd made no attempt to evade, boring in hard to get to the Avengers.

They couldn't stop them all. One section of Avengers had to break off when two Oscars raked them from astern. The Corsairs chased them away but one Avenger trailed behind the rest, a thin wisp of white smoke coming from the cowling. It had to dump its bombs to stay in the air.

Contrary to every expectation and the carefully considered plan, the Japanese fighters had not chased after the first strike as they withdrew. Too late to catch them up, the survivors had rallied over the refineries to protect them in case there was another attack from the south. When a spotter on the north shore spotted the second strike coming in, they had rushed to intercept them.

Callicoe watched the whirling mass of aircraft from above, judging the moment to come in. His eyes hunted the sky around them. He glanced towards the sun and squinted, spreading the fingers of his left hand to filter some of the light out. He snarled, there could be fighters up there, he couldn't tell. He had a final look around before he committed his section.

"Joker Green Leader to all Joker Greens, here we go. Wingmen, stick to your leader and for god sakes, don't follow them through the turns."

He stood his Corsair on its port wingtip and went into the attack. He headed for a pair of Green Japanese fighters roaming around the flank of the Avengers. He made sure his gyro sight was set for a Ki-43. He'd heard some of the other pilots screaming about Zero's but he'd seen the subtle differences, the smaller canopy, the more slender rear fuselage that distinguished the two types.

He lined his sight up on the big red circle on the fuselage and then angled off for deflection. He squeezed the trigger and the Corsair juddered from the recoil of the six guns. Tracer trailed behind and before he could adjust, the Oscars rolled and peeled off to the left. Callicoe let them go, staying with the Avengers.

Two Oscars went down, one to the Corsairs, one to the Avengers. Flak blotted the sky and started walking up to their height as they got close to the refineries.

The fires on the ground made it difficult for the second strike. Thick pillars of black smoke obscured their view and the Avengers went lower than they should have done to see what they were bombing. More than one dropped their load blind rather than risk it.

"Keep your eyes peeled," Callicoe warned his section as they turned for home. "Reform on me, we're going to have to fight our way out of this."

He wasn't wrong. The Japanese managed to put some extra fighters up and they were waiting for them on the way back. The radio descended into a cacophony of noise as sightings were called out one on top of another.

"Fighters! Three o'clock level."

"Zeroes, ten high."

"All Joker sections, buster, buster," cried Goodfellow. "We've got to cut a way through for the bombers to get out of here."

The Corsairs went into the attack. These Japanese pilots were canny. They weren't interested in the Corsairs; they wanted the bombers. They broke their dives off early and then reformed before coming in again from another direction. The Corsairs hared around, burning up fuel.

Goodfellow saw what they were doing. He called up Matthews on his R/T.

"Shady buggers this lot."

"Smarter than the average Nip, aren't they?" Matthews agreed. "Heads left, tails, right?" he joked.

"We'll take left," Goodfellow agreed. He pulled up, keeping above the Avengers.

Four Zeroes came in from astern as staggered pairs, the first pair slightly in front and below the second. Callicoe wheeled to meet them. Cannon shells flashed across his nose and he stamped on his rudder. He felt the flutter in the controls and caught it in time to stop going into a high speed stall. Shaken, he rolled out to settle the

Corsair and then came around to go after them. Gabby was on the far side, above to his right.

"Watch it Joker Green Two," Callicoe called. "Coming back in."

He dived after the Zeroes, gaining on them all the time but he was too late to stop them raking the Avengers. One of the bombers staggered under a well aimed burst and went down, flame streaming out of the cowling. Callicoe chased after them, his blood up at letting him through.

A Zero climbed hard to setup for another attack and Callicoe closed the distance. It had a black engine cowling and green fuselage and wings. He fired, missed and carried on after him.

"Don't let him go," Gabby called.

Callicoe had no intention of doing so. He grabbed the stick with both hands and hung on its tail. The Zero was tight in the turn, nimble but delicate. All he needed was one hit. The Zero rolled off the top to come back in and for that one instant, it hung perfectly in his sight. Callicoe pulled the trigger and sawed it in half.

"Behind you!" Gabby shouted. Callicoe's eyes snapped to his mirror. A bullet smashed it and more thudded into his Corsair. Callicoe slammed his stick the left and pulled back. He sagged in his seat as the G-forces built up. He tried tensing his legs to keep the blood in his head where it needed to be.

There was another thud. They were still behind him and Callicoe reversed his roll before going down. The world revolved. Sky became ground and he dived; throttle wide open. The Corsair went down like a rocket, engine screaming. The altimeter span around the dial. Callicoe pulled back on the stick, grunting as his lungs were squeezed. His vision narrowed, black flickering at the edges. Colour bleached from his eyes as the Corsair bottomed out of its dive.

Gabby had called out his warning and gone straight after the two Oscars that were on Callicoe's tail. The first one broke off as soon as he got behind them.

The Oscar fired and he saw hits sparkle on Callicoe's tail as he broke into a hard turn. Gabby strained to follow him. His speed was higher and he couldn't match the turn. He eased the roll and kept the stick back in his stomach. As the Oscar closed in for the kill, Callicoe took it down and Gabby went with them.

He got behind the Oscar and fired off a snapshot. He missed but it got the Oscar's attention. The pilot looked over his shoulder, saw the bent wing fighter behind him and pulled out of the dive. Gabby stayed with him, firing short bursts to chase him off.

"You're clear Joker Green Leader," he called.

The Oscars and Zeros chased them all the way, harrying them until they were thirty miles off the coast. They only turned back when their fuel ran low but it had been a gunfight all the way. They'd lost another two Corsairs covering them.

They were lucky to have the tail wind shoving them along. They got within seventy miles of the carriers before the first Avenger had to ditch. The second one managed another thirty before it too went down. Callicoe and Gabby circled the second one while the crew got into their dinghy. It looked awfully lonely floating on the water down there.

They kept watch over them until their fuel ran low. Callicoe rocked his wings one last time and they waved back before he set course for the carriers. A destroyer got to them two hours later after a hard sprint. They didn't hang around; they dropped the scramble nets over the side and hauled them up. A Lewis gun shot up the dinghy to sink it. A submarine picked up the other crew.

The carriers headed west. There was no time to rest. As soon as the fighters touched down, they were turned around, rearmed and refuelled. The pilots were debriefed and then put back into their aircraft. Moore put up half the fighters, the other were half held on deck ready in case the Japanese came to play.

The enemy fighters stayed away and by dawn the next day they knew they were clear. They rendezvoused with the tankers to refuel before heading for Trincomalee.

1771 licked their wounds, two pilots and three Corsairs down. Apart from Richardson, one of the new replacements, Bob Thomas had gone down during the fight back to the carrier. He'd made a rookie mistake. Low and slow; he'd committed the cardinal sin and tried to follow a Zero through a turn and paid the price. It had got behind him and cut him to pieces.

Goodfellow got Callicoe to pack up their stuff. Thomas' didn't take long; he'd not been on board long enough to get settled. Callicoe shoved his uniform into his kit bag and put his personal items on top, some silver backed brushes, a bible and his flight logs. Richardson's effects took longer. Farthingdale leaned over the edge of the top bunk while Callicoe dumped everything on the lower one.

"Any socks?" Farthingdale asked. Callicoe passed two pairs up.

"Underwear?"

Callicoe gave him a look.

"Unusual, but here you go." He passed some briefs up.

"Money?" Farthingdale ventured.

"Nice try," said Callicoe. He rummaged in the sponge bag and came up with an old fashioned cut throat razor. He opened it up, the blade was polished and sharp. He fingered it gingerly.

"Jesus. Did he actually use this?"

"Every day," Farthingdale assured him. Callicoe closed

it with a snap and put it back in the sponge bag. He found a bundle of letters tied with string and a diary.

The envelopes all had American stamps and post marks. He flicked through the diary. A photograph fell from between the pages. Callicoe picked it up off the deck and saw a beautiful brunette with a dimpled smile.

"Nice girl," he commented.

"A bitch," Farthingdale said.

Callicoe shrugged. He shoved the photograph back into the diary and sat there, tapping the spine, pondering what to do. He put the letters and diary on a separate pile and carried on sorting things out.

Once he was done, he brought the diary and letters back to his own cabin. He was flicking through them when Gabby came in.

"God it's hot," he moaned. He climbed onto his bunk and asked Callicoe what he was doing.

"Making sure there's nothing embarrassing for Richardson's parents," he explained. Gabby's ears pricked up.

"Come on then, read me the sexy bits. Any photos?"

"No." Callicoe said shortly. He wished he hadn't mentioned anything now. He couldn't find any reference in the diary that Richardson had mentioned the engagement to his parents. Still, the tone of the last few weeks was bleak; he didn't think it was something Richardson's family would want to read.

The letters were all from his girl, full of love and longing. Knowing she'd thrown Richardson over, Callicoe thought he spotted the subtle shift of tone in the letters when she must have moved on to someone else.

With that prompt, his thoughts turned to Jane. *Victorious* had delivered a bunch of mail and newspapers when she got back from Bombay. Callicoe had spent an hour gloating over the photograph she had sent him. The envelope also included a packet containing a small golden elephant. Kaylani had told her the Indians considered the elephant a good luck charm. His hand strayed to where it hung on its chain around his neck. He wondered when he'd get back to Bombay to see her. God alone knew when he'd get some leave.

"What?" he said, realising Gabby had asked him a question.

"I'll look after those if you want," Gabby offered, a salacious grin painted on his face.

"No, I think I'm fine, thank you."

He used some string to tie the diary and the letters together. Carrying the bundle to the stern he threw them over the side and watched them disappear. He went into the Wardroom for a drink.

Chalky White was starting another telling of his dip. How he'd survived after going over the bow was pure good luck. As soon as he'd started rolling, he knew he was in trouble. His engine cut out as he lifted off and the Corsair had gone straight in. He'd just had time to kick the rudder pedal and angle slightly to starboard before he plunged into the sea.

He already had the hood back and he hit his harness release as water started to fill up the cockpit. He kicked off from the fighter, swimming frantically to get away. The carrier had loomed above him and White began to panic. There was a crunch as it ploughed the Corsair under, then the bow wave washed over him, shoving him under. White had swallowed sea water, choked, went under, surfaced and choked again. His legs and arms thrashed as he'd tried to get away. A freak wave pushed him clear as *Lancer* rushed past at thirty knots. He was going under for the third time when a boat from the guard destroyer dragged him aboard, half drowned.

He went to see the Padre as soon as he was back aboard the carrier. After a close shave like that, he thought it prudent to say a few Our Fathers.

Goodfellow spent a few hours writing two letters, thankful that he didn't have to write three. He sat for a while, thinking long and hard about what to say. He didn't like writing a standard letter. He always imagined what his own mother would feel like when the Admiralty telegram dropped on the doormat. He thought about what words of comfort would she would want to see in a letter. Composing the words in his head, he started writing.

Callicoe found a quiet spot on the cable deck to think about his own brush with death. That Oscar had nearly got him today. He'd had a look at his Corsair when he got back and found a dent in his seat armour. He thought about the fighter he'd shot down. He'd killed a man; he could so easily have gone the same way only moments later.

They had a New Year's party when they pulled into Trincomalee. Drink flowed freely. They sang songs and gave a stirring rendition of Form A25 that made Callicoe think of Williams. They played mess games, starting with the ever popular relay up and down the length of the Wardroom.

It wasn't a simple relay race. Players had to down a pint first, spin five times around a broom handle before running up and down. Drunken pilots crashed left and right. Tug of war was little better. 1771 played off against the 1783 mob. They lined up, the man up front holding onto one end of the broom handle. Each man behind wrapped his arms around the one in front.

Barrett felt like his arms were getting pulled out of their sockets as the broom handle was yanked back and forth. He held on for grim death, his hands getting sweaty. He lost his grip and fell backwards in a heap.

They played another round with Goodfellow up front.

1771 won that one so they had a decider. Callicoe hung on like a limpet as Matthews ragged the broom handle around. Changing tactics, Matthews pushed forwards with a roar. Callicoe's grip went slack and the broom handle caught him square in the balls. Callicoe let go of the broom and collapsed in a heap clutching between his legs. He wiped tears from his eyes as Gabby helped him to a chair.

"Come on you dozy bugger," he soothed. "Get this inside you, it'll make the pain go away."

Callicoe gagged as Gabby upended the shot glass and poured neat gin down his throat.

They played shells cases after that. A polished brass shell case was put in the middle of the Wardroom and the players stood in a circle with their back to it. Linking arms, the name of the game was to move and pull and tug so that someone touched the shell case before you. If they did, they were out and had to leave the ring. A player could also be eliminated if he lost his grip and broke the circle.

The circle pulled back and forth, pulling on each other. As men were eliminated, the circle got smaller and smaller. Callicoe led a charmed life as he was jerked around like a rag doll. He danced around like a marionette, his body swerving round the metal tube, missing it by inches. Finally, he was dragged into it and he was out. Sixth, a creditable finish.

They counted down to midnight and cheered when they got to zero. It was the 8th January 1945, but who cared, they were alive.

24 – Road To Palembang

Rumours started to circulate that the Fleet would be transferring to Australia. Nobody complained. The limited delights of Trincomalee had worn thin and most were looking forward to the move. Callicoe wasn't one of them.

"Let me guess," said Gabby. "Mooning over your WREN."

Callicoe made a face while he thumbed through a maintenance report for one of their Corsairs. It really needed a thorough overhaul but *Unicorn* and *Minerva* were still away so they were reduced to using their own resources.

"I'll just be further away," he said, trying not to get himself worked up at the situation. He might not have made a formal declaration to Jane but it didn't mean he didn't care about her. "At least at Trincomalee there was an outside chance we'd get back to Bombay."

"I wouldn't worry mate," Gabby told him. "Out of sight, out of mind is my motto. Just think of all that virgin territory in Australia. The girls haven't seen anyone like me."

"No, you're right," said Callicoe. "Exactly what their reaction will be when when a Norfolk dwarf undresses in front of them is anyone's guess."

"Don't be rude," Gabby said. "Live in the moment," he chided. "There's plenty of war left."

Callicoe stewed in silence, thinking about Jane.

"I've got it all figured out," Gabby continued, chattering away to himself on the top bunk. "White's an

Aussie, he's got to be good for something. He can give us the lay of the land, line up a few girls, a cool beer or two and Bob's your uncle."

A mere four days after getting back from the raid on the oil fields, they were told in so many words that the move was on. Everyone packed up at *China Bay* and put their stuff aboard. The Fleet got up steam and put to sea. The official word was that they were doing manoeuvres but no one believed a word of it. Oilers had been busy doing the rounds for the last few days topping up the tanks. Barges had come alongside and put aboard food and munitions; they didn't do that for nothing.

The tannoy called the crew to harbour stations and *Lancer* put to sea with four destroyers as escort. *Reliant* followed her out, then all the other fleet carriers.

To their surprise, ten hours out from the harbour, Oates briefed them for a series of mock raids on Trincomalee. They would attack the airfield from altitude, then they'd come back and do it again at low level. If there was enough time, they might fly off a third strike as well. The RAF would put up their fighters in defence and attempt to intercept them coming in.

"Good practise for everyone," Oates beamed. "Anyone who collides in mid air, don't bother coming back to fill out your A25's," he told them in good humour, trying to underscore how crowded things would be up there.

It was the biggest strike they had ever seen, even if it was just for practise. Vian certainly didn't believe in doing anything by halves. Aside from the CAP to cover the carrier force, everything went in. The Fireflies led the Avengers. The Corsairs and Hellcats and Seafires stacked above them to provide cover. Some of the fighters were tasked with keeping the RAF's heads down, buzzing the field at *China Bay*.

In the face of overwhelming numbers, the RAF boxed clever. They launched everything they had as soon as they picked up the incoming aircraft on radar. The Beaufighters and Spits orbited to the north, waiting for the strike to commit and then came charging in. It was a mad house. Callicoe was mystified no one was killed.

Some fighters shadowed them back to the Fleet. The search radar picked them up late and the CAP raced in to head them off. The Beaufighters had timed it well. If that had been for real, they could have lost most of the returning strike. While an attack was coming in, the carriers couldn't steam into the wind to land on aircraft.

Before they peeled off to Ceylon, a Beaufighter flashed them a message with their signal lamp.

"B-E-T-T-E-R, L-U-C-K, N-E-X-T, T-I-M-E," Gilliard murmured under his breath as he spelled out the morse to himself.

"Cheeky buggers," he said as he waved a fist at them.

He turned his attention back to landing the aircraft back on. He braced his legs on the deck and held his arms out as the first Avenger came in.

Callicoe was on the downwind leg to land when all hell broke loose on *Lancer's* flight deck. There was a flash of yellow and then a huge ball of orange flame broke out by the island. The carrier sent up a red fare and gave Callicoe a red light.

He orbited while the crew fought to get the situation under control. Smoke billowed in the air. Callicoe kept glancing at his fuel gauge. He was fine but some of the others might not be. He called up the remaining aircraft in his section to get their fuel state. No one was hurting yet, but they weren't flush either.

The minutes crept by as the fire was brought under control. Oates called up the circling aircraft and ordered them to land on the other carriers. A rock settled in Callicoe's stomach with that announcement. If *Lancer* was badly damaged it would mean missing the action. They might even have to pull back for repairs.

Some went for *Reliant* but Callicoe felt more comfortable landing on *Illustrious*. The same class of carrier, all of his landing cues and references would be the same so he wouldn't have to worry about adjusting to something different. He landed without fuss and was welcomed aboard. Barrett landed behind him.

"What's going on?" he asked.

"Someone's caught it," Callicoe said. "I saw fire on the deck."

"Christ, I hope they're okay."

The second mock strike was delayed an hour while the situation on *Lancer* was ascertained. Her deck was cleared and she was ready for flight operations to continue. When Callicoe and Barrett came on deck, they saw *Illustrious's* deck crew had not passed up the opportunity for some japes. Each aircraft had a large letter on the tail to identify which carrier it was from. *Lancer's* ID letter was T. Some wag had painted a black X over the letter and put a smaller Q for *Illustrious* in front of it on the vertical stabiliser.

"Very funny," said Callicoe, shaking his head.

"We even threw in a free tank of petrol," the Deck Officer told him. Callicoe nodded.

"Yeah, yeah. Thanks for the assist."

"Any time."

Callicoe started up for the second strike and joined on with his own squadron once he was in the air.

"Are you sure you're with the right squadron?" Goodfellow asked as he formed up.

"I'm sure," Callicoe said shortly. The grief continued when they got back to *Lancer*. A crowd gathered in the hangar to see the handiwork. Callicoe was about to take a scraper to the paint when Gabbby interrupted.

"Ah, ah," he said, wagging his finger. He held up Callicoe's camera. "We've got to record this moment for posterity."

"Bollocks," Callicoe replied as he started scraping the black paint off.

It was a light moment in an otherwise grim end to the day. The deck fire had been Fortescue missing the wires on landing. Coming in too high, he'd ignored the wave off and dived for the deck. The undercarriage had folded like skittles and the engine had stubbed the deck, like a toe on the stairs. Shoved backwards by the impact, the engine went into the fuel tank and back into the cockpit. Fuel spilled onto the hot engine and it went up like a roman candle. Fortescue didn't even have time to undo his straps as the cockpit was filled by a wall of flame. He just screamed as the Corsair slithered into the crash barrier.

The fire parties had fought like trojans to get him out of the cockpit but it was already too late. Fuel from the drop tank leaked across the deck and they sprayed foam to stop it getting out of control. They got what was left of Fortescue out of the cockpit and dumped it onto a stretcher. The radio and guns were stripped out of the wreck before it was pitched over the side, there wasn't anything else worth saving.

The mood was sombre in *Lancer's* wardroom that evening. Fortescue had been well liked, "a solid chap," Barrett had said and he was right. Not a star, nor the best shot, Fortescue was someone you could depend on to cover your back. There was only one cure for this; a thrash. They toasted the recently departed and sang a few songs while Wicklow played the piano. That took the edge off things. After another song, Goodfellow called for some quiet.

"I know it's been a grim day, but I didn't think it right to let the day pass without highlighting the sterling efforts of our Senior Pilot and our esteemed Section Leader."

Callicoe groaned. Barrett was making for the hatch when Gabby stopped him.

"I'm sorry, but when two experienced pilots let those twerps on *Illustrious* get one over on us, then there has to be a forfeit."

Glasses and bottles were thumped on the bar.

As the fleet headed east, the weather turned. The easy conditions turned into a rough swell with twelve to fifteen foot waves. Coming in on the front quarter, the carriers rolled uncomfortably in a stomach churning undulation; up and to the right, down into the trough and left and then up again. Refuelling was interrupted as ships found it impossible to maintain position. Hoses parted and pumping gear was damaged. Smaller destroyers crashed into the oilers hulls and had to pull off. The fleet had no choice but to reduce speed and come into the wind. Resupply was suspended until it passed.

It took two days to calm down. Flying was restricted to a light CAP and a few Fireflies on extended anti submarine patrol. They all took a turn and Callicoe found it amongst his more hairy experiences. The only thing he could compare it to was his landing practice on the old *Argus* the year before.

Lancer could only make twenty knots, but the lack of speed was made up for by the stiff wind over the deck. As Callicoe started his take off roll, it was like being at the top of a water slide in a swimming pool. Ahead of him was water as the carrier plunged into a trough. As he took off, the bow rose up and he soared into the air. He circled the fleet for two hours doing endless circuits back and forth. Rain hammered off the canopy like bullets.

If the take off had been an experience, the landing was hairy. The stern was moving up and down twenty feet and more. Callicoe equated it to trying to get onto a trampoline when someone was already jumping on it.

He left the throttle alone and kept a firm grip of the stick as he made his curving approach. Flying with one wing low into the wind caused all sorts of problems. Callicoe needed to see the batsman and keep the deck in sight but the gusts kept wanting to drive him down.

With gusts of thirty to forty knots, the turbulence around the island played havoc on his final approach. As he came over the round down the stern was dropping away from him and he opened up at the last second to get clear. There was a tremble in the controls as the wing threatened to drop but he caught it smartly and thundered above the deck, coming round again. Gabby's landing was just as risky in reverse, the deck was rising. He caught the number one wire and almost stood his Corsair on its nose.

Callicoe got down on his second attempt. He caught a middle wire and then hung on as his Corsair slid on the slick deck. After he came off the wire, the deck crew rushed out and shoved some chocks under the wheels and told him to cut his engine where he was. Callicoe got down on shaky legs. Rain stung his cheeks as he ran head down for the island.

"God above," he breathed.

"Exciting wasn't it?" Gabby grinned as he wiped water off his face.

Up top, his Corsair was wheeled forward level with the island and then lashed down. With the strong wind there was no way they were risking pushing it back to the stern lift.

Flying operations were suspended as the wind increased and they battened down the hatches. The pilots gathered in the Wardroom and gripped their drinks tightly as the ship rolled. They gave up playing Uckers, the counters kept sliding across the table. Even three card brag was a push.

Oates went from group to group, talking with them for a few minutes before moving on. He leaned into the rolls like an expert.

"I saw your landing," he told Callicoe.

"So, it was you on the gallery."

"I wanted to see for myself what the flying conditions were like."

"In a word, dreadful."

"If you think this is bad, try winter in the Atlantic," Oates told them, grinning madly. "I flew Swordfish in worse weather than this. Waves as tall as a house, rain coming down in sheets. The wind was so strong you were almost hovering in mid air, deck like an ice rink." He shivered at the memory of it.

Callicoe baulked at the thought of flying in driving rain in an open cockpit, hands frozen on the controls because of the cold.

At dusk, he went up to the bridge and stood at the back, watching what was going on. Rain lashed the island and the windows were caked in salt. Water burst over the bow and rushed along the deck. He looked to starboard at one of the destroyers keeping station on them.

How it survived was beyond Callicoe, the crew must have had balls of steel. It was almost a submarine. It would plunge down into a trough and as it climbed up the other side, the waves would crash over it as far back as the bridge.

It went on for hours. Visibility dropped so much that the ships had to turn their station keeping lights on. It was a risk but the chances of a submarine spotting them in this was very slim indeed.

In the early hours, the skies finally cleared and as the sun crept over the horizon it was like someone had poured oil on the water. The waves dropped to a gentle rolling swell and they could breathe again.

25 - Graduation

Rain drenched them all the way across the Indian Ocean. The stiff wind shoved bands of cloud west as the fleet pressed on. Vian wanted to be in position by the 21st but the weather frustrated him. As they approached Sumatra from the south west, the weather conditions deteriorated again. The seas climbed and thick rain moved in. Visibility dropped to a few hundred yards and they were dependent on their search radars to see ahead.

Vian took them south in a wide orbit, waiting for the weather to clear. They did it two more times to no improvement but on the 24th they finally got a break in the weather. The rain cleared but there was barely a breath of wind, making launch conditions marginal.

Leaving the big ships behind, the carriers turned into the wind. The Captains called down for all the speed the engine rooms could muster.

Goodfellow kept the flight assignments the same as the last practice. This time, Callicoe was parked at the back of the deck and had to wait for everyone else to go before he got his turn. The air thundered as the aircraft started up. Ratings rushed around the deck, shining torches in the gloom of the rising dawn.

One by one, they launched. A Corsair or Avenger would start rolling, the tail would come up and they climbed away to join the growing armada. The last Avenger refused to start. Callicoe saw Birkenfield get down with a face like thunder as black smoke billowed out of his aircraft's cowling. There was a moments delay as it was wheeled back onto the forward lift and struck down to the hangar.

It was Callicoe's turn. He started his engine and choked on the thick smoke of the Koffmann starter cartridge. He locked his wings and did his final checks. The green torch did a circle and Callicoe ran up the engine, holding the brakes on. The airframe shuddered from the raw power of the Double Wasp as it turned that massive propeller. He let off the brakes rocketed down the deck.

Even at height it was still dark so he flicked his navigation lights on. Three flashes, pause, three flashes, pause, so his section would know where to go.

He spotted *Reliant's* Avengers, with their V ID letter on their tail and took up position above them. Callicoe was twitchy. With this many aircraft in the sky, there was a very strong chance of collision. He kept his eyes peeled as he maintained position above the Avengers, weaving left and right to keep pace with them. His section was flying top cover today, Barrett's section was up front, Goodfellow's was the close cover.

Goodfellow had given them a detailed briefing before take off. On *Illustrious* they'd had a model to refer to. Goodfellow had made do with a blackboard.

Palembang had been one of the key targets for the Japanese when they'd invaded Sumatra. In 1942, the Japanese army had swept in to take the oil refineries. Although retreating allied forces had tried to wreck the facilities during their headlong retreat, the Japanese had them working again by the end of the year. The Royal Dutch Shell refinery at Pladjoe was the largest facility in the Far East. To the east was Soengei Gerong, built by Standard Oil. Between them they produced more than three million tons of crude oil a year. Seventy five percent of the Japanese supply of aviation fuel came from them.

They climbed hard all the way. They had to get over the mountain range to reach Palembang on the north side of the island. For once, Callicoe had a chance to enjoy the scenery. The Barrisan Mountains had wisps of mist on the lower slopes. The jungle below was lush and green.

He smiled as he remembered an old recruiting slogan, 'Join the Navy and see the world'. As they cleared the tops they levelled off and headed direct for Palembang.

Callicoe's head was on a swivel as the Avengers increased speed. Now would be the time if he was a Jap. He'd dive out of the sun and come screaming in, guns blazing. He was well aware they were flying into a hornet's nest.

The jewel in the crown of the Japanese war machine, the Japanese had over one hundred aircraft around Palembang. There were more in Java and Singapore if they started shrieking for help. With this many aircraft in the air there was little point in being subtle anyway. The Japanese were bound to have them picked them up on radar on the way across.

Up ahead, the jungle gave way to a spider's web of roads that converged on the city of Palembang. On the horizon, the blue water of the Banka strait shone in the bright sun. The Musi river was a silvery line winding down to the coast. Their targets were on both sides of the river.

Callicoe was concerned that he couldn't see the Fireflies. They were supposed to be going in first with a bunch of Corsairs to strafe the three airfields around the city. If they arrived late, it could get very hot indeed.

The raid Commander sent the Avengers in. The tubby bombers shook into line astern to make their approach. The Japanese started putting up barrage balloons over the refineries and storage tanks. They weren't the big oblong gas bags they were familiar with. They looked like big weather balloons; silver globes suspended on a wire. It would make the Avengers job much more difficult. A cable could snick a wing off like a cheese cutter. Guns of all calibres sent up a barrage of flak as they made their runs. The raid Commander came on the air.

"Greyhounds, take care of those balloons." There was no response. "Greyhounds, take care of the balloons!"

Somebody had to lend a hand. He made a decision.

"Beagle Leader calling, my section, follow me in, we need to clear out these balloons."

He checked his safety was off and dived into the attack. The world tilted in front of him as he stood his Corsair on its wingtip and went swooping over the refineries. The balloons bobbed on their cables in the breeze as Callicoe lined up on them. He fired from way back in short bursts, using his rudder pedals to spray bullets at the balloons.

A balloon jerked on its cable, then collapsed like a souffle. Another deflated. A third drifted off, its cable cut by some shrapnel.

Callicoe pulled clear, his section hot on his heels.

"Christ, that was hairy," said Gabby as he glanced at a hole in his wingtip.

"Cut the chatter," Callicoe ordered, annoyed at the lapse of discipline. He came around in a wide orbit considering making another pass, but the Avengers were already coming in, weaving left and right to avoid balloon cables.

Bombs started spilling from their bays on the Pladjoe refinery below. Pipes fractured; buildings were toppled as the 500lb bombs detonated. Storage tanks were set ablaze and thick smoke billowed into the air.

The Avengers were briefed to head west but Callicoe had trouble picking them out. The smoke was making it difficult to see them. Now was the vulnerable time, when the bombers were strung out from their bombing runs.

He got some height, leading his section west to get out of the way of all the flak and smoke. More flak was exploding ahead and Callicoe raced to get there. He saw

Avengers at low level getting a good shellacking from some flak batteries. Fireflies buzzed around them, diving to fire on the guns before coming around for another pass.

The Avengers were hard pressed as Japanese fighters put in an appearance. Their timing was perfect as the Avengers had not yet reformed. Callicoe shoved the throttle through the gate and went for it, the bit between his teeth as he called his section in behind him.

They dived on five fighters that were harrying a group of Avengers trying to get back into formation. Their turret guns were firing back but it was a pitiful defence in the face of cannon armed Zero's. One Avenger wobbled as a Japanese fighter picked lumps out of his tail.

Callicoe closed on that one. Seeing two Corsairs over his shoulder, the Zero peeled off. Callicoe let him go and tightened his turn to come back in. Broadside on to two Zeroes, he banked hard and fired a high angle deflection shot. A mere moment and they were past him but he put a few rounds through the fuselage of one of them.

Tracer flashed over his head. Callicoe didn't wait to find out who it was. He broke off and climbed hard. His head sagged on his shoulders as he came over the top and rolled out. He came back in, engine roaring at full throttle.

Japanese fighters came in from two directions. An Avenger went down; one parachute appeared, then a second. Two Zeroes went down in flames, followed by a Corsair.

Flak continued to explode amongst the bombers. An avenger reared up as a shell went off under its wing, taking away the wingtip. It started to lag behind the rest. A Zero pounced on the cripple and Callicoe moved in to head it off. The Zero was so focused on its target it didn't see him get into position behind them.

Callicoe nudged the stick and opened fire. Six lines of

tracer reached out and slammed into the Zero. Bits flew off and it turned into a fireball, spinning away. It was hot work. He flung his Corsair around like a man possessed, chasing a Japanese fighter away, running around like a sheepdog protecting its flock.

The Section split up, there were too many Japanese fighters for them to stay together. They broke into pairs, hunting around the Avengers with other Corsairs and Hellcats.

Cook fell to a Zeroes guns. Farthingdale avenged him but then got into trouble himself, chased north by two Oscars. He called for help but no one could get there. On his own, he threw his Corsair around, dodging the cannon fire. He dived, letting the speed build up before bottoming out over the jungle and then hauling the stick back into his stomach. He grunted as the Corsair went up like a rocket. The nimble Oscars tried to stay with him but couldn't maintain the climb.

Farthingdale stamped on his rudder and rolled to come back down, chasing after them. They split off, one each going left and right. Farthingdale put the throttle through the gate and chased after the one to his left. The powerful Corsair ate up the distance and he started firing, sniping short bursts at the fighter as it jinked in front of him. He never saw the other Oscar slide in behind him. Too late, he realised his mistake as cannon shells thumped into the fuselage.

The Japanese fighter walked its fire into the cockpit and took Farthingdales head off. A thin trail of smoke came out of the cowling as the Corsair went into its final dive. It slammed into the jungle going full tilt.

More aircraft fell on the fight back to the coast. The Japanese pressed home their attacks, boring in close and paid the price. A line of little fires marked the route south. The strike didn't get off scot free. Two of *Reliant's* Avengers had gone down. One over the target, another on the egress west.

Callicoe had lost two, Cook and Farthingdale. Barrett lost one, Anson, one of the few regulars the squadron had. It had been an expensive day.

On the route home, Callicoe took up the rear guard position with a Section of Hellcats. They had their work cut out for them as the Japanese continued their pursuit. As time wore on, Callicoe had to be careful. Running around at full throttle had put a strain on the engine and ate up fuel and his ammo was running low. The last thing he wanted was to feel the thunk as the breech blocks closed on empty guns.

The aircraft landed on and the fleet withdrew to the south west. For the next two days they struggled to refuel. Rough seas interfered and it took longer than the Admiral liked. When it was complete, Vian had to face an unpalatable truth. All the time hanging around waiting for good weather had eaten into their fuel reserves. Even with resupply from the oilers, there wouldn't be enough left for a third strike as he had planned. The next raid would have to be enough.

Although the refuelling had taken longer than intended, the delays allowed the hangar crews to patch up the aircraft and get everything that could fly on the line. The squadrons losses were keenly felt. They had lost one or two over the last few months, but the strike on Palembang had been a sharp reminder that they were at war. The fighting had been vicious with no mercy and no quarter given. Out of necessity, Goodfellow folded the survivors of Callicoe's section into the other two.

After the replenishment, the fleet crept into position off the coast every night but the weather remained poor. Heavy rain, low cloud and high seas prevented the launch of another strike. The Admiral fretted. Every day's delay allowed the Japanese more time to strengthen their defences. Each morning the tannoy would announce a twenty four hour postponement and everyone knew they had another day to live.

The squadrons played hard in the Wardroom. Drinking to blot out the raid, remember the dead and enjoy themselves, perhaps for the last time. Gabby played Uckers for six hours straight, beating all comers. A CPO from the engine room was wheeled in to take him on. Even he fell after Gabby got two double sixes in a row and got all his pieces home.

While they waited for the weather to improve, Vian called a tactics conference and Goodfellow and the other CO's went over to *Indomitable*. It was an experience, bobbing around in a tiny boat to get over to the carrier.

The problems with the first raid were thrashed out. There were some very frank comments from the Avenger CO's who felt the escorts could have picked them up quicker after they dropped their bombs. *Zooming around like blue arsed flies,* was mentioned at one point.

The fighter CO's responded, protesting that a ten mile plus train of bombers was too much and the Avengers needed to reform quicker after the strike. Everyone agreed radio discipline had been atrocious. A good example was the Fireflies not being able to hear the raid commanders call to attack the barrage balloons.

The thick smoke after bombing had been identified as messing with the pull off the target. It was decided that the Avengers would rendezvous more to the south to also avoid the flak they'd had over the city. Other than that, there were few changes to the first plan.

The CO's returned to *Lancer* and laid down the law. Better radio procedure at all times. Neither Matthews or Goodfellow made a particular comment about close escort. Although Birkenfield hadn't been on the raid due to his engine problem, none of his crews had complained about the fighter cover so he wasn't going to labour the point.

The Fleet crept back to the Sumatran coast to get into launch position to find a thick belt of rain off the coast. Rain lashed the deck, turning it into an ice rink. Vian had to face a stark choice. There wasn't enough fuel to keep coming back. The Borrisan Mountains were visible in the distance, so he gambled and hoped the rain would pass. The launch was delayed while the Fleet hunted for a gap in the weather. The rain continued to fall but they found a patch where the visibility was slightly better. The order was given and the carriers turned into the wind.

Up on deck, Callicoe looked at the low clouds. Launch conditions were marginal at best. It would be a nightmare forming up once they were airborne. He was proven right when they circled the carriers. The low cloud base made it difficult for the numbers of aircraft in the air. Eventually they had to climb above the clag as they headed north for the mountains.

Goodfellow led his section as top cover with Callicoe on his port side, tucked in a little behind. Gabby was to Callicoe's left. It was almost a repeat of the first strike.

There were barrage balloons over the refineries but the Avengers went in regardless. They blasted a power house to bits and chucked bombs amongst the heavy equipment and storage tanks. The defences were more alert this time and the flak barrage was terrific. There were also fighters in the air over the city and from the get go, the fighting was fierce.

Palembang was too valuable for the Japanese to sit back and take it. The damage to the Standard Oil works had been severe. They couldn't allow it to happen to the Shell facilities as well.

The Corsairs and Hellcats were hard pressed to defend the Avengers as they cleared off the target. The Japanese were ferocious, pressing home their attacks with determination. Some didn't even break off when a

Corsair got on their tail and started firing. Goodfellow and Barrett both bagged a sitter like that. It descended into chaos as more enemy fighters came in.

Callicoe found himself on his own after breaking hard to port to avoid a two engined fighter that had reared up in front of him. By the time he cleared his tail, he couldn't see Goodfellow and he had no idea where Gabby was. Feeling vulnerable on his own, he dived for a group of Avengers being circled by some Oscars and a Japanese fighter that looked like an American Mustang.

He cut inside the turn and blasted it apart. It blew up and Callicoe flinched as he flew through the fireball. Something hit him underneath and he pulled up to get clear. The Oscars broke off, looking for easier game.

Callicoe flew alongside the Avengers, pulling up next to the leader of the group. Half his rudder was missing and there were holes in the fuselage. The pilot had his hood pulled back and gave him a wave. Callicoe waved back before getting some height to maintain position above them.

The Avengers were strung out over more than ten miles and the escorts struggled to cover them. The Fireflies did sterling service, working hard to keep the Japanese back.

Two Hellcats formed up on Callicoe's right as he shepherded this group of Avengers away. He needed their help as a group of six fighters came in from ahead. Callicoe shoved the throttle forwards and accelerated to get in front of the bombers. The Hellcats followed him. Callicoe licked his lips. Two to one was a tough proposition.

The Japanese fighters opened fire, gun flashes winking on the top of their cowlings and on their wings. Callicoe returned fire, his Corsair vibrating from the recoil. One round glanced off his canopy. Callicoe held his course and the Zero roared overhead. He came round hard to get on its tail but had to break away as a flash of red appeared in his rear view mirror. Tracer flickered around him and he felt the familiar tick as a round hit him. There was another bang as a bullet hit his seat armour.

Sweating, Callicoe barrel rolled to the right and then climbed hard. He did a full loop, giving the Corsair its head as it carried him up and over. Coming back down he saw two Oscars in front of him. He held the trigger down, spraying the air in front of him. One fighter shuddered under the weight of fire as hits sparkled on its fuselage. Petrol streamed out of a split tank. He saw the hood go back and the pilot had one leg over the side of the cockpit as he tried to bail out. Callicoe held his fire for a moment, giving him a chance to step out when the Oscar burst into flames. The pilot was wrapped in fire and fell out of the stricken aircraft. Callicoe craned his neck as he watched the body tumble end over end until they were out of his sight.

Climbing hard, he looked around. The Avengers below him were still there. So were the Hellcats. Two Japanese fighters were haring north. It looked like they were clear. More aircraft were ahead and the Avengers pushed to catch them up. The four bombers slotted in on the tail of the formation. Callicoe saw ID letters for *Reliant*, *Victorious* and *Illustrious* in the mix. When you were fighting for your life, it didn't really matter which carrier you were from.

As the Barrisan Mountains drew near, Callicoe could feel his engine starting to run rough. The temperature was nudging into the red and he fiddled the engine controls to eke every ounce of power out of it. If he could get over the mountains, it was all downhill from there.

In the briefing they had been told that if they were brought down over the island, they were supposed to head for Lake Ranau, east of their exit track. A Sea Otter amphibian would come in to pick up any aircrew that needed rescuing. Callicoe preferred to risk it. If he bailed out or tried a landing in some jungle clearing, he could get injured. If that happened, there'd be no hope of making the lake in time.

Once he made it over the mountains, he backed off on the throttle and traded height for speed to keep in the air. As he passed Enggano Island, he knew he wouldn't make it. The fighter simply had nothing left to give. He looked around and saw an Avenger in similar trouble and drifted over to them. It was the one he'd seen before with half his rudder missing.

They ditched together and Callicoe got out of the cockpit like a scalded cat. He inflated his Mae West and sculled backwards to watch his Corsair go down. She sank like a stone and Callicoe was a bit miffed, he'd hoped to see the damage before she went down. He swam over to the crew of the Avenger, bobbing in their dinghy.

"I say," Callicoe said, panting from the exertion. "Room for one more?" he asked in good humour. He was grateful when they pulled him on board. He lay on the bottom of the dinghy for a moment, his feet dangling over the side.

It felt like an age since they'd taken off but when he glanced at his watch, it wasn't even lunchtime. He saw the second hand wasn't moving and he gave his wrist a shake.

"Busted." He shrugged and lay back down, getting his breath back.

"Welcome aboard," said the pilot, a smiling sort with rosy red cheeks called Glennister. He tugged off his flying helmet. "Thanks for the escort."

They looked up as a Corsair circled round their position. Callicoe hauled himself to a sitting position and waved. The pilot waved back as he stood guard overhead. They saw another dinghy in the distance. Every time they topped a wave, they saw the splash of yellow on the water. They didn't bother trying to paddle towards it, it was too far away. They sat and slowly dried out under the beating sun while they waited to be picked up.

The Avenger crew were from *Reliant*. Callicoe hadn't known before because of the hole where the ID letter had been. They shot a line with each other, arguing the merits of their respective ship, the friendly rivalry buoying them along.

After half an hour, their escort reluctantly left them. They watched it go up into the clouds and disappear. Glennister's Observer noticed they were drifting closer towards the island. That got their attention. They took turns paddling over the side of the dinghy with their arms. It made little difference.

"Christ, I'd hate to end up in the bag," Glennister said. He took his revolver out of its holster and checked it was loaded. "Bloody Japs," he said with some venom. He looked at the island, seeing waves cresting over some offshore rocks.

Smoke appeared on the horizon to the south. Minutes dragged and Glennister kept looking from the island to the smoke, trying to judge time and distance. They didn't seem to be getting any closer but that was probably his imagination playing tricks on him.

Callicoe debated firing off a flare. He decided to wait until the ship got closer. If he fired one off now, he'd just be telling the Japs they were there. After another hour, they could see it was a destroyer coming up fast. It paused only long enough to pick up the occupants of the other dinghy and then dashed towards them. A mile out, they started waving their arms. Callicoe launched a flare. He got another one ready before an Aldis lamp flashed in their direction.

The destroyer didn't lower a boat. The scramble net went over the side and a rating climbed down halfway to help them up. Callicoe lay on the deck after helping hands pulled them over the side. A blanket was put over their shoulders by a tall Lieutenant and they sat at the stern while the doc looked them over.

"Nothing a good tot won't cure," he announced. "Come below when you chaps feel like it."

They watched the mountains recede in the distance as they steamed south.

26 – Down Under

It was three days before Callicoe got back to *Lancer*. He was put to work. *An officer was an officer, even if he was a pilot*, as *Whelp's* tall First Lieutenant had put it. He helped out on the bridge, keeping a lookout, supervising a party of ratings during a fire drill. Callicoe was happy to oblige. Anything that kept him above deck was most welcome. After the gentle roll of the carrier, *Whelp* pitched around even in a moderate swell. Callicoe had found it difficult keeping his lunch down when he was below decks.

They caught up to the fleet shortly before they got to Fremantle on the coast of Western Australia. *Whelp* lowered a boat and delivered Glennister and his crew to *HMS Reliant* first before coming up to *Lancer*. The big crane behind the island swung over the side and lowered a scrambling net. Callicoe grabbed it, shoved his arms through the ropes and was hauled up like a sack of grain. He was deposited on the deck where Gabby and the others were waiting for him. They'd formed a side party and Gabby gave him a salute, tongue clamped firmly between his teeth, his peaked cap back to front on his head.

"Welcome aboard, SIR!"

Callicoe saluted towards the bridge and then waited for the crane to come back up with his flying gear. *Whelp's* cox'n had tied a bag with his gear in to the scrambling net. He retrieved it and went below to the Wardroom.

Before he could get a drink, Goodfellow sent him to the doctor. Callicoe spent an hour getting prodded and poked in all the usual places. The doctor asked him to stand on one foot to test his balance.

"Didn't bang your noggin?" the Doctor asked him with his broad Scottish accent. Callicoe shook his head.

"It was like being at Brighton beach," he lied.

"You seem fine to me laddie." The Doctor put his stethoscope back into its case and signed a form. "Fit to fly," he said.

Callicoe was welcomed back into the fold. Goodfellow stood him a drink and Callicoe related his tale. The Intel officer had a chat with him later. He'd already been credited with his kill. Gabby had confirmed it, he just filled in the blanks about what happened next. Goodfellow read the report and added his endorsement. He flagged it for the Admirals attention for a mention.

Callicoe was brought up to date on the final tally. They'd lost one, jolly Jack Frost covering the Avengers on the way out. Chasing two Zeroes down low, he'd strayed over a flak battery and been blown to pieces. Wicklow had been shot up. He wasn't hurt but it had been touch and go to get his Corsair back to the carrier. The port undercarriage leg had folded when he touched down and he'd slithered into the barrier. His Corsair had been dragged clear and was down in the hangar on chocks, awaiting attention.

1783 had lost one pilot as well. Duncan was the only family man amongst the pilots. Twenty two and out, he left a wife and two children behind.

Birkenfield's Avengers had lost two themselves, but no criticism was made of the escort they'd had. Both of them had gone down on their bomb runs. One had collided with a balloon cable and gone straight in. The other had caught a flak burst in the bomb bay and gone off like a firecracker.

All told, *Lancer* had lost eleven aircraft and eight pilots since leaving Trincomalee. That was nearly twenty percent of the Air Group. In compensation, they'd wrecked the oil facilities and claimed nine kills, six probables and four damaged. It helped, but there were plenty of missing faces when they got to Fremantle.

Overall, Commodore Moore had mixed feelings about the two strikes. They had been their final chance to practice before heading into the Pacific. Operations would be far more intense once they were with the Americans. The recce photos taken by the Hellcats showed extensive damage but it was frustrating they'd lacked the fuel to launch a third strike. They'd accomplished their task; just. It would be months, if ever before the Japanese were producing fuel again.

The bag of enemy aircraft had been a big extra to compensate for their losses. Taking into account the over inflated claims that pilots always made, they'd destroyed over seventy aircraft, in the air and on the ground. That was fair compensation for the fifty aircraft they'd lost.

While some things had gone well, the biggest failure had been the refuelling. Once again, the Auxiliaries had been the weak link. The speed of fuel transfer wasn't fast enough and even when they did connect the hoses, they kept breaking. They had lost a day between strikes because of the resupply problems. When the Fleet got to Sydney, there'd be little time to make the necessary changes, it needed to work.

The other issue had been problems with the strikes themselves. Moore thought some of the difficulties had come from overly complex planning, almost as if Vian was trying to be too clever for his own good. Another problem had been the Ramrod attacks on the airfields. Attacking each one in turn had given the Japanese a chance to get their fighters in the air. Moore had argued that they should be hit simultaneously but had been over ruled. He took no pleasure in being right.

The stay at Fremantle was brief; just long enough to

take on fresh supplies before they pushed off. Callicoe took photographs of the fleet at rest

They saw up to date newspapers for the first time in weeks. There had been big advances in Burma, shoving the Japanese out of the Arakan. Eastern Fleet had covered an amphibious landing on Ramree Island. Back in Europe it looked they were rolling the Germans up.

It was a three thousand mile run to Sydney. They had seven days to spruce themselves up to make a show. Captain Austin had the crew over the side painting the hull.

The British Pacific Fleet swept into Sydney harbour with all the pomp it could muster. When the Klaxons sounded, the crews manned the rails and raised their hats, giving three cheers for the population of Sydney. The Air Groups had flown over the harbour in an endless procession of aircraft, a display of power.

Illustrious went into the massive drydock at Woollamalloo to sort out a shaft problem. *Lancer* went into the other graving dock next to her. All of the ships submitted lists of requirements.

After the air display, the squadron split up to different airfields. 1771 went to the air station at Nowra, a dusty little fly speck place eighty miles south of Sydney. The town shook to the sound of aero engines as they came in. Mechanics got to work overhauling the aircraft.

Nowra might have been basic, but there were simple pleasures to hand, like fresh milk and bread. After weeks of powdered milk and hard tack it was glorious. Replacement men and aircraft arrived to bring the squadrons back up to strength. Six new pilots walked into the hut the squadron was using as an informal Mess. Three were fresh from Canada, two had come from England. A sixth had come from Colombo on a cargo ship, missing the fleet by two days when they had sailed from Trincomalee. Goodfellow was grateful to have them and split them up between the three sections.

Callicoe felt uncomfortable with one of the new boys in his section, a regular who had seniority on him. Kendall had joined the Navy a month before the war had begun and spent the first three years on the convoy routes.

He'd had to fight tooth and nail to get flying training. He'd passed through *Pensacola* six months before Callicoe and Gabby. When he got back to England, he ended up at a test station that evaluated aircraft for the FAA. Kendall had been tearing his hair out. He'd wanted action. When he saw a notice in the Wardroom asking for volunteers for the Eastern Fleet, he'd jumped at the chance.

If it bothered him, Kendall didn't show it. Five foot eight, medium build with mouse brown hair, he was a handsome fellow. His hazel eyes crinkled in good humour when he heard a joke or told a funny flying story of which he had many. He gained Gabby's approval when he matched him drink for drink and offered to partner him in as many games of Uckers as he liked.

Callicoe's other new man was a Wavy Navy Sub Lieutenant called Christopher Guest. With his arrival, Wicklow was no longer the baby of the squadron. Guest looked even younger if that was humanly possible with platinum blonde hair and powder blue eyes. He swore like a trooper and smoked like a chimney but he looked like butter wouldn't melt.

They spent a few days to get the measure of each other. Callicoe took Kendall up for a mock dogfight to see what he was made of and wasn't disappointed. Kendall might not have seen actual combat yet, but he was a good pilot, deftly handling the Corsair.

He scared hell out of them when he showed off what he called his party piece. From a standing start, he shoved the throttle forward and rocketed down the runway.

Lifting the nose early, he'd held the Corsair down to gain speed and blasted across the field at nought feet. He snap rolled left and pulled the Corsair into a maximum rate turn, using the rudder to hold the nose level with the horizon. Callicoe's heart had been in his mouth as he watched the fighter skim over the ground, inches from piling in.

He'd torn a strip off Kendall a mile wide when he got back down.

"I don't want to write to your mother, telling her she had a bloody idiot as a son," Callicoe had raged. "I've seen some bloody stupid things in my time but that-" Words failed him. Barrett had interrupted him at that point and saved him from saying something he'd regret.

"Kendall, Skipper wants to see you," he'd said, putting his best Senior Pilot face on. Goodfellow tore another strip off him.

"What the hell were you thinking of?" Goodfellow had asked in a similar vein to Callicoe.

"Show that I'm ready, sir," Kendall said. He stared into the middle distance while he braced at attention in the middle of Goodfellow's office. "I just want to kill Japs, sir," he added.

Word got out about that, Killer Kendall, that's what they called him. Kendall couldn't care less. He'd been serious. His older brother had been killed on the *Repulse*. He wanted to balance the scales and kill a few Japs in recompense.

The squadron absorbed the new blood, folding them into their little family. It took all sorts to fight a a war.

The weather at Nowra was hot, but it was a different kind of heat to Ceylon. In the southern hemisphere, they were in the waning summer as time advanced towards autumn. Still hot by English standards, the air was much drier and that was a relief.

Eighty miles outside of Sydney, entertainment in the evening was sparse. The place was dairy country with lots of wide open spaces. The station had a football pitch and the squadrons resumed the inter Group league that had existed at Trincomalee. It wasn't taken too seriously. No one wanted to break a leg in a foolish tackle and get grounded.

There was a reasonable selection of films available and after weeks at sea, anything was new. Apart from the films they had the usual things to keep them occupied, Uckers, poker, three card brag, cribbage and a sing song around the piano.

The word came that it would be a while before the fleet put to sea so Goodfellow handed out leave passes by section. Callicoe's section went off first. Transport took them to the Warwick Racecourse in Sydney. Horse racing had been suspended for the duration and the place had been turned into a large transit camp with wooden huts. The canteen turned out good solid food and lots of it.

Callicoe dumped his gear and with Gabby, caught a train to town and then a bus to the docks. Half of the crew had been granted leave and *Lancer* felt empty. Civilian workers were aboard with a snag list a mile long.

Callicoe sorted through a few messages that were waiting for him. One was a bill for the Wardroom. He winced when he read it. Even allowing for Duty Free prices, that was a lot. He wrote a cheque and left it in the message slot.

The other message was a mystery. It had come from the Admiralty supply depot at Woolloomoolloo. He was required to report to office C8 in the admin block between 1000 and 1200 hours Monday to Friday. Perplexed, he'd checked with the hangar deck crew but no one knew anything about it. Making sure his uniform was clean and creased in the right places he'd ambled along to find out what was going on.

"I'll come with you," Gabby had offered.

"I appreciate it, but if I'm tasked with some duty on board ship, there's no point both of us losing our leave. I'll catch you later at one of those pubs, White told us about."

Callicoe got directions to the admin block. He went inside and roamed the corridors until he found C8. It was marked, Logistics Support. He knocked on the door and a female voice said, "come in."

The door opened on to a big office. There must have been upwards of twenty desks in there. A mixture of WRENS and Navy ratings sat shuffling papers and tapping away on typewriters. The windows afforded a splendid view of the harbour, the Sydney bridge and the city beyond. Two offices with frosted glass were to Callicoe's right. He was about to knock on one of the office doors when a WREN came over. She was strangely familiar and Callicoe was rooted to the spot as she walked toward him.

"You got my message then?" said Jane.

27 – Good Fortune

Callicoe blinked, not quite believing what he was seeing in front of him. His mouth didn't quite flap Guppy fashion but it wasn't far off. Jane cocked her head to the left and smiled, her cheek dimpling like he remembered.

"You *can* say something," she said as she took her glasses off.

"But-how?" he stammered.

She walked him towards the door and deposited him outside.

"Wait here. I'll be a minute."

She disappeared back into the office and reappeared with her tricorn hat.

"Come on, a quick walk round the block," she said briskly.

He fell into line and walked after her, still a little shocked. She squinted as she looked up at a vibrant sapphire blue sky without a cloud in sight. It was going to be another warm day.

"How on earth?"

"I've been here for weeks," she explained. "A bunch of us got posted before Christmas. I did write to tell you," she said, her voice a little subdued, he obviously hadn't got the letter. He nodded as it sunk in, she was here.

"I saw the fleet come in," she said.

"I think everyone must have seen us," he replied with a smile. It had looked like the whole city was on the streets when they'd flown overhead.

As soon as *Lancer* had docked Jane had drafted the signal requesting his presence. She'd had to be careful; she knew there wasn't much privacy on board which was why she had to make it so circumspect. She hadn't anticipated the Air Groups being so far from the city or that he'd be gone so long. It had been agony waiting for him to show up.

"I've missed you," she told him, meaning it.

He brightened at that. He looked round quickly before giving her hand a squeeze. He'd recovered from his initial shock now.

"When do you get off?"

"Five, but I can swing it. I've got an easy approach with the Lieutenant Commander."

Callicoe's eyebrow shot up.

"Have you now?" he asked in good humour.

He stood outside the admin block for a while afterwards, grinning like an idiot. He sailed out of the dockyard and found the street White had told them about. He found his section in the third pub along lining the bar, Gabby, Wicklow, Kendall, Guest and White. There had already been arguments in each pub when the staff refused to believe that Wicklow and Guest were old enough to drink.

"Madness," Gabby said while he caught Callicoe up with what had been going on. The pub was half full with sailors. The locals wouldn't start appearing until 4pm onwards when they knocked off for the day. With it being Friday, they always slid out a bit earlier to get a few drinks in before the pubs shut up at six. Callicoe delighted in the ice cold beer and ran a finger up the condensation on the side of the glass.

"Best bit about home," White said. "A nice ice cold beer after a hard days graft."

"Beer is better than women?" Gabby asked in mock outrage.

"Yeah, well, it's drinking time at the moment," White

assured him. "We'll get that out of the way, then we can explore the night time delights and see the lovelies."

Gabby perked up at that. Nowra had been a total bust as far as he was concerned. He was looking forward to meeting a few girls, having a dance and anything else he could get his hands on. Sydney was Whites home town. Gabby was expecting great things after having his head filled with images of long limbed women with big smiles and an accent.

They occupied a table and slumped in the seats; legs stretched out in front of them. A cool breeze was coming from an overhead fan and Callicoe closed his eyes, thinking about Jane. His reverie was interrupted when Gabby asked him the one question he didn't want to answer. He grunted.

"Waste of time. It was something about spares for the Corsairs. Nothing that can't wait," he said, hoping the lie would satisfy enquiring minds; it did.

They couldn't drink forever. For a start, beer was rationed. Second, if they kept going from pub to pub, they wouldn't be vertical by mid afternoon, let alone tonight. They went exploring for somewhere to eat.

Woolloomoolloo was a working class area around the docks, a bit rough and tumble but it was clean and tidy. The shops and pubs made decent money from all the sailors. When ratings went drinking, they preferred to remain within staggering distance of the main gate.

If you wanted something a bit more upmarket there were regular buses to other parts of the city. There used to be a tram line in Woolloomoolloo but it had been closed in 1935. White had been upset when that happened. He used to ride down to the docks with his Grandma to see the ships come in at Finger Wharf.

They found a small restaurant which had a good line in fresh fish from the harbour. They had it with chips and some fresh buttered bread. Callicoe licked his top lip after taking a long pull on an ice cold glass of milk.

They whiled away the afternoon with desultory conversation, making plans to see a show or go to the cinema. White had to see his parents at some point and decided to go tomorrow. His father would be home from the rail yard in the middle of the afternoon.

"Anyone want to come?" he asked, more to be social than expecting anyone to take him up on it, but Wicklow said he would.

Kendall craved seeing some sport. He'd enjoyed playing Rugby at University and was a reasonable spin bowler when he was in the mood. First class Cricket had stopped for the war but there must be some games being played somewhere. They asked around and found an army XI was playing a dockworkers XI on the Sunday so Kendall was sorted.

They rode a bus into town and pottered about the shops for an hour but soon got bored. Shopping wasn't their thing. As the clock ticked round to four, men began to emerge from offices and factories and yards, heading for the nearest pub. It was incredible. It was like the floodgates had opened and there was a press of bodies on the street. Men pushed past Gabby and Kendall without a word of apology, they were focused on getting to a pub as soon as they could.

"Don't let us get in anyones way," Wicklow muttered as he stepped back, watching men go back and forth.

Callicoe took the opportunity to disappear. He'd been wrestling for a while about how he was going to get back to the docks without attracting attention. Pleading a headache would have sounded ridiculous. When the crowds appeared, he just stepped back, took off his peaked cap and started walking.

He got back to the docks, flashed his pass at the sentry and then hot footed it to the admin block. She was waiting for him when he got there.

"Sorry, the crowds were pretty big."

"They do like their alcohol," she agreed. "It's called the six o'clock swill."

She led the way and they walked up to Hyde Park, a big area of green separating Woolloomooloo from the central business district. Callicoe didn't see any other uniforms around so they risked bumping shoulders. They settled on a bench under the shade of some big trees. Callicoe felt nervous, like he was meeting her again for the first time. He rubbed damp palms on his legs.

She hooked a finger under the epaulette on his left shoulder, her thumb lingering over the two wavy gold stripes.

"Lieutenant now," she observed with obvious warmth, pleased for him. She smiled as his chest puffed up slightly with pride.

"Yes. You don't outrank me anymore," he said with a grin, nudging her on the shoulder.

"No longer prejudicial to good order and discipline," she teased. She hitched closer to him and linked her arm through his.

"It's been a very long day, waiting for the clock to wind around to the finish, while you," she dug him in the ribs, "have been out having a good time."

"Hey, I'm on leave," he protested. "I earned it," he said joking, but it dampened her mood suddenly.

"Was it very bad?" she asked him, not wanting to hear him say yes. He lied and said it had been fine but she heard the brittle edge to his voice, the sudden tightening around his eyes.

It had been months of hell for Jane in Bombay. Being in supply, she only heard things second hand and even then the information wasn't always accurate. It had been hard, waiting for one of his letters to arrive, wondering if it would be the last one.

Kaylani had been her rock, her level head calming

Jane when her imagination got the better of her. It was no better when she transferred to Australia. The Sydney press had trumpeted the successes over Palembang and glossed over the casualty figures, merely mentioning losses. She'd been biting her nails until *Lancer* docked.

She'd felt foolish, chasing after him when she found out the fleet was going to move to Sydney. Her department had been preparing manifests for equipment to be transferred when they asked for volunteers to help with the build up. She'd put her hand in the air. She'd berated herself on the way over. She'd wanted to escape Australia and now she was willingly going back.

"How about, we go and see some sights, catch a movie?" he suggested.

"All right," she agreed, liking his enthusiasm. They went back to Woolloomooloo so she could get changed. The WRENs and WRANs were berthed in some boarding houses a few streets away. Callicoe arranged to meet her at the park, he wanted to go back to *Lancer* and get a shower.

He got back, cleaned up and was gone without bumping into Gabby or anyone else. Feeling refreshed, he saw her waiting for him in the park. She walked up and down, a vision in a mint green knee length dress. She was holding on to some white kidd gloves and a dark green clutch bag to stop her fidgeting, she was nervous.

She'd added some inches to her height with some heels and was taller than him. He made a joke of it, standing on tip toe to look into her eyes. He took his chance and kissed her.

"I've waited a long time for that," he said. She didn't reply with words, instead kissing him in return.

They walked slowly, Jane hanging off his arm while she pointed out a few places. Sydney wasn't that different to England he thought. The style of architecture was similar, it was just cleaner. London always seemed to have the weight of ages on every street corner, in every building. Sydney seemed fresh, more exciting somehow. Callicoe knew his present company had something to do with that.

They had a light supper. Neither of them were particularly hungry and they got tickets for the first cinema they came across. They weren't interested in the film either, only each other. In the dark, they let their hands do the talking. They were in good company, quite a few other couples were doing the same thing.

They emerged into the gloom of the gathering night and walked to the Royal Botanic Garden. It was shut but they didn't let that stop them, the fence was more for decoration than security anyway. Callicoe helped Jane over the low wall, holding her hand while she did her best to preserve her modesty.

Walking across the gardens to Farm Cove they followed the path round to the right, a rocky point that overlooked the entire harbour. They sat down on a bench. To their left was the big steel harbour bridge, to their right, the great span of the harbour with the fleet at anchor.

The evening breeze rustled the trees and Callicoe put his arm around her shoulders, pulling the girl in close. Jane didn't object, liking that he took the lead. They sat like that for a while, watching the ships on the water.

He told her little bits about life on a carrier, the funny things, avoiding the obvious tragedies. Talking about it made it more real, reminding him what he loved about flying and life at sea. It might have been scary at the time, but being on *Lancer* during the storm had given him a visceral thrill, that jolt that told you that you were still alive.

Her hand walked up his leg, feeling around something in his pocket.

"What's that?" she asked.

"This?" Callicoe shifted and pulled out his pipe, holding it up for her to see. Laughing, she took it and put it in his breast pocket.

"Old men smoke pipes," she teased.

"I am *not*, an old man," he insisted. He clamped it between his teeth and assumed a lofty air. "Calms the nerves. Provides a distraction when I need it."

She snorted in good humour.

"If you say so."

She put it back in his top pocket and patted it. He placed his hand over hers and she looked at him, a mischievous glint in her eye. She kissed him and and pushed him back onto the bench, her fingers undoing the buttons of his shirt.

She slid her hand inside and them stopped when she felt something metal. She pushed the folds of material aside and saw something glint in the night.

"What's this?"

"A little gold elephant someone sent me," he murmured, pulling her on top of him. "It brought me luck."

She kissed him hard, eyes squeezed shut.

He saw her home safely, remembered where it was and just managed to get the last bus out to Warwick racecourse. Gabby gave him what for when he got back.

"Where the hell have you been?"

"Out," he said breezily, twirling his cap on his finger.

"We spent an hour looking for you. Up and down we went. We thought someone had nabbed you."

"I'm a big boy." Callicoe blew him a kiss.

"Clearly."

Callicoe took off his shirt and stretched out on his bed. Gabby glared at him.

"I was worried."

"Sorry."

"Well then," he huffed, slightly mollified by the apology. "You gonna tell me about it?"

"Nope. I'm not ready to share yet."

"We're thinking of going to the beach tomorrow. Get some sea, some sun, go for a swim. You coming?"

"No."

"You're no fun anymore."

Callicoe laughed.

He spent the day with Jane, keeping her to himself. They were made welcome wherever they went, the uniform and the wings on his chest getting them a cheery greeting and good service. It was Saturday and Sydney was a bustling place. They went to George Street and Callicoe waited while Jane browsed in some shops.

They looked at the Queen Victoria Building. A grand Victorian shopping centre, it still had some interesting shops and the central arcade was still impressive, even if a lot of its features had been ripped out. Jane took him to Gowings at the junction of George Street and Market Street.

"Everyone goes to Gowings," she told him.

Built in 1868, it was a modest department store over several levels. It specialised particularly in gentleman's clothing and camping gear. She dragged him to the shirt department and had him try some on. He grumbled at the prices for a uniform shirt.

"Nonsense," she told him. "A good shirt says a lot. I want my man to be smart. He'll have it in tan," she told the sales assistant.

"I will not," he said. "White."

"Tan," she repeated. She'd seen the requisition order from Fleet headquarters. Admiral Fraser had decided that his men would all wear tan uniform like the Americans did but with British badges of rank. "Stop complaining," she chided, knowing she was right.

The sales assistant took some measurements. Callicoe was a good fit for off the peg.

"Just one adjustment on the sides, sir. We can pull that in for you."

Callicoe paid and was promised it would be ready in a hour. They lunched in the restaurant on the top floor while they waited. Jane sat close to him, her foot going up and down his leg under the table. She looked at him innocently as she ate her piece of cake.

They went back to the Botanic gardens in the afternoon and strolled round, hand in hand. A stall was selling apples and Callicoe bought a bag.

"This is something you miss on board ship," he said, crunching his way through an apple. "Fresh fruit. Bread. Milk. God, milk, did I tell you about the milk?"

He had, but she let him tell her the story again, happy to hear his voice. He told her about Nowra, the rolling countryside. He had a way with words, a lyrical turn of phrase that made a bleak little place sound like a paradise.

They passed the bench they'd sat on the previous night and burst out laughing. They sat down again while Callicoe polished off another apple. They watched two destroyers heading out.

Jane liked seeing the ships. In Bombay, she'd had a view of buildings while she shuffled paper. Seeing them like this made them more real. They became more than just names on bits of paper but living breathing ships filled with men.

She glanced at Callicoe as he looked at the harbour. He'd changed since she'd seen him last and she tried putting her finger on it. He'd lost weight but she expected that. His cheekbones were a little more prominent, his frame a little more gaunt.

In Bombay, he'd been nervous. He still was in some respects, but he seemed older somehow. She put it down to months of operations. Fighting for your life would affect anyone. He'd seen things no one should have to see and how many of his friends had died? She wondered. He didn't speak of it, but he also hadn't mentioned a few people that he'd written about in his letters. She could guess why.

They whiled away the hours in the gardens until closing time, sitting on the grass. She was content to do things at his pace. He liked having the room to take his time for a few days. Callicoe wasn't tired, but he was in no hurry either.

Fleet operations were like that, days spent getting into position, then a mad dash into the wind and then a strike. He'd tasted fear, that dry catch at the back of the throat when a landing approach was going bad or when he ditched on that strike off Palembang. That had been the worst, that moment, bobbing up and down on the water thinking the Japs would get their hands on him.

They had pie and mash down by the docks. She laughed as she wiped some gravy off his chin.

"What are we doing tomorrow?" she asked.

"Depends," he said round a mouthful of food. He wiped his hands on a small paper napkin. "My mob might be doing something. They talked about watching cricket at some place near here. Near some rail tracks? An army XI playing the dock workers?" he suggested, dredging his memory. "Do you want to go?" he asked.

He knew Cricket wasn't everyones cup of tea. It wasn't his either particularly but watching some sport made a change. It was a normal life, something he'd left behind when he joined the Navy. Jane nodded.

"I think I know the place," she said. "There's normally a game every other Sunday. It's not bad. Gets a good crowd."

They got back to her boarding house again.

"Here we are," she said.

The house was a big three floor terraced town house

in the middle of the street. Light peaked out behind curtains. They'd have been fined by the ARP's back home for breaching the blackout. It wasn't a bad place. It was clean and tidy. The landlady was less strict than the one she'd had in Bombay but there were still rules. Having male company in rooms was one of them.

He put his arms around her and she moulded herself to him. Her perfume filled his nostrils and Callicoe could feel the heat stoking up inside of him. She could feel it too and she bit her lip in anticipation.

"I could come up," he offered. She shook her head slightly.

"Rules," she whispered in his ear.

"Break them," he whispered back with a husky chuckle. He kissed her neck and she groaned in anticipation.

She must have been crazy for thinking it, but she gave in and led him up the three steps that took them to the front door. She fished out her key and put a finger to her lips.

"I'll be quiet," he promised. She laughed, a nervous lilting laugh. She made shushing motions with her hands.

"You'll get me thrown out," she said with a smile. He kissed her again.

"But it would be worth it." He nibbled on an ear.

"I must be mad," she breathed. She put her key in the door and winced as she heard it click it in the lock. She moved the slowly. The door opened on a hall eight feet wide and over twenty deep. The floor was tiled. The stairs were dead ahead on the right hand side. They were carpeted, Callicoe could see the brass rods on each step glinting in the gloom.

"Top floor, end door," she hissed.

Jane paused at the entrance and cocked her head, listening. The house was quiet but not asleep. She could hear a radio playing some music at a low volume. Light showed underneath a door at the back of the hall that led to the kitchen and a small parlour.

"Don't stop for anything," she told him. "Avoid the fourth step, it creaks. And stay to the right." Before he moved, she grabbed him by his shirt's lapels. "You better be worth it," she breathed and kissed him.

He crept down the hall like some cat burglar, hugging the right wall all the way. He planted his feet carefully, staying on his toes. He put one foot on the stairs and moved fast. As he neared the top of the flight, the stairs creaked and Jane slammed the front door closed to cover the noise.

Callicoe froze but she made shooing motions and he carried on. She walked down the hall, the heels of her shoes clicking on the tiles. The hall was bathed in light as the door to the parlour opened. Her landlady was backlit, a dark and shadowy figure.

"Oh, it's you my dear," she said. "I hope you've had a nice day."

"Good enough, Mrs Willis," Jane replied. "It's been a long day. Could I get a glass of milk before I go up?" she asked.

"Oh all right dear, come on through."

The landlady stepped back to let her through to the kitchen. Jane made a noise, opening a cupboard door, putting a cup on the counter top, getting a milk bottle from the cold store. More than enough noise to cover Callicoe going up the stairs. At least she hoped it was.

She found him sat on the floor outside her door, waiting. She opened the door and he went inside and sat on the end of the bed. She put the cup of milk on the small table and sat on the chair next to it. She pulled the curtain closed and struck a match, lighting two candles, one by the bed, the other on the table. The room was bathed in a dim warm glow.

Her bedroom was about twelve feet by ten. The single

bed was in one corner. There was a small fire in the chimney breast but it wasn't lit, not in this weather. The room was in the eaves of the house, so one side was angled with the slope of the roof. A double wardrobe was behind the door for her things. Two suitcases sat on top of it. Another one was shoved under the bed. A chest of drawers was next to the wardrobe. It doubled as a dresser, the top of it covered in bits and pieces. A basin and jug with water sat on the table so you could wash in the morning without leaving the room.

She took off her shoes, placing them neatly at the foot of the bed before sitting back down and rolling her stockings off. Callicoe watched silently, almost transfixed. She grinned as she took off her earrings and necklace and put them on the table. She reached behind and undid the buttons to her dress, sliding it off her shoulders. The dress spilled to the floor as she stood up, just in her slip.

Callicoe kicked into gear and stood up himself, undoing his own shirt. They met in the middle of the room, staring at each other.

His eyes were hungry for her, months of thought and feeling crystalising at that moment. She could see the need in him.

He backed up to the bed and lay down, pulling her with him. She got on top, her legs straddling either side of him, her arms either side of his head. She reached down, fumbling to undo his trouser belt. He lost patience and did it himself, hitching the trousers down.

"We've got to be quiet," she said. He nodded, his brain short circuiting as she lifted up slightly, rocking her hips back and forth.

Neither of them were virgins but it had been a while for both of them. It felt like being a teenager again, fumbling in the gloom, stopping when the bed creaked too much, giggling at the ludicrous situation. The first time was quick as they went over the cliff together. The moment came in a rush, a tightening of muscles, wrapping their arms around each other. Callicoe buried his face in her shoulder, Jane muffled her voice against the pillow as they both shuddered and tensed up. They held on to each other, hearts hammering, stroking, whispering to each other.

They waited for a bit and then went at it again, slower this time, keeping the fires stoked and burning on a low heat. Finally, with the candles guttering as they burned low, they took a break. Callicoe hitched over on the bed, his back pressed against the wall. Jane lay on her left side, facing him, her face silhouetted from the low light behind her.

She ran her hand up and down his chest and stomach, following the line of his muscles. Her nails traced a line from his navel up to his neck.

"How will you remember this?" she asked. She threw her head back theatrically and put the back of her hand to her forehead. "And when you think of me, be kind," she said, deepening her voice to try and sound like Marlene Dietrich.

Chuckling, Callicoe frowned as he thought about a suitable response. He ran his hand up her side, pausing at each rib before cupping her breast with his palm. She shivered under his touch, ticklish on her side.

"How about, her gossamer sheer panties dropped to the floor like the morning dew?"

Stifling a laugh, she lightly thumped him on his right arm.

"Idiot."

"I'm quoting poetry," he protested. She sat up and swivelled, putting her feet on the floor, her back to him.

"Really? Who?" she asked, looking at him over her shoulder.

"Shelley," he said a little too quickly.

"Liar." She crossed the bedroom to the table and drank some of the milk. He admired her stood there, her lithe frame limned in the last of the candle light, a sheen of sweat on her tanned skin.

"Byron then."

"You liar." She came back to the bed and she dove into his welcoming arms. "You know you're lying."

"Okay, I give up, I surrender."

He dozed lightly, exhausted from their lovemaking. She was draped over him, her legs intertwined with his. Her hair tickled his neck and shoulder. They whispered quietly to each other in the dark. The candles had gone out a while ago. Callicoe had no idea what time it was but he didn't want to leave. He was cosy here with Jane next to him. They stroked each other as he talked, their fingers making circles, lulling, soothing one another.

"You know what?" he said. She grunted a *what?* her brain half asleep. "We don't know much about each other."

"Wasn't that deliberate?" she said, coming alert like her face had been splashed with ice water.

"Maybe it was. But things have changed; for me anyway."

She shifted and levered herself up, leaning on her elbow. She looked down at him, her gaze searching, intense. His face was hidden, unreadable.

"Is that a declaration of love I hear?" she asked, her tone teasing. Callicoe avoided the question by pulling her on to him and kissing her, her breasts pressed against him. She sighed and came up for air.

"How did an Australian girl end up in the WRENS anyway?" he asked.

"Exile, escape?" she said, settling herself back into the crook of his arm. Maybe it was time to tell the story, she decided. She let the drawbridge down and opened a door that had been firmly closed for a long time.

"I told you I was from Kalgoorlie, but I never told you how or why I left. I got married," she said simply, watching for Callicoe's reaction. His eyes widened in surprise but he had the good sense to keep quiet. "Oh, he was dashing and exciting at the time. He'd found his gold and he was going home to England. He proposed and I accepted."

She made it sound simple but it was more complicated than that. It had been January 1940. She had been twenty years old and she thought she knew better.

She'd grown up in Kalgoorlie, a place miles from anywhere. A gold town for over fifty years, people came to dig in the outback on a single claim or work the mines, chasing that elusive buttery yellow metal. Fortunes were made and lost out in the red dirt of the outback.

Jane's family were well known in the town. Her father was a senior administrator at the big mine and they lived in one of the grander houses. They spent their summers in Perth. From a rough background, her father wanted better for his daughters. He got her an education and expected good things in return, a good match that brought with it connections and advancement. Jane had been horrified, seeing her whole life mapped out in front of her. Her younger sister embraced that life wholeheartedly. Her head had been stuffed with facts and history and then she was expected to knuckle down to a domestic life.

Jonathan Mandeville had swept her off her feet. He was that lethal mix of rough and tumble and English sophistication that took her breath away. With a veneer of sophistication herself, he had played to her vanity. He'd shown her his mine and the riches he'd accumulated and promised to treat her like a queen and she fell for it. With his mine played out, he took his spoils back home. They eloped, married in Perth and took a slow boat to England.

"I only really found out what he was like on the boat trip to England," she said with some bitterness. "He was charming enough when he wanted to be. I thought his hard manner was a show to get his men to work for him. Australians are stubborn you know," she told him. "Out in the wilds, you threaten, you cajole, bribe and drive men to bend them to your will. It's hard out there in scorching hot, flint dry air." Her voice grew distant with the memories.

Her father was like that. She'd seen him one day when she went to the mine. Dressed in his suit, he looked out of place amongst the navvy's in their work clothes, covered in dust and sweat. Her father swore worse than they did, bearing down on them to get back to work.

She rolled over and backed up against him. His arm circled her waist, holding her close.

"By the time I got to England I realised what a mistake I'd made." She squeezed her eyes shut, feeling the tears gathering. Her cheeks tingled with remembered pain. "There I was, thousands of miles from home, alone with a swine as a husband."

He kissed her shoulder and she blinked back to the present.

"Strange as it may sound, the war saved me," she said, her voice shuddering. "He thought it would all be over by the time we got back to England. When Churchill took over and talked about fighting them on the beaches, he took his money and fled to America like the mongrel he is."

"And you joined the WRENS," Callicoe finished for her. He was sure there was more story to tell but she'd said enough tonight. She nodded and pressed herself against him, taking strength from his presence.

"Popped my jewellery to get some money and used my maiden name to get in. I never dreamed I'd get posted to India. Well, I wasn't to start with. I did two years down at

Felixstowe, then I was in Durban and then Bombay."

Callicoe held her close, willing his feelings into her, wanting her to feel she wasn't alone anymore. A lot of what she said seemed to mirror his own experience, that feeling of being trapped. Were all children rebels to their parents he wondered? Would his own children be like that in the future?

Freedom was a very precarious thing. People were fighting and dying for it now, putting themselves in the firing line for an ideal. How many people worked in jobs their entire lives that they hated, yearning for something else? He realised he was in a more privileged position than most but even he'd swum in small narrow ponds until his own act of rebellion.

Her breathing was low and even and he realised she'd fallen asleep. Gritting his teeth, he extricated himself and shifted down the bed. He covered her with a sheet and got dressed. It wasn't easy in the dark and he stubbed his toe twice before pulling back the curtain to let some light in.

It provided just enough to see where the rest of his clothes were. He shrugged on his top, pulled his pants and trousers on and his socks. He wrote her a note on a scrap of paper and left it on the table before creeping out onto the landing. He took his time going down the stairs, carrying his shoes and cap in one hand. He strained his ears to hear the slightest noise.

He froze on the second landing. He could hear music playing somewhere. He looked down the stairwell but there was no light visible. Hugging the wall, his heart was thumping in his chest worse than it had in a dogfight. The music was coming from the parlour where Jane had said the landlady was. He wondered if it had been left on by accident or if someone was actually awake down there. There was no way of knowing.

It was six feet to the front door. There was a chain on but he had no idea if the door had been locked. He slid one foot in front of the other to get there. He breathed a sigh of relief when he saw a key in the lock. He turned it agonisingly slowly until it clicked open. Tongue clamped between his teeth, he inched the chain off and then opened the door. He slid through the smallest gap onto the street outside.

28 – Back And Forth

Callicoe had a small argument with the sentries at the gate before they let him in. They shone a torch in his face, scrutinising a Lieutenant of rumpled appearance that was trying to get into the docks at 3am.

"Do I look like a bloody saboteur?" he asked.

"Doesn't pay to be too careful," the sentry said. Callicoe noticed there'd been no, sir. He also noticed the thick Australian accent which explained it. "But I reckon you're okay," the man said at last, snapping off the torch. "Good night-sir."

Callicoe anticipated another argument at *Lancer's* gangway but the Marine recognised him. He shared a look with the other guard and shook his head as Callicoe went aboard. Officers. They'd been coming back all night in a steady trickle.

"Randy buggers," he muttered. And it was the officers that preached clean living when on leave, how typical.

It was warm below decks and Callicoe lay on his bed, thinking about Jane until sleep claimed him.

He smiled as he was gently shaken from side to side.

"Hey darling," he murmured. Then he remembered where he was and he opened one eye a crack. Gabby loomed over him holding a steaming mug of tea.

"You are alive after all," he observed. "You were sleeping like a dead man."

Callicoe yawned and got up, stripping off his uniform and fishing out some fresh clothes. He needed a shower and his face felt rough, maybe a shave as well.

"I'm not even going to ask," Gabby said, handing him a mug of tea. Callicoe took it gratefully.

"Good, because I'm not telling," Callicoe replied, rolling his neck. He was a strange mix of physically groggy and mentally awake. He glanced at his watch and figured he'd had about three hours sleep, no wonder he felt rubbish.

Once he'd breakfasted and had a shower, he felt vaguely human. He read a newspaper in the Wardroom over another cup of tea while he waited for the rest of his Section to assemble. Wicklow had gone with White, leaving himself, Gabby, Kendall and Guest to amuse themselves for the rest of the day.

"The Four Musketeers," Guest said in good humour, "ready to do battle."

"Are we still on for cricket?" Callicoe asked.

"Gosh, yes," said Guest with youthful enthusiasm. He'd been looking forward to seeing a good game.

"Just gotta pick up the girls first," Kendall reminded him. Callicoe arched an eyebrow in query.

"You haven't hung around," Callicoe observed.

"Neither have you," Gabby accused. "Shagging last night, were we?"

Callicoe sniffed and folded the newspaper.

"A gentleman never tells," he said in lofty tones. He swatted Gabby over the head with the newspaper. "As it happens, I did meet someone."

Gabby snapped his fingers.

"Ha, I knew it!"

"You'll see her at the cricket," he told them, pleased there would be some female company around. He'd had visions of Jane being surrounded by his section licking their lips like lions in the arena.

While he'd been out with Jane, the others had gone to the beach and had a lazy day on white sands at Bondi Beach. Gabby had equated the place to a hunting ground and him the mighty hunter. Being a Saturday, the place was jammed and they'd almost been spoilt for choice.

Gabby and Kendall had met sisters while they were queueing for ice cream. Gabby's patter and easy manner had the desired effect and they were invited to join the girls on their spot where they'd laid out some towels on the sand.

Guest had met his girl entirely by accident. They'd been bowled over by a big wave and ended up spluttering and coughing as they got back to safer ground. He'd given her a hand back to her family and been prevailed upon to stay and share a sandwich.

When they found out he was a pilot he almost became royalty. Her father worked in the graving yard where *Illustrious* was and fired questions at him all afternoon, how fast the planes went, how many Japs he'd shot down, what it was like landing on a carrier? Guest answered as best he could, fudging a few answers. When he mentioned the cricket game, the father announced they were already going and he was cordially invited to accompany them.

After they got back from the beach, they'd showered to get rid of the sand and gone to a dance. They'd missed the last bus or train to the racecourse and trailed back to *Lancer* in the wee small hours.

They had a leisurely morning and organised a few bits and pieces to take to the cricket. They borrowed some blankets to sit on and picked up some bottles of drink on the way to the ground.

Kendall and Gabby disappeared around eleven to meet the sisters. Kendall half expected to be stood up but the girls were there waiting for them. They got the tram to the cricket ground. Guest went with Callicoe.

They met Jane round the corner from the boarding house. Her face lit up when she saw him and she gave him a wave.

"Darling," she said, kissing his cheek. She'd worn flat shoes today so she was the same height as him. She wore a patterned blue dress and a wide brimmed straw hat and some sunglasses. It was going to be a warm day sat watching cricket. She carried a string bag with some sandwiches wrapped in greaseproof paper.

Callicoe made the introductions and Jane looked at Guest and felt like mothering him. He looked about fifteen and was all gangling limbs and chubby boyish cheeks. The cigarette hanging from his lips looked strangely out of place.

They walked to the cricket ground, following the crowd. Guest kept an eye out for Agnes and her family. She spotted him first and waved to get his attention.

They weren't hard to spot. Two bright white navy uniforms and peaked caps stood out amongst the press of people walking to the ground.

"Boss, this is Agnes Richards and her family. Her father, Paul, her mother, Norma and sister, Pauline."

"Good to meet you fella," the older man said, crushing Callicoe's hand in a vice like grip.

Agnes was a mousy blonde with a pretty smile. She wore a bright red dress and a straw hat similar to Jane's.

They went into the ground and Mister Richards got his usual spot, midway round the ground on a little rise about ten yards back from the boundary. Blankets were laid. Agnes got a flask and some sandwiches out. Her mother produced a book and started reading. Callicoe wouldn't have been surprised if it was the bible.

"You sit by me, lad," Mister Richards told Guest.

Callicoe set up with Jane a short distance away.

"We don't want to interfere with young love," Callicoe said with a grin. Jane playfully slapped his arm.

"I think it's sweet."

They sat together welded from the shoulder down.

"Was, er, anything said this morning?" he asked. Jane

shook her head.

"No. I suppose we'll know for sure if my suitcase is in the hall when I get back," she laughed. "Oh, by the way," she reached into her bag and gave him his pipe. "Exhibit for the prosecution," she said, handing it to him.

Callicoe blushed and shoved it into his top pocket.

"I wondered where that was."

It wasn't a bad game. The army had obviously got themselves a few County players in the mix or a few talented types from school. They put up a respectable score off an iffy wicket that favoured spinners. They put another fifty on after lunch before they declared to put the dock workers in. The dockers struggled manfully, lost their leading lights early and rallied with the middle order. The army switched to a fast bowler and took the last two wickets for ten runs, winning by twenty eight.

Kendall and Gabby never did appear, they only came across them on their way out of the ground. There were more introductions and then everyone went their separate ways. They had three hours to get back to Warwick before transport was taking them back to Nowra.

Callicoe dropped Jane back at her digs. There were no suitcases in the hall so that was one question answered. She gave him his new shirt he'd left behind.

"Write?" she demanded.

He nodded, not trusting his voice and kissed her.

He was quiet on the drive back to Nowra. The truck ate up the miles while they talked amongst themselves. A good time had been had by all although Callicoe thought Guest looked a bit haunted. He didn't imagine the lad had as much time alone with Agnes as he would have liked.

Gabby and Kendall were exchanging notes on the two sisters. White handed round a bottle of home brew cider his father had given him before he left. Wicklow extolled the virtues of family living in Australia. White's family had been very welcoming to a stranger turning up out of nowhere.

"We're very pleased to meet one of, Stan's friends," his mother had said in the hall. The house was a narrow two up, two down terrace in the suburbs of Sydney. Wicklow had been given a camp bed in the box room where White was sleeping. Since he'd left home, White's younger brother had graduated to the bigger bedroom at the back of the house and wasn't giving it up for anyone. White didn't care, they were only sleeping in the room anyway.

They caught up on the news when they got back to Nowra. One of the new replacements had been killed already. Norman had tried a daredevil take off like Kendall and pulled a tight turn just that bit too far, stalling in from twenty feet. The Corsair had crumpled around him, killing him outright. Goodfellow was fuming. A Corsair had been written off and a pilot lost for no good reason. He'd had the squadron in a hangar and read all of them the riot act this time. There was to be no stunting, no Flat Hatting.

"If I catch even a whiff of someone doing it, they won't be flying again," he told them, meaning it. He had Kendall and Callicoe in his office.

"I blame you for this," Goodfellow said, his voice hard. He'd had two days to build up a head of steam before Kendall got back. "Stunting around like this is some kind of game." He came round from his desk and stood behind Kendall, his chin jutted forward, his face taut.

"Line shooters and idiots, I can do without. Flying off carriers is dangerous enough as it is without this to think about. Hang that one on your conscience." Kendall flinched but had the good sense to keep his mouth shut. Goodfellow sat back down and bowed his head for a moment.

"But I have to bear some responsibility as well by not grounding you immediately. You're dismissed," he said, his rage barely controlled. Nothing more was said, but the threat was clear, Kendall was on thin ice.

Callicoe unpacked and hung up his new shirt. He hoped Jane was right about that. Sandwiches were laid on in the Wardroom for them and he ate late, reading a newspaper and enjoying a glass of cold milk.

Gabby sank next to him with a subdued Kendall in tow. Gabby saw what he was drinking and wrinkled his nose.

"You and your milk," he said in disapproval. Callicoe spoke round a mouthful of food.

"If you had to donate blood," he said, "they wouldn't be able to use it, one hundred percent proof."

Knowing the reason for Kendall's mood, they rounded up a fourth and roped him into a game of Uckers. They kept the conversation light, focusing on women, sea and sand. Callicoe was sorry he'd missed the beach, it sounded like somewhere to take Jane the next time they got to Sydney.

Barretts section went on leave and left in a truck in the morning after Divisions. Goodfellow had Callicoe's section up the following morning, partly because he thought they needed the practice, partly to get Kendall out of his sight.

Callicoe took them on a long cross country and swapped everyone around. After Palembang he'd thought a lot about the final stretch when he was on his own.

"The sky is a big place," he told them over the R/T. "A minute or two at full throttle and you can be miles from help, all on your own. What if I get shot down? Who takes over?"

He had Gabby lead for a while, then Wicklow, then Guest and the others. When they got back to Nowra,

Callicoe flew a carrier landing pattern. He wanted to give Guest and Kendall as much practise as possible for how they did things. After they landed, he went to see Goodfellow and asked permission to practise deck landings the following day.

Goodfellow had no problem with that. All of the new boys needed the practise and everyone needed to do a few of them to keep their hand in.

In the morning he had his two sections together.

"I have an announcement to make. What I have to say is the result of considerable reflection. I've watched how we've operated as a squadron the last few months. Sometimes it takes operations to highlight things that need attention."

"So, from this point forward, I have an expectation that our flying will be the best in the Air Group. Our radio discipline will be the best in the Air group. Our landing record will be the best in the Air Group."

There was an uneasy shift amongst the pilots. The CO's demeanour did not radiate his usual charm. He was serious, deadly serious about some things that were not entirely under their control.

"I want you to look back on this time with a great deal of pride, and we'll achieve that with hard work and application. We'll break for an early lunch and then this afternoon, we'll start with practice deck landings like Lieutenant Callicoe suggested." Heads turned in Callicoe's direction and he flushed under the scrutiny.

"Oh, thanks a bunch," he thought in his own head.

"The runways marked out and a batsman will help you down. Off you go."

That was the way of things for the rest of the week. Goodfellow had them practise launches, squadron attacks, dogfights, landings, extended navigation exercises.

The Corsairs with the big white T on the tail became a regular sight over Nowra. As much as it pained him to reign in a subordinate who was doing things for the right reasons, Oates was forced to curtail the frequency of the flying. There was only so much fuel allocated for training and Goodfellow had consumed a lion's share in a short space of time.

"I just want the men ready, sir," Goodfellow had protested.

"I don't doubt it," said Oates. "But go easy. We're going to be here for a while yet. No need to maintain such intensity at the moment."

Stung at the rebuke, Goodfellow had them in the classroom instead. He had them go over the technical aspects of the Corsair and carrier operations in general. He tested their aircraft recognition and then the same for ships. He knew they could spot a carrier, anyone could, but the Japanese had a lot of destroyer and cruiser types. They needed to be prepared.

Even when Barrett got back with his section, they didn't get a breather. Goodfellow sent his section for a break to Sydney, but he didn't go himself.

Callicoe got a letter from Jane. He wasn't the only one. Guest got four letters from Agnes; each one dated a day apart. Kendall received a letter from the sister he was seeing and waved it under Gabby's nose in delight.

Once Goodfellow's section got back, the CO worked the entire squadron hard for three days in a series of exercises. He finished off with a six mile march. Trucks dropped the men off outside town with a canteen and a compass.

"If you get shot down, it'll be jungle you have to wade through. You might be injured." He gestured to the green countryside. "This is a doddle. See you later," he said.

Callicoe kept his section together and they started walking. Unused to covering such distances, they stopped in a grove of Acacia trees until the sun was past its zenith. Sheltering in the shade they dozed and talked.

"You gonna see, Agnes when we get to Sydney tomorrow?" Kendall asked Guest.

The young lad shook his head.

"I don't think so," he said with little enthusiasm.

He'd been quite excited when the first letter arrived. His ardour had begun to cool when the second one came. Agnes was nice enough but she'd devoted two whole pages in one letter to how she brushed her hair. By the fourth letter, there was a strident note asking why he'd only replied once. Maybe if he didn't write back, she'd get the message.

29 – Logistics And Damn Lies

Admiral Fraser wasn't stupid. The arrival of the fleet had caused a stir, but the sudden descent of thousands of men could also bring with it certain complications. There could even be some resentment in the local population. A demonstration of what they could do would do wonders for confidence and tolerance.

The flyover of the Air Groups had been a good start. A gunnery exercise that people could see and hear sealed the deal.

Some of the bigger ships went out and participated in a shoot a mile offshore. A hulk had been towed out to sea and the cruisers and battleships had blasted it to pieces. It made an impressive show and the papers had been full of it the following day, emphasising the firepower of battleships like *Howe* and *Jellicoe*.

For the last two years, the people of Sydney and other parts of Australia had been at risk of attack. The Japanese had even managed to sneak a submarine into the harbour in 1942.

The arrival of the Fleet told Australia that the boot was now firmly on the other foot.

The attacks on Palembang had barely rated a mention back in England. The Australian press had trumpeted the success with big headlines and photographs. More headlines would need to follow to maintain that confidence. They needed to get into the action and soon.

While the ships were brought to a peak of operational efficiency, the problem for the planning staff at fleet headquarters was the Fleet Train. Admiral King, the god of Naval Operations in Washington had decreed that the British Pacific Fleet had to be self sufficient in terms of supply for provisions, ammunition and equipment. The one concession they had been able to get concerned access to the American bulk fuel supplies. They would be allowed to use it, provided they put in what they took out.

Due to the shortfalls in the Fleet Train, they'd been compelled to advance plan operations assuming that the resources to support the fleet would be available. Moore hated the duplicity. He'd actually met Admiral Nimitz and admired him immensely.

Despite the official line, Moore knew that Nimitz was keen to have British ships alongside his. Extra carriers were a valuable resource not to be sniffed at. The Admiral had given the nod to his commanders in the field to lend them what assistance they could but that goodwill would only stretch so far.

The lynchpin in this whole affair was Admiral Fisher. He'd had to scour the globe and find the ships to support the operational effort. When he'd started looking at the operating requirements himself last year, Moore doubted if it could be done. Somehow, Fisher had achieved the impossible and brought it all together. They were still short of ships in every category, but they had enough to get started. The Fleet Train was a masterpiece of British improvisation. Compared to the Americans, they were the poor cousins in the Pacific and they knew it, but they would make it work; they had to.

The final piece of the puzzle was selecting the location of an advanced supply base. Sydney was over three thousand miles from the action. They needed to have somewhere close to the combat zone where the fleet could withdraw, refuel and resupply and then get back into the action again. The Manus Islands were selected as the intermediate stop. Leyte and Ulithi atoll would be the forward stations.

The Fleet Train would run constantly from Sydney to these forward bases and then from there, meet the ships to resupply them. The small escort carriers would roam this area to provide security, giving the Air Groups on the fleet carriers a rest from having to fly CAP duties. The escort carriers would also be used to ferry replacement aircraft around although the presence of *Minerva* and *Unicorn* as mobile workshops was a huge boon. Moore knew the Americans eyed the maintenance carriers with thinly disguised envy, having nothing similar in their own inventory.

The Americans were gearing up for the next stage of their advance across the Pacific. Okinawa would be next and the British Pacific Fleet expected to be a part of it.

30 – Sydney Blues

Oblivious to what was coming, Callicoe was glad to be heading back to Sydney, he needed the break. He'd sent Jane a letter he was coming so it wouldn't be a surprise when he showed up, but he doubted she'd be able to get any leave. Besides, even if she could, he wanted to plan it a little better so they could actually do something. They couldn't sneak around like last time. They'd get caught sooner or later and that would cause her all sorts of problems.

The first thing they did when they got to Sydney was go down to the docks for a look. *Lancer* had been moved into the harbour. *Unicorn* and *Minerva* had returned from their cruise. They'd picked the depots clean of everything they could lay their hands on. Between them they'd brought back over one hundred aircraft; spares, tools and engines. For now, that was it until more equipment arrived from the UK.

The atmosphere on board *Lancer* was upbeat. A few mechanical niggles had been put right and everywhere smelled of fresh paint. Worn out equipment had been replaced and the ship was at her peak, she was ready.

Callicoe had a look in the hangar. Wicklows wrecked Corsair had been swapped for a new one from Minervas stocks. Two others were being worked on by the mechanics. For the moment, they were the only aircraft on board.

He walked over to the nets on the port side at the back of the flight deck where Gilliard and the other batsmen worked. The gallery at the side of the deck had been extended and the dock workers had been busy. Ten extra 20mm cannons had been added. Eight more had been fitted to starboard, effectively doubling the carriers short range AA defence.

"Do you think they know something we don't?" Gabby asked when Callicoe mentioned it later in the Wardroom.

He'd gone up to the bridge and chatted with the officers on duty. Callicoe looked out of place in his whites, they were all wearing new tan uniforms like those he'd worn when he was training in America. Jane had been right after all.

He dodged down to the ships stores and found three sets of uniform waiting for him. He'd take them to Gowings in town to be tailored and have his rank braid and wings sown on.

The other addition on board was a party of American liaison staff. As they would be working closely with the Americans, someone had decided it would be a good idea to have some of them on board to smooth out the differences. Somehow space had been made for them amongst the ship's myriad compartments.

Callicoe found the new additions in the Wardroom, Gabby was treating them to a retelling of the Palembang strike while they topped his glass up. American ships were dry so the officers were taking advantage of the facilities while they could. Aware they needed to foster an air of cooperation; they'd made themselves universally popular when they brought two ice cream machines with them. Considering *Lancer* lacked open hangars and air conditioning systems, the availability of ice cream went a long way to making things more tolerable.

They settled themselves down with a drink in the Wardroom and made plans for their leave. Wicklow had a noodle with the piano and was pleasantly surprised to find that it had been repaired. Two broken strings had been replaced and a civilian had been hustled aboard to retune it.

The blokes were all for the beach and Callicoe agreed to join them. A soak and a swim sounded just the ticket to relax. They split up. Wicklow went with White, Guest tagged along with Gabby and Kendall.

Callicoe changed into the new uniform, glad he'd bought the shirt now. He dropped the other shirts off at Gowing's and went down two floors. He bought a pair of swimming trunks and some metal rimmed sunglasses. He caught a bus to meet up with Gabby and the others and passed a pleasant hour in a pub with high ceilings and low prices not far from the Queen Victoria Building.

He left them to it when they pushed off to see their girls. With time to kill, he went back to Gowings and settled in the restaurant with a cup of tea and some scones. There was no clotted cream, but the jam was excellent. After four, he collected his shirts and went back to the docks, waiting outside the admin blocks.

He was reminded of that day in Bombay when he'd waited in the Jeep to see her. There was that sense of anticipation. He felt the same thrill when he saw her come out the door, deep in conversation with another WREN. Tucking the brown paper parcel under his left arm he pushed off from the wall where he'd been waiting in the shade and walked towards them.

The other girl, a first officer saw him coming and slowed her pace to throw him a crisp salute. Jane was about to do the same until she recognised him.

"You rotter," she said. "This is him," she whispered to her friend. The girl gave him a fast up and down appraisal. A ghost of a smile passed her lips and she put her hand on Jane's arm before leaving them in peace.

"Lieutenant," she said. Callicoe watched her walk off.

"Eyes front," Jane ordered. He grinned. "Nice shirt," she commented.

"Yes. Spot on, someone told me they were the new fashion."

She gave him a knowing smile and they walked to the dock gates.

"I imagine you're all quite busy at the moment?"

"Rather," Jane nodded. "Something bigs brewing that's for sure."

"They don't move us thousands of miles for nothing."

They had dinner at a hotel. The place was full but the maitre'd shoehorned a small table into a corner. Callicoe broke his usual rule and told her about Norman's crash. Jane was subdued, imagining it was him in the Corsair instead.

"What was he like?"

"Oh, a nice enough lad. I didn't really talk to him. He was only with us a few days."

"Then why-"

"Because I'm worried about Greg. The skipper as good as accused him of killing the lad." His face wrinkled in disapproval. "I didn't like that."

"Didn't he?" Jane said quietly. "It seems to me he set the example for others to follow."

Callicoe fiddled with the stem of his wine glass.

"We're all adults. I'm not blaming anyone else for things I do wrong. I don't think Goody can speak for the dead that's all."

Kendall had been subdued all week at Nowra and that bothered Callicoe. A pilot needed to have confidence and Kendall's had taken a massive dent.

"A telling off would have been sufficient. He could have had me do it as Section Leader."

"I'm sure he had his reasons," Jane said. She didn't like hearing about this, hearing him work himself up.

They rode the tram to Hyde Park and then walked amongst all the green. Both of them liked it there. Callicoe had missed plants and trees on the carrier. As much as the wide expanse of the oceans was awe inspiring, just hearing the wind through the trees was relaxing. Jane liked the parks because she was an outback girl. There wasn't much green in Kalgoorlie. That had been another hook for her to go to England with her new husband.

They walked back to Woolloomoollo, her arm linked through his. That wasn't strictly proper for two officers but Callicoe couldn't care less. He was a reservist, this wasn't his career, they'd hardly throw him in the brig.

Jane told him not to come to her boarding house.

"Jim, there can't be a repeat of last time."

"She didn't throw you out," he said, teasing. He held her hands, stroking her knuckles with his thumbs.

"No, but I'm sure she suspected something. She made a devil of a fuss that the front door was unlocked and the chain was off."

"I'll figure something out," he assured her. They kissed goodnight. He stood watching her walk into the distance before catching the train back to Warwick Racecourse.

Kendall and Gabby were deep in conversation in the hut when Callicoe came in. They sprang apart like startled cats.

"You're back," Kendall said, stating the obvious. Callicoe tossed his cap on his bed.

"Good night?" he asked. Gabby coughed.

"Not bad. Want a nightcap?" he said, changing the subject. Callicoe caught the look pass between Gabby and Kendall as he turned for the door. He figured they'd tell him when they were ready.

Thursday morning, he rang a few hotels to book a room. Two weren't interested in a single night booking midweek but the third said they had a room available. Callicoe made the reservation. Once that was taken care of the whole section went to Bondi beach.

With it being a weekday, they practically had the place

to themselves. The only other people in view were other sailors from the various ships that were in harbour. Callicoe made a fuss of keeping his towel free of sand.

"I hate getting sandy," he complained, which was the wrong thing to say. Gabby and Kendall grabbed a leg each and ran, dragging him across the beach to the water. Callicoe struggled and kicked but it made no difference. He stalked back to the towel dripping and plonked himself down.

"As my old nan used to say, if you don't like something, try, try again," Gabby beamed while Callicoe flicked at the sand between his toes.

They caught some sun, horsed around in the water and splashed around like kids. For a few hours, the war seemed very far away.

She met him at the park out of uniform wearing the same dress she had worn last week. The only difference this time was that she had a hat to go with it. He picked up her suitcase and asked if she was ready. She nodded.

"I am. I'm a little curious what you've got in mind."

"We're not going far," he told her. "If we had more time then maybe we could plan something more elaborate."

It was close to six when they walked into the lobby of the Percival Hotel. On the far side of the business district, it was a two storey corner building in the italianate style with a brick exterior and tin clad roof. It had been a pub and boarding house for years, but after the Great War, a new owner had spent money to take it more upmarket. It retained the large open space downstairs but turned into a restaurant for patrons and dining room for guests. The rooms had been refurbished and the whole place had a facelift. Just as the work was completed, the great crash wiped out any chance of making it a going concern. It had languished for years before a new owner had made something of the place.

The lobby was bright and breezy. The walls were adorned with photos of Sydney throughout its development. Jane hung off Callicoe's arm as he strode up to the reception desk.

"I made a reservation earlier by telephone?" he said, hamming up his accent. "I'm joining a new ship in the morning and my wife's come down to see me orf."

The receptionist hardly gave them a second glance. There had been a number of officers staying here lately. He span the register round and leaned back for a room key. Callicoe wrote their names and for address put *HMS Lancer* after he saw other people had done the same.

The receptionist gave them the room key and pointed the way to the lift. "Dinner service stops at nine," he said as they walked off.

The corridor leading to their room had a mustard carpet, white oak panelling halfway up the wall. Silk print wallpaper was on the upper half.

On the west side of the hotel, their window still caught the light of the setting sun. There was a double bed, a dresser, a chest of drawers and a single wardrobe. It was a bit on the snug side but adequate. The decor from the hall carried on into the room, with the same mustard carpet and wood panelling. The curtains were a dark red heavy fabric. He pulled the net curtains to give them some privacy.

Alone, he gathered her into his arms and kissed her. She sighed, resting her forehead on his.

"I've come to see you orf have I?" she asked with a smile, mocking the posh accent he'd put on. Callicoe shrugged.

"Yeah, well. I lied a bit."

"A bit?"

"Just a little white one." He put her suitcase on the bed and undid the clasps. Jane stopped him opening the lid.

"Not for you," she said. "Us girls have to keep our magic secret.

He shrugged and sat on the bed bouncing up and down, rocking back and forth.

"Nary a creak or a rattle," he announced. "It'll do."

Jane blushed.

"I'm hungry," he announced.

"Do you want to eat downstairs or shall we have room service?" she asked over her shoulder as she put a few things in the drawers.

He hitched up the bed and stretched out, hands behind his head while he looked at the ceiling.

"Hungry for you. But as to dinner; downstairs? We may as well have a slap up meal. I'll be having rations and god knows what on board ship soon enough."

Dinner was good. The service was prompt, the food was hot and hearty, rather than stunning. With the war in its sixth year, rationing had curtailed certain luxuries and the Police had cracked a few black market rings recently. Callicoe held his meat up on a fork.

"It's a bit of a stretch describing this as a cutlet," he said, his tone pitying. "More like a morsel."

"There is a war on," Jane chided, using the common refrain with a smile.

"Gosh, really?" replied Callicoe. He cleared his plate and attacked the sponge and custard like a starving man. He finished Jane's as well after she declared she was full.

Rather than retire to the bar for a few drinks, they went out. Callicoe felt like a dance, at the worst, a movie. As long as he was close to Jane he didn't really care.

With the fleet in, the nightlife in the city had ramped up. Dance halls had opened their doors and there were signs advertising events every night of the week. Gabby had nattered non stop about how good the Trocadero on George Street was but the place was jammed. People were packed in cheek to jowl which was no good at all.

Another dance hall a block away caught Callicoe's eye. They had a live band playing and there was a good atmosphere so they went in there. Seats and tables were arrayed around the outside. The band played at the end on a stage.

Wasting no time, they hit the floor, moving around, close together. She trod on his feet, he trod on hers.

"I'm hopeless," he said.

"I'm not much better," she agreed. They kept at it, moving slowly to their own rhythm.

Callicoe was nudged on his shoulder. He was just about to tell them to get lost when he saw who it was.

"I thought it was you," said Gabby.

"I thought you were all for the Torcadero?" Callicoe said.

"Too busy," Gabby said, shimmying back and forth with a girl, his arm around her waist. "Evelyn, meet my boss," he said with a cheeky grin.

Callicoe introduced Jane. Gabby thought she was knockout.

"So this is your mystery WREN."

"Mystery woman?" Jane asked.

"You're his best kept secret, luv," Gabby said with a wink as they danced close together.

"Am I now?" she said sagely, her mouth quirked in a lopsided smile. Callicoe shot daggers at his friend.

The band took a break and they retired from the field, sitting around a table. The girls went to freshen up. As soon as they were out of earshot, Callicoe leaned forward and dropped his voice.

"What are you playing at?" he hissed.

"Laying the groundwork," Gabby shot back. "If I play my cards right," he said, his voice trailing off. Callicoe laughed.

The girls came back. Jane crossed her arms and leaned on Callicoe's shoulders.

"Have we all made up now?" she asked with a grin.

They danced for an hour or so but the place began to fill up. The dancefloor became a crush, the heat in the hall increased and they knocked it on the head.

They went outside. Gabby and his girl were all for moving on to another place but Jane and Callicoe bowed out. They had other things on their mind.

They enjoyed the walk back to the hotel after the heat in the hall. Callicoe lit his pipe and blew clouds of sweet smelling smoke to the heavens It was the last of his tobacco from England. He'd been saving it for a special occasion, this seemed to qualify.

When they got back to the hotel, she had thought to change into something silky but when it came to it, her nerve failed her. She was suddenly shy and she asked Callicoe to turn the light off before she got into bed. He obliged without asking why.

Her feelings were a swirling maelstrom. They barely knew each other, but she knew she needed him now. A warning voice sounded at the back of her head that this was what she did last time but he wasn't Jonathan. He wasn't even remotely like him and could never be.

She was taking another leap of faith but did it anyway. She knew all the preparations that were being made behind the scenes for the Fleet. He'd made no promises to her. She may never see him again, but she had tonight.

Callicoe could see the emotion in her that bubbled beneath the surface and could feel the conflict within himself as well. He'd been straining to be his own man for so long, he'd never stopped to think about what he was doing to himself. He'd gone from one goal to the next with blinkers on, to join up, to go solo, to get his wings, to land on a carrier, to get operational. Now he was a Section Leader with responsibilities, not just to himself but the others too. He hadn't left any space for him.

In Bombay, Jane had been a distraction at first, but it had grown into something else in the intervening months. He'd let himself be swept along, the compacting of time intensifying their snatched moments, amplifying their importance. He'd crossed over a line at some point. He couldn't quite put his finger on when it had occurred. Perhaps it was when she'd told him her story. Perhaps it was before then.

As they lay in bed with his arm around her waist, he talked to her, really talked. She'd shared her story, it only seemed fair he shared his. He told her about his mother and Joan and his father and brother and Ariadne; all of it. The *'whole rotten mess'* as he described it. It was like a confessional in church.

Jane listened, sifting the words, making the connections, hearing pieces clicking into place. Many things made sense to her now, the way he held himself in check, his reserve. Kaylani had suggested Callicoe was shy but that wasn't it she realised.

As she had been trapped by her own upbringing, so had he. People made light of the notion of keeping a stiff upper lip, not making a fuss or an overt show of emotion even if you wanted to. Callicoe was the living embodiment of it almost. There would be no angry outbursts from him like there had been with Jonathan.

She knew he cared. The way he'd talked about his man Kendall, the concern he'd expressed had shown her the kind of man he was. No, he was nothing like her husband. Jonathan would have been like this Commander Goodfellow she thought. He'd have torn a strip off Kendall with relish and rubbed it in for good measure, that had been his way.

She rolled over and faced him. In the dark, she couldn't see his face. She reached out a hand and gently stroked his cheek.

"Darling, when you get back-"

He put a finger to her lips and felt her damp cheeks.

"Shhh," he soothed. "I'm coming back, Jane. I've just found you, I'm not losing you now."

She buried her face against his chest as sobs took her. She'd never felt so alone as she did then. During dinner he'd raised his glass and said, "to us and the future."

He'd said it almost as a throwaway, like he was stuck for something to say. She had found the words a little ominous. With him about to go to war, it sounded like he was tempting fate.

God, keep him safe, she prayed.

31 – Taffy 57

It took them two weeks to get in position to join the Americans at the Ulithi Atoll anchorage. They'd left Nowra on the 7th March and flown over Sydney, a great procession of aircraft. It was a display of strength, a show and a thank you for the reception they'd had from the Australians. Callicoe knew at least one person would be watching, willing them to come back safe.

As they went north, Vian took the opportunity to exercise the carriers. Nothing too strenuous, just enough for them to get their sea legs back. For Callicoe, seeing the Great Barrier Reef from the air had been worth the trip in itself. Then they went through the Coral Sea to New Guinea and into the Bismarck Sea to reach the Manus Islands.

The stop was a brief one and Callicoe was grateful for that. The place was a furnace. The sun beat down making metal too hot to touch. Deck crew had to put a towel down to stop themselves getting burnt when working on the aircraft. The armoured deck radiated heat throughout the ship. Even in the squadron office which had portholes and a mild breeze off the water, it was over 100 degrees. Below decks, men wilted, stripped to the waist, sweat streaming down their bodies as they worked ship.

With over seventeen hundred men on board, the ship's evaporator plants were overwhelmed, unable to produce fresh water fast enough for showers and cold drinks. The ice cream machines worked overtime. The men swam to cool off as often as their duties allowed. They splashed and shouted like kids. There was something to be said for taking a dip at the end of a long tiring day.

They refuelled, took on some stores and went after three days. No one was sorry to go, the anchorage was hell on earth. Callicoe was sorry for whoever was stationed there.

Ulithi was even more bleak. A huge atoll it was barely above sea level, a massive ring of rock and coral twenty miles across. Its one saving grace was a strong fresh breeze that blew in night and day regardless. The place was jammed with ships, American and British. Callicoe shuddered at the chaos if a Japanese sub managed to penetrate the anchorage. The Germans had done it at Scapa Flow, sinking the *Royal Oak*. The booms were heavily patrolled and destroyers and sloops roamed off shore on constant alert.

The crew started muttering about Kamikaze. They'd heard about them on newsreels, but at Ulithi the word was muttered in hushed whispers, like some kind of bogey man. In February the US Fifth Fleet had been roughed up by Kamikaze's at Iwo Jima. An escort carrier had been sunk, another damaged. A number of support ships were hit as well. *USS Saratoga* had been severely damaged in an aerial attack.

Only the week before, the Japanese had staged a long range Kamikaze attack on the Ulithi anchorage itself. The Essex class carrier *USS Randolph* had been damaged and her flight deck put out of action. She had remained at Ulithi to be repaired; a very real reminder of the threat suicide attacks posed.

While the losses were unfortunate, it provided Admiral Nimitz the leverage he needed to make use of the English carriers. His five task forces had been reduced to four, leaving him short for the advance on Okinawa. Washington could hardly object to the British carriers being used as a flexible reserve in those circumstances.

It didn't sound very glamorous, but Fraser seized the opportunity. While the fleet had been sailing to Ulithi, they'd only had Nimitz' assurance that a use would be found for them. Recent events had shown they needed every carrier they could lay their hands on. Conspiring together like two old women, Fraser and Nimitz agreed that the British carriers would operate in support of the Fifth Fleet off their left flank. The Japanese had airfields at the three islands Sakishima Gunto and Formosa. They would need to be neutralised while the main attack went in. There wouldn't be much glory, but there would be action.

Once the fleet got under way, they were told their destination. Oates had the whole Air Group in the hangar, not just the pilots, but the gunners and observers as well. Standing on a ladder the mechanics used to get to the engines, he laid it out for them.

"Our little jabs at Sumatra last year were mere footnotes in history, practise. You've been wanting action, now we're going to get it. Okinawa isn't even three hundred miles from the Japanese mainland. If the Americans take Okinawa, then bombers can range at will all over Japan, bomb them to oblivion. The Nips are going to fight tooth and nail to defend it with ships, planes, subs, you name it."

"On the left flank is Formosa and the three islands of the Sakishima Gunto group, Miyako, Ishigaki and Iriomote."

"They've got airfields there chock full of aircraft and AA guns. Our task will be to keep them busy and keep their attention focused on us. It's going to be hot work gentleman." That raised a laugh. Even with the lifts down, it was stifling in the hangar. They could do without any more heat.

"No doubt you'll hear radio calls referring to Task Force 57, or Taffy 57 in the vernacular of our American friends." He dabbed himself in the chest with a thumb. "Task Force 57, that's us. *Illustrious*, *Indefatigable*, *Victorious* and *Indomitable* are 57.1. *Lancer*, *Reliant* and *Minerva* will be operating as 57.2. So, remember, anyone landing on another carrier by accident will have me to answer to."

The hangar echoed to another laugh. The Wardroom was a lively place that evening. Most of it was for show. No man wanted to reveal his nerves in front of his friends. This was finally it, everything they'd been working towards.

All of this was fabulous material for the latest addition to the crew. Throughout the run north, he had roamed over the ship, talking to ratings, engineers and pilots. He spent hours asking questions. If you were having a conversation about something, he would be hovering in the background, his eyes gleaming behind his wire rim glasses while he wrote copious amounts of notes.

When Charles Cullen had arrived in Sydney, he'd been afraid that he was too late but he'd got there just in time. Two days before the BPF had set sail, he'd presented his credentials and the letter of introduction from the Admiralty.

As the Fleet was going into the Pacific and taking the war to the Japanese, they were keen that the people at home got to hear about it. Some of the carriers already had Pathe news crews aboard, Cullen was a late addition.

Cullen had seen more action than most. Since the beginning of the war, he'd sniffed out human interest, going wherever the front line was. He'd covered the war in France following a Blenheim squadron. He'd been in North Africa watching the Army and the RAF struggle to contain Rommel. After that he'd returned to England to see the bomber war, striking deep against the Nazi war machine.

Cullen couldn't get copy from the the war in the

Atlantic. It was a grim unrelenting grind; the cruel sea was as much a villain as the U-Boats. He hadn't been allowed to go on a convoy run to Russia or Malta. He was reduced to spending time with some MTB's on the south coast. He fell in love with the pint pot boats, riding with junior officers who dashed around like it was some game. They were like seaborne cavalry, dashing across the Channel to hunt for enemy shipping at night.

He learned that ships were personalities just as much as people were. *Hood*, *Ark Royal* and *Illustrious* had achieved an almost mythic status during the war. Cullen wanted to produce a legend of his own, weaving a story about a ship and her crew.

He was given his pick and Cullen chose *HMS Lancer*. He didn't choose her by accident. He was experienced enough to know that any reporter worth his salt did their research beforehand. He'd done a lot of that during his journey east. He'd asked questions in Bombay. In Ceylon he'd spent two days at Eastern Fleet Headquarters to find out a few things. Junior staff officers had a tendency to talk about senior officers no longer able to answer for themselves. He got enough material to write a book.

Admiral Vian was the dashing commander of *HMS Cossack* fame. Cullen wasn't interested in him, not wanting to add to the legend. He was intrigued by minor characters who made everything possible. He wanted to put a human face on things, to bring the reader along with him and get them involved.

There was one other man who was well satisfied. On *HMS Reliant*, Commodore Moore toasted the Admiral for acceding to his suggestion. Before leaving Ulithi, Admiral Rawlings and Admiral Vian had held a conference to go over what lay ahead of them.

To ensure as much coverage as possible on the left flank, Moore had proposed spreading the Task Force wider, three groups centred around two carriers apiece. Rawlings said no. The benefits were obvious but the Fleet lacked sufficient escorts for three groups. In addition, he'd been hearing cautionary tales from the Americans about skies full of Kamikazes. Moore countered by suggesting two groups, the main group under Vian's command, with *Reliant* and *Lancer* on the far left under his.

"I'm sure it will work, sir. The ships have worked together for a while, we know how each other thinks and the Air Groups are well matched."

"I'm not so sure," Vian said. "You could be very exposed on the left."

"We're already exposed, sir. If you think two carriers aren't enough, let me have *Minerva* as a spare deck. She can also replenish our losses without having to call on the escort carriers for support."

"It'll make the Japanese think twice. When we attack from two different directions, they'll think there are far more of us than there actually are. We can also position to mask our operations, taking turns to mount strikes and spread the load."

Vian couldn't argue with that. When he'd first been told what their role would be, he had always feared that operating as a single Task Force would make their point of threat very one dimensional. Every day they would creep in and fly off a strike. The Japanese would know roughly where they were to mount counter strikes. With the Sakishima Islands north and Formosa to the west, they were almost boxed in on two sides. Putting carriers to the west would give them better radar coverage and spread the risk.

Moore got his way.

Callicoe was turfed out of bed at 0300 hours. He didn't need rousing; he was already awake. He'd snatched a few hours of sleep but the sense of anticipation had woken him up not long after midnight. He'd tossed and turned in the muggy heat, trying not to think about what was waiting for them.

So far, their strikes had almost been a cake walk. Apart from the last two raids on Palembang, the Imperial Japanese Air Force had barely put in an appearance. Callicoe wasn't worried about the Japanese fighters too much. They were so lightly armoured; they literally flew apart if you even sniffed at them. Desperation made men fight hard.

Callicoe was sure RAF pilots had fought tooth and nail over England's skies during the Battle of Britain. He was sure the Japanese would be the same defending their homeland.

The ship closed up to action stations at 0500 as the fleet crept closer to the islands. They were in Kamikaze country. The guns were cleared and the sky was scanned for anything remotely suspicious. Pickets of destroyers and cruisers ranged ahead to extend the radar coverage.

Callicoe perked up after a cup of tea and got himself a seat at the back of the Wardroom so he could lean back against the wall.

Oates was disgustingly energetic as he swept into the room. He looked at the tired faces in front of him and gave them a beaming smile as he balanced a map board on a table and leaned over the top of it.

"The Fleet is moving in until we reach a point, one hundred miles south of Miyako Jima, here." He circled the area with a pointer.

"First launch will be from 0600 hours. Fighters will be going in for a sweep over Ishigaki and Miyako Jima. The task is to clear the way for the bombers. *Reliant's* Seafires will fly CAP and cover the strikes coming back in. We're picking up the slack and covering the Avengers."

"If you have to ditch, there will be submarines out

there to pick you up. We have to make the Japanese keep their heads down and keep on doing it."

He started going through the timings and squadron assignments, rattling it off fast. Twelve Corsairs would go in on the sweep; the rest would escort the Avengers. When the sweep got back, they would be on fast turnaround, made ready for the next strike.

They would be going in on Ishigaki.

The centre of the three islands in the Sakishima group, it looked roughly like a pan with a handle sticking out, heading roughly north west. It had three airfields. Hegina and Miyara were satellite fields. The main strip was Ishigaki on the south end of the island. None of them would be a pushover. Recce photos showed pens for aircraft, hangars and they were bristling with AA guns.

As Oates went through the details it was clear that the tempo of operations would be on a bigger scale than anything they had done before. It would be hard work from first light until dusk when the carriers would withdraw for the night. The hangar crews would be pushed hard. They'd have to service the aircraft all day and at night make good any damage and get them ready for the next day's work.

Goodfellow and Matthews had agreed that they would rotate those on the early starts to give people a chance to get some rest. This operation was going to be a long slog, they had to pace themselves.

After all the build up, the first strike was a bit of an anticlimax. The Corsairs went rushing in, guns blazing and ranged up and down the airfields. There was little of interest. When he got down low, Callicoe saw that they were either dummies or aircraft so damaged, they were up on blocks of wood to act as decoys.

The second strike of Avengers provoked little interest either. They flew over the airfields and dropped their bombs practically unmolested. The Japanese woke up for the third strike of the day. No aircraft rose to meet them, but the AA gunners had been stung into action and the sky was laced with explosions and big glowing balls of tracer.

One Avenger went in over the target, another one from *Reliant* had to ditch on the way back. They were picked up by the submarine on rescue duty. Birkenfield wrecked a third Avenger after getting back to *Lancer*. A flak burst close aboard had peppered his legs with shrapnel and damaged the undercarriage. Coming in with only one leg down, he did a beautiful job of keeping the wings level until the last moment. The Avenger didn't even end up in the barrier. He got out under his own steam and hopped over to the island before he let the medics get their hands on him.

The CAP had been busy too. Throughout the day, radar picked up aircraft coming in from altitude trying to find the fleet. They were vectored to intercept but made no contact. It was expensive. Three Seafires had crashed on landing, highlighting how delicate they were for carrier operations even in calm conditions.

The fleet withdrew at dusk. It was a bright moonlit night. There was a very real possibility that long range Japanese bombers could stage a night raid if they caught the fleet at sea. They stayed at alert for most of the night. They had to rotate the gun crews and give the men a chance to rest otherwise they'd never last through another full day.

Callicoe got little sleep either, still keyed up from the days efforts. He knew something was coming. The Japanese wouldn't sit back and do nothing for long, but he also knew they rarely let themselves be drawn into rash action. They moved when they were ready and not a moment before.

They were roused again at 0330. Action stations was sounded and Lancer was closed up by 0500. The aircraft were brought up from the hangar and spotted on the deck, ready for the first strike. It was more of the same, jabs at the airfields and other facilities while the AA guns fired back.

There was little discernible return for the effort expended. Runways hit the previous day had the holes filled in and only dummies and wrecks littered the fields. Two more Avengers fell to flak and Matthews lost a Corsair on the early morning sweep. Coming in at thirty feet, three lines of tracer had converged and blown the cockpit apart. The fighter had gone in at full speed, careening through a line of decoys.

They claimed thirty aircraft destroyed. That was lowered to ten once the intelligence types had picked over the gun cameras and the Hellcat recce photos.

The Firefly's had more success attacking a barracks north of Ishigaki airfield. Their rockets turned it into a smoking ruin for no loss.

Reliant's Seafires outdid themselves after the previous day's effort. The last one aboard bounced hard, missed the wires entirely and went over the crash barriers straight into the deck park. It was carnage. The pilot was killed as well as three deck handlers. More importantly, three valuable Seafires and one Avenger were written off. Replacements were flown off from *Minerva* to make up the losses.

Callicoe picked at his food that evening. All the cook house had produced was soup and sandwiches. The ship had been closed up all day so despite steaming at speed, the decks hadn't been ventilated. It was hot and stuffy until cool air began to penetrate below decks. There was no sing song in the Wardroom, no one had the energy. All Callicoe wanted to do was have a shower and crawl into bed.

A third day of fun was cancelled after a typhoon warning came through from Guam. The Admiral decided to withdraw early for fleet replenishment. The American assault on Okinawa was scheduled to start on 1st April and he wanted the fleet back in position to support them when everything kicked off. They went south east to rendezvous with the Fleet Train.

Once they were clear of the combat zone, the Air Groups got a rest. As soon as contact was made with the auxiliaries, the escort carriers took over the CAP duties. Replacement aircraft were flown over to get them back up to strength and two Avenger crews and a new Corsair pilot for 1783 came aboard.

While there was no flying, the pilots were busy as all hands turned to getting supplies on board or servicing the aircraft. It took three days to replenish the carriers before they turned around and headed back in.

They had the routine down cold when they went back in. Up early, briefing and then sit in the aircraft ready to go. Callicoe wasn't the only one to nod off until startup time.

They went over, caused mayhem and gave Johnny Jap a bloody nose and got nothing in return. No aircraft came up to meet them. It was distinctly unsatisfying, particularly when they continued to lose one or two aircraft a time to flak and accidents. The fact they could have lost just as many to training didn't matter. They were expending blood sweat and tears and the Japanese were not obliging their efforts.

At dawn on the 1st April, battleships, cruisers, assault craft and aircraft plastered Okinawa while four divisions were put ashore. On the western coast, the XXIV Corps and III Amphibious Corps went ashore at Hagushi. The

10th army swept up from the south, capturing airfields at Kadena and Yomitan in hours. In the face of light opposition, the Americans pushed north towards the Motobu Peninsula.

"Bloody feather merchants," Gabby complained in the dark of their cabin that night. "I was promised action."

"Stop moaning," Callicoe shot back. Maybe the Japanese were played out and had nothing left to fight with. "If this is as bad as it gets, I'll take it. They can chuck the towel in and we can all go home."

He was to be sorely disappointed. No sooner had the early morning fighter sweep headed north, than the radar pickets picked up a mass of aircraft coming in from the west.

Klaxon's sounded as the signal FLASH RED went around the fleet. Gun crews trained their weapons in the right direction. Callicoe sat up in his cockpit, coming alert. *Lancer* increased speed, her engines going flat out. The CAP shot off, vectored towards the raid while both carriers launched more aircraft.

Callicoe was waved forward and he went through his routines with practised ease. He unfolded his wings, locked them and shuffled forward. There was no time to wait for the niceties. Callicoe got a green and he was off, engine screaming at full power as his Corsair clawed for height.

32 – Divine Wind

The CAP were the first fighters to intercept the incoming raid. Seafires from *Reliant* and Hellcats from *Indomitable* went barrelling into the approaching intruders. They dived from ten thousand feet out of the sun. Three Zeroes fell on the first pass. Two others were damaged but pressed on. As soon as they were engaged the aircraft split up, spreading themselves far and wide gunning for the ships. The CAP couldn't stop them all.

Callicoe was up to six thousand feet, Gabby was on his left wing but they were on their own. There'd been no time to form up the section before heading off to intercept the raid. They listened to the frantic radio calls as they spotted them coming in. A clump of Zeroes were diving hard with some Seafires haring after them. The Japanese fighters dodged left and right as lines of tracer filled the air around them. One Zero staggered under the hammer blow of 20mm shells and came apart, shedding its wings as it turned into a flaming comet.

Callicoe spotted four or five Zeroes below him and rolled into the attack. He lined up on the last man in the line, a Zero in bare metal and sprayed with random green lines. He opened fire at three hundred yards. The Zero went straight down, a dead hand at the stick. The remaining aircraft scattered. Callicoe went left, Gabby following close behind.

Ships started firing, lacing the sky with a blizzard of shells, everything from 5" down. Some Zeroes dropped to wave top height to get in close. One gaudy Zero with a red nose and a white tail went the length of *Lancer's* deck, spraying bullets as it went. He veered right, hugging the waves. While the gunners focused on it, two Zeroes rolled on their backs and came down vertically from four thousand feet.

Spotters picked them up late. Captain Austin ordered the helm hard over and gritted his teeth. The carrier heeled to the left as she turned to starboard. In the terminal phase of its dive, one Zero tried to adjust its path but the controls were stiff. It hit the sea just off the port bow. A huge plume of water shot into the air as its bomb went off and soaked the crew on deck.

The other one was nailed by the flak as it started its dive. The port wing was wreathed in flame and it began to spin, getting faster and faster as its dive steepened. It went into the water short of *HMS Hawke*.

The fighters followed the raiders into the barrage, flinching as flak went off around them. They grimly held on, desperate to chop the Zeroes down before they could hit the ships. It was brave but it was reckless. The AA gunners on the ships weren't interested in aircraft recognition at a time like this. A diving aircraft was an enemy and they fired on anything within range. Two Seafires and a Corsair were chopped from the sky before they could get out of harm's way.

HMS Lamian turned hard to avoid the attentions of a Zero that came in above. Aiming for the funnel, the Zero hit just astern of the bridge. It went through two decks before the bomb slung underneath exploded deep in her heart. The explosion blew out the side of the ship, rupturing the bulkhead between the boiler room and the engine compartment. The sea rushed in and she began to list immediately.

Two more Kamikaze were stopped short of the carriers before the remaining aircraft broke off. The fighters chased them as they headed west, back the way they had come.

HMS Laurent came alongside her stricken sister and lowered boats to get her crew out of the water. As she settled, the destroyer broke her back. The stern and bow pointed vertically before slipping below the waves.

Ten miles away, smoke billowed from *Indefatigable's* flight deck. A zero had come in from above, similar to the one that had attacked *Lancer*. Coming down vertically it had hit amidships alongside the island, destroying the sickbay and starting a fire in the hangar. The crew set to with houses and the fire was under control in a matter of minutes. Within forty minutes she was ready to recover aircraft.

One of the escorting destroyers had also suffered damage but *HMS Ulster* had dodged a Zero at the last moment and the Kamikaze had gone into the water along her starboard side. Shockwaves from the exploding bomb had caused major damage but she had survived. *HMS Gambia* took her in tow to keep her moving.

The fighter sweep had been recalled to intercept the raid but arrived too late to intervene. They only saw the aftermath. One carrier wreathed in smoke, one destroyer listing badly and a patch of oil and bubbles where *HMS Lamian* had been.

They circled the fleet and stood guard while the CAP and the aircraft that had been launched were recovered.

The raid had interfered with the days schedule but the Fleet managed to get a strike off within two hours. The Avengers went in for revenge, pressing their attacks in the teeth of heavy flak. They plastered the airfields again for little discernible result.

While they were over Ishigaki and Miyako Jima, nuisance raids continued to harass the fleet. Radar picked up small groups of aircraft that came in from the north west, then the west. Each time, aircraft from the CAP were vectored to intercept.

"They're using up our fighters," Captain Austin explained to Cullen. "They know we can't ignore them so the CAP has to rush around and burn fuel. It's not wasted effort, they're probing our response, looking for weak spots. We have to use fuel as well. Every time they show up on radar, we have to increase speed, it wastes our fuel as well."

Cullen nodded, filing all of this away for future reference. He watched from the Goofer's gallery as the aircraft were recovered. Oates explained Gilliard's role and how the arresting wires worked. Cullen was a sponge, trying to absorb as much as possible. Carrier operations were totally outside his realm of experience.

The practise strikes had given him a flavour of what went on but they were nothing like full operations. There was an air of urgency that was lacking in the practises, an edge that made it more real.

He watched from the forward gun mounts as the second strike launched to go for Hirara airfield, hoping to catch the Japanese on the ground. He ducked as each one went past, engine roaring.

The strike was another bust. Callicoe hadn't seen much. The Japanese AA gunners were very good. Their AA posts were well sited, giving them an excellent field of fire. You had to come in on the deck, thirty feet and no more with the engine wide open. All they bagged was a single Zero outside a hangar. The fact it was in plain view made Callicoe think it was another decoy.

They got back and landed on fast. There was no time for leisurely landings here. You slammed your aircraft down and cleared the way for the next one coming behind you. The deck crew worked their socks off. Recovered aircraft were refuelled and rearmed immediately.

While he waited for his Corsair to be made ready, Callicoe collared Guest and found a quiet spot by the after pom pom's on the starboard side of the deck.

"Look, I'll make this short because quite frankly there isn't time to analyse this down to the littlest detail. I'm worried you're not going to last," he told the youngster in genuine concern. "We've already lost Abbot today; I don't want to lose you too." Abbot had been in the Corsair shot down by the AA barrage during the last raid.

"I saw you when we were strafing the airfields this afternoon. There's no point swanning around at eighty, ninety feet, you're serving yourself up on a plate. You've got to get lower."

"I can't get an angle if I get too low and that's not how we were taught," Guest said. Incredulous at the logic, Callicoe pinched the bridge of his nose.

"Look, forget what you were taught," he snapped. "Get lower or you're going to get killed."

Guest just blinked at him.

Before the conversation could go any further, the klaxon went off and the tannoy sounded FLASH RED again. *Lancer* cranked on full speed. Overhead, some of the Seafires peeled off and headed west at full tilt. The mechanics increased their pace, desperate to get some aircraft cleared to fly.

The Japanese had been canny, they had radar of their own and they knew when the aircraft were returning to the carriers. They sent their Kamikazes in, hoping to catch them with their pants down.

Callicoe grabbed one of the deck gang asking if anything was good to go. He flinched as *Lancer's* 4.5" guns opened fire. His chest vibrated from the shockwave, the deep boom hammering his ears. He ran to the left side of the deck and huddled next to one of the Oerlikon mounts.

"Officer on deck," shouted a Marine on the gun. "Welcome aboard, sir," he said with a wry smile. Callicoe gripped the rail as the raid came in.

The Japanese had staggered their aircraft this time, sending them in three waves, with a few minutes between each wave. As the CAP dealt with one, the next one blew through.

The cruiser astern of *Lancer* opened up, her superstructure sparkling as guns of every calibre started their barrage.

Callicoe looked back across the deck. The mechanics had taken cover. There would be no aircraft going up. He was going to have to sit this one out.

Callicoe curled into a ball, trying to push himself into the ships plating. Up in his Corsair, he had something to do. He felt naked here on the deck.

The Oerlikons started firing, a repetitive dull thud as round after round was stripped from the magazine. Callicoe made himself useful. He picked up a magazine from the ready locker to hand to the loader when he needed it. Brass casings clattered to the deck as 20mm shells spat out of the barrel.

Callicoe pointed as two Zeroes came into view through some cloud. Black puffs of smoke started to explode around them.

Callicoe had to hand it to the Japanese, they were brave. The two Zeroes bore in, not deviating one inch as they made their runs. Every gun on *Lancer's* port side turned on them.

The first Zero was blotted from the sky as if it never existed. The second one opened fire and Callicoe ducked as bullets lashed the deck. The Oerlikon stopped firing and he glanced up to see the Marine still attached to the gun mount, minus his head. The loader lay on his back, a hole in his chest the size of a fist.

On the bridge, Captain Austin saw it coming in, willing it to fall. He couldn't believe it was still in the air as lines of tracer converged on it. At the last moment, the

Zero reared up and then rolled onto its back. It cleared the flight deck by inches, its wingtip clipping the starboard fire director before it dived into the sea.

Three thousand yards away, *Reliant* heeled over to starboard as a Kamikaze dived on her from above. Commodore Moore could only watch helplessly as it came screaming down at them. The pilot must have been hit because it veered off and plunged into the sea, missing by a good two hundred yards. Metal fragments showered on the deck.

Eleven Zeroes were shot down. The CAP claimed six of them, the rest had been downed by the AA barrage. Unfortunately, the gunners had also blown two Seafires out of the sky. One pilot was picked up, the other one wasn't.

Callicoe shouted for help to deal with the two bodies lying next to him. After they were carted away on stretchers, he went looking for Guest. He found him by the island. He'd been frozen to the spot with fear.

He wasn't the only one. On the bridge, Cullen had a grandstand view as the fleet defended itself. Everyone else had a job to do. All he could do was stand there as a witness as hell was visited upon the earth. Guns roared and the beautiful blue sky was turned black with explosions. The water was churned up by shrapnel and shells. Aircraft wheeled overhead in a deadly dance.

He saw courage beyond description. He watched a Seafire cling to the tail of a Zero that was headed for *HMS Hawke*. The Seafire ploughed through the flak and raked the Zero from stem to stern. The Zero lurched and cartwheeled across the water. Seconds later, Cullen saw the Seafire perforated by an eight barrelled pom pom. Carried away with it all, the gunner kept on firing long after the Seafire plunged into the sea.

That was it for the day. After the raid the fleet withdrew to the south east to refuel. It had been an expensive few days but also lucky ones. Only *Indefatigable* had been hit by a Kamikaze but it could have been quite different. *Lancer* and *Reliant* had a lucky escape as did *Victorious*.

As they steamed south east, *Indefatigable's* damage was assessed. The island had been peppered by shrapnel and the R/T office damaged. Two of her crash barriers had been wrecked and there was a three inch dent in the deck about fifteen feet across. Quick setting concrete was poured in the dent to level everything off.

R/T equipment could be replaced, the big issue was the loss of the crash barriers for flight deck operations. Having only one would make life interesting if anyone missed a wire on landing.

At dawn, the auxiliaries weren't where they were supposed to be and a few aircraft were sent out to find them. By the time the fleet made the rendezvous the weather had changed. The swells were too big to start refuelling and they hove to, holding position waiting for it to change.

It improved the following day but there were still the usual problems. The British Fleets lack of modern tankers was becoming an impediment. Hoses broke and slow pumping speeds hampered operations. They never made up the lost time. By the end of the third day, some of the destroyers still didn't have full tanks and the carriers were only half full which put them in a bad position.

As Admiral Carriers, Vian had tactical command, but Admiral Rawlings had overall strategic command of the Task Force, it was his decision. This was their debut; they'd promised Halsey and Spruance and Nimitz that they'd be on station. A promise was a promise, Rawlings had them set course back towards Sakishima.

They were exactly where they should be at dawn and the fighter sweep went in. They found the Japanese had been industrious little souls. Even under the harassment of an American Task Force to keep up the nuisance raids, the Japanese had filled in the holes and made the airstrips operational again.

Gabby threw his flying helmet across the Wardroom when they got back.

"Why bother?" he shouted in frustration. He turned to the rest of them as they walked in for a cup of tea and a sandwich. "I mean, why bother? We go over, we drop bombs and the little bastards just fill the bloody holes in again."

They went back and escorted the Avengers who dropped 500lb bombs in the usual places and nary a Japanese aircraft was to be seen. Back on the carriers the only conclusion they could reach was that the Japanese were using the airfields at night and moving them before the daily strikes went in.

Towards the end of the day another enemy raid came in and used building banks of cloud to avoid interception. The CAP caught them late but drove them off. Only one broke through and missed *Illustrious* by a whisker. It was their only taste of the Kamikaze that day. They found out the reason why later on.

They hadn't seen any more aircraft because the Japanese had been marshaling their forces to strike directly against Task Force 58 around Okinawa. At sea they sent the Battleship *Yamato* and a light screen of destroyers straight at the American fleet. In the air, they dispatched over five hundred aircraft, three hundred of them were Kamikaze's.

There had been persistent attacks on the Task Force around Okinawa ever since the landings began, but the Americans had never seen anything like this. Their radar screens were full as the armada of aircraft closed in. The anti aircraft defences were swamped and the fighters couldn't stop them all. The outer picket of destroyers caught the worst of it. The *USS Bush* and *Colhoun* were struck multiple times and sank. Fourteen other ships were damaged.

Sailors had become convinced the Japanese were finished, that it was all over. To see the skies filled with so many aircraft, attacking with such abandon and crazed fanaticism had a massive psychological effect. It showed that they weren't done yet. Like Pearl Harbour four years before, the Japanese had missed the vital target, the carriers.

The following day, the Americans sent a Divine Wind of their own. A submarine had spotted the *Yamato* and her destroyer screen in the Bungo Strait. They sent over three hundred aircraft from sixteen carriers. For over two hours, wave after wave of attack planes battered the battleship from all sides. Hit by more than eleven torpedoes and countless bombs, *Yamato* finally succumbed. Down at the bow, she rolled over and her forward magazines blew up.

33 – Taketh My Name

The massed Kamikaze attacks showed the Japanese were still a force to be reckoned with. Task Force 58 had the high ground, but despite the pounding of the Sakishima Islands it hadn't stopped the Japanese making nuisance raids against the Fleet. As Moore had anticipated, the island of Formosa was a threat that needed to be dealt with. After pulling back to resupply, Task Force 57 were ordered west with Moore's division on the far left flank.

In reaction to the increased air attacks they went into battle in a new formation. More radar equipped destroyers were put on outer picket to provide depth of coverage and more advanced warning of attack. Miles from the main force, they were in an exposed position out on their own. The carriers had the added burden of providing a constantly rotating CAP for each ship. Close in, the ships were clustered around the carriers to provide better AA protection. As a lot of Kamikaze attacks had come from astern, a destroyer or a cruiser was stationed behind them to provide extra firepower.

As the BPF got into position, low cloud, rain and heavy swells stopped operations for twenty four hours. That delay came at a cost as the Kamikazes scored again. They hit the Task Force around Okinawa and scored big. The fleet carriers *USS Essex* and the famous *USS Enterprise* were both hit by Kamikaze. The pressure was on for the Brits to do something about it.

Oates could see the pace of operations starting to affect his pilots. In the Indian Ocean they'd flown one or two strikes and then retired from the field. Here, it was an unrelenting grind, day after day of operations that began at the crack of dawn and extended until dusk. If you weren't flying a strike then you were either flying CAP duty over the fleet or spotted on the deck on standby in case of an incoming raid.

Pilots were martinets. Carrier pilots even more so. Normally they had a healthy interest in their landing performance and a sense of pride at being able to land on a postage stamp after a difficult mission. They were so tired; they weren't even bothered when they snagged a late wire or bounced hard on the deck. They were just grateful to get down. That was not a good sign.

Callicoe was so tired from non stop flying, the days seemed to blend into one another. The take offs and landings had become routine, the strikes were only memorable when they were punctuated by moments of sheer terror.

He would get up too early, eat something and then get his flying gear on before the hatches were closed. Hair became stiff from sweat after hours of flying. Laundry was a memory and they began to get ripe as they sat in the Wardroom waiting for their turn to fly.

Gabby pushed his luck even further than that, rising at the last moment and forgoing a wash, shave or even breakfast. Goodfellow's eyes bulged when he saw him come up on deck in his pyjamas to fly the morning sweep.

"You've got to be comfortable when you fly," Gabby protested. Goodfellow thought he looked terrible. There were dark patches under his eyes and his cheeks were gaunt.

"You know, I don't like being a bore, Veriker, but you do push your luck sometimes. I always knew you Wavy Navy types took liberties but there is a limit."

Goodfellow had to let it go, the ship was closed up for action so he couldn't send him below deck to get changed.

He wasn't impressed, the squadron had a reputation to uphold.

"Stay out of sight," he ordered and stalked off, muttering to himself. God knows what Oates or the Captain would say when they saw him.

A lot of the Japanese raids had come out of the west, staging from Formosa and the fleet went in hard. Staggering the strikes to give them no chance to recover, *Illustrious* and *Indefatigable* went first, then *Victorious* and *Indomitable*, then *Reliant* and *Lancer*. The Japanese barely started clearing up the mess from the first strike before the next raid appeared over the horizon.

Mid morning, Callicoe led his section as they covered sixteen Avengers on the way to Shinchiku airfield. Barrett was above and behind flying top cover.

Heavy cloud had forced them to go in low and they were twitchy. Callicoe felt hemmed in with the water below and the clouds above. Fighters could burst on them out of nowhere and they'd have little chance to react.

The flak started from far out. Big guns filled the air with shrapnel and Callicoe took his section in ahead to soften them up. A blizzard of shells came up at them. It was horrific, there were AA guns all over the place. There were gun pits clustered at the end of the runways. Bigger guns were scattered around firing at the bombers at altitude.

Unwilling to risk his section in line astern, Callicoe brought them in line abreast. They would only make one pass at this and then clear the way for the Avengers.

They came screaming in, their props almost carving a channel across the ground. Callicoe worked his rudder pedals, nudging the nose left and right, spraying his fire around. Men fell like skittles. Boxes of ammunition exploded as the Corsairs cut a swathe across the field.

"Keep it tight, chaps," he said through gritted teeth. He

kept his touch on the controls light, well aware that one twitch would put him into the ground. He risked glances left and right to see his section blazing away at targets as they tore across the ground.

They climbed to clear the trees at the far end. They hadn't caused much damage, but it was enough of a distraction for the Avengers to make their run. They opened their bomb doors and dropped their loads at fifteen hundred feet and peeled off to the south.

He levelled off at two thousand feet and ordered his section to form up and report. They'd all been hit but nothing seemed serious. He circled round and climbed to escort the Avengers out. The flak chased them all the way until they were out of range.

The Avengers landed on first when they got back to *Lancer*. Callicoe was circling overhead when fighter control vectored the CAP towards an incoming raid.

"They've bloody timed this right," Gabby said over the R/T. Callicoe gave him a terse 'roger' and told him to keep the air clear. Callicoe listened intently as he heard the controller direct the CAP towards the raid. They were coming in at fifteen thousand feet from the west, a mixed bag of bombers and fighters.

The radio traffic got chaotic as they made contact with the Japanese. It was a real mixer, thirty plus bandits coming in hard. The Seafires couldn't contain them and Barret and Callicoe's sections were detailed to assist. *Lancer* and *Reliant* increased speed and turned into the wind to get the standby aircraft in the air.

They headed west, climbing hard to head off the raid before it made it to the fleet. They were still too low when they made contact. The Zeroes and Tony's dived at them. Head to head was extremely dangerous, particularly when you faced an enemy that considered it an honour to die for their Divine Emperor.

The sky became full of milling aircraft. Every time the Japanese fighters pushed towards the fleet, the Corsairs and Seafires tried to stop them. It became a turning fight that got lower and lower. A Tony went down, closely followed by two Seafires. Parachutes blossomed as their pilots bailed out. The Japanese pilot didn't jump, a parachute wasn't needed on a one way trip.

Barrett broke right as a burst went through his starboard wing. He tightened his turn and then dived as more bullets thudded into his tail. The Zero followed him down. Not all of them were Kamikaze and the escorts had their work cut out trying to clear a path for their blessed compatriots.

Callicoe turned hard to get on the tail of a Tony as it broke out of the melee. Silver, with red Hinomura on the wings it was lethal and pretty. Callicoe dived after it as it headed for the Task Force. More fighters broke through and the Corsairs and Seafires chased after them.

The ships started firing as they got close. Callicoe fired and missed. The Tony juked left, rolled and bore straight in. Callicoe had to fire short bursts. He didn't have much ammo left after their strafing run over the island. He closed the range and got the Tony lined up bang to rights and fired. Tracer reached out, clipped the tail and then stopped as his guns ran dry. Cursing, Callicoe broke off.

"I'm out," he called as he peeled off.

Gabby had the bit between his teeth and clung on, diving into the barrage to chase after the Tony.

Callicoe had his heart in his mouth as he saw Gabby's Corsair plunge into the maelstrom of flak. Gabby flinched as shrapnel pinged off his canopy. He fired and cursed as a long burst missed underneath the Tony. Before he could adjust, his Corsair shuddered as pom pom shells punched into her. He dived away, fighting the controls as his engine began to make noises like a rusty mangle.

The pilot of the Tony mistimed his approach and dived too soon on *Reliant*, coming in at a shallow angle. It was the only thing that saved her.

The Tony slammed into the deck like a skimming stone. It hit amidships and broke up, ricocheting through the deck park, destroying a Seafire and three Avengers. The third crash barrier was torn to shreds. The forward gun director on the port side was ripped away and men were swept from the deck like crumbs off a tablecloth.

Two other Kamikaze fell short of *HMS Hawke*, plunging into her wake. The Fleet got away with it. They'd shot down fifteen for only four of their own.

Illustrious and *Indefatigable* launched their second strike of the day, doing their best to hammer the airfields despite the weather. Heavy clouds moved in and they had to plough through intermittent rain squalls to make it to the target.

The poor visibility forced them lower and the flak claimed two Avengers as they pulled off their bombing runs. The Fireflys revenged them, slathering the AA guns with 60lb HE rockets.

Reliant was operational again by the time she had to fly her second strike. The hole in the deck was plated over and bits of Tony were pitched over the side.

As the light began to go the Fleet pulled back for the night and the squadrons licked their wounds. In the Wardroom they sat, drained of energy while they talked in monotones. Callicoe fell asleep in the Wardroom, his pipe clamped between his teeth. Gabby shrugged off his flying gear and crawled straight into his bunk. He was asleep before his head hit the pillow.

Down in *Lancer's* hangar, the mechanics patched holes and slaved to make the aircraft ready to go again in the morning.

34 – Hot Work

When he woke up the following morning, Callicoe felt like death warmed up. His neck was stiff and his eyes felt like hot ball bearings. He dragged himself outside as the sun was peaking over the horizon. It was his turn to fly the early sweep. He said good morning to Barrett who would be on standby.

Callicoe promised himself to ask what Barrett's secret was, he must have had some kind of iron constitution because he looked fresh as a daisy. He was devouring a bully beef sandwich and slurping on a mug of tea while he enjoyed the morning breeze.

Callicoe walked around his Corsair. One of the mechanics pointed out a neat line of holes along the underside. He'd acquired them when he strafed the airfield. Satisfied it would fly, he gathered his section together by the tail.

Having felt Goodfellow's wrath yesterday, Gabby was suitably attired. All of them looked exhausted. Guest had put years on his youthful face, his complexion sallow, stubble dark on his pale cheeks.

"I know we're all tired, but we've got to stick in there. Stay alert, watch each other's back and we'll all get back. Guest, you're with me. Gabby, I want you to lead the second element."

Gabby nodded silently, too tired for a quip. They went to their aircraft and strapped in. Callicoe went through the start up routine with practised ease. The silence was shattered as the engine burst into life. He leaned back and closed his eyes, waiting for the time to launch. The carrier leaned into the turn and he opened his eyes, refreshed from the few moments repose.

The sun was over the lip of the horizon, a glowing disc low in a sky chased with purples and blue as night became day. The rain squalls had passed in the night and it looked like it was going to be a nice day. Perfect to rain death and mayhem on the sons of Nippon. Callicoe shook his head at that thought, it was the kind of thing Gabby would say.

Cullen was stood next to the Flight Deck Officer. He wanted to see a dawn launch. There was a romantic air to it. The aircraft were warmly lit by the sun, painted in pastel shades, their propellers glowing discs. Deck crew rushed around. To Cullen's untrained eye it looked chaotic but every man had his task, moving with practised ease.

It was a still day with barely a breath of wind. Captain Oates rang down for more speed and *Lancer* vibrated as she topped thirty one knots, her engines going like the clappers.

Callicoe unfolded his wings and locked them in place, ready to go. Guest did the same. The chocks were removed and Callicoe was waved forward. The Deck Officer waited until the bow was bottoming out of the wave and then he flashed a green.

Callicoe let off his brakes and brought in the power. The Corsair started rolling, the tail came up and he was off. Guest was right behind him.

He orbited to the right and chopped back the throttle, giving the rest a chance to form up on him. He stacked Gabby's element behind his and they headed west for Formosa in two vics. Callicoe kept it low, he wanted to come in on the deck.

Formosa loomed ahead of them on the horizon. The eastern side of the island was dominated by five peaks that towered over ten thousand feet high. Off to starboard he could see the Firefly's from *Reliant* going over at three thousand.

Callicoe's lip curled in satisfaction. If they wanted to go in where everyone could see them that was fine by him. they'd draw all the fire. It was a brutal thought but he could only focus on himself and his own section.

Close to the coast, they flashed over three fishing boats. Blink and they were gone. Callicoe cursed, hoping to god none of them had a radio on board. He dropped lower, screwing every ounce of power out of the engine. He kept glancing in his mirror and then over his shoulder. Kendall was on his left, but Guest was out of position, forty feet or so above everyone else.

Callicoe shook his head. He'd told Guest again and again to get lower but the youngster just couldn't do it. Callicoe thought he had a fear about going in and wanted to leave himself a cushion for error. None of that would do him any good if the AA guns caught him. He took a reference from the coast as they roared across the land. They were only minutes away and he flicked his safety off, hunkering down in his seat.

They'd taken off thirty minutes earlier than normal. Oates had hoped to catch the Japanese out and this time they'd scored. As they crossed the airfield boundary, there was a smorgasbord of aircraft on offer. They'd come in just in time, some of them were on the runway with their engines turning.

"Tallyho!" he called, "Let 'em have it."

With the sound of their own aircraft on the runway and the wind coming from the west, the AA gunners picked up the Corsairs late. Coming in just above the top of the surrounding jungle, the grey and green painted Corsairs almost blended into the background. The first warning the Japanese had was when the first Oscar on the runway blew up as he started his take off run.

Another one lurched left as his pilot was killed, a dead foot on the rudder pedal. It went through a half circle and dropped into a slit trench. The Corsairs spread out and shot up anything in sight. A two engine bomber blew up. Fighters started rolling in all directions, trying to get in the air.

Their surprise was so complete, Callicoe was happy to make a second pass. As the AA gunners trained their guns on the Corsairs, the Fireflies came in and fired their rockets. Two ploughed into an Oscar just as it lifted off. The fighter blew up and folded around itself.

The section came in again. The AA gunners fired in all directions as they tried to get organised. Callicoe skidded through a turn, spraying a big two engine bomber. Bits flew into the air, then it burst into flames.

"Keep low!" he warned as the gunners started to get themselves into some sort of order. He banked hard right as lines of tracer shot across his nose.

Kendall and Guest trailed behind as they followed him through the turn. Kendall hugged the ground, his world tilted sideways. Higher up, Guest was looking down at the two Corsairs as they mowed the grass. It was the last thing he saw as cannon shells smashed through his canopy. His Corsair rolled through ninety degrees as the nose dipped and it cartwheeled across the airfield.

Oblivious to the tragedy behind him, Callicoe reversed his turn and climbed to get clear. As he pulled away, his Corsair staggered from a hammer blow.

The Corsairs sped east skimming the jungle, back the way they had come. The Fireflies followed hot on their heels.

Callicoe stayed low. He didn't want to climb until they were back over the water but after a few minutes, he was forced to as his engine temperature started to shoot up.

He knew Guest was gone. Gabby had seen him go in. There was nothing to say, he'd told the kid to get lower.

He couldn't think about the dead now, he had to get himself and the rest of his section home alive.

Even before he cleared the coast, his engine began running rough. The temperature was jammed in the red and Callicoe knew his engines life was measured in minutes. There was no way he was going to last the hundred miles back to the carrier. He started to think about ditching. The important thing now was getting as far as he could before the engine packed in for good.

After a few more minutes, the Pratt and Whitney started to thrash itself to death. Callicoe decided to put her down before it stopped entirely. He dropped the flaps and flattened out over the water. He was grateful to find the calm conditions had remained and the sea was almost glass smooth. He made a normal landing approach. Holding it straight and level he just flew the Corsair into the water. He flared at the last second to lift the nose and bring her in on her belly. The prop threw up a massive amount of spray and Callicoe was drenched as the Corsair slithered to a stop.

As soon as she stopped moving, he undid his straps and was over the side, inflating his Mae West. After the roar of the engine for the last fifty minutes it was suddenly very quiet, floating in the middle of the Pacific. He watched as his Corsair gave a final sigh and sank beneath the waves.

The water was nice and balmy, it was like floating in a giant bath. He changed his mind when he did a circle of his surroundings and saw how close to shore he was. He was lucky if he was five miles away. He started kicking with his legs, feebly trying to get further out.

Callicoe looked up as his section circled in a wide orbit overhead. He waved his arms as he bobbed up and down and one of the Corsairs came in low to buzz him. They circled the entire time he was in the water so he never felt alone.

After half an hour an aircraft appeared low on the horizon from the east. Another five minutes and he saw it was a Walrus amphibian. He started waving frantically until his arms wore out. The Corsairs led the Walrus right to him.

Never pretty, the Walrus looked like it was out of the ark. It had a blunt nose, two wings, wire and struts and an engine mounted back to front. Callicoe couldn't care less how ugly it was. It touched down sweet as a nut and circled round to taxy back towards him.

Before it got to him, there was a roar like the sky was falling in and then a huge spout of water magically appeared a few hundred yards away. Callicoe started swimming faster. There was another roar and another water spout. Shore based guns were firing on them.

His Corsair's peeled off and headed towards the coast. Callicoe kicked, frantic to close the distance to his saviour. The Walrus didn't slow down as it got closer and for a moment, he thought it was going to run him over. At the last minute the pilot threw on right rudder and turned. The gunner at the rear hatch tossed him a line as the Walrus went past. Callicoe grabbed it with both hands and clung on for dear life. The gunner pulled on the line and hauled him aboard like a sack of grain.

"God am I glad to see you guys," he said after he stopped coughing up sea water.

"Hot work was it?" the Observer asked.

"You have no idea."

As he was hauled aboard, the Walrus continued its turn into the meagre wind and the pilot opened the throttle. The Walrus gained speed. It kept going, skimming over the calm waters. The pilot was willing it to lift off.

A millpond might have been good for boating, but it wasn't very good for seaplanes to take off. They needed a bit of a swell to break the surface suction of the water.

They kept going, bumping along as shells continued to explode around them. The Japanese gunners were getting the range and it was getting kind of hairy.

"Come on old girl," the pilot muttered to himself. He patted the side of the fuselage. "Be good to daddy."

He got his miracle when a shell went long and churned up the water ahead of them. The Walrus scudded over the waves and lifted into the air.

Callicoe crawled to the cockpit and shook the pilot's hand.

"Thanks for the assist."

"No problem, mate," the pilot replied. "It's what we're here for. Just the one of you?"

Callicoe nodded.

"As far as I'm aware, just the one." He stood behind the pilot the entire trip back. His section escorted them all the way.

They landed back aboard *Victorious* as graceful as a butterfly. As soon as the engine was shut down, the deck crew folded the wings and manhandled it forward.

It was a very grateful Callicoe who got back down on a friendly deck. He'd missed some excitement while he was floating in the middle of nowhere. Another raid had been intercepted but this one had been stopped short of the fleet. The CAP had caught them twenty miles out and torn them to shreds.

An Avenger flew over to pick him up and take him back home. He got back at dusk as they were pulling off to resupply. Cullen was waiting for him with his pad and pencil poised. He'd heard all about the day's events from his section when they got back. A rescue at sea under the guns of the enemy was just the kind of story he was looking for.

35 – Again, Again, Again

Guest wasn't the squadrons only casualty for the day. Douglas, one of the replacements they'd picked up in Sydney had been killed during the raid. In the rush for some Corsairs to get off the deck to meet the incoming attackers, he'd run into a prop. It was as quick as that.

"Such a bloody waste," Callicoe muttered in the Wardroom. "All of them, such a bloody waste."

He thought about all the faces that had gone since the squadron had first gathered at *Quonset Point*. Ten of the original eighteen had been lost due to accidents and enemy action. He stopped counting after that.

He rolled his neck and had another drink and tried to think happy thoughts. He didn't want to go down that rabbit hole. Even Wicklow was a little down. He sat at the piano and prodded the keys but he wasn't much in the mood for a party.

As they weren't flying in the morning, they did their best to relax after a really hectic three days. Matthews banged the bar with a glass for some quiet.

"God almighty, what a moody bunch you are." The big Canadian stood on a chair. "Everyone get a drink," he demanded. He waited until they all had a glass or a bottle in their hands. "To the honoured dead," he said, his glass held high. He finished his bottle.

"Right, that's that shit out of the way. Line up, tug of war!" he barked. Matthews dragged them up by their boot straps whether they wanted to or not. They might be doing this for weeks yet. He wanted to shake them out of their stupor.

He managed it in the end. They were kids mainly and kids didn't need much encouragement to forget their troubles. After a few more drinks and a game or two they had their tails up. They weren't exactly cock a hoop, but it was a start.

After a hard day hauling supplies, bombs and fuel on board, Captain Austin bent a few rules and issued an extra tot of rum to thank them for a job well done. He put a movie on in the after lift well for anyone who was interested. After the intensity of operations, it felt good to have a laugh for a change.

In the morning, four replacements pilot were flown over from one of the escort carriers. Goodfellow and Matthews took two each. They weren't exactly given the warmest welcome. They hadn't been blooded yet. Even Kendall and Mitchell who'd come aboard *Lancer* in Sydney were distant. For now, they were rookies who had to prove themselves. They didn't have long to wait.

Admiral Rawlings had got away with his calculated risk by the skin of his teeth. When they pulled back from Formosa to resupply, some of the destroyers were almost running on fumes. *Victorious* was scraping the bottom of the barrel as well.

It wasn't the only thing they were running short on. Enemy action, ditchings and deck landing accidents had taken care of twenty five percent of their available aircraft. Only the fact they had *Unicorn* and *Minerva* along to help service and repair aircraft had kept some of them in the air.

They'd got lucky with the Kamikazes. If three hundred had turned up like over Okinawa, Rawlings doubted if a single ship in the Task Force would have been afloat by the time the attack was over. As it was, the carriers had survived despite some very close shaves.

He was grateful when he saw the low sleek shape of *HMS Formidable* waiting for them at the rendezvous. *Illustrious* had been starting to struggle mechanically and she had been operating in the Far East for months longer than any of the other carriers. She had reached her limit. *Formidable's* arrival allowed him to send her back to Sydney for refit and repair.

Even so, for all the difficulties, they'd had it easier than the Americans. While they'd been attacking Formosa, the Kamikazes had claimed some more victims around Okinawa. None had been sunk, but two more carriers, three battleships and fifteen destroyers had been damaged. The carriers had to withdraw to Leyte for repairs, reducing Fifth Fleet to three carrier Task Forces.

Strained as they were, Rawlings contacted Admiral Spruance and offered to stay longer on station. Spruance gladly accepted. The BPF had gained itself a convert. While his men tried to relax, get some sleep and reset, Admiral Rawlings had put them back on the game board.

Callicoe had managed to rally himself over the last two days. He'd slept like the dead, which wasn't a term he liked using with all its negative connotations. He wondered if his ability to sleep was because he'd become used to the pace of operations, or he'd become resigned to his fate. Either way, he felt like a new man when he stepped out on the flight deck with his parachute harness slung over his shoulder. It was like that first strike on Sabang back in July all over again.

They flew three strikes that day to the old haunts of Hegina, Miyara and Ishigaki. They plastered the airfields with bombs, cratering the runways and shooting up anything that moved. In the afternoon, they went to a radar installation for a bit of variety and left it a smoking ruin.

By the end of the day, Callicoe's newfound energy was

starting to fade away. He'd flown four times, the morning ramrod, cover on a strike and two stints flying patrols over the islands and outer pickers and he was tired. Shots of adrenalin could only last so long and when they wore off, he was more fatigued than before.

He always loved flying. It was good to get up for some fresh air away from the persistent stifling heat below decks, but the monotony of patrol duties was particularly tedious. He was starting to fidget as well. After seven hours and more, his body was reminding him that being sat on a parachute was not the most comfortable place to be.

He was looking forward to a shower when he got down. His shirt was stiff with sweat and he was hungry. He put the binoculars to his eyes and looked down at the ships of the Task Force. They'd turned into wind in preparation to recover the CAP before steaming south east. Another hour and they would be safe for the night, covered by the shroud of darkness.

He kept glancing at his watch as time dragged. It always did when there were only a few minutes to go. He took the section in one last wide orbit before the FDO called them in.

They dropped down and flew over *Reliant* before heading for *Lancer*. On his horizon were the other four carriers. All around them were the escorts, the cruisers, destroyers and battleships that protected them.

They landed in turn, Callicoe coming in last as was his way. He was so tired, there wasn't even the usual thrill of making a deck landing to wake him up. He wound back his canopy, dropped the flaps and hook and gear on the downwind leg and made his final turn. He made a decent enough approach and Gilliard was making all the right signals as he flew down the slot.

As he got close, Gilliard gave him *'You are fast!'* but Callicoe didn't respond at all. Gilliard's bats got more frantic, trying to tell him to slow down but Callicoe's Corsair came in hot. In a funk, he straightened up, missed the cut entirely and roared over the stern at nearly ninety knots.

Callicoe snapped awake, the moment captured like a mosquito in amber. He was slightly off line to port, sailing over the wires straight towards the crash barrier and the deck park beyond. He slammed his throttle closed far too late and pulled back on the stick. There was a nasty jolt that snapped his head back and he thought he'd got away with it and caught the last wire; then his Corsair ploughed into the crash barrier.

Dragged to an abrupt halt, Callicoe was slammed forward, bashing his head on the gyro gunsight. The undercarriage was ripped off, the big prop turned into a whisk and the engine came to a cylinder shattering stop. He had a distinct memory of a detached wheel go bouncing down the deck, hit the tail of a Corsair in front and then go over the side.

Nostrils filled with the stench of leaking petrol and burnt wiring, he scrambled over the side and helping hands got him clear. He leaned back against the island; palm pressed to his forehead.

The Doctor crouched down next to him and waved his hand in front of him.

"How many fingers am I holding up?" he asked.

"Very funny." Callicoe took a swig from the proferred hip flask and winced, his teeth hurt. "Christ, what's in that?"

"Laphroaig, single malt, the best. Emergencies, for the use of," the Doctor replied with a grin.

Callicoe stood up on shaky legs and Barrett appeared.

"What happened?"

"Not sure." Callicoe rubbed his neck. He remembered the jolt before he'd gone into the barrier. One of the deck hands came over with a lump of metal.

"Found this, sir," he said, handing it over to Callicoe.

They looked at it. It was the end of his hook.

Gilliard stomped across the flight deck.

"You lucky bastard," he said. Callicoe wasn't sure if he was mad or not. "High, fast, I thought you were going to miss the barrier as well."

Gilliard had been frantically signalling as Callicoe crossed the stern. At the last moment, the tail had dipped, there were sparks as the hook struck the deck and snagged the last wire. It held for a moment, then the hook had broken and the fighter slammed into the barrier.

In the Wardroom, Gabby added Callicoe's accident to the tally on the right column of the blackboard he'd put by the piano. Since they'd started operations, he'd been keeping a score of how many aircraft they'd claimed, and how many they'd lost. It had all been a joke at first. They shot up so many Japanese aircraft on the ground, the scores were terrific. Then the losses had started mounting up. It wasn't so funny anymore. Gabby put a chalk line through four lines to make it five.

"There, up to date," he muttered darkly as Callicoe came into the Wardroom nursing a lump on his forehead.

"Bloody hell, you don't hang around," Callicoe muttered, trying to keep his tone light.

"Fairs, fair," Gabby said. "Got to keep the scores square."

Callicoe put the bit of hook on the top of the piano.

"Souvenir."

"What's that?"

"My hook. I broke my plane," he said, his tongue felt thick in his mouth, his gums still hurt. He walked to the bar and asked for some ice. He knew there wasn't any but it didn't hurt to ask. He snagged a cold bottle of beer instead.

Condensation ran down the outside and he put the

bottle to his forehead, closing his eyes, enjoying the soothing effect of the cold glass. He pulled his sweat stained shirt off his chest. "I need a shower."

Gabby watched him go. He polished off his own bottle of beer before standing up, a little shaky on his feet.

"I'm for bed," he announced. No one replied and he looked hurt as he left the Wardroom.

"Good riddance," someone muttered darkly from the corner. Goodfellow looked over and saw the new boys sat nursing their drinks. He fixed them with a piercing gaze until they found something intensely interesting on the floor.

He levered himself up and walked over to the piano to look at the blackboard. *Butchers Block (Aircraft Only)*, had been written above the two columns of numbers. It was morbid and Goodfellow didn't like it but it had become a fixture of the wardroom. It was gallows humour, a tilt at mortality almost. One in the eye for Davy Jones perhaps. He went to find Barrett.

The pickings were slightly better the next day. They caught two transport planes on the ground, chopped an Oscar that was trying to take off and lost three Avengers in return, one over the target and two ditching on the way back to the carriers. Like a fox, the Japanese air force had gone to ground again.

Cleared to fly, Callicoe led his section in a CAP in the afternoon. He had a nice bruise developing on his forehead and he wiggled his jaw from side to side. His teeth still felt loose. *Reliant* had lost so many Seafires in landing accidents she barely had enough to maintain a decent CAP over the Task Force so the Corsairs were having to take a turn at that too.

His R/T burst to life and the controllers vectored them to intercept an intruder. He turned to the desired heading and led his section up into the clouds. They popped into the clear at fifteen thousand feet. Callicoe blinked as bright sunlight hit him after the gloom of the clouds. He continued climbing, wanting plenty of height if he was going to make the interception.

At twenty thousand, Callicoe sucked down the oxygen like a starving man, shivering slightly at the cold. They rarely went so high and with the warm weather, he'd gotten used to wearing a short sleeve uniform shirt without a flying suit over it. He shuddered again and jerked the controls.

He scanned the sky, looking for what they'd been sent to find. They headed west, eating up the distance. Kendall saw their intruder first.

"Tallyho, Sturgeon Leader. Two o'clock low."

Callicoe had to squint to see it. Kendall had good eyesight indeed. The Judy was painted a dirty white, making it almost invisible against the clouds. Its shadow was a dark stain as it flew over the fluffy plain underneath it.

The Yokosuka D4Y, or Judy as it was better known, was a fat bodied dive bomber not to be underestimated. It was as fast as the Zero fighters that escorted it so it was often pressed into the reconnaissance role.

Callicoe played the odds. They were far enough from the fleet that it wouldn't be spotted by this solitary aircraft yet. Besides, they'd operated so often off the Sakishima Islands now that the Japanese would have a fair idea of where they were anyway. If they dived straight at it, it would be able to dive away in a matter of seconds and either escape or come back for another look.

He kept on course, letting the Judy slide past them to starboard. When he had the sun above him, he made his move.

"To the spotter, the spoils. Sturgeon Three, he's all yours. Sturgeon Four back him up, the rest of us hold here."

Kendall didn't need telling twice. Callicoe watched with a critical eye as he broke right and went into a dive. He was smooth and efficient, not one of those pilots who yanked on the controls and slammed his kite around. The new replacement, Bell followed close behind. The two Corsairs went down like a rocket, gunning for the Judy.

With the benefit of the sun, Kendall got close, but it still wasn't quite good enough. Just before he got into guns range, the Observer caught a glint of sunlight above him and saw the two fighters coming down.

The Judy flicked over and did what it did best, dive. Kendall started firing as it rolled over, picking bits off its tail and wing before it disappeared into the fluffy clouds below it.

He carried on his pursuit, but when he popped out below the clouds, it was nowhere to be seen. They shouted up for a vector from the Fighter Controllers, but the radar contacts had merged on their plot. When they picked it up again, it was heading northwest like a bat out of hell. That was all they saw in the air in two days, that one solitary Judy.

Spruance asked Rawlings for one more rotation and reluctantly, he agreed. The fighting on Okinawa was bogging down and the casualties were mounting up. Spruance's Task Force was going to have to stay on station longer than planned. They needed the cover the BPF provided to the west.

Minerva provided some replacement Seafires when they pulled back to resupply. There were no Corsairs or Avengers left at all, the cupboard was bare. Flagging spirits were raised when mail was delivered along with some out of date newspapers and some new films. Spirits were further raised with the rumour of a withdrawal to San Pedro Bay at Leyte or perhaps the Ulithi anchorage. God forsaken as that place was, anywhere was going to be better than here.

Callicoe got four letters from Jane. They were short but heartfelt and he felt guilty for not writing her one himself. The photograph she sent, he put in his wallet to carry with him. He rallied his thoughts and wrote a letter, making sure it went over to one of the supply ships before they went back up the line.

The days passed in a blur for the crew. It was long days, short nights and lots of work in uncomfortable heat. *Lancer* started to show signs of being worked to her limit. A steam pipe ruptured in the engine room and for two hours she could do no more than fifteen knots. Goodfellow's had a barrier engagement when the fifth arrester wire snapped. It paid out to its maximum and gave way with a twang.

Finally, *Lancer's* stint at Sakishima Gunto came to an end. They gratefully steamed south towards Leyte for an extended period of rest and resupply. They'd operated for thirty two days at sea, a prolonged feat unmatched by any other British naval unit since the war had begun. The crew were strained, the equipment on board had been pushed hard.

For three days, Captain Austin let the crew work at their own pace. The lifts were let down and they stayed down, helping fresh air get below decks. Extra tots of rum were issued and they even played deck hockey to relax. Cullen watched from the rail of the bridge as boys laughed and joked after going through the hell of combat. They spent their free time clowning around to remind themselves they were still alive.

Austin knew once they got to Leyte there would be a lot to do. The ship needed to be put to rights. Bombs, fuel, food, ammunition and spare aircraft all needed to be sorted out. Engineers would need to come on board and see if the broken arrester cable could be replaced.

There was almost a collective sigh on board as they dropped anchor in San Pedro Bay. A large sheltered anchorage, the place wasn't as hot as Manus and a pleasant breeze rolled in form the south east.

It was a busy place, with a number of ships coming and going. Both the Seventh and Fifth Fleets staged ships through here to support operations towards Japan and MacArthur's push in the south. *Illustrious* was still there, having her damaged hull examined. She was in worse shape than anyone had realised. The concussion of a number of near misses had cracked and depressed her hull plates during her hectic career.

Before *Illustrious* left for Sydney, everything not nailed down that was spare was offloaded. *Lancer* was the recipient of several of her aircraft as replacements. As a joke and a tribute of sorts, Callicoe had the mechanics put a small Q next to the T when they were repainted to have their carrier ID letter changed.

Contrary to expectations there was no shore leave. Nimitz wanted them back on station by the 4th May and Rawlings didn't want to let CINCPAC down after he'd gone to bat for them.

Every day, the ships boats went back and forth, bringing crates and boxes to be loaded on board. Stores ships did their best to fill the shopping lists the supply officers gave them but there wasn't enough to fulfill every need. Items were distributed as far as stocks went.

Engineers plated over the dent in *Reliant's* flight deck and replaced her crash barrier. They couldn't repair *Lancer's* broken wire. The recoil drums had been torn from their mounts. That was something that would have to be rectified when they got back to Sydney.

Callicoe had his hands full supervising the squadrons aircraft. Duds, including the Corsair he'd gone into the barrier with were hoisted over the side and put onto lighters alongside. They were ferried over to *Unicorn* and

Minerva so they could be repaired in their better equipped workshops. Together with the engine repair ship, *Deer Sound* they worked around the clock to put as many aircraft back on the line as possible. Any that weren't ready by the time the Fleet put to sea would follow on later as required. The storage depots in Sydney had been cleared out of spares and they were brought forward to Leyte by the escort carriers. These were distributed around the carriers to help bring them back up to strength.

Even though there was no shore leave and it was hard physical work, the change in routine did wonders for morale. Captain Austin made sure the mess decks served up as much fresh food as possible. Once they were back on the line, it would be bully beef sandwiches and soup again. There was a movie every evening and the ships traded their films back and forth after each showing. There was deck hockey and relay races on the flight deck and even two swimming contests.

Even before they got to San Pedro, the ugly spectre of politics reared its head. Back in Washington, Admiral King was still keen to limit the BPF's involvement in the final push on Japan. He issued a directive that he wanted them to cover the landings of Australian troops in south west Borneo at Tarakan. The catch was Admiral King needed the approval of Nimitz and Spruance and he didn't get it.

Nimitz lobbied hard to retain the services of the English carriers under his command. His forces around Okinawa had taken a pasting. The Kamikazes had revealed the weakness of US design and they'd lost too many carriers already. In the push for Japan, Nimitz was going to need every available deck he could lay his hands on. The British carriers had shown an unusual resilience where Kamikazes were concerned.

At dawn on the 1st May, the BPF headed north back towards Japan, rested, if not refreshed.

36 – Tooth And Nail

While they were at San Pedro, Rawlings and Vian had held a conference with their air staff to discuss tactics, what had worked and what hadn't. What everyone had agreed upon was that the CAP over the carriers needed to be strengthened. Experience had shown a section down low, a section around seven thousand feet and a high section at twelve to fifteen thousand wasn't enough. Every time a raid had come in, the Japanese had pressed their attacks and scorched past them.

Poring over the after action reports from the big raids over Okinawa, it was clear that no matter how good the CAP was, some aircraft were always going to get through. Although it would put pressure on the pilots, they had no choice, they had to increase the strength of the CAP. To free up sufficient fighters, the Fireflies were roped in to provide cover for the outer destroyer cordon.

Lancer was back on station on the morning of the 4th May. She was in company with *Reliant* and *Minerva* again out on the left flank. The reporter had moved on. After filing his stories, Cullen had packed his bag and transferred his kit over to *Reliant*. In the last few weeks he'd decided to make his story the carriers. He'd been on *Lancer*, now he had to see how the other half lived.

Callicoe was pleased he'd gone. He'd hovered around like some angel of death, seeing everything and filing it away for future reference. It had made Callicoe twitch.

He was twitching now. He was taking three new men up today in his section and apart from a limited amount of landing practice on their way back north they were total unknowns. No one had bent anything, which was a start but they were just going to have to learn on the job. It was unfair but there was little else they could do.

They were stood by the tail of his Corsair now waiting for him. Lysander the swarthy Welshman, a spare dark haired lad called Sparrow and Sam Cash, a loud Londoner who was like Gabby used to be, full of beans and larger than life.

He told them to stick to his tail and follow his lead. Just because it had been quiet before didn't mean it would be this time. There had been more Kamikaze attacks off Okinawa and their job was to go back in and pummel the airfields. Even if the Japanese filled the holes in, they had to keep going back and batter them to deny them use of the runways.

He sat in his Corsair parked down the flight deck by the island. He was behind four Corsairs from 1783 who were going to do a stint on CAP duty. *Lancer* got up to speed and turned into the wind to launch while Fireflies and Seafires launched from *Reliant*.

Even as Callicoe got into the air and formed his section up, *HMAS Naturi* picked up incoming aircraft. The sweep was cancelled; the enemy was coming to them.

He climbed hard with his section circling *Lancer* while he gained height. The Fighter Controllers reeled off course and speed as the raid came in. A section of Seafires made contact first at seven thousand feet and picked off two Zeroes before they split up. They chased after one group, the controllers vectored Callicoe onto the other, keeping the rest of the CAP over the Fleet.

There were at least twelve of them still coming in. Callicoe had the high ground but there were bands of cloud at different altitudes limiting his visibility.

The Fighter Controllers led them right to them.

Coming out of the sun, the six Corsairs went into the attack.

"I told you you'd get your feet wet," cracked Gabby as he drifted left to give himself some space.

"Keep it tight and let's break them up!" Callicoe ordered. He glanced once to his right to make sure Sparrow was still with him and then they were on the fighters.

They took out three on the first pass, Kendall and Cash broke their duck. Callicoe stitched a Judy in an efficient two second burst, shattering the canopy and mangling the engine. The dive bomber lazily rolled over as it fell out of the sky. The remaining nine aircraft broke into two groups.

"Cute," Callicoe snorted to himself. This was obviously their new tactic to limit the chance of being stopped. Callicoe wasn't going to play that game. "Sturgeons Two, Three and Four on me, Five and Six to the right."

Gabby and Lysander went after two Zeroes and two Kates, Callicoe led the rest after the other five.

"Don't let them go. Stay with me, Two."

Callicoe got a terse 'Roger' from Sparrow and then focused all of his attention on the two Oscars. They were running interference for the three bombers. The Oscars turned to face them head on. Callicoe gritted his teeth and opened fire. With ammunition to spare, he could afford to. The Oscars broke off and then turned back in hard. Sparrow went high and then rolled over, trying to get inside the first one. The Oscar saw him coming and reversed his turn, pulling tight. Sparrow wasn't going to be sucked into that game and pulled up to gain height and advantage.

Callicoe caught a piece of his Oscar, taking a few lumps out of his wing. The Oscar dived trying to shake him off. Kendall and Cash pushed in for the Judy's. The bombers didn't wait around flying straight and level, they took it down, diving for the cloud bank below them.

Kendall and Cash lost them before they could get close. Like a coordinated dance, as soon as the Judy's disappeared from view, so did the Oscars. They broke off from the Corsairs and went for the deck. Callicoe let them go and reformed the section. As much as he wanted to chalk another one off, their job was to protect the Fleet, not go chasing glory.

The Controllers called them back. The raid had broken off fifteen miles short of the carriers. One had dived on *HMS Hyperion* in the outer picket but missed, crashing into her wake one hundred yards short. Her stern had been pelted by bits of shrapnel but that was all.

Callicoe's sweep was cancelled and his section was kept as an outer cordon up at twelve thousand feet. They landed on after the later strike launched, formed up and went in. They were cock a hoop as they went down for interrogation. Their Corsairs were moved up to be refuelled and rearmed. They would have CAP duties at ten.

The atmosphere in the Wardroom was better than it had been for weeks, seven days rest had made all the difference. Their tails were up, the enthusiasm of the new men had rubbed off.

Callicoe took the chance to get a sandwich and a cup of tea. He was ravenous. Sparrow was talking fast, still riding the adrenalin high of his tangle with the Zeroes he and Gabby had chased after. Gabby had nailed one but the rest had got away. Sparrow hadn't hit a thing. It had all happened so fast; all he did was spray empty air.

Callicoe grinned, pleased to see that he was buoyant and open. The ones who shrank into themselves were the ones to watch. Gabby was tucking into a cheese and onion sandwich with lots of butter.

"The new kid was all right then?" Callicoe asked.

Gabby shrugged, which from him was high praise. To him, sarcasm was still his first line of defence to maintain his sanity.

Lancer turned into the wind to get ready for the returning strike. Before they came into the circuit, Callicoe was launched for his second stint of the day. He got a treat to send him off. With a blare of klaxons, he saw the *Hawke* and *Jellicoe* and the cruiser *HMS Nessus* swing out of line and put on full speed to rendezvous with *King George V*, *Howe* and the other cruisers. The 25th Destroyer Flotilla went with them as cover. It was an awesome sight, watching the capital ships head in towards the islands.

An hour later, six groups of bogeys were detected closing on the carriers. One group drifted south, skirting the outer edge of their radar range. The Controllers thought this was a decoy but it couldn't be ignored. Some of the Fireflies were sent after them to keep the main CAP in place.

Callicoe's brain went into overdrive, listening to the Controllers read out the positions of the incoming groups. They were stacked at different heights, the leading groups lower than the ones coming behind which was clever. Any fighters engaging the ones down low would be out of position to go for the next wave after that.

Sections of fighters were detailed to head after them. Seafires or Corsairs would pounce on a small group, sometimes shooting one down before they peeled off into the clouds only to then turn and come back in again from a different vector.

The cover was whittled away as fighters wheeled to intercept. They kept on coming, wave after wave from different directions. Run ragged, the radar controllers started to lose track of targets.

Callicoe's section was one of the last left covering

Reliant and *Lancer*. Out of nowhere, five Japanese aircraft emerged from a bank of cloud and were diving below them. They had come in low and then climbed into a bank of masking cloud for the final run in. The ships woke up and the sky turned dark as flak went off all over the place.

Callicoe didn't wait for instructions, he broke hard and took his section down with him but he was already too late.

One Zero was blotted from the sky but the rest came straight in. The aircraft carriers were their target. One went for *Lancer*, two went for *Reliant*, one went for *Minerva*.

Callicoe's Corsair jolted as flak exploded around him. He flinched as shrapnel tore into his aileron. He fired almost blind but got lucky. The Judy rolled to avoid his fire and blundered into a string of shells from *Lancer*. Callicoe broke off to get clear and Cash went with him, scared witless by the maelstrom in front of him.

Kendall fared little better. He was about to nail a Zero when a 4" shell went straight through the outer panel of his starboard wing. The Corsair sheered to the left and the Zero was forgotten as he struggled to stop his fighter going into a spin.

Diving almost vertically, the one left heading for *Reliant* misjudged its speed. The controls had stiffened up and it went in straight as an arrow. *Reliant* turned hard to starboard as it commenced its dive. The Kamikaze sliced into the water fifty yards from the island. The ship shook as the bomb went off. Shrapnel penetrated the hull and slashed through steam pipes from the central boiler before burying itself in the bottom of the hull.

Steam vented in the boiler room and scalded crew ran before their skin was flensed from their bones. Two dynamos shut down and *Reliant* slowed down to eighteen knots.

Minerva went to port and increased speed. She didn't have as many guns as *Lancer* and *Reliant* and they weren't as well sited. She needed to manoeuvre to unmask the batteries in front of the island. Crew hugged the deck as 40mm pom poms fired above their heads. The Zero heading right at them came in from astern, misjudged its dive and roared across the bow. It reefed into a hard turn to make another run. It never got the chance; *HMS Siren* blasted it from the sky.

Up above, Gabby clung to the tail of the Judy in front of him. He'd fired twice already and missed. It was diving for *Lancer* and he wasn't going to let them go. The bomber was coming in from dead astern and it rolled slightly to cut inside *Lancer's* turn.

Gabby hunched up inside his cockpit, it was getting tight. The flak was a solid wall in front of him. *Lancer* was flinging up everything she had and he was plunging into the teeth of it. Snarling, he shoved the throttle through the gate and closed in.

His world shrank to the gunsight and the dark green aircraft in front of him. He fired, clipped it, kicked his rudder and fired again; his finger jammed on the trigger. His Corsair juddered as six .50 cal machine guns stripped bullets from belts and flung them down their barrels.

He hit the Judy and kept on hitting it. The canopy exploded, the pilot died and slumped forward, jamming his stick in place. The Judy screamed down and continued its slow roll, slamming into *Lancer's* armoured deck just astern of the island.

It crumpled on impact, then its two bombs exploded within a second of each other. The blast sent out sheets of flame that scorched the island and everything else within fifty yards. Splinters scythed across the deck, cutting men down. A Corsair was blown bodily over the side and an Avenger was cut in two. Fuel spilled from ruptured tanks and burst into flames. Ammunition cooked off and started spraying bullets all over the place. Men ran for cover. Blazing fuel slid across the deck, starting a chain reaction amongst other parked aircraft. Two more Avengers and a Corsair went up before they managed to put it out.

Barrett was sat in the cockpit of his Corsair when the Kamikaze hit the deck. He was scorched from the explosion and lost his eyebrows to flash burns. Temporarily blinded by the flash, he started screaming as he was wreathed in flames. Fumbling blindly, he fell over the side to the deck into more fire. Burning from head to toe, he staggered into the arms of one of the fire crew. Flesh hung off him like strips of bacon, his face a melted blob that screamed silently.

Stricken at not managing to nail the Judy in time, Gabby hauled back on the stick to pull out before he went in himself. Doing close to 450mph, he banked left to clear the carrier. The pom poms and Oerlikons on *Lancer* and the destroyer to her port side followed him all the way. He presented a perfect target, a full profile of wings and fuselage and tail and was perforated from all sides. Gabby screamed as his Corsair was turned into a blazing fireball and plunged into the water.

37 – All Hands On Deck

As the carriers came under attack, hell rained down on the airfields of Miyako Jima. They were hammered by shells from the battleships and cruisers as they steamed along at a steady 15 knots. In line astern like the battle fleets of old, the big 14" guns sent shell after shell to air burst over the runways. Dark clouds of smoke and dust hung over the island as the airstrips were reduced to dust. Admiral Rawlings looked at the Flash signal in his hand and ordered the rate of fire to be increased. The damage had been done; the carriers had been hit. All he could do was complete the bombardment and get back as soon as possible. Forty five minutes after they started, the big ships turned back. It had been a good shoot, but at what cost. Rawlings would only discover when he got back to the Task Force.

Callicoe could only watch in horror as fire blazed on *Lancer's* flight deck. The carrier was wreathed in smoke as the crew fought to get the deck fire under control. In the hangar, a fire was contained by the steel curtains before it could take hold. Choked by smoke the carrier turned to put the wind off the bow. Damage control parties rushed inside the island to put out a fire in the Wardroom. The Air Intelligence Office was abandoned as the steel walls got hot.

Reliant seemed little better. White smoke plumed out of her funnel and she had slowed to a crawl. A slick of oil trailed in her wake, it looked like the ship was bleeding.

He had his section check in and came up one aircraft short, Gabby. Lysander had lost sight of him when Gabby had started his mad dive into the flak. Callicoe went silent, trying to wrap his head around what had happened. Gabby had been with him since the very beginning at *Saint Vincent* over two years ago. It just didn't seem possible. It hurt even more that no one had seen him go in. Callicoe knew what it was; the bloody flak had got him. To die at the hand of your own side was like some sick joke, poor reward for such bravery.

He shook his head to clear it. He'd have to think about Gabby later. He had others in need of him. He looked warily at his fuel gauge, wondering how long he could stay up. He got the others to provide their fuel state and called *Lancer* up to find out what was going on. They were ordered to orbit and maintain the CAP as long as their fuel state allowed.

On *Reliant*, Commodore Moore had gone below deck to damage control to find out what was going on. Up on the flag bridge, he was surplus to requirements in situations like this. He watched silently as the crew fought to get the ship operational again. She had to get up to speed to be able to recover her aircraft.

He returned to the bridge and scanned the horizon. He didn't need binoculars to see the scale of the disaster. Dark smoke climbed from two carriers in the other group. *Formidable* had been hit amidships and forced to reduce speed. Another Kamikaze had skidded off *Indomitable's* deck, taking a number of aircraft over the side. Fire raged on her deck as one aircraft after another cooked off, adding to the flames. Only *Victorious* and *Indefatigable* were operational. He brooded in silence as Admiral Rawlings came back with the battleships and cruisers, too little, too late.

As time ticked by, some of the CAP fighters low on fuel started to land on *Minerva*. Her flight deck began to stack up with aircraft from *Lancer* and *Reliant*. There was even a Hellcat from *Indomitable* recovered. With his carrier force crippled, Rawlings ordered them to withdraw. They turned south east.

On *Reliant*, the repair parties managed to reconnect the steam pipe and within two hours her dynamos were brought back on line. She accelerated to twenty six knots and started to recover aircraft. Callicoe landed last and took his time. He'd never landed on *Reliant* before and it was a little odd. His usual references were different as her deck was higher off the water. He touched down gingerly and caught the third wire. He released the brakes, rolled back to clear the hook and then taxied past the barrier, folding his wings. The deck was jammed with aircraft, Fireflies, Seafires, Corsairs and Avengers.

Callicoe got down on shaky legs. He felt sick. Kendall put a hand on his shoulders and asked him if he was all right. Callicoe nodded, not trusting his voice. They had an impromptu debriefing on the deck. No one felt like going below in case anything else happened. They watched as deck crew refuelled the aircraft and did their best to sort them out. There was so little room up top some of them were taken below to make space. Some Corsairs were positioned for launch in case they were needed.

In the middle of all that, someone announced that Hitler and Goebbels were dead. There was a buzz at the thought that the war in Europe couldn't last much longer. They were one step closer to it all being over. That thought was tempered by the realisation that they still had the Japanese to deal with. They weren't done yet.

The fire on *Lancer* was like a cut to the head, it had seemed worse than it was. Fast actions by the crew saved the day. Burnt aircraft were dumped over the side. Wounded were carried below.

The Doctor had his work cut out for him. Most of the casualties had flash burns of some description. The most seriously burned were given morphine to dull the pain but there was little else he could do.

Up on the bridge, the first officer tried to shrug off an orderly as he helmed the ship. Blood was streaming down his leg and he stood barking orders while a bandage was wrapped around his thigh. Captain Austin was down in the hangar to see how much damage the fire had caused.

Up top, there were two big dents in the deck armour. The biggest was over twenty feet across and nearly a foot deep. There was a hole in the middle the size of a football. The other dent was ten feet wide and only a few inches deep, a frame beam directly underneath had taken the worse of it. Once the deck had cooled sufficiently, a steel plate was welded over the hole and quick drying cement poured over to level it off.

Callicoe landed on *Lancer* and saw the extent of the damage when he got down from his fighter. It looked bad but scorched paintwork could be dealt with. The island was peppered with holes and the two patches of concrete stood out against the green and grey deck. Below, the Air Intelligence Office, the Flight Office and some workshops had been burnt out. The air stank of smoke, burnt wiring and scorched flesh. Two blanket covered bodies were brought out of the Flight Office on stretchers.

The Wardroom was a charred hollow. The side of the piano was blackened, the lino tile on the deck had curled and shrunk from the heat. The chairs were no better than matchwood. Callicoe kicked one out of the way and a piece of metal clattered across the deck. He stooped to pick it up and rolled it over in his hands. It was the piece of his Corsair hook. He put it on top of the piano. He took Gabby's blackboard off its hook and stared at it. The bottom of it had been burnt and the layers of wood had delaminated but the chalk was still legible. Boots crunched on the debris behind him. Callicoe didn't bother to see who it was.

"I just heard about, Gabby," said Goodfellow, his voice muted. Callicoe nodded as he searched the floor. Amongst the debris he spotted what he was looking for. He picked up the piece of chalk and added one more mark on the 'Aircraft Only' column. He put the board back on its hook.

"Not so funny now, is it?" Callicoe said quietly, gesturing to the board.

Goodfellow took the piece of chalk out of Callicoe's hand and added another mark to the board.

"Barrett's gone too," he said. "Well, he's not dead but he's out of it. I want you to be Senior Pilot."

He couldn't bring himself to describe what had happened. He'd seen Barrett down in the Sick Bay, whimpering on a stretcher shot up with enough morphine to fell a horse. His face and arms and upper body were wrapped in blood stained bandages. He would be transferred to a hospital ship as soon as they made the rendezvous. Goodfellow wondered if it would be considered lucky, or unlucky to survive something like that.

The pilots gathered in the hangar and looked at each other, a little shell shocked. It had been one of those days. All of them took the loss of Gabby and Barrett hard. To be shot down in combat was one of the risks they all ran. Flak over the airfields was an occupational hazard, even landing accidents were a part of life because they were under your control. To be burnt to a crisp like Barrett had been, to be cut down by your own flak was a bitter pill to swallow.

Morale on a ship is a complex thing. At sea, they were a community with the Captain as the father figure. A good Captain could make or break a ship. Austin was a good Captain. He did the rounds deck by deck, trying to gee the men up. He spoke to them by name, asked them how they were and made them feel valued.

Austin could see the strain etched on their faces. He knew they were tired. Even the rest at San Pedro had only alleviated the symptoms; it was the pace of operations that had worn them down. The day's events had just piled the pressure on. But, as tired as they were, he could see a pride there. They had survived, the ship had survived and they'd done it together.

Later that night, Austin walked the deck to look up at the stars. It was the first moment he'd had to himself all day. He stood near the bow, listening to the sound of the waves, the thrum of the engines, the clang of steel on steel as work parties kept at it below. *Minerva* was two thousand yards to port, her bow wave shimmering in the moonlight. He'd been glad to have her today or it could have been a disaster.

He turned when he heard someone come up behind him. It was Lieutenant Commander Webster, one of their American liaison officers who'd come on board in Sydney.

"I'm sorry, sir, I didn't realise it was you," said Webster, his southern burr strong. "Up on the bridge we just saw someone up forward."

"I was just taking a moment," said Austin.

Webster stood next to him and shoved his hands in his pockets. If someone had told him he'd never have believed it. He'd been on the *Ticonderoga* when she'd been hit by two Kamikaze. They'd torn through her deck like tissue paper and caused major damage. She'd survived and limped back to Pearl, but it would be months before she'd be ready again. Today he'd seen Kamikaze's bounce off *Lancer's* deck like ping pong balls. All it had taken was a few brooms to sweep the bits off the deck and they were ready to go back in.

"I tell you one thing, you Limey's sure build them tough."

Austin laughed, a great barking laugh that shook his shoulders as the tension of the day came bubbling out.

"We've got to, old boy," Austin got out between gasps, "we don't have as many toys as you."

In a small cabin next to the torpedo workshop, Cullen sat at his typewriter with a blank look on his face. His clothes smelt of smoke, his eyes stung, he had no eyebrows and his arms felt raw. The Doctor had given him some cream for the flash burns but it still hurt. When battle stations had been sounded, he'd gone to one of the pom pom mounts by the island. He'd been leaning over the rail looking up at the Kamikaze diving on them when a loader had grabbed him by the scruff of his neck and hauled him backwards. There had been a loud bang, a huge plume of water and then a big flash.

When he came to, the pom poms were still blazing away and Cullen was laid on the deck, his arms and face singed.

He tried to marshal his thoughts but for once he was struggling. When he was in North Africa, he'd talked the CO of a Wellington squadron into letting him go on two raids. Flak in the dark wasn't the same as being in the middle of a barrage in the day. He'd tasted real fear when he saw that Kamikaze coming down, he just couldn't put it into words.

Another person having trouble putting things into words was Callicoe. He lay on his bunk with his pipe clamped between his teeth. He couldn't be bothered to light it. He tried to take solace in the familiar but a gaping hole had opened in his life. He couldn't go to the Wardroom; it was a burnt out husk. The squadron had gathered in the hangar for a wake of sorts but everyone would look at him and there would be an endless round of muttered platitudes about keeping his chin up.

He knew he should write a letter to Jane but couldn't summon the enthusiasm. If he put it in words, it made it real. If he could just delay a little while, he could sleep and then it would be something that happened yesterday, he could deal with that.

Goodfellow came through the hatch into the cabin.

"May I?"

Callicoe gestured to the chair to his left. Goodfellow sat down heavily. He put a bottle of something on the table top, the glass banging on the wood. He held a tin mug out to Callicoe.

"The one and only bottle of gin that didn't get blown to bits. I figure we deserve it."

"What about everyone else?"

"They've got beer. After today's trials, Captain Austin issued two cans per man."

Callicoe sipped his without tasting it. He didn't sit up either, balancing the mug on his chest. Goodfellow watched him. Callicoe was wound as tight as a drum. Goodfellow had been here himself once. Brooding in silence, trying to deal with the unthinkable.

In 1942 he'd seen his best friend ditch his Swordfish on their way back from a strike. He'd circled twice and saw him get into the dinghy. He'd even waved at him before going hell for leather back to *Victorious*. They never did find him.

Goodfellow often thought about what it must have been like, freezing to death in a dinghy in the middle of the ocean, waiting for help that never came. It had taken him a long time to get over that. He always thought he could have done more but that was just whimsy. That didn't stop the demons come knocking in the dark of night though.

"How many aircraft will we have in the morning?" Goodfellow asked. He already knew the answer, but he wanted to drag Callicoe out of his introspection.

"Counting the two we lost on deck and…Veriker-uh-Gabby's, fourteen."

"About average then," Goodfellow grunted. "Everybody lost a few today." Callicoe didn't bother asking him if he meant aircraft or people.

"Who do you want to take Barrett's section?" he asked. "We're spread a little thin."

Goodfellow nodded, pleased Callicoe had got to the nub of the issue.

"How about Kendall? He's good," he suggested.

Callicoe couldn't argue with the suggestion although he was surprised by it. Not so long ago Kendall had been on Goodfellow's shit list but he'd calmed down since then. He was aggressive in the air; a good pilot and he knew the drill. He remembered what Jane said about time, a day was a week, a week a year. It had been quite a few years since Sydney.

"Do you want to tell him or shall I? I'm his Section Leader but you're the boss."

Goodfellow leaned forward and patted his knee.

"I'll leave it to you to give him the good news," he said as he left the cabin. He'd left the bottle of gin behind as well.

38 – The King Is Dead, All Hail The King

Callicoe was groggy when he was roused at 0330 hours for the early start. His limbs were heavy as he put his flying boots on and shambled up to the Flight Office. It was smaller than the Wardroom but they had to go somewhere to brief. It didn't take long, they'd done it so many times before; fly out to Miyako, fly the flag and come back.

Putting the controversy of the shore bombardment aside, it had worked because there was virtually no flak when they got over the airfield. They made short work of the few guns that did fire at them and Callicoe led from the front, pouring all of his rage and hate at the enemy. He even broke his own rules, making a second pass to come down on a gun post, only pulling up at the last second. From above, his section thought he'd left it too late, watching the Corsair mush lower as it pulled out, clearing the ground by a few feet.

Kendall was just as bad. Leading a section for the first time, he went roaming the island after his passes over the airfield. The lack of AA guns wasn't enough for him. He chased a train and blew it off the track before following the line and shooting up a camouflaged depot, leaving it in flames.

Callicoe got back with fire in his eyes, a new intensity to take the fight to the enemy. He briskly asked his flight if there were any questions and stalked off to make his report. Kendall landed on thirty minutes later full of beans. Goodfellow watched them critically, trying to gauge the mood. They'd been tired at briefing but there was no substitute for action to get the blood flowing

Oates found Goodfellow on the Goofer's Gallery watching aircraft come in. He was dressed in his flying gear, ready to take his turn on CAP.

"Scopes are clear," said Oates. He rolled his neck and breathed deep. It was stuffy in the Fighter Controller office and he needed a break.

"They've got to come soon," Goodfellow said. "I would. I'm surprised they haven't already."

"If I was them, I'd have come at first light to finish us off," Oates replied sagely.

He'd been on edge all morning, waiting for the other shoe to drop. The waiting was agony.

There was no big raid. The only excitement was a radar contact in the afternoon from the west. Goodfellow chased it for two hundred miles before he lost it. Disgusted with himself, he landed back on the carrier to report.

They withdrew that night to resupply and Callicoe let out a sigh of relief. They'd dodged a bullet.

The casualties were transferred to a hospital ship at the resupply rendezvous. Goodfellow saw Barrett over the side. The orderly gave him a slight shake of the head as Barrett was sent over by a breeches buoy. Goodfellow doubted he'd last the night.

They refuelled, replacement aircraft were flown over from the escort carrier and they went back to Sakishima Gunto with the bit between their teeth. The Japanese had missed their chance, now it was their turn.

Hell and retribution was rained down on the islands from the first light of day till dusk. When the Avengers weren't dropping bombs, patrols of Corsairs and Hellcats roamed over the islands firing at anything that moved.

Callicoe settled down into his new role. As Senior

Pilot, he was involved in mission planning and flight assignments. It kept him busy. He was often seen down in the hangar or roaming the flight deck as he haggled with the mechanics to keep the Corsairs serviceable.

Kendall slipped easily into his role as Section Leader. He led from the front and attacked whenever the opportunity presented itself. The Corsairs were now carrying 500lb bombs when they went over on their sweeps and Kendall was getting very good at placing his eggs where he wanted them. He blew a radar station to bits, dropped a bridge and chucked the bombs into hangars when he attacked the airfields.

Callicoe got his undercarriage up smartly and circled the carrier while he waited for the rest of his section to launch. He was on the final CAP of the day before they pulled back once more for fuel and ammunition. He was in a grim mood. They'd received word at breakfast that Barrett had died during the night. Maybe it was a small mercy. Callicoe didn't think he'd want to survive himself if he'd been like that.

That was his greatest fear, fire. He could face being wounded, but fire made a man into a parody of himself, a withered ruin. He'd seen Williams burned alive and he knew if that happened to him, he'd find a pistol or something to finish what the flames had started.

The Corsairs formed up and Callicoe flew north to the outer picket. Since the carriers had been hit, they'd supplemented the CAP even more. They spread them out to provide more coverage, particularly to the west because that was where most of the raids had come from.

Callicoe spread his section out as they ran round the race track, covering their assigned sector. Visibility was mixed. Clouds had moved in and there were rain squalls on the horizon or Callicoe was no judge, perfect Kamikaze weather.

Back on *Lancer*, the radar operators got a twitch, intermittent contacts to the west and to the north. They were moving fast and were very low, typical Kamikaze technique. Twenty five miles out, the contacts firmed up and there were more following behind. FLASH RED went out. Standby aircraft were launched and held in reserve, positioned over the carriers to respond to any that leaked through.

Once the aircraft were up, *Lancer* and *Reliant* cranked on full speed and went east to make the raid chase after them. It wouldn't make much difference, but anything that gave them more intercept time was useful.

Four Seafires from *Reliant* made first contact, breaking up a group of Zeroes. Fireflies went in next, mixing it up with them. Another wave came behind them as they came on in the same old style.

The numbers started to stack up as more and more of the CAP were sucked into the battle, a rolling furball that kept drifting east as the Japanese pilots pushed in. The Fighter Controllers worked hard to manage the engagement but it was slipping out of their control.

Callicoe was called in when they got within fifteen miles. He was in a bad position as he went into the attack. They'd been vectored in when they were almost due north of them and the Japanese fighters weren't waiting around for anyone. Callicoe ran on emergency power but the gap closed slowly. The temperatures began to creep up but he had no choice. He'd rather blow up his engine than let a carrier get blown up.

He got on their tail just short of the fleet and fired. Two Oscars peeled off and turned hard. Callicoe ignored them and fired again, shredding the tail of a Zero with a bomb slung underneath. It wobbled, jinked left and then reared up. Callicoe gave it a long burst and hit it dead centre. It burst into flames and Callicoe broke hard right to avoid colliding with him.

"Nice flamer, boss," said Cash. For a moment, Callicoe thought it was Gabby's voice, the two sounded so similar.

"Three and Four, keep our back clear," he ordered. He couldn't worry about those two Oscars. If they tried to dogfight with you then they were escorts. He wanted the Kamikaze's.

He closed in as they began their attacks. Ahead, a second group were making an approach from the north. Radar had picked them up late and they'd had an almost clear run flying low before they popped up to seven thousand feet to make their attack.

The AA barrage started up, big explosions as the 5" and 4.5" guns fired first. Callicoe gritted his teeth. He was going to have to follow them into that. There would be no pulling back this time, he was committed.

The two Zeroes he was chasing split up. Callicoe stayed on the one in front of him. His Corsair started to jolt as the AA barrage crept higher. Once it got directly over head the carriers, the Zero snap rolled and pulled hard, diving almost vertically. Callicoe fired, missed, and went after it. His world tilted and he had the carrier laid out below him like a plan drawing. Guns sparkled at her sides. *HMS Howe* was throwing up an enormous amount of junk to try and bring the Kamikaze down.

Callicoe rolled as he went down, trying to get an angle on the Zero. Coming from dead astern, the slender wings and thin fuselage made a difficult target. The altimeter was unwinding at a frightening rate. Callicoe knew he only had a few more seconds before he was going to have to pull out of this.

Reliant turned hard to port, the great hull heeling to the right. The Zero tried to roll to adjust but it moved agonisingly slowly as it reached terminal dive speed. Callicoe took his chance. His next burst sawed the port wing in half and the stricken Zero span away out of control. It plunged into the water and blew up.

Callicoe closed his throttle and pulled back on the stick. He had to use both hands to get it back an inch as the Corsair plunged into the barrage. The nose came up slowly and Callicoe levelled off at nought feet going like the clappers. He hugged the waves to get clear, the water around him churned up as gunners chased him away.

The other Zero had commenced a shallow dive, heading for *Reliant* from astern. When the carrier turned to port to avoid the one from above, it put this Kamikaze on her beam. The pom poms and Oerlikons added to the hail of fire. The Zero was hit multiple times but kept on coming. It pulled up to adjust its attack but the pilot wasn't quick enough. The Zero ripped across the rear of the flight deck. He released his bomb just before he hit and it slammed into the side of the ship, just below the fire director. Fire blossomed as the Kamikaze tore through the deck park and slammed into the starboard 4.5" gun mounts, wiping out the crews.

Splinters scythed into the hangar below. An Avenger burst into flames and and fire spread across the deck. The steel curtains were dropped to try and keep the fire from some bombs that had been stored amidships.

The carrier shook as some of the ready ammunition in the gun turrets detonated, peeling back a corner of the deck like a tin can. Shrapnel penetrated the hangar floor and started small fires in the boiler room. Engineers ran around throwing buckets of sand to put the flames out. A few minutes later, there was an explosion and the men grabbed foam extinguishers and worked their way into the bilge flat. Somehow, they managed to keep it from spreading until a damage control party could reach them.

Callicoe had to keep low until he was clear of the destroyers. Every time he tried to gain some height, the gunners went berserk, mistaking him for a Kamikaze. He was well to the south before he could get back up to height. On his own, he checked he was clear before heading back in.

On the other side of the Fleet, Kendall was jammed between two fighters. He had one in front and one behind him. The Oscar juked to the left and he went with him, sticking to him like glue. The one chasing him cut inside his turn and took a piece out of his wing. The controls jerked in his hand.

"Can anyone get that bastard!" he shouted. "Can anyone get him off me?"

He let the Oscar go and dived. He lost two thousand feet and pulled out, but the one behind him was still there. He rolled left and almost lost it, the damaged panel on the wing acting like an airbrake. As he eased out of the turn, the Oscar closed in for the kill. At the last second a Seafire gave it a concentrated burst and dived past, almost vertical. Kendall breathed a sigh of relief as he levelled off.

He worked his controls, eyeing the damage to his wing. The rudder was a little soft as well. He turned left to get back into the fight.

Two more Kamikaze got through and went for *Reliant* from dead ahead. With flame and smoke pouring out of her stern, she reversed her turn, unmasking the port guns to fire. The first Kamikaze fell short and cartwheeled into the water, sending up a sheet of water that soaked the deck. The second was hit at the last moment and went in at an angle, slashing across the bridge before slamming into the deck. The Zero crumpled and rolled across the ship before sliding over the side. The crew later found a red rubber dinghy partially deflated and wrapped around the mast.

The front of the bridge was caved in, only Captain Manson and a Midshipman made it out alive. Steering control was passed to the emergency conning position. The carrier slowed down as the fire in her boiler room raged and dynamos tripped out.

A 250lb bomb exploded at the base of the island and tore off the front plating. The interior was peppered with shrapnel that tore through the Fighter Control office and wrecked the radar repeaters. The gun crews on the forward pom poms were cut down and three Oerlikon mounts were blown clean off the ship along with their gunners.

Commodore Moore was killed. A wicked piece of shrapnel went scything through the island and hit him in the chest. He'd stood stock still, transfixed by the sight of a jagged piece of metal buried in him. He just had time to mutter, "good lord," before he collapsed to the deck, his eyes wide in shock.

Reliant was afloat, but she was in poor shape. She could barely make 10 knots as the damage control parties below deck struggled to keep the fire in the main boiler room from spreading. Backup diesel generators were brought on line to provide electrical power and keep the pumps going.

The escorting Japanese fighters peeled off and headed for home, chased by some of the Corsairs. The Seafires stayed close to the carriers. Worried pilots saw their ship covered in smoke and listing slightly to port. They started nervously watching their fuel gauges, contemplating having to land on *Minerva* again or diverting to *Lancer* before they went into the drink.

That wasn't the Kamikaze's only success. Both *Formidable* and *Victorious* had been hit. *Victorious* caught the worst of it. A hit on the bow knocked her accelerator out of commission and ruptured aviation fuel lines that caught fire. Blazing fuel spilled across the deck and through the hole in the armoured plating into the workshops. Her forward lift was also damaged but remained operational. A second Kamikaze struck the stern a glancing blow on the port side, destroying an arrester cable and wiping out a gun director for the 40mm pom poms.

Formidable was only lightly damaged but she lost a lot of her aircraft. A Kamikaze had slammed into the rear deck park and the carrier had shook from the force of the impact. The rear of the ship was engulfed in a massive fireball as the aircraft went up one after another like a string of firecrackers. Burning fuel leaked into the hangar below but the fire was put out by the sprinkler system. Eleven aircraft were drenched in corrosive salt water and four more were destroyed on deck. The fires were out in fifteen minutes and within half an hour she was back up to speed.

Admiral Rawlings had the Fleet close up for mutual protection as they limped south east to the replenishment point. *Reliant* was the worry. She could barely make fifteen knots. Her flight deck was warped at the rear and the bent plating would have to be cut away. Five of her arrester cables were destroyed and she couldn't receive aircraft.

Lancer's flight deck was crowded as she'd taken some of her Avengers on board. Two of them were wrecked on landing. The other five were parked at the stern.

While the crews worked hard to keep the carriers operational, Admiral Rawlings had a real dilemma on his hands. Admiral Spruance asked for the BPF to remain in action off Sakishima Gunto until May 25th.

Admiral Rawlings sighed and looked at the signal again. He was flattered that Spruance regarded their efforts so highly but the way things were going, he wondered if he would have any carriers left by then.

Only *Lancer* and *Indefatigable* were fully operational. *Indomitable* couldn't maintain full speed. *Formidable* had lost a lot of aircraft although replenishment should make those losses good. *Victorious'* flight deck equipment was in a precarious state and she was experiencing rudder problems again.

Reliant was done. Her flight deck was wrecked. She would need major repair if she was going to get back into the fight and the only place she could get that was Sydney.

He knew some of the blame for this could only be laid at his door. He'd let himself be lulled by the lack of air activity to make his worst blunder, the shore bombardment. Hindsight had shown how crucial the battleships and cruisers were for AA and radar coverage to protect the carriers but he couldn't change what had happened now.

Moore had warned him more than once and he hadn't listened. He regretted his loss bitterly. Moore might have been a little overbearing sometimes, but he'd been the voice of caution that he needed in his ear.

He leaned on the chart table in his flag cabin.

"Two more weeks," he muttered to himself. "Two more weeks. Three more rotations."

They would stay, he owed Spruance that, but he also knew that their position was precarious.

39 – Carnival

Coming back from another sweep, Callicoe cursed his stupidity as they got back to the carriers. The Japanese had been their usual sneaky selves and started using smokeless ammunition. He'd let himself get suckered into going for a line of aircraft parked in plain sight. The Japs had waited until he'd brought the whole flight down to lay their bombs before they gave them both barrels, literally. Lysander had made a new crater on the field. Callicoe couldn't even remember what he looked like.

Callicoe knew there was something wrong with his Corsair because there was a flutter in the stick. On the way back saw his hydraulic pressure was nudging zero. He knew the hook dropped automatically when the pressure went and he could blow down the undercarriage with the emergency Co2 bottle. He just wouldn't know how much he'd be able to drop the flaps which would make it a heavy landing.

He called up *Lancer* to give them the news. Gilliard was game for anything so Oates left it up to him. He could ditch, bail out or give it a go. Corsairs were in short supply so Callicoe was damned if he was going to ditch something that could be fixed.

On the downwind leg he blew down the wheels and got about thirty degrees of flap before he ran out of pressure. He knew he was too fast when he came in but didn't have much choice. Everything happened far quicker than normal. He straightened up badly and put her down off line. The Corsair bounced the wire and hurtled towards the island. At that point, Callicoe knew he was just along for the ride.

He braced his arms over his head and squeezed his eyes tight shut. The stern pom pom crew dived for cover as the Corsair crashed into them. The starboard wing sheared off at the fold, the Corsair swung right and rolled over into the crash barrier. He ended upside down in a screech of metal. He was showered in splintered perspex as the canopy broke around him. Callicoe started screaming when petrol started sloshing all over him.

He spluttered when the deck crew sprayed him with water to stop a fire. He was dragged out of the wreckage and lay on the deck, panting at such a close shave.

"Nice landing," said Gilliard. Callicoe looked up at him upside down.

"I was trying to save the plane," he replied.

Gilliard looked at the wreckage.

"I can see that," he said, deadpan.

Victorious went for the record and suffered three landing accidents in one day that just about finished off her strained deck equipment. A Corsair ripped out two arrester cables, bounced through the barrier in flames and went into the deck park before going over the side. The pilot never made it out in time. Two more heavy landings wiped out the jerry rigged cables they had remaining.

Formidable suffered a careless accident that wiped out what was left of her Air Group. While servicing a Corsair below decks, the fighter's guns had gone off and shredded an Avenger parked across from it. That had sparked a major fire. When it was all over, the hangar was lit only by emergency lights. Over twenty aircraft had either been burnt out or damaged by salt water from the sprinklers. With virtually no aircraft left, *Formidable* left station to follow *Reliant* back to Australia. Then there were four.

Admiral Rawlings had always promised himself that four was the minimum numbers of carriers he would operate with. He didn't even have that really. *Indomitable's* central shaft had overheated reducing her top speed to twenty knots and the parlous state of *Victorious'* deck equipment barely made her operational.

Rawlings was tempted to consider another big gun shore bombardment, but he wasn't prepared to risk his carriers again. They'd not been able to hold the Kamikaze's off when they had six, let alone four damaged carriers on their last legs. Moore's warning banged at the back of his head and he erred on the side of caution.

Increasingly bad weather saved them from pushing themselves too far. In the following days they launched some strikes but fog and rain squalls restricted flight operations. Callicoe was glad. The tired faces of the squadron told its own story. Even when they didn't bend their Corsairs, they were taking more wave offs and making simple mistakes.

They withdrew to the replenishment points one last time and then withdrew to Sydney for rest, repair and refit.

On the trip back Callicoe had to hunker down with Goodfellow and Oates and make some hard decisions. They all knew they would get leave when they got in. What they had to decide was if anyone went home.

There weren't enough complete squadrons to rotate the units like the Americans did. The Admiralty had proposed a six month tour but the Fleet Surgeon Commander had said no. By the time they got back to Sydney, the pilots and crews had flown more sorties in the last three months than the entire Fleet Air Arm had in the last two year's worth of operations. It was going to have to be a decision made by Doctors and Squadron Commanders about who had reached their limit and needed a rest.

Callicoe and Goodfellow had looked at each other

when Oates read that signal out. By that rationale they were both time expired and then some. They weren't the only ones. Wicklow was due too, and Gardner. They were the last of the original pilots that had formed the squadron at *Quonset Point* last year.

"I can't let you all go," Oates said, his face grim. Command decisions had to be made and it pained him to have to make them. "There's not enough experience among the new men. Hell, some of the replacements are barely even deck qualified," he said in frustration.

"I know I've got no right asking you this," Oates said with pain in his eyes.

"I'll do it," said Callicoe.

"And me," Goodfellow agreed. "But Wicklow and Gardner go home. They've done enough."

"Agreed."

Wicklow and Gardner were in the Flight Office playing snap when they were given the news. Their mouths hung open guppy fashion; they couldn't believe it. Both of them protested the decision as Goodfellow knew they would.

"I'm finishing this," Gardner had said.

"But Japan, sir," Wicklow complained. "It doesn't seem right somehow, not being there at the end."

"I'm not sorry," Goodfellow said. "You've done more than anyone can ask. You'll be missed, but some of us deserve to make it."

Goodfellow let them argue some more to get it off their chests but he wouldn't let himself be swayed. He was touched their first instinct was to stay, but they were too close to it. So was he, Oates was right.

The Fleet refuelled at Manus and were cheered when they saw the brand new fleet carrier *HMS Implacable* floating in the anchorage. The sister of *Indefatigable*, she had made good time from England. Vian put her to work on an intensive training program. She'd be ready when they went back into action.

Admiral Rawlings wasn't there to see them in when they got to Sydney. He'd sailed on *King George V* to Guam to meet with Admiral Nimitz. Commander in Chief Pacific Fleet was piped aboard with all the ceremony the Royal Navy could muster. One thousand sailors stood in brilliant sunshine to hear Admiral Nimitz say they were not forgotten and that the United States valued the contribution the Royal Navy was making. That made the newspapers.

More importantly, Rawlings was able to discuss the next phase of operations with CINCPAC directly, without the delays of signals going back and forth. They thrashed out the broad strokes.

Planning for operations over Japan had started even before the Fleet got back to Sydney. The general idea was that the BPF would operate with Admiral Halsey and Third Fleet, joining up with him by the 16th July. Halsey would commence operations off the eastern coast of Japan on the 10th July.

If the Japanese didn't surrender after the first phase, the fleet would withdraw to refit. The next step would be Operation Olympic in October, the invasion of Kyushu, the southernmost of the home islands. Once their forces had a toe hold there, the invasion of the main island would commence in the early part of 1946.

Rawlings said they'd be ready, promising Nimitz four carriers at a minimum. Depending on the extent of the damage, he might have more. Rawlings also knew he had more carriers on the way. *Implacable* had arrived and by the time of Operation Olympic he could promise a second full task force.

Nimitz was well pleased. After the pasting his carriers had taken off Okinawa he needed after deck he could get.

Nimitz wanted them despite any machinations from Washington and Admiral King. Rawlings sailed for Sydney, secure in the knowledge that the BPF would get to play a part.

There was no fancy fly over like the last time they got to Sydney. The aircraft were flown straight ashore. *Lancer's* survivors went north of Sydney to *HMS Nabiac*, a sparse airfield next to the mining town of Kurri Kurri. A rough and tumble town, the place had one of the largest coal mines in Australia, producing thousands of tons per day. The South Maitland Railway connected the town to the city of Newcastle and the coal trucks ran straight from the mine to the harbour.

A special train was laid on to transport them to Sydney and trucks brought them back to Warwick Farm Racecourse. After the heat of the carriers, they relaxed in the cool winter weather, grateful to not broil in their huts while they slept.

Callicoe followed on a day later after coordinating some maintenance work with the staff. He test flew a brand new Corsair painted in a new all over dark blue paint scheme. The blue and red roundels were gone, replaced by large white circles and bars.

He'd got up to height and hit full throttle, hearing the engine purr. He stunted around and enjoyed the taut controls of a brand new aircraft. He touched down neatly and taxied to dispersal, folding the wings before he parked it. They had six more like that on the line, painted with *Lancer's* T on the tail.

Once he was happy they had everything in hand, he got the train to Sydney to catch up. He arrived just in time, they were having the send off for Wicklow and Gardner. Their orders had come through to return to England. They were going on a freighter that was heading to Bombay for the first stage of their journey. From there they hoped to get a Liberator to Aden or Cairo.

It was the thrash to end all thrashes. They went into town on the train and after going in two places, they washed up at a pub called the The Magpie. They entered like a human tide with Gardner and Wicklow in the vanguard. Cold beers were lined up at the bar and they toasted the departing heroes, all of them jealous they weren't going in their place.

Wicklow took up his position by the piano and started cranking out the usual hits. They finished with Rule Britannia, sixteen pilots and a collection of locals joining in at full volume. Glasses banged the tables. The only ones not participating were a small knot of American officers at the other end of the bar. One of the new boys, Ritchie lurched over and nudged an American Lieutenant to join in.

The Lieutenant had been propping up the bar quite happily before his peace had been so rudely interrupted. He shoved Ritchie in the chest, grabbed his beer glass and threw it on the floor.

"Fucking Limey!" he said with some vehemence.

The singing came to an abrupt halt.

"Rule Britannia? You guys are so stupid you don't know when you're beat. You don't rule the waves. Not anymore." He dabbed himself in the chest with his thumb. "We rule the waves out here."

Before anyone could make a move, Ritchie squared up to him. He tapped the Lieutenant on his shoulder.

"You know, old chap. I think I take exception to that."

An Ensign tried to calm things down.

"Excuse my friend here, he's just had some bad news."

The Lieutenant shrugged off his pal with one arm while he started pulling his tie off with the other. He was drunk so he didn't even bother getting off his stool, he just swivelled to face Ritchie. His eyes glittered; his mouth fixed in an evil grin.

"You know what, old chap? I kinda hoped you'd say that."

He cracked his knuckles. Ritchie was steeling himself for the first punch when the Ensign took matters into his own hands. He had the legs of the stool out from under his friend and dumped him on the floor.

"Do excuse us, we'll find someplace else. Come on you."

He grabbed one arm, and the Americans exited the pub before anything else happened. The Lieutenant roared and struggled but he was too far gone to put up much of a struggle. The Ensign came flying back in, put two pounds on the bar and tipped his hat before running out again. The Landlord scooped up the money and put it in the till.

"Well that was odd," Wicklow said. He shrugged and carried on playing.

"What the hell are we gonna do?" said Callicoe. "No bugger else plays on the squadron."

"You could always keep me," Wicklow replied with a grin as he tinkled the ivories with a flourish. "Sort of like a squadron mascot. Unbox me for special occasions."

"Far be it from me to spoil a good idea," said Goodfellow, "but home you go youngster." He patted him on the head.

Gardner was prevailed on to have more than one or two drinks for once. He let himself go, singing like the rest of them. It was only then that Callicoe could see just how much the strain had been playing on them. It had sloughed off and they were carefree, cracking jokes like little kids.

They stayed until closing time and went back to Warwick Farm where they polished off some more bottles of beer. When they finished the beer, they moved on to gin. At the end, Gardner was miraculously still vertical and conscious. He sat on the grass with his back to the hut. Wicklow and Callicoe sat next to him.

"I'm going to miss you two," Callicoe said.

"Easy changed," said Wicklow with a grin. He took a long pull on his bottle of beer.

"Out of my hands laddie," Callicoe told him.

He knew what Wickolow was thinking. There was that pull to see something through to the end. It was the perennial paradox of operational flying. Any sensible person would refuse to go up, but they did it every day. Grown men never admitted to being scared, you'd be accused of being twitchy. If someone had told him he was grounded, Callicoe was sure he would have protested too, however ridiculous such protestations might be.

"Where will we be in a year do you think?" Gardner slurred. He closed one eye and squinted at his bottle of gin, trying to see if there was any left.

"Drinking beer at home I hope," Wicklow said. His father had a boat building business at Teddington. He'd go back to creating something instead of destroying things. Callicoe baulked at the idea of returning home to his tangled family web but he struggled to see how he could avoid it.

Come the morning, everyone was there to see Wicklow and Gardner off in their jeep. Regardless of hangover, it was three cheers and caps were thrown in the air. Callicoe captured the moment with his camera.

Jane walked back and forth in the park, hands fidgeting, her heart hammering in her chest as she waited for him. She already had some idea what he'd been through after *Reliant* and *Formidable* had made port the week before.

Cullen had filed his copy as soon as he got ashore, giving his stories to whoever was interested. Even allowing for censorship, the *Herald* and the *Telegraph* had been full of tales of derring do, Kamikaze attacks and heavy raids on enemy positions. She didn't even need to read between the lines, they'd all been to hell and back.

She was shocked by his appearance when she saw him. He was tanned but his face was drawn and there was a haunted look she'd not seen before. He kissed her and just stood there with his arms wrapped around her.

"Hey you," he said, his voice cracking. He'd managed to hold himself together just long enough until he saw her.

"Darling," she breathed, her eyes damp with tears. They stood, heads bowed, foreheads touching. Finally, Callicoe gathered himself. He wiped his eyes and clamped his pipe in his mouth.

"Right, what's for dinner?" he asked, his voice gruff.

Jane held his hand and led him to a little place she'd found. They talked about everything except the obvious question, 'how long have we got?' He asked her when she could get leave and she replied she was overdue. She'd been waiting for him to get back.

For the next few days Goodfellow imposed some order. He had them on the grass doing PE in the morning, sweating the alcohol out of them. There were classes on ship and aircraft identification. An Intel type came gave them an overview of Japan and its history. He pointed out the islands on a big map and discussed escape and evasion.

"It's not like Europe," he said. "You're not going to be able to blend into the background amongst the local population." That raised a laugh. The average Japanese was just five foot tall so Goodfellow would be like some sort of mountain stood next to them.

"They revere the Emperor and have been taught from birth that they're a superior race in culture and military prowess. You're the barbarians and you're cowards to surrender. Don't expect any help from civilians. It'll be a toss up that they kill you or hand you over to the army."

Goodfellow gave them the afternoons off and they couldn't get out of Warwick Farm quick enough. They rode the train into town to go to the drinking or swimming on the beach. They were on their best behaviour and there was no grief from the local Constabulary.

Kendall saw his girl, Marjory. He had to break the news to her sister Evelyn about Gabby, it was the hardest thing he'd ever done.

Goodfellow asked Callicoe to sort out the squadron's appearance. They'd gotten raggy the last few weeks. Pilots wanted to be comfortable when they flew. With the limited laundry facilities on board ship, they'd taken to wearing a kaleidoscopic variety of outfits under their Mae Wests and parachutes. Some of them wore green Aussie jungle fatigues. Others wore a mix of American and Royal Navy pants and shirts. More than one wore a thin all in one flight suit and who could forget Gabby's episode in his pyjamas. Few of them had a complete set of uniform. Callicoe managed to prise some new kit out of the supply department.

When they'd had their hair cut and tidied themselves up a bit, Goodfellow had the squadron paraded for a photo. Callicoe remembered the one taken at *Quonset Point*. He was the only one left now. He sat in the middle of the front row next to Goodfellow on the left. Commander Oates sat on the right.

Callicoe pottered around in the afternoons. Sometimes he snatched an hour or twos peace and had a nap or did some admin. He rang *HMS Nabiac* for their progress on the aircraft. Callicoe went up one day to see for himself. He drove up to save time. It was a wasted trip really, they knew what they were doing, but he took the opportunity to take a Corsair up for a flip to keep his hand in.

In the evenings, he went out with Jane. They went to the movies; they went to dinner. One evening he made up a four with Kendall and his girl.

"The place is supposed to be quite good," Kendall had said. "Cheap booze, loud music."

Callicoe met Jane at the park as usual. She did a small pirouette, lifting one heel, arms posed.

"How do I look?" she asked him.

She looked stunning, in a knee length figure hugging red dress, pinched at the waist. She wore the sweetheart pin he'd bought her, the miniature pair of Fleet Air Arm wings on the left lapel. She completed her look with white gloves and white peep toe heels.

They met Kendall and Evelyn by the Queen Victoria building. Kendall's date was a pretty blonde, tall like Kendall. She was wearing a dark green dress with matching heels. She had a showy hat with a long feather that made her look like something out of an Errol Flynn swashbuckler. Callicoe felt a little self conscious, he was the shortest one there.

It was a good dance. The band played a variety of music and the floor was jammed with couples as they danced. Callicoe did his best and only managed to stand on Jane's toes a few times.

"You've improved," she said as they circled close together.

"I practised."

"Who with? Gabby?" she said automatically without thinking. "I'm sorry," she said as she saw his face drop.

"It's all right," he said, holding her close.

Callicoe danced with Evelyn a few times. He thought she was very nice. She had a long face set off by wonderful cheek bones and crystal blue eyes. Her hair was cut to shoulder length, styled in bangs to frame her face beautifully. She was a very good dancer too, naturally guiding him without making it obvious.

Kendall stared wistfully at her shapely behind as she and Jane went to powder their noses.

"Smashing girl," he said.

"She is," Callicoe agreed.

He produced his pipe and packed the bowl with tobacco from a small drawstring pouch. He struck a match and lit the pipe, luxuriating in the smell of the tobacco. He'd found a small tobacconist on Bueler Street and bought himself a whole pound of a Virginia mix with hints of applewood and cherry.

Callicoe regarded Kendall, pleased that he'd risen to the challenge of running a section. His earlier wobble was long forgotten.

"So when's the skipper going to give us leave?" he asked.

"Next week I think," Callicoe replied. "I'm sorting the paperwork at the moment."

He was looking forward to it himself. Seven days off. It had been the longest time he'd had to himself since the squadron shipped out last year. He was going to tell Jane later; it would be a nice surprise.

"What do you have planned?"

Kendal shrugged.

"Not much. Something lazy. I know some of the lads fancy a bit of adventure but Evelyn's folks have a place at somewhere called Manly Bay. There's a beach, it sounds perfect. What about you?"

"Something similar I imagine." Callicoe grinned. "Jane wants to keep me to herself I think."

All of their carefully laid plans went out of the window the following morning when orders came for the squadron to report to *HMS Nabiac* immediately. It wasn't just them; it was all of *Lancer's* Air Group. They packed their bag. Callicoe just had time to scribble a note for Jane get one of Reliant's lot to promise to deliver it.

There was pandemonium at the train station as MP's commandeered two carriages on a northbound train. They crammed aboard and it was two hours north to the tent city of *HMS Nabiac*.

On the train ride, speculation was rampant but Oates wouldn't be drawn on what was going on. He had his orders just as they had and operational security topped everything.

They found the mechanics were working flat out on the aircraft. They spent the rest of the day alongside them, putting in a short flight test and satisfying themselves that they were ready.

Oates didn't like being rushed. It was times like this that things got missed or there were accidents.

At dusk, he gathered the Air Group together by one of the Corsairs. He looked at the faces of the men that he'd gotten to know over the last few months.

"You know, I always thought we were special. We've shown that we can get the job done when it matters so some of you might look on this as a reward. There's a rush job on and the Admiral's decided we're the only ones that can do it."

"We've got one more day to get ready, check the kites over and make sure they're top of the line. So, knock off now, get your tea, we're going to be burning the midnight oil."

40 – The Next Generation

Callicoe circled the Task Force waiting for the Avengers to form up. When they were ready, he spread his section out and climbed, clawing for height to provide top cover for the strike going in. Goodfellow was out front, Kendall was the mid cover. Two sections from 1783 were bringing up the rear. Seafires from *Minerva* and the other section from 1783 would provide CAP while they were gone.

Vice Admiral Hallows watched from *Lancer's* bridge as the aircraft headed north east. The launch interval was good and there were no delays. It was everything he'd been promised when he was appointed to be Commodore Moore's replacement.

Even the launch from *Minerva* had gone well. It was no easy thing coordinating aircraft operations with two such disparate types of carrier. He was impressed considering this whole escapade had been laid on at such short notice.

The Americans had asked for some assistance. With *Implacable* already committed to operations off Truk Lagoon, *Lancer* had been sent instead. She was the most ready of the carriers but they didn't want to risk her on her own so *Minerva* was sent to provide a spare deck.

The Air Group came aboard when they were thirty miles off the coast of Nelson Bay, the land a smear on the horizon. Once they were on their way, Hallows addressed the ships company for the first time.

"I suppose you're wondering what all the flap is? Now we're at sea, I can tell you."

"Two and a bit thousand miles northeast of here is Tuara Atoll, a mere speck in the middle of nowhere. The Japs have had it since 1942. When the Americans started taking islands back, places like Tuara were bypassed and isolated."

"They've been a bit naughty, causing some problems. The Americans have asked us to lend them a hand. Get some rest. I think we're going to be busy for the next few days."

Kendall and Callicoe shared a look. They had hoped it was just going to be some training, the new Admiral flexing his authority.

"Terrific. So much for our leave," Callicoe muttered.

"God knows what, Evelyn's going to say. I had my leave all set up," Kendall complained. "You can just imagine what she thinks I'm up to."

Callicoe shifted in his seat, constantly scanning the sky as they got nearer to the island, nervous at what might be waiting for them. The briefings and strike planning had been comprehensive enough. The Americans had provided plenty of photographs of the islands themselves, but accurate intelligence of what was currently there was a bit thin on the ground.

Aside from Nauru Island further north, Tuara had one of the largest phosphate deposits in the world. A German mining concern had relocated Chinese workers there to commence mining in the middle of the last century. After the First World War, it had become a British concern. It exported its produce to Australia and New Zealand for mining. A small rail line was built on the south side of the island to go from the mine to the dock so ships could be loaded. When the Japanese took the island in 1942, they had turned the place into a fortress. They built an airfield, another dock and warehouses to store supplies. The coral atoll four miles to the west became a fleet anchorage. Fuel storage tanks were built there for it to provide a stopping point for the large fleet ships of the IJN.

Reconnaissance had shown there was at least one destroyer at the island, some patrol boats, a few fishing boats and some aircraft. Intelligence had assured them the islands had been cut off for months and were probably low on fuel. Callicoe took that with a pinch of salt. The islands weren't checked that often, anything could have been shipped in. Obviously, they must have received some fuel, otherwise the Americans wouldn't have bleated about some of their transports being attacked a few days before.

They decided to go for the airfield first. If they could take care of whatever the Japanese had there and crater the runways, then they could range at will. If ships got underway, the Task Force had more than enough firepower to take care of them.

Tuara came in sight on the horizon, a dark smudge against the bright blue sea. It was a beautiful day with clear skies and visibility for miles.

Callicoe reminded his section to go on to oxygen as they passed twelve thousand feet. He put his own oxygen mask on and did a radio check, the other five of his flight checking in crisply as he insisted on.

Even if fuel was in short supply, the Japanese clearly weren't rationing ammunition. They threw up a blizzard of fire as the aircraft got closer. It was far heavier than anything they'd seen over the airfields at Sakishima Gunto, big balls of black smoke and orange fire.

The Avengers didn't wait around. As soon as the flak started, they went down into the attack. The AA fire was ferocious. Two Avengers had to dump their bombs on the run in. Smoking, they turned out to sea back towards *Lancer*. Both ditched short of the carrier on the way back.

The rest laid their eggs on the airfield. Explosions blossomed as they flew the length of the runway. A bomb went through the roof of one hangar and huge tongues of flame shot out of the doors and windows. Huts burned. A fighter was blown to pieces. Callicoe kept an eye out but no enemy fighters put in an appearance all the way there and back.

The radar controllers picked up a solitary blip thirty miles to the west going in circles. It didn't come close enough to warrant sending the CAP after them.

They landed and rearmed. Kendall's section was fitted with two 500lb bombs so they could leave some parting gifts of their own.

They made another pass at the airfield and left it a smoking ruin. Kendall dropped his bombs and roamed at will. He picked off gun emplacements and shot up any aircraft he found on the ground. Men were chopped down as they ran.

"My oath, it's almost too easy," he said at interrogation with a gleam in his eye. "They can keep lining them up all day like that as far as I'm concerned."

Callicoe drank cup after cup of tea. There was an itch at the back of his head. He was nervous, expecting a surprise. Goodfellow tried to reassure him.

"Come on, Jim. If they were going to do something, they'd have done it by now. It's not like it was last time."

"I hope you're right," Callicoe replied. "I really hope you're right."

The Task Force steamed east while they were being rearmed for the third strike. Hallows wanted to keep some distance between himself and the anchorage in case the Japanese did have any operational ships there.

On the third strike they went for the mine dock on the southern shore. There wasn't much there at all. The Avengers ignored the accommodation blocks and flattened the warehouses by the dock. The flak was light, just a few pop guns around the dock itself.

The freighter that was tied up alongside was hit by at least three 500lb bombs. They left it burning, its decks awash. Callicoe shot up a bunch of junks that were tied up and a small launch with a machine gun fitted on the bow. He left them burning but it was distinctly unsatisfying. They were using a sledgehammer to crack a nut, at least that's how it felt to him.

Callicoe, Kendall, White and a few others gathered at the stern under the flight deck. It was cooler here. After a week and more ashore, it was stifling hot being back on board ship. Callicoe enjoyed his cold beer. It was one of the improvements the docks had made at Captain Austins direction. The ships water plant was completely inadequate to provide enough cold water or ice, so when the Wardroom was being rebuilt and the mess decks overhauled, he'd had some extra refrigeration units installed. It wasn't much, but it was a definite improvement since they'd last been on board.

"Why are we here?" asked White.

"My word, you don't hang about do you?" Kendall said. White was in his Section now, his dogged Aussie determination a good match for Kendall's aggressive tactics.

"What I mean is, anybody could do this. It's almost practise, and we don't need the practise."

"I don't care," said Kendall. "I'll take any chance to kill a few more Japs."

White could understand that sentiment. He'd known a few mates the Japanese had killed at Singapore. A few more were POW's, he didn't know if they were alive or not.

Callicoe didn't comment, not wanting to be drawn into the conversation. White was making a fair point. Escort carriers could have done what they were doing.

Later on, Hallows gathered Oates, the intel bods and the senior staff of his squadrons together. It was Callicoe's first chance to see Hallows up close and he listened carefully as the Admiral outlined his intentions for the morning.

He was tall, brown haired with a face creased by staring into too many suns on deck. Slight in build, the broad gold shoulderboards hung off him. His voice was soft and Callicoe found he had to strain to hear him.

There was general agreement that there was minimal air threat. They'd gone in strong and not seen a single aircraft in the sky all day. This wasn't like operating off Formosa and Sakishima Gunto. There was nowhere for a sneaky force of hundreds of Kamikaze to hide. They could afford to relax their precautions somewhat. *Minerva's* Seafires would fly the CAP, two sections of Corsairs would escort, the rest could roam targets of opportunity. Overnight, *Hawke* would close in with the Cruisers *HMS Nessus* and *HMAS Mildura* and three destroyers running a screen to bombard shore installations. Some of the Corsairs would spot and call fall of shot.

Callicoe turned in, tired. It was stifling below deck so he got three blankets and his pillow and slept on the quarterdeck. He wasn't the only one. The tannoy called them to stations at 0330 hours. Callicoe dragged himself up. He didn't bother changing, he was still wearing what he had on yesterday.

He assigned Kendall's section to escort. His own section would strafe today. Callicoe ducked underneath his Corsair and looked at the two 500lb bombs on their racks.

It might have been bright and early but the Japanese gunners weren't asleep. The AA fire over the anchorage was lighter than it had been over the airfield but it was still accurate.

There were three exits to the anchorage which was about three miles wide. On the eastern side, the widest spit of land had some oil storage tanks and a number of huts and small buildings. No effort had been made to camouflage them, there was no point as they were completely in the open.

Callicoe dived into the attack. He'd lay his eggs first and then come back to strafe the AA guns to clear the way for the Avengers.

A destroyer in the harbour added to the weight of fire and he sheared off as a pattern of shells exploded in front of him. Rolling back, Callicoe steepened his dive and lined up on a cluster of gun pits by one of the long wooden jetties. He released his bombs at fifteen hundred feet and pulled up, turning to the right to clear the way for the next one in.

His bombs bracketed the gun pits. Sandbags and pieces of men were tossed into the air. Two guns fell silent. He brought his section down to almost mow the lawn, their .50 cal machine guns scything the ground and kicking up sand. Callicoe came in at thirty feet and shot up a patrol boat tied up at the dock, it burst into flames.

The Avengers flew doggedly through the flak and lined up on the destroyer. It was a sitting duck. It made no attempt to move. It just sat there at anchor, spitting its defiance at them as bombs hit the water around it, soaking the deck. A bomb exploded on the stern and another hit near the bridge of the port side. It was smoking when they left.

They were back two and a half hours later to finish the job. The Destroyer didn't go down without a fight but unable to manoeuvre, it was in no doubt. Hit by four more bombs, it rolled onto its port side and slid beneath the waves leaving men bobbing amongst oil and debris. The storage tanks were cracked open like eggs but they didn't burn, they were empty.

During the second attack, a Zero floatplane went speeding across the water after it emerged from a camouflaged position. Callicoe was on its tail in an instant as it tried to get airborne.

Just as it lifted off, Callicoe closed to point blank range and gave it a two second burst. The nose dipped, the float caught a wave, it wobbled and then the wingtip float dragged. It disappeared in a mass of spray.

HMS Hawke opened fire at 1100 hours and kept on going for two hours. The cruisers contributed to the barrage. They pummelled the mine, the warehouses and the dock before moving west and switching targets to the airfield. By early afternoon there was nothing left to shoot at and the big ships withdrew to take up escort position around *Lancer*.

The last action of the day was a final sweep by the Corsairs over the island. It was almost a waste of fuel, there was literally nothing left to shoot at. Whatever had harassed the American ships before was either long gone or dead and buried.

The only excitement was when they came back to land on. Callicoe thumped down hard and there was a moments panic when his drop tank broke loose and shot into the deck park like a torpedo. Men scrambled to get out of the way while it left a trail of petrol behind it. Luckily it didn't ignite but Callicoe had a moments panic remembering what had happened to Barrett and Williams.

41 – When You Think Of Me

When they got back, Callicoe and Goodfellow spent hours sorting the admin out for the leave passes. They'd double checked everything with Oates first. Although the Fleet would be in for weeks yet, Oates said they better get away while they could. *'Don't sign a lease,'* was how he put it. Goodfellow decided he better get the men away quick before anything else happened.

The city council had organised a hospitality centre where sailors could go when they got leave to be fixed up with a holiday. For men far from home, there were things as diverse as riding on a sheep station, climbing in the Blue Mountains or relaxing on a beach. They scattered to the four winds, desperate to get away for a few days.

As soon as she got the call, Jane cleared the arrangements with her boss. She dodged back to her digs for the bag she had packed and was waiting outside the station for him. He appeared round the corner ten minutes later, his kit bag slung over his shoulder.

"Sorry, last minute stuff, you know how it is."

She kissed him lightly on the cheek.

"That doesn't matter. You're here."

"Right, shall we go?"

She nodded and they went into the station to find the right platform for the train to Newcastle. It was almost a reverse of the journey he'd taken from Kurri Kurri. They sat together in an empty compartment and talked the entire way there.

He helped her down to the platform and they showed

their ticket to the inspector as they left the station. They stood at the exit waiting to be picked up like he'd been told.

Callicoe noticed a man and woman off to the right staring at them intently. They looked at each other and she gave him a little nudge. He made a calming motion with his hand and walked towards them. Callicoe thought he was in his early fifties, wearing a well tailored tweed three piece. He doffed his fedora.

"Lieutenant Callicoe?" he asked, a little unsure of himself.

"That's me."

The man held out a hand in obvious relief.

"I'm, Tom Fair." Callicoe shook his hand as the woman came over. She reminded him of a little mouse, her gloved hands held diffidently in front of her. She was petite, barely coming to the man's shoulders, "This is me wife, Judy."

"Pleased to meet you," Callicoe said. "This is, Lieutenant Fisher," he said, gesturing to Jane.

Tom Fair looked between them.

"Lieutenant Fisher?" he said slowly.

"That's right."

Callicoe steeled himself for the protest. Judy Fair gave him a knowing nod and asserted herself.

"Oh, Tom, it's not an interrogation. I'm sure these officers have had a long and tiring trip on the train. You come with me dearie," she said, looping her arm through Jane's and leading her towards their car. It was a red long nosed Austin with a big gas bag fixed to the roof.

Tom shot his wife a look and then picked up Jane's small suitcase. He put it in the boot. Callicoe put his kit bag next to it. He got in the front passenger seat, the women in the back.

They drove out of town, up the coast, round Nelson Bay to their home at Hawks Nest, Playfair House. Judy asked them questions the entire way, thrilled to hear about Kalgoorlie and London. Tom didn't talk much. He was a nervous driver and kept his eyes fixed on the road.

Callicoe expressed surprise when Tom said he'd made his money sheep farming and then branched out a bit.

"I didn't think there was so much money in farming," he said.

"Yeah, well. It all depends on the scale," Tom said.

"Don't boast dear," Judy said, cutting him off.

Just outside of town, their house was in manicured grounds. Clumps of Gymea Lily sprouted from flowerbeds. The house was built in the Federation style. It had red brick walls, with a broad veranda under a large sloping roof of galvanised tin providing plenty of shade. The gable ends, fascia and veranda columns were painted white.

Tom parked the car and got the bags, taking them into the house. Judy went in with him. Jane clung off Callicoe's arm, eye's shining. The sound of the waves on the beach was magical and she loved the fresh air.

In the house, Tom was talking in hushed whispers as he looked at them through the screen door.

"I'm not happy about this, Judy," he muttered.

"Nonsense," she said, looking at the two of them in their uniforms. She was amused at her husband's prudish stance. Eminently practical, she'd seen the situation for what it was as soon as Callicoe had made the introductions.

"Now you listen to me, Thomas Fair. You're not to say a word to them," she told her husband sternly. "They're here to enjoy a hard earned leave. Don't you remember being in love once?" she asked her husband. He snorted but she carried on without waiting for him to say anything else. "I'll go and make the beds up," she told him.

Callicoe came into the house and took his cap off. It was light and airy inside. The hall had a polished wooden floor adorned with rugs. The walls were painted a pastel yellow.

"You know, it's awfully good of you to let us stay like this," Callicoe said. Tom Fair clicked his tongue and went up the stairs to his den to stew. Jane appeared, looking around. She spotted a mirror on the wall and went over to fuss with her hair. Judy reappeared all bright and breezy.

"Now my loves, you've got the bedrooms at the end of the hall. Our two eldest are in Burma so they won't be needing them at the moment. Mark this, you've got the run of the house. If you need anything just call and we have dinner late; after seven."

She left them to it. Callicoe went down the long hall, noting the rooms as he went. To the left was the dining room and a living room. To the right, the bedrooms and bathroom. At the end of the corridor was the door to the kitchen. Their bedrooms were next to each other.

Jane went for an explore outside. The garden was huge, a good two hundred feet either side of the house. White wooden steps ran down to the beach. There was a small beach house by the steps.

The beach at Hawks Nest ran from Yaccaba Head in a great curve nine miles north to Sandy Point. It would be good to go for a long walk, she thought to herself.

They got changed. Callicoe couldn't get out of his uniform fast enough. He put on a shirt and some tan slacks he'd bought at Gowings. Jane emerged from her bedroom in a simple green dress and brown shoes. She smiled and put on some sunglasses.

"Lovely."

"Would you do me the honour of a turn?" Callicoe said with mock solemnity.

They went outside to the garden. After months cooped up on the carrier, he wanted to stretch his legs.

Tom was reserved at dinner but Judy carried the conversation easily. She asked Callicoe all sorts of things about England.

"It must be so hard being from home," she said.

"Oh, it's not too bad. They've got the mail sorted. One of my squadron got a letter from his mother in twenty five days."

"And what about your family?"

"Not much to tell," he said, making light of it. "One brother, married, with children. One father, one step mother. All very normal."

"You said you had a sheep station, Tom?" he said, changing the subject.

"I do. I've got a few places a long ways from here, out around Temora. Family business for a long time."

Callicoe could see Tom was the outdoor type. Even with the veneer of wealth he could see he'd worked for a living. His face was lined from squinting in strong sunlight and no aristocrat ever had hands like that. He'd wager a guess that the he had more than just a 'few' places. He'd caught the hint of pride in his voice when he'd spoken about the sheep station in the car.

"Course, Judy's from Sydney so we've got this place for holidays, things like that. She likes the sea."

"Yes. We used to come here for holidays when I was a girl so Tom bought this for me," she said, preening with pleasure.

They were an interesting pair, Callicoe thought. Judy clearly wore the trousers at home but he had no doubt that Tom was the master when he was working. She'd just polished off some of his rough edges. Jane was less impressed, seeing shades of her father and her husband in him.

Tom and Judy retired early after dinner, the matriarch wanting to give them some space on their first night.

Callicoe sat on the veranda, enjoying the cool of the evening. Jane sat next to him on the wicker sofa, legs tucked up under her.

"Do join me," he said with a grin.

"You know this thing is called a love seat?" she told him. He shot her a sidelong glance; sure she was teasing him.

"Good lord. You learn something new every day."

She shivered and rubbed her arms. "Cold," she said. He lifted his right arm and she snuggled up against him. They sat like that for a while, lulled by the sound of the surf on the sand.

She yawned and stretched like a cat.

"I'm for bed," she said, sleepy. She kissed him and slipped inside the house.

Callicoe sat for a while yet, doing his damnedest not to think.

Jane found Callicoe in Mark Fairs bedroom, the eldest of the Fairs sons. Jane had heard all about him from Judy the last few days. He was a Chemical Engineer before he'd volunteered for the army. He was a handsome boy in his photograph on the shelf. Jane wondered what kind of man would return from the jungle.

Callicoe lay on the bed, his back to the door, whether that was a deliberate move on his part, she couldn't guess. His right hand was propping up his head while he read a book.

"I was thinking of going for a swim later," she said, trying to keep her tone light. He didn't move, he just turned a page, eyes focused on the book.

"If you feel like it," he said.

He half turned as she sat on the bed behind him, placing a hand on his side. The silence was deafening. She sighed.

"Are we going to talk about it?

"Should we?" he asked, his tone brittle. He knew if he rolled over, he'd see the tears gathering in her eyes and his own defences would come tumbling down.

"James. I don't want this to spoil things."

"Neither do I." He turned another page.

"Then why-"

"-because I don't like being pushed," he bit out, regretting his tone as soon as he said it.

It had started innocently enough like most arguments do. They had been on the beach, relaxing in the lee of a dune in between a quick dip. She'd been sat in front of him and he'd wrapped a big towel around them both, keeping the wind off. He'd rested his chin on her shoulder as she leaned against him.

He wasn't even sure how the argument had started. They'd been talking about how long *Lancer* would be in port and what they could do and how they could see each other. His memory clicked. That was it. He'd said something like, "I can meet you every day if you'd like."

"And later?" she'd asked, her tone coquettish, teasing.

"What do you mean?" he'd asked, his brow furrowed.

"I mean, what happens when it ends?" she'd said quietly, suddenly tense in his arms.

"Um, I go back to England I expect."

She'd stiffened and Callicoe knew he'd said the wrong thing. She shifted forward away from him. It was just a fraction but the distance became a gulf.

"England. Back to your family I suppose?" she said, more a statement than a question.

"Well, yes," he'd replied slowly, his brain struggling to switch gears and catch up.

"The loving family you wanted to get away from," this last was said with a bit of a sneer which he didn't like.

"Darling, one needs money. One needs a job to make their way in this world. I don't imagine there's going to much call for a retired carrier pilot with five kills to his name and few other skills."

"And there's no place for me in all of that, is that it?" She stood up in a flurry of limbs, fighting to get free of the towel before running up the beach. He tried to stop her but she fought him off and left.

The ground could have swallowed Callicoe at that point. He didn't mean to hurt her. He knew he should have gone after her, said something, but his natural caution hauled him short as the question rattled around his head.

He realised he hadn't thought of Jane in all of that. It wasn't that he didn't like her, he did, very much. The thought of getting back to Sydney and her waiting for him had sustained him during those long days off Formosa and Sakishima Gunto. He sat for a while after that, staring at the waves as they crept further up the beach as the tide came in. Shivering, he'd picked up the towels, shook the sand out and walked back to the house.

After showering and changing, he'd stayed out of the way to get some space until Jane came looking for him.

"I'm sorry, Jane. It was a careless remark, I'm sorry. I don't want to fight."

"I'm not pushing. I just asked what the future held for us, for me," she said with a hard swallow, almost scared of what his answer was going to be. They'd been happy the last few days, now the bubble had shattered.

"Do we have to complicate things?" he asked. He could feel the intake of breath as she stiffened and he spoke faster, getting the words out. "What I mean is, there's not many of us left. You know, that's something I never thought about before. It was all a game; flying, some giddy boys adventure. You never think it'll happen to you."

His voice choked and he rubbed his eyes. Jane lay down behind him, fitting herself to his body, legs tucked in underneath him, her arm over his waist. She kissed his shoulder.

"After Gabby went, it made me realise I'll be lucky to see the end of this."

He didn't mention the nightmares. He'd died so many times in his dreams it was a wonder he got to sleep at all. Now he was Senior Pilot, a shepherd for the others. Looking after a section had been stressful enough. Now he was having to watch the others and how they coped with the strain of combat. He had to be the one who remained calm or had a word to buck someone up. It was hard having to be the strong one all the time.

"James, you'll get through this. I know you will," she said. "It's just a day at a time."

"I'm trying, Jane. When I'm with you, nothing else matters. You're the rock I'm clinging to. I need you."

She broke down then. "I need you too," she said quietly. She buried her face in his back as the tears came.

Callicoe had dozed and Jane had stayed with him, watching him. He slept fitfully, twitching. Judy Fair had come in with a cup of tea for her.

"Leave him for a bit dear. He won't wake for a while."

They talked in the kitchen, Judy listening as it all came pouring out. She nodded, a good listener, encouraging Jane to carry on when she paused.

"Its difficult," she agreed. "Men are like horses. You can lead them to water…"

She handed Jane a plate of biscuits.

Callicoe emerged late in the afternoon, groggy from sleeping at a funny time. He pinched the bridge of his nose, trying to clear his head. He coughed into his hand to announce himself. By the time he got to the living room, Jane and Judy were talking about rugs and wallpaper. Judy had been thinking of redecorating for a while and was running combinations past Jane.

"In a house of men, you have no idea what a treat it's

been talking to someone about colours."

She turned as Callicoe went over to the bookcase, putting the volume he'd been reading back on the shelf.

"Tom'll be along in a minute," Judy said. "He was going to go to town for some supplies,"

Callicoe took the hint and went outside to find him. They made the short drive into Hawks Nest. Tom Fair picked up a few things, Callicoe was the gopher, fetching and carrying and putting them in the car. Neither of them talked very much.

Callicoe had found him to be quite reserved over the last few days. He used two words when most people would have used six or seven.

"Do you think it'll be long now?" he asked.

Callicoe shrugged and stared out of the window on his side of the car.

"I think the sons of Nippon are going to fight to the death," he said sadly. "Okinawa's been a bloody affair and they're only going to fight harder the closer we get to home."

"Little yellow bastards," Tom Fair growled. It was the first time Callicoe had heard him talk with real passion and conviction all week.

"What times the train on Saturday?" Callicoe asked, getting him off that subject.

"One thirty."

"So what time do we need to leave?"

Tom figured out some times and distance. If they started about eleven, they should be okay. He'd get the gas bag filled tomorrow and check the oil so the car would be ready.

He parked in front of the house. Callicoe helped him bring the bags through to the kitchen and then went to get changed for dinner. He sat with Jane, listening to records in the living room. Neither of them mentioned earlier, drawing a veil over it. Fresh slate, she'd said.

The final full day, things were back to normal. The mood between them had lifted, both of them pushing the argument to the background. It was a blip, nothing more and nothing to lose sleep over. Jane persuaded him to take his camera when they went for their last stroll up the beach. She walked barefoot, wanting to feel the sand between her toes.

He took some photos of her sat on a dune, hand holding her hat in place. She took some pictures of him to finish the roll.

"Did you take many pictures?" she asked him.

"No. I, er, stopped. Too busy."

He took the camera and hung it off his shoulder. When he bought the camera, he'd wanted to capture what life was like on the carrier. As time had gone on and the casualties had mounted up, he'd stopped using it. It didn't seem right somehow. He'd felt like a ghoul, lurking to capture an interesting photo.

They turned around when the wind got up and walked back to the house. Callicoe had a bath before dinner, filling it until his nose was just above the water. There'd be no baths when he got back to sea.

It had been a magical week. Tom and Judy had left them alone, giving them the run of the house. There had been no word of complaint when Callicoe rose late or walked around at night, chasing the fidgets that denied him sleep.

He woke up in a cold sweat, eyes darting around the room. He'd been diving into a sky full of flak and tracer. Jane was stood at the door, barefoot.

"I heard you screaming," she said quietly.

He sat up and rubbed his face, coughing.

"I'm fine," he protested.

"You're not." She sat next to him and put her hand to

his forehead. He was soaking.

"You're not fine. Why do men have to be so tough all the time?" she asked him as she over rode his objections and got under the covers.

He dozed for a while as she watched him, scared for the future and losing him. He woke again and as the sky began to lighten, they made love, slowly. It was like being back in the boarding house, jumping at every small creak expecting Tom Fair to come charging through the door like some raging bull.

Rocking her hips back and forth, she moulded herself to him, breasts mashed against his chest, her lips welded to his. He responded, pushing back, his arms gripping her as she increased the tempo of her movements. She could feel his breath coming in small gasps, shuddering as her muscles tightened around him, her legs clamped to his sides.

Tom and Judy saw them off at the train station. She gave Jane a paper bag with sandwiches and bottles of ginger beer for the trip. Tom crushed Callicoe's hand in a bear grip.

"Good luck son. Give them what for, eh?"

Callicoe promised he would. Then Judy smothered him in a tearful hug, pulling him down towards her.

"Take care of yourself."

Callicoe found himself quite emotional that she would care.

He saw Jane to her boarding house when they got back. The closer they got, the more her anxiety ratcheted up. It was back to reality when she stepped through that door. She told herself she was being silly but there was an awkward moment as they kissed. They bumped noses, pulled back and did it again. He didn't say goodbye, that was too final and it wasn't how he wanted to part.

"I'll call tomorrow," he assured her. "Dinner?"

She nodded; eyes wide. She looked stricken. After a week together, she didn't want him to go.

"Goodnight, Jane." He kissed her again, hard, burning the moment into his memory.

It was busy back at the transit camp. Men coming back from leave were full of beans and the huts were loud as pilots and crews talked over each other. Goodfellow was there to see every man in, welcoming them back, glad to see them refreshed.

He'd spent his leave walking in the Blue Mountains around a place called Wentworth Falls. He chose it because he was told it had lots of green and they weren't wrong. The rolling hills and terrain reminded him of the Lake District.

He'd gone out early every day and enjoyed the peace and quiet. His favourite spot was a walk through the Valley of the Waters which had a succession of waterfalls at the junction of two creeks. To start with, he'd found it hard going but by the end of the week he was tanned and toned, shaking off the rust of shipboard life. Some other aircrew were staying at his guest house and they played Uckers in the evenings to pass the time. One day, a few of them came with Goodfellow and he walked them into the ground.

The only spanner in the works was that Bell was out of action. He'd gone riding with two other new lads, Cash and Newey and broken his leg. The ridiculous thing was that he hadn't even been moving when it happened. Getting down from his horse, he'd caught his foot in his stirrup and fallen at an odd angle, twisting his leg and breaking it at the bottom of the bone.

He hobbled into Goodfellow's room on crutches to tell the story. The lad put a brave face on things but Goodfellow could see he was crushed at the thought of being left behind.

At Sunday roll call, Oates gave them notice that they would be going back to Kurri Kurri. The morning service was very well attended as men put their spiritual affairs in order. Callicoe went too, it seemed prudent somehow.

He met Jane in the afternoon. It was her shifts afternoon off and they went to the Botanical Gardens for a walk and then to a restaurant for dinner. Callicoe couldn't think of a way to sugar coat it so he told her about going back up to *HMS Nabiac*. Jane visibly paled.

The date she'd feared was looming large. She'd known it was coming, she'd seen the ships moving around in the harbour since they'd been away. *HMS Reliant* had come out of the dry dock freshly painted with her new flight deck. All sorts of requisitions had come through her department as the ships made themselves ready for sea.

When the fleet had first returned to Sydney, she thought they'd have weeks together. His going on that operation had snatched him away from her for most of it. She felt cheated.

She was very glum as he walked her back to the boarding house. Both of them knew that tomorrow would be their last day together.

He did his best to make it memorable. He tarted his uniform up, giving it a brush down and running an iron over it to give it some creases. Jane made an effort too, appearing at the door with a sunny smile and a new dress Callicoe hadn't seen before.

They went to dinner and Callicoe pushed the boat out, going somewhere he'd heard about from Kendall. It was very grand, with silver service and liveried waiters. They had soup, a fish course, roast lamb and then Peach Melba to finish. The prices were appropriately high as well but he didn't care.

They retired for drinks, his departure looming like an

elephant between them. Callicoe sighed, this wasn't the girl he'd first met in Bombay. Her shoulders had dropped and she'd shrunk into herself, her fingers fiddling with the stem of her glass.

Callicoe thought he had something that might cheer her up. He swapped seats and sat next to her. She leaned into him and he put his arm around her.

"I realised I have been remiss," he said. Her head lifted off his shoulder, her interest peaked. He pulled a small long box from his tunic pocket and presented it to her. "So I got you something until I'm back."

Hands trembling, she opened the box and gasped when she saw what was inside, a gold bracelet inset with opals. Her eyes widened in shock as he took it out of the box and put it around her wrist.

"What's more Australian than gold and opals for a special girl?" he said with a grin. She looked at it, seeing the opal glitter, the stones shot through with blues and purples and veins of orange. She wrapped her arms around him with a sob, holding him tight.

"Oh darling, it's wonderful."

Her mood lifted, knowing that he cared now. She'd been very nervous since coming back from Hawks Nest. The argument had played on her mind non stop and she'd spent hours staring at the ceiling wondering where things had gone wrong. None of that mattered now and she chided herself for doubting him.

42 – Gathering Storm

They rendezvoused with the American Third Fleet two hundred sixty miles off the coast of Japan. It was a sight to behold. Over two hundred ships were spread out over a vast area, including nine fleet carriers and ten fast battleships. Callicoe looked down at the BPF contribution as it steamed towards them and it seemed pitiful in comparison. He remembered the mouthy Lieutenant in the pub and the fuss over Rule Britannia. Perhaps he had a point after all.

The BPF might be making a small contribution, but it packed a lot of punch. Five carriers and a maintenance carrier, protected by battleships and cruisers. More than enough to hold their own he thought. *Reliant* was made ready in time to sail and she was again in company with *Lancer* out on the right flank with *Minerva* following behind. *Victorious*, *Implacable* and *Indomitable* were in the other wing. *Indefatigable* had been left behind after problems with her air compressors. She would catch up later. The escort carriers and other support ships of the Fleet Train brought up the rear.

As soon as they got there, Rawlings and Vian went across to see Admiral Halsey to find out what he had in mind for them. The great man was sat in his flag cabin on the battleship *Missouri* and laid out the general plan of attack.

"I mean to hit those Jap bastards hard," he said bluntly. "I don't want to give them a chance to catch their breath. We're going to roam up and down off their coast and show them that we own these waters and there's nothing they can to do to stop us."

All Halsey wanted to know was how Rawlings wanted to play things. Nimitz had told him at Pearl Harbour not to tread on the Brits toes. Halsey did what Nelson would have done, he turned a blind eye and left the choice up to them. He gave them three choices. They could operate in close company with Third Fleet as one of his Task Forces, they could operate near Halsey as a semi independent force, or they could operate entirely on their own.

Rawlings had heard all about Halsey. At Guam, Nimitz had jokingly warned him that he'd better hang on to his coat tails if he wanted to keep up with him.

Of Nimitz's two fleet commanders, Spruance was the caution one, Halsey was the bulldog. From the very beginning of America's war, Halsey had been at the forefront of the action. While the bombs had been falling on Pearl Harbour, he'd been hunting for the Japanese carriers. It was Halsey who'd taken *Hornet* and *Enterprise* within seven hundred miles of the Japanese coast to launch the Doolittle raid.

Rawlings knew the only way to keep up was to work close together. He didn't hesitate, he accepted the first option.

In the afternoon, the mighty fleet headed east to the land of the rising sun. The final reckoning for Pearl Harbour, Singapore, Hong Kong and a host of other places was not far away.

Halsey expected the skies to be filled with Kamikaze. British ships were a little light when it came to AA defences so he put them to the north, on his right flank. *Lancer* found herself the furthest out with *Reliant* and *Minerva* as Task Force 37.2. The other three carriers, four when *Indefatigable* caught up were TF37.1. Each Task Force would operate twelve miles apart with battleships and cruisers in a protective circle around them.

Destroyers were further out to provide extra radar coverage.

Halsey intended to keep up rolling attacks all day, every day. Every two hours, his ships would turn into the wind to launch strikes recover aircraft. If you fell behind, then you'd just have to catch up on your own.

43 – Land Of The Gods

Callicoe sat in his cockpit and yawned. His head was stuffed full, whirling with the briefings they'd had on the drive north. The topics had been as diverse as geography, weather, strafing techniques, fleet manoeuvres, aircraft and ship recognition. Great emphasis had been placed on strafing and Callicoe had rolled his eyes at the thought of more ground attacks. Goodfellow hammered home the need to adopt the best approach for the target, he wanted them to get in and out; fast.

Four Corsairs were ahead of him on the deck, their engines ticking over. Callicoe started up as *Lancer* turned into the wind. They were launched fast, the Flight Deck Officer literally flinging them off the deck.

Callicoe led Cash, Sparrow and Ritchie. He was nervous with them behind. He'd not flown with them much and it wasn't the same when you didn't know what someone could do. With Gabby and Wicklow and the others, he knew he could fling his Corsair around and they'd be there, glued to his wing.

Goodfellow took them in low under a heavy cloud bank. They headed into the dark, the sky getting lighter behind them as the sun crept over the horizon. That wasn't ideal; they would be silhouetted against the sky when making their run in. Some fishing junks and a patrol boat loomed out of the dark and they were gone in an instant.

Crossing the coast a few minutes later, they popped up to two thousand feet and tore into the attack. The flak barrage was terrific and Callicoe clung grimly behind

Goodfellow's section.

"Ten to one the patrol boat had a radio," said Cash.

"I'm not taking that bet," Callicoe bit back as they spread out to get some working room.

He drifted right, heading for a line of fighters he'd spotted. Under three hundred feet, he released his bombs, literally tossing them at the target as he pulled up hard. He rolled off the top as the bombs went off down below.

Cash lofted his bombs through the front of a hangar. A pattern of flak exploded in front of him. He cursed as his Corsair was bodily lifted upwards and the engine shook fit to bust. He sheared off and headed east to get some space.

After they dumped their bombs, Sparrow and Newey hunted as a pair, going for the AA guns. They blasted two heavy guns to bits and were working on a third when Newey took a burst in his starboard wing.

They left the airfield honours about even. They'd caused some damage but the AA gunners had kept up a spirited defence and the field was still operational.

Goodfellow's section closed around Callicoe's to cover them home. Callicoe was the only one to get away scot free, all of the others in his section had been hit. Cash had caught the worst of it, his engine sounded like a collection of bits rattling around a drum. His stick juddered in his hand and he had to keep hitting it to keep the nose pointed in the right direction.

When he got back to the carrier, he could barely keep it going in a straight line and there was no way he'd able to make a landing. He circled in a wide orbit keeping out of everyones way while the rest of them put down. Callicoe scrambled out of his Corsair and went to the stern, standing next to Gilliard so he could see Cash make his approach to ditch. *HMS Siren* was standing by as guard destroyer to pick him up.

The Corsair was wobbling around, its nose drifting

left and right as Cash was trying to keep it going. As he flattened out over the water, he cut his switches and pulled the stick back to flare into the trough of a wave. The tail clipped a wave and pitched the nose forward. The Corsair came to an abrupt halt and Cash slammed forward, smashing his face into the gyro gunsight.

He came to as the Corsair was going under, the cockpit full of water. He spat out blood to clear his mouth and pulled at his harness. He started to panic as he caught his foot on the rudder pedal, screaming as he was dragged under water.

Callicoe had front row seats as he saw him struggling to get free. The Corsair plunged under the water and disappeared, taking Cash with it. Callicoe turned away, feeling sick to his stomach until Gilliard pointed.

"Christ, he made it!" he said.

Callicoe turned to see Cash thrashing around in the water, waving his arms. His Mae West had saved him. As he went under for the final time, he'd pulled the toggle to his life jacket and it had inflated, dragging him to the surface.

A boat from *HMS Siren* fished him out. He was put back aboard after the next strike launched but he wouldn't be flying for a while. He'd broken his nose and knocked out his two front teeth.

Callicoe flew CAP while 1783 had their turn. Matthews Corsairs blitzed another airfield and got away with barely a shot fired, the AA gunners strangely silent.

The weather got worse. Heavy clouds built up on the hills and played havoc with navigation. The Avengers couldn't find their target and dropped ten tons of bombs on a factory that appeared through a break in the clouds.

They flew five strikes that day, small raids of ten to fifteen aircraft at a time, a constant rolling harassment of the enemy. They only lost the one Corsair and three aircraft were damaged.

Cash was the centre of attention in the Wardroom that evening. His face was an angry purple with wads of cotton wool shoved up his nostrils.

Sparrow kept his glass topped up with gin to dull the pain. Cash didn't say much, he didn't like showing off his gappy grin and it hurt every time he moved his jaw. It felt like he'd gone ten rounds with Len Harvey.

The weather worsened overnight. Cold rain lashed the deck and it was miserable when Callicoe came up on deck for the first ramrod of the day. The deck was slick and he picked his way carefully over to his fighter. The kite had three propellers and all the bits were there, he was happy to leave it at that. He trusted the mechanics enough to know they'd have checked everything. He got into the cockpit, distinctly soggy.

Big fat drops of rain spattered off the canopy, making crazy patterns as they slid down the perspex. He rubbed the lenses of his goggles on his shirt and settled them on his head. He wouldn't be needing his sunglasses today.

The Corsair took off with a roar into heavy rain. Callicoe went north of his planned track before heading in. After yesterday's experience with the fishing junks and patrol boat, he wanted to give himself a fighting chance of making it without being spotted. He crossed he coast and adjusted course to take them over green hills where there was nothing marked on the map.

They came over the crest of the last hill and dived on the airfield from the north. There were a few moments of surprise in their favour and then the AA gunners opened up. It was even worse than yesterday.

Callicoe opened up with his guns, trying to get them to keep their heads down. They had no choice but to go in. If they orbited to come in from another direction, it would just give the gunners more time to nail them. They dropped their bombs and streaked across the airfield at nought feet, the tracer chasing after them all the way.

Callicoe flinched as a cannon shell smacked into the tail. He wobbled from the shock, dropped and recovered himself just in time. He was so low; his slipstream blew up a cloud of dust and debris behind him. They pulled off the target one short. Sparrow was left behind in a smoking crater.

Callicoe heard the story when they got back aboard. They were sat around the Intel officer giving their reports.

"I dunno what the hell happened," said Ritchie. "We were tearing along when I caught a flash out of the corner of my eye. When I looked, he was just gone."

Callicoe was grim. He wondered if that was how it would be for him one day; blink and he'd be a footnote in the squadron diary. *'Attack on Japanese airfield near Tokyo, one casualty, Lt Callicoe KIA'.*

He bent some thought on the whole problem of strafing airfields but couldn't come up with anything that would make a difference. Guns were scattered all over an airfield so it didn't matter which direction you came in from, someone would always have a perfect shot at you.

Speed and height were the only things that he had control of. The thing to be avoided at all costs was making a second pass. Callicoe had been lulled into doing that once or twice over Sakishima Gunto. He wouldn't dare do it here, the gunners were just too good.

The 1783 boys came back one short as well, but their pilot had ditched off the coast. They'd circled for an hour until a sub picked him up.

There was a brittle air in the Wardroom that night. Two down in two days was not a good start. Callicoe went to his spot under the flight deck at the stern. The ships wake shone under the moon light; the water pitch black. The ships around them were dark shapes, running blacked out.

He lit his pipe and was wreathed in smoke while he pondered his fate.

Kendall appeared at his shoulder and held out a bottle of beer. Callicoe took it.

"Bloody rough day," he said.

"Japs," Kendall said with a sneer, a catch to his voice. "Any one of ours is worth two or three of theirs."

Callicoe glanced to this right and saw Kendall's eyes burning with hate.

"Strafings a mugs game," he said, taking a slug of beer. "If we were hitting something, I'd say otherwise but we just seem to be blasting empty airfields." He shrugged. "What's the point?"

"We're killing Japs, aren't we?" Kendall said sharply.

Callicoe clamped his mouth shut, not wanting to get into an argument. He'd noticed that Kendall was half cut and he could be quick to anger when the mood was on him.

"Maybe we'll get something more juicy when we come back in," Kendall speculated. Callicoe shrugged and nodded agreement.

"I hope so, I hope so."

Replenishment took longer than expected. The Task Force met up with the tankers and auxiliaries easily enough but the weather conditions deteriorated further. They even got a typhoon warning. All refuelling was suspended as the wind increased and the sea whipped up, spray coming off the top of the waves. The ships turned into the wind and rode it out. The sea came in as long rollers and the carrier ploughed into them, rearing up before dropping into the trough and then rearing up for the next one.

There was a tragedy when *HMAS Naturi* was shoved into the side of a tanker by a rogue wave. She drunkenly lurched clear minus three Carley floats and two ratings who'd gone over the side. They found one body; they never did locate the other one.

It took them two days to complete refuelling. As the bad weather continued, Halsey shifted operations to the south. They would be hunting down ships in the inland sea between Honshu and Shikoku. Callicoe felt like this was a case of be careful what you wish for. If the flak over the airfields was bad, god knows what it would be like over harbours.

They were turfed out of bed early and had a detailed brief of the area around Osaka. There were blow ups of the harbour area and anchorages and if the photos were up to date, there were juicy targets all over the place.

There was a real buzz in the Wardroom as Oates went through the target assignments. It was going to be a maximum effort in every sense of the word. The delays due to the weather had allowed *Indefatigable* to join up and get in on the action. The Avengers would go for the big stuff, the Corsairs would go for the harbour facilities and the smaller ships.

It was impressive. Everything that could fly was up and they went straight in. Destroyers lay at anchor in the middle of the harbour. A cruiser was laid up in dry dock. The prize was a carrier, not a big one, but it was tied up to a buoy in the open.

The flak was terrifying. Callicoe hadn't seen anything like it. He bit his lip and shoved the stick forward. The Avengers went in from five thousand feet in shallow dives, throwing armour piercing and HE bombs at them.

The Corsairs covered the Fireflies as they launched their rockets and strafed AA guns. They bombed cranes and warehouses, workshops and anything else that could float. They had a field day, roaming the length of the harbour.

Bombs exploded around the carrier. Four bombs went

down the length of the flight deck. The second one went through the lift, through the hangar floor and exploded deep inside. The carrier started taking on water and the pumps couldn't stay ahead of it. Fires raged out of control in the hangar.

A destroyer exploded. A bomb sliced deep into the ship and detonated inside the magazine. A massive hole was blown in its side. The shockwave crumpled the hull of the destroyer moored next to it and it rolled over onto its side.

Callicoe skimmed over the water at 400mph, the engine going full blast as he charged towards the dry dock. He toggled his bombs and hauled the stick back into his stomach. He grunted at the G-forces as his Corsair went straight up. The bombs shot forward, skipped off the water like a stone and went straight into the gates of the dry dock. They weren't armour piercing bombs, but with the speed of release it was enough. They detonated and punched a hole in the side of the gates. Water flooded into the dry dock.

They only lost two Avengers which was a miracle considering the curtain of flak the defences had laid down. The squadron formed up and took the rear flanking position, covering them on the way out.

They went back in the afternoon to polish off what they'd missed the first time. The carrier was listing badly and blazing from stem to stern when an Avenger slammed a bomb into the bilge amidships. That finished it off and it rolled over, settling on the bottom of the harbour.

The cruiser was stuck in the dry dock. Callicoe's bombs had jammed the gates. The Fireflies went after it like a pack of wolves. They fired volley after volley of rockets and the Avengers plastered it with bombs. It blew up in the dock, the armoured deck tearing apart.

The Corsairs headed inland and went for an airfield

west of Kobe and caught them on the ground. Fighters were lined up on the runway about to take off.

"Beautiful!" Kendall shouted as he rolled into the attack. He went down almost vertically, took a quick sight and then planted his bombs in the middle of the runway. There was no mercy. All those times they'd shot up airfields over Formosa and Sakishima Gunto for little gain, this was payback. They streaked over the airfield and left it a burning wreck.

The final raid of the day was an attack on the outskirts of Tokyo itself. There had been almost a reverential hush in the Wardroom when Oates had announced the target. One thing he made abundantly clear was that no matter what happened, they were to go nowhere near the Imperial Palace, not even fly over it.

"They revere him as a living god," Oates said. "We all know they're fanatics, they consider it an honour to die for the Emperor. If word got out that we'd shot up or bombed the Imperial Palace there'd be hell to pay come the time we invade."

Goodfellow shot Kendall a dirty look, convinced he'd try it anyway.

Flying to Tokyo was an almost surreal experience. They flew over verdant green countryside and a succession of small towns and villages full of quaint little houses with steep tiled roofs. The countryside seemed to be a quilt work of paddy fields and irrigation dikes.

As the big city came into view the terrain changed. The size of the place was staggering. London was big, so was New York and Miami. They were nothing on this. The city went on for miles and miles into the distance, the city was enormous.

Tokyo had clearly been hit before. The American B29's from Iwo Jima had come over in their hundreds, dropping thousands of tons of incendiaries in their raids, blanket bombing whole districts into oblivion. Made of wood and packed together, Japanese houses burned well. You could still see where the narrow streets had been in the charred outlines on the ground.

Callicoe wondered if it was worth bothering as he dropped his bombs on a factory that was missing most of its roof. He blew out one of the walls and watched the building collapse in on itself.

"Rats! Rats! Five o'clock!" was the call and Callicoe snapped back. He looked over his right shoulder and could see the enemy fighters coming in.

"Yellow Section, break, break!" He ordered. He went right and Ritchie followed him close behind. The other two went left. Callicoe climbed to face them as the Japanese fighters came in. He fired and sent six lines of tracer at them. In a flash, they were past one another and Callicoe kept climbing to get position on them. The Oscars, Callicoe thought they were Oscars went after Kendall's section. He chased after them. Firing short squirts to get their attention. One broke off and Ritchie went for him.

Kendall dumped his bombs and his section turned into the attack. Suddenly, the Oscars found themselves trapped in front and behind. Callicoe closed on them from the rear. He took the next Oscar in line and blew its tail clean off. The hunter became the hunted and the Japanese fighters scattered to get away.

44 – Paper Tiger

New pilots came aboard when they pulled back to resupply. Callicoe could barely summon the enthusiasm to care enough to know their names. It wasn't fair and he knew it but it was the only way he could get through the day. Sparrow and Cash were replaced with two new rookies fresh out of the gate called Hollister and Nevis.

Callicoe talked to them at his spot by the stern, they could get some privacy there. He had few words of wisdom to share. The Corsair could be a killer if it wasn't treated with respect and there were plenty of little quirks that would get you killed quicker than winking. He could see they were scared but the kids would never admit it.

"When we go in, just stick with me," he told them. Hollister nodded, swallowing hard. Nevis just stared at him, his eyes wide like saucers. "I don't care if you don't get a bomb on target. Don't worry about hitting anything. All I want you to do is follow me and get back in one piece."

Callicoe knew that was going in one ear and out the other. They'd fly in the morning and they'd fire their guns, spray bullets everywhere and probably get themselves killed.

In the morning Callicoe took his section on a sweep over Shikoku, hunting for targets. Nevis took off okay and formed up but his formation flying left something to be desired.

They came across a train and made short work of it then moved onto a bridge, blowing it to match wood.

They came across a factory by a small town and went into the attack.

The only defence it had was a solitary 40mm gun on a hill top overlooking the factory. The gun crew scrambled to get it ready and opened fire as the Corsairs came in. Untrained, they were hopeless, but even an idiot can hit a target on any given day. They kept feeding clips of shells into the gun and caught Hollister nose to tail.

He pulled up out of range, but the damage was done. His Corsair was trailing oil and a hole as big as a fist was in the fuselage. They beat it back to the coast but Hollister never made it. His engine cut out, seized up due to lack of oil.

He had no choice but to put his Corsair down in a paddy field. He made it thirty feet before a bunch of farmers took hold of him. Callicoe was sick to his stomach as he saw them put a rope around his neck and drag him off towards their village.

After their success over Osaka, Hollister's fate put a dampener on things. They all knew what the Japanese did to prisoners. He hadn't even unpacked his kit. Callicoe needed a drink but he had a mission to fly.

Goodfellow sent them back to the same area. Callicoe obliterated the 40mm gun on the hill on general principle. He dropped his 500lb bombs on it and left a stinking crater where it had been. They flew over Hollister's crashed Corsair on the way back and torched that too.

It was almost embarrassing. For months they'd been told about the massing of force in Japan for a suicidal last stand against the barbarian invader and they'd seen nothing. Their ships didn't move because they had no fuel. The air force had barely put in an appearance and the American bombers had already torched anything of strategic interest.

The battleships ranged up and down the Japanese coast bombarding shore targets at will. The carriers struck with impunity, their bombers ranging across the land.

Callicoe led a sweep along the southern coast of Shikoku and bagged a submarine running on the surface. They caught it in the open, a mile from shore. Their first bomb struck it on the bow to stop it from diving. It turned to try towards the shore to try and beach itself but it never made it. The Corsairs shot it to pieces. One bomb nearly blew the conning tower clean off. Another mangled the deck gun. They watched the crew scramble over the side into some dinghies as the submarine went down for the final time.

Kendall made coastal traffic his speciality. He shot up anything that moved, ranging from junks, to fishing boats. He even took on a destroyer. Kendall made no distinction, a Jap was a Jap, dead ones were even better.

The Fleet withdrew to refuel and ran into another storm off the Japanese coast. It was an uncomfortable four days as the waves ran broadside to the wind. It was the worst time Callicoe had in his entire time in the navy. Below deck, the stuffy heat inside the ship got too much for him. He had to go to the Goofer's Gallery at the back of the island for fresh air.

In the beam sea, the tankers could barely make five knots, just enough to maintain steerage way as they rolled around like drunken sailors. One of the tankers hadn't been converted to beam refuelling and they had to wait for the seas to drop before they could take on fuel.

Getting munitions on board was an all hands affair, knots of men manhandling crates of bombs below deck. Two ratings were injured when they lost their footing and a crate landed on them. By the time they finally completed their replenishment, they were out of position by over eighty miles.

They raced to catch up only to have Halsey postpone operations around the Hiroshima area. Captain Austin didn't care. The delay gave him a chance to take on more aviation fuel.

Lancer wasn't the only ship to have problems. Some of the destroyers were getting very low on fuel. Admiral Hallows had to order *Lancer* and *Reliant* to transfer some of their own fuel oil over so the destroyers would have enough to make the next rendezvous.

The bad weather dogged them as they went back north east. Rain and fog restricted air operations and Callicoe flew nothing more than a CAP or a short patrol. The coast was blanketed in dense banks of fog and they went further north to find clear skies.

Even though sailing conditions had calmed down, Callicoe still felt queasy. As the sun went down, he went to the stern to smoke his pipe and get some time to himself. The Wardroom was noisy and he felt strangely detached from it all. He brooded in his solitude.

A corvette had brought a load of mail and Callicoe had three letters from home and one from Jane. Frank had been his usual pompous self.

There was little real news, just gossip from the department, a query asking how he was and then at the end, a mention that he had been promoted. Callicoe was pleased for his brother but wondered why Frank hadn't put that first.

Ariadne's letter was full of woe. She wrote, pages of stuff detailing what Frank had been like in recent months. Even with his promotion he still wanted her to have another child. She finished at the end saying she was determined to leave him if he didn't stop. Callicoe was sorry to hear that, he'd hoped things would get better.

Callicoe didn't recognise the handwriting of the third

letter and he had to turn to the last page to see who it was from. His eyebrows shot up when he saw it was from Margaret. He'd never had a letter from his step mother in his life, even when he'd been away at school. The letter was just like her, dry, cold and sparse in detail. In plain language she informed him that His father hadn't been well and he'd gone to the Lake District for a rest.

Callicoe knew it must have been serious for his father to take a rest. He'd hated doctors and hospitals all his life. Margaret asked if he could write a letter to his father to buck up his spirits.

None of them mentioned each other much. Read in isolation, it was like trying to piece a puzzle together with half the bits missing. Once he'd read all three, he was able to get some idea of what was going on with the family.

He knew he should write a reply but he couldn't be bothered but their concerns seemed so petty. He'd have plenty of time to send them something later.

He heard someone come through the hatch behind him but didn't turn around. He enjoyed his pipe and listened to the swirl of the water below, the thrum of the engines deep in the hull.

"I thought I'd find you here," said Kendall.

"Just taking a moment to gather my thoughts," he said. "If we've got months of this like last time, then I'm pacing myself."

"We might be doing this for less time than you think," Kendall said with bubbling enthusiasm. Callicoe glanced at him and saw his eyes shining, a smile plastered over his long face.

"Oates came into the wardroom with a signal that was sent to the Admiral. The Americans have dropped a bloody great bomb on one of the Nips cities. Wiped them out!" he said with some relish.

Callicoe just blinked, his brain trying to absorb what he was saying.

"What do you mean, wiped them out?"

"I mean exactly that," Kendall said excitedly. "One bomb. It's killed everything in a ten mile radius."

"I don't believe it," said Callicoe. "What bomb could do that?"

"An atom bomb they're calling it."

Callicoe put his pipe out and headed for the wardroom. Kendall hadn't exaggerated. Callicoe was appalled at the thought of such destruction from one bomb.

"This'll bring the buggers to their knees," said Kendall, gloating over the signal. Oates had let him read it and his eyes hungrily devoured the words.

"Do you think it'll be over soon, sir?" Nevis asked Goodfellow.

"Let's hope so. How much longer can they go on? If the Yanks can drop bombs like that we may as well pack up and go home."

Clearly Admiral Vian didn't think the same way. The following day, the Task Force closed the shore to launch another day of strikes. The orders were to keep on battering the Japanese until they saw the light and threw in the towel.

Callicoe was decidedly twitchy when he went on deck. He slapped his gloves from hand to hand as he walked around his Corsair. He took extra time looking at the hook and the undercarriage. He put a hand on the drop tank and rocked it on its mounting. His heart wasn't in it.

He got in the cockpit with a sense of dread. For the first time it felt like a coffin and he wound his seat up to the maximum so he had more of a view. It was ridiculous but he felt trapped inside, even with the canopy back.

He took off to fly cover over the battleships while they went on another shore bombardment. He had a grandstand seat as these relics of the first war fired their big guns. For *Hawke* and *Jellicoe*, it was the only time they had fired their guns in anger. They'd never engaged a target at sea and they'd spent their war escorting convoys or covering invasion forces. Every time they fired there was a huge gout of flame out of the barrels. Callicoe was fascinated to see great semi circular shockwaves ripple out from the side of the ship on the surface of the water.

It went on like this for days, just like at Sakishima Gunto. It was a grind of days of air strikes and shore bombardment and a short pause to resupply. Reconnaissance spotted some untouched airfields in the north and they went up there to pay them a visit.

Even with heavy flak it was a massacre. The aircraft were lined up in neat lines like they were ready to be inspected. They tore into them, blasting them to bits with bombs and rockets and tracer. They went back in the afternoon to do it to another airfield ten miles away from the first one.

Two Corsairs went down over the target. Davis crashed into a hangar at over 300mph. Nevis was hit at low level. There was a massive thump and then he was in a flying ashcan. He just had to time to scream before his Corsair blew up and scattered him over the airfield. They felt the loss keenly, but it was a small price to pay for claiming over one hundred aircraft.

45 – Tilting At Windmills

"This can't go on," Callicoe said to Goodfellow as he slurped on a cup of tea. He was tired and all he wanted to do was sleep.

"Buggers don't know when they're beat," Goodfellow replied offhand. He was shovelling a handful of raisins into his mouth. The Americans had dropped another one of their atom bombs a few days ago but it didn't seem to have made any difference. The AA guns still fired at them when they came over and they'd even seen an enemy fighter in the air once or twice.

"To the death, Oates said, remember?"

Callicoe grunted.

"I hate to think you're right. It's been five days since they dropped the second one. What are they going to do? Wait until the Yanks wipe every city off the face of the earth?"

"If that's what it takes," said Kendall, sliding into the conversation.

"I just don't see the point of us carrying on with this," Callicoe scowled. "Our dinky little bombs aren't going to make any difference now."

He thought about the AA fire over the airfields. It was still lethal and it seemed foolhardy risking the men like this. They grabbed their gear and were about to go on deck when Oates appeared.

"Hang on you two, change of plans."

Kendall and Callicoe looked at him, past caring. Any target could kill them.

"Intel's got two photographs of a destroyer in a

secluded bay east of Tokyo. Its got steam up but its just sitting there. Some bright spark thinks it might be used to spirit the Imperial family and the government away before the end. We've got orders to go in and sink it."

"Their timing is impeccable as always," Kendall commented. The Avengers were up and weren't due back for at least an hour. "It'll be at least two; three hours before we can send a full strike off."

"I know, but it's a priority target. The Admiral wants us to take a tilt at it."

Callicoe winced and pinched the bridge of his nose.

"You're not serious?"

"I'm afraid I am. Your kites are being bombed up now."

They went back into the Flight Office while Oates showed them the photographs. It wasn't an easy target. The harbour reminded Callicoe of a beaker from science class, a big circular bowl with a long narrow neck. The bay had a narrow entrance and was surrounded on all sides by steep slopes. The destroyer was docked to a jetty on the north west side. There was a boom of anti torpedo nets rigged around it. Not including the guns on the destroyer, they could see at least five or six other guns for sure but there could have been more hidden away, camouflaged under nets.

Grim faced, Callicoe stumped out to his Corsair. He patted the side of his fighter and strapped himself in.

"Come on old girl," he said as he started the engine.

Callicoe was steaming. Here they were, eight Corsairs going in half cocked against a difficult target. He was sick to his stomach when he taxied forward and unfolded his wings. He could see the coast of Japan on the horizon and he hated the place. They launched under the noonday sun and headed due west.

When they got to Kosuko Bay, he could see the Japanese had chosen the place well. The bay was a basin that had been scooped out of the surrounding hills. A mile across, the sides of the bay were steep and thickly wooded. A small road went down to a village near the jetty. Some fishing junks were pulled up on the beach.

They didn't go straight into the attack, Callicoe wanted to get the lay of the land first. The gunners saw them coming a long way off and the sky was dotted by bursts of flak as they got closer. Callicoe spotted more guns. There were a number of flak posts on the rim of the bay they hadn't seen in the recce photos.

The destroyer was a typical Japanese tin can, very long and slender with a graceful superstructure. They looked delicate but they were very fast. Callicoe remembered from the recognition lectures that these things could do thirty five knots or more in a straight run. A wisp of smoke drifted out of its funnel. Bottled up like this in the harbour, it was vulnerable.

They made an approach on the entrance to the bay but broke off when a wall of flak came up to meet them. The Japanese had positioned their guns well. Anyone flying down the funnel would be shot to pieces long before they got in position to drop their bombs.

They went back up to five thousand feet while he pondered what to do next. He'd have given anything for a dozen Fireflies armed with rockets at that moment.

He thought he saw another way to do it. He called Kendall up over the R/T and explained his plan. Kendall looked down, considering angles and distances.

"You're crazy. You'd be taking a hell of a risk."

"Better that than no chance at all," Callicoe bit out.

"I'm coming with you then," Kendall said. "We can't send these children into this. Two aircraft stand a better chance than one."

Callicoe reluctantly agreed.

"Yellow two. Orbit up above. I need you to keep the gunners occupied. We're going to need all the help we can get."

"Roger, Yellow Leader."

Kendall ordered his section to do the same and the six Corsairs peeled off and went into the attack. They hunted in pairs, circling the bay and making passes at the AA gun positions. They wheeled and dived, firing their guns before climbing away and then coming back down to make another pass. White worked the rim of the bay. He came down in a steep dive and chucked a bomb at a gun post. As he flattened out of his dive, he was hit and he headed east to get out of the way.

Callicoe judged his moment and then went in. He circled inland, using the terrain to his advantage. He headed for the bay from the south, hugging the ground. Kendall was right there with him on his right side.

As he went over the rim, the bay was spread out in front of him. He throttled back and shoved the nose down. The altimeter unwound at a frightening rate as they plunged into the bay. They flattened out at thirty feet, going straight at the destroyer like a rocket. The gunners on the destroyer picked them up late. They frantically turned their cannon and machine guns on the Corsairs.

A bullet tore through the sleeve of Callicoe's shirt. Then a round took him in the left arm. He gritted his teeth and shoved the throttle through the gate. He gripped the stick with both hands as the Corsair leapt forward. Blood ran down his arm, making his grip slippery. Bullets thumped into his Corsair from all sides. He could feel his fighter shudder under the hits, then his fuel tank was hit. Callicoe clung to his course as flames obscured his view. He was committed. If he pulled up now, he'd just be showing them his belly and would make an easy target. He hitched to the side to see anything at all. Fire licked past the canopy and smoke began to fill the cockpit. Flames licked at his boots. There was a thud underneath him and the Corsair rocked. He wrestled her back to level and bore in, his guns raking the decks.

Kendall couldn't believe Callicoe was still in the air. The front of his Corsair was wreathed in flames but she was still going, the big prop turning. He tried to distract them with his own guns but it was no use. They were focused on Callicoe, pumping round after round into the stricken fighter. Kendall released his bombs and hauled back on the stick to clear the hills beyond.

The pain was excruciating. Callicoe bit his lip so hard he could taste blood. He couldn't feel his legs but he still had control of the Corsair. He held her steady and dropped his bombs. In the final seconds, he laughed at how stupid it all was.

From above, they could only watch as Callicoe and Kendall raced across the width of the bay. Callicoe's Corsair ploughed into the side of the destroyer mere seconds before his two bombs did. Thinly armoured, the fighter tore through the destroyer's side and exploded. His bombs skipped off the surface of the bay and went into the boiler room and detonated. It was like a giant had plucked the ship out of the harbour. It reared up and then snapped like a twig amidships as the explosion blew out the keel.

The Corsairs circled, watching as the destroyer sank. There was a series of explosions as its ammunition and torpedoes went up in secondary detonations. It burned from stem to stern, Callicoe's funeral pyre.

"Job's done," Kendall said bitterly. "Let's go home."

The Corsairs formed up on him and they went back to *Lancer*. Kendall went into the barrier, his undercart had been shot out. He was taken below to have a bullet dug out of his shoulder.

The next day, Kendall was flat on his back in the sickbay when the ships tannoy burst into life. Doing his best to contain his excitement, Captain Austin announced that the war was over, the Japanese had surrendered. Kendall covered his face with the crook of his good arm so no one could see him crying. He wasn't crying with relief, or for his dead brother. He cried for Callicoe and the waste of such a good man. He'd been right; it hadn't made the slightest difference at all.

46 – In The Navy, He Was

That wasn't the end of it. Some die hards refused to accept the surrender and carried fighting. For the next two days, the ship kept going to Action Stations as groups of Kamikaze made last gasp attacks. None of them got within touching distance. As Admiral Vian had instructed in an earlier signal, they shot them down in a *friendly* manner.

They missed the signing of the surrender in Tokyo Bay. *Lancer* and *Reliant* were sent back to Sydney and took part in the victory parade held at the end of August. The crews marched through the city, their heads held high, arms swinging, chests puffed with pride at all they had accomplished.

Lancer's aircraft were put ashore. Workmen went on board and converted the hangar into a massive dormitory, capable of taking over a thousand men. The carriers were going to pick up POW's and bring them back to Australia for the first leg of their trip home. Extra facilities were added. Kendall had to smile when someone saw fit to install some air conditioners.

He went to see Jane. He knew where to find her because Callicoe had left her a letter amongst his personal effects. She met him outside the admin building. When she saw Kendall standing there with his cap tucked under his arm, she just knew and the bottom fell out of her world. They sat on a bench outside while Kendall told her everything.

"So, you were with him at the end?" she asked, her voice quiet, head bowed.

"I was there. I've never seen anything like it. Someone said his controls must have jammed but I know what he did. I made sure they knew what he did," he said fiercely.

Jane nodded. He gave her the letter. He'd read it, but he didn't tell Jane that. He'd only glanced at it to make sure there was nothing in it that would cause offence. Maybe it would give her some peace but Kendall doubted it. She didn't seem the type to him. Duty done, he took his leave. He had a bad taste in his mouth and he wanted a drink.

Jane sat for a long time on the bench, looking at the words on the paper. Tears dropped from her chin and smudged the ink. She was alone again, her thoughts full of what might have been.

Goodfellow recommended Callicoe for a VC. He didn't get it. Some paper shuffler in the Admiralty decided throwing yourself at a destroyer wasn't good enough. That created the thorny problem of what to do instead. You couldn't get a DSO posthumously; the same went for the DSC so he was mentioned in dispatches.

Kendall got the Distinguished Service Cross. When he looked down at the medal on his chest, he felt undeserving. It didn't seem right that he had a medal to show for that day and all Callicoe got was a little bronze oak leaf pinned to the ribbon of his campaign star.

Their citations were printed in the London Gazette in March 1946. To Margaret's eternal disappointment, there was no investiture at Buckingham Palace. Callicoe's medals were sent in the post in a small card box with a little leaflet saying what medals he was entitled to. She had them mounted court style in a frame, 1939-45 star, Pacific Star and War Medal.

They took pride of place over the mantlepiece in the reception room next to a photo of Callicoe in his naval uniform. His father kept his sons white peaked cap and a photograph on his desk at work. Whenever people came into the house or his office, they asked about them. His father's voice would choke with raw emotion and say, "they were my sons. In the Navy, he was."

The End

Authors Note

How an author gets inspiration for a book is always a strange thing. Run The Gauntlet, my 2nd book was inspired by a magazine article, my third, Maximum Effort by a photograph. This one was the title. I was casting around for something new, considering my last three books had been about the RAF in Europe and thought about Aircraft Carriers. I did a bit of reading and became aware of the British Pacific Fleet. The thought of covering carrier operations was interesting. I always try to find a story about an aspect of war that is less well known and that was it, I was off and running.

It is often written in history books regarding the Burma theatre that the troops there regarded themselves as the forgotten army. The same can be said for the Royal Navy in the Pacific.

Compared to the forces the American Navy could put in the field, it was small potatoes. The BPF contribution amounted to no more than one of the US Navy's task forces but they fought hard in the Indian Ocean, during the Okinawa campaign and off the coast of mainland Japan. More pilots flew off the carriers than had been in the entire Fleet Air Arm at the beginning of the war.

While my story is nested within the events that took place, lots of things are fictional. There was no HMS Nabiac at Kurri Kurri for example. Real persons do feature in the novel, such as Admiral Fraser, Rawlings and Vian who commanded the BPF. Admiral Nimitz was CINCPAC and Admirals Halsey and Spruance commanded the Third and Fifth Fleets respectively. In all cases, my characterisation of them has been done to suit the story and drive the narrative along.

I don't like to tread on courage, so all of the ships the characters serve on did not exist. A number of other ships are also figments of my imagination to serve the story. For fictional ships, I have not used any ships name that was in use at the time. When real ships and units are mentioned, I restrict myself to mentioning them within the context of historical events that actually occurred.

Printed in Great Britain
by Amazon